MORE THAN PEN PALS

Books by Dana Wilkerson

Throwback RomComs
More Than Pen Pals

Books by D.A. Wilkerson

Totally 80s Mysteries
A Totally Killer Wedding
Most Likely to Kill
Of Heist and Men
A Totally 80s Christmas

Mystery Journals
Mysterious Musings
My Totally Suspect Notebook

MORE THAN PEN PALS

A Throwback RomCom

DANA WILKERSON

*Dedicated to the ladies at The Collective
for always cheering me on*

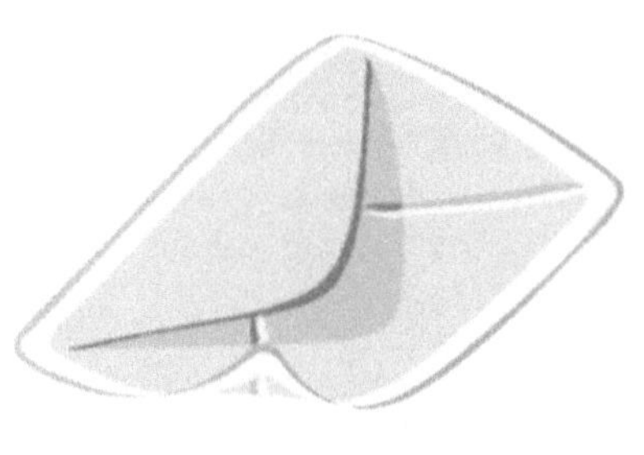
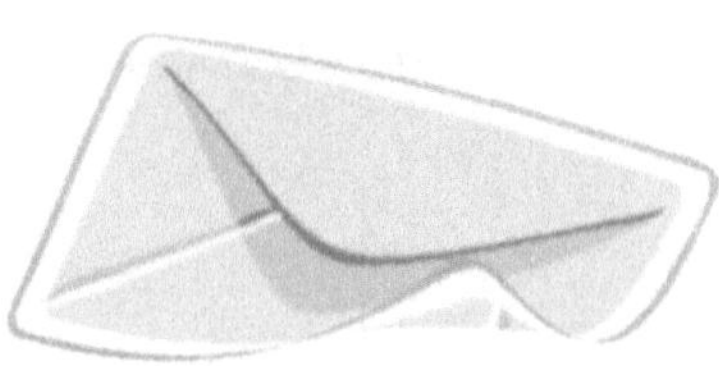

Prologue

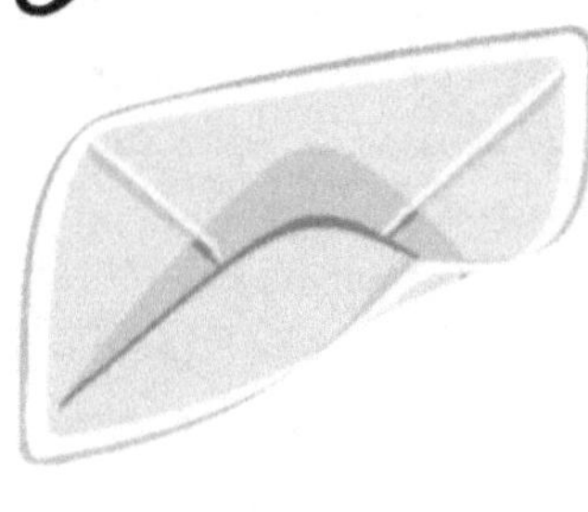
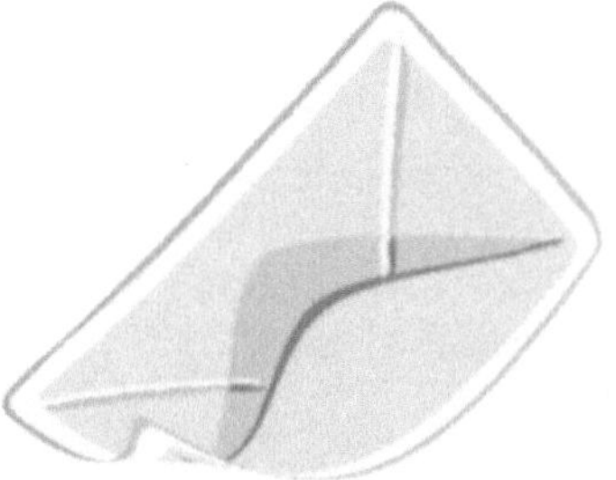

Leslie Beckett
147 Rural Route 2
Oakville, Ark.

Ashley Hamilton
5000 Lakeside Place
Evanston, Ill.

January 27, 1973

Dear Ashley,

Hi, I'm Leslie. I've never had a pen pal before. Have you? I think it's neat you live near Chicago (my dad told me Evanston is north of Chicago). I love big cities. I live outside a small town in Arkansas, but I guess you know that, because you have my address. My dad works in Little Rock, but that's not a very big city.

I'll be ten on Valentine's Day. I don't like having a birthday on a holiday. Everyone forgets about me. Plus, I'm a twin, so I have to share my birthday anyway. I know you're also in fourth grade, but are you nine or ten?

What do you like to do for fun? I enjoy sleepovers with my friends, playing tennis, and watching baseball with my dad. My favorite team is the Cardinals. Since you live in Chicago, do you cheer for the Cubs or the White Sox?

I'm sending you a picture of my family. That's my parents, me, my twin Shannon, and my little sister Cynthia. How many people are in your family?

Please write back soon.

Sincerely,
Leslie Beckett

Ash Hamilton
5000 Lakeside Place
Evanston, Ill.

Leslie Beckett
147 Rural Route 2
Oakville, Ark.

February 10, 1973

Dear Leslie,

I've never had a pen pal. My teacher made us do it this year.

Chicago is fine. My dad's office is in the city. He's a lawyer. I go to work with him sometimes when I'm not in school.

Have you ever been to Chicago? I've never been to Arkansas.

I play tennis, too.

The Cubs are my favorite team.

I'm ten. My birthday is on Halloween, so I know what you mean about people forgetting you on your birthday.

What's your favorite subject in school? Mine is history.

Sorry I don't have a picture to send. I'll ask my mom if she can get me one.

I have two baby sisters and one brother who's a year older than me. His name is Randall.

I hope you have a good birthday.

Sincerely,
Ash Hamilton

February 16, 1973

Dear Ash,

Ash is a funny nickname. Does everyone call you that? Some people call me Les, but Les isn't a real word. Ash is.

My birthday was fun. I had some friends over. We played Boggle and Uno and Twister and we listened to music. I like the Osmonds and Stevie Wonder. What music do you like?

My favorite subjects are English, reading, and writing. I want to work at a newspaper when I grow up. What do you want to do?

I have never been to Illinois. Does it get really cold in Chicago in the winter?

Since you're a Cubs fan, I don't think we can be friends. Just kidding. Who's your favorite baseball player? Mine is Lou Brock.

Please send a picture. I want to see you in my head when I write to you. Right now I imagine what you look like, but I'm probably wrong. I would ask you what color your hair is, but I'll see it when you send that picture.

Your friend,
Les

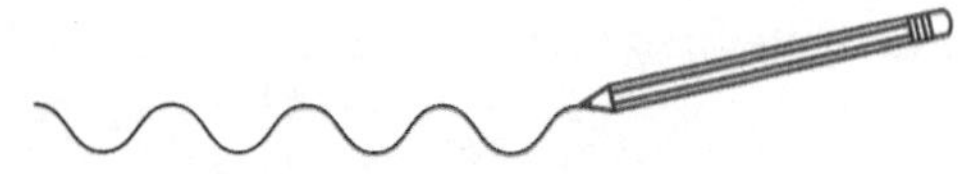

July 9, 1973

Dear Les,

I'm finally sending you a picture of my family. I'm sorry I didn't send one before, but my dog chewed up the first one my mom gave me and then I forgot to get another one. I'm the one in the blue and red striped shirt.

I haven't written to you in a month because I was at camp in Wisconsin. Randall and I both went. It's fun being outside all the time and playing sports and stuff. I don't like making crafts, though. I wish they didn't make us do them, but if we complained we got in trouble.

The other thing I didn't like about camp is there were a couple boys that were mean to me, and the counselors didn't care.

Do you and Shannon go to camp?

Is it strange having a girl as your twin? I think it would be.

Sincerely,
Ash

July 16, 1973

"Aunt Star, I need your help." I settle next to my aunt on her couch with the envelope from Ash.

"What is it, Les? You know I'll always help you, kiddo."

"I have a pen pal. We've been writing to each other since January."

"That sounds fun. What's her name?"

I bend the envelope back and forth. "Um, Ashley. I thought she was a girl, but she's not. She's a boy."

I show my aunt the letter and photo I got in the mail the day before I left home to visit her and my grandparents in Missouri.

"See?" I hold up the picture. "The kid in the blue-and-red striped shirt is a boy."

"Yes, he is."

"And look at what he said in his letter about being twins with a girl." I point out the last paragraph. "I'm pretty sure he thinks I'm a boy and Shannon is a girl. Both of us were in the picture I sent him, so he has us mixed up."

Aunt Star nods. "I think you're right, so you need to tell him you're a girl."

"Do I have to tell him?"

Her eyebrows raise. "Why wouldn't you want to?"

I lean my head against her shoulder. "I like having a pen pal. And I like Ash, even if he's a boy. I'm afraid he won't want to keep writing to me if he knows I'm a girl."

"Maybe so, but you need to be honest with him, honey. That's the most important thing in a friendship."

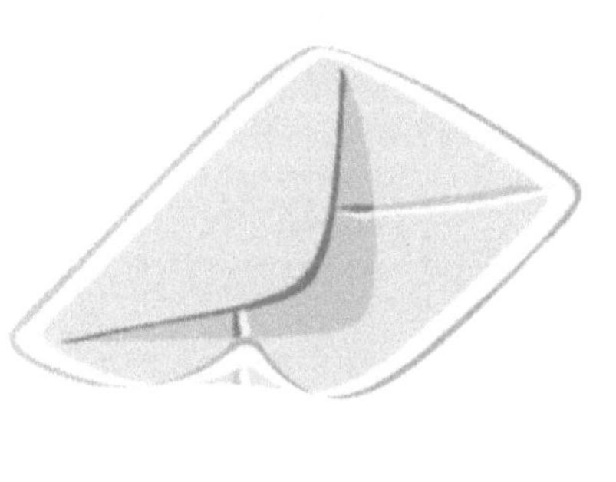

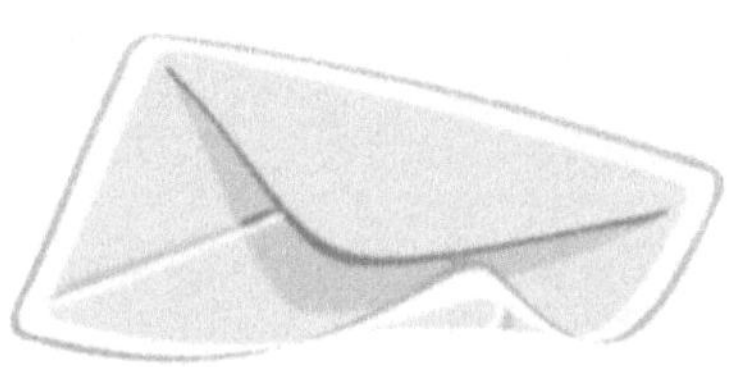

May 1988

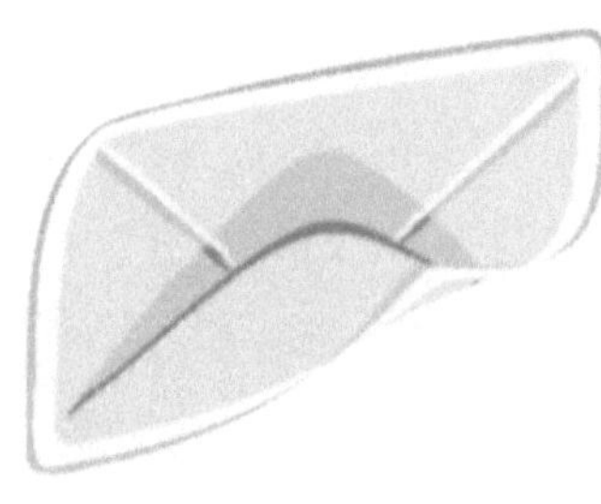

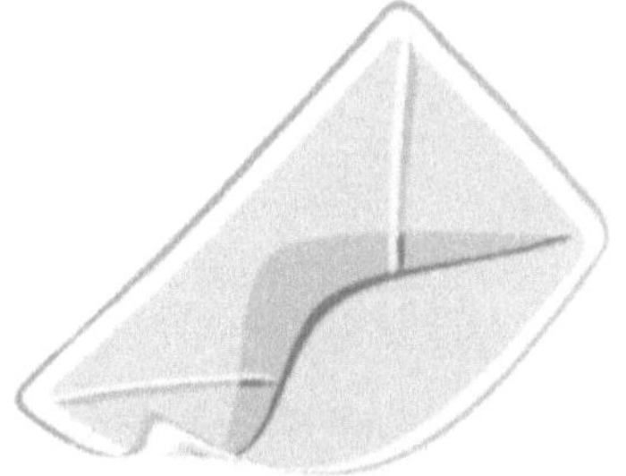

one

. . .

Chicago, Illinois

"Do you have a boyfriend? You *must* have one. You're simply gorgeous." My new co-worker Wendy stops to take a breath and then starts right back in. "Please tell me you have a boyfriend. I don't want to compete with you for a man. If you don't have one, we need to find you one, pronto."

I like to talk, but this woman is in another league. Wendy is a cute, gregarious redhead who took me under her wing the second I walked through the door of my new job at Carter-Jenkins Public Relations last week, and from all appearances, she's a fast-rising star at the firm.

"No, I don't have a boyfriend." I tuck my blonde curls behind my ear. "And I don't intend to compete with you for one. You have plenty of fine qualities. You don't need to worry about me."

She quirks an eyebrow at me. "If you say so. Anyway, tell me everything about yourself. Start at the very beginning and go all the way through moving to Chicago a few weeks ago."

While I consider exactly where to begin and how much to share, I marvel at how Wendy reminds me of my cousin Beckett. She's adorable, she confidently wears brightly colored clothes few women could pull off, and she wants nothing more than to help people.

Before I can delve into my life story, the waiter arrives at our table at Sapori D'Italia with our entrees. Wendy dives into her fettuccine alfredo the second the waiter's hand leaves the plate.

"Oh my goodness, this is so delish! Have you ever tasted anything so good?"

"I'll tell you after I've had a chance to take a bite of mine." I smile at her.

She giggles. "Sorry. I get worked up about my pasta."

"I get it. I love Italian food, too." I fork up some lasagna and moan when the flavors assault my taste buds.

Wendy stabs her fork in the air. "Told you!"

"Yes, you were right."

"I'm always right. Including about needing to find you a man to get you off the market."

"I don't need a man." Especially not so soon after Glenn, but I have no intention of dwelling on that situation or talking to my new co-worker about it.

"Well, maybe you don't *need* one, but don't you want one?"

"No," I say more grimly than I intended.

Wendy's eyes narrow. "Who hurt you?"

The woman is perceptive.

I sigh. "I don't want to talk about it."

"All right. We'll get there one day. But for now, tell me everything else—including where your adorable Southern accent came from."

During the seven years I've lived in Illinois I've tried to tamp down my Arkansas twang, but it inevitably slips through.

"I'm from Arkansas," I say, "which isn't really the South. It's one of those weird states that's not sure where it fits."

"Oh, it's the South." She gives a firm nod to emphasize her point.

"Don't let someone from Alabama hear you say that. That's the *real* South. Where are you from?"

"Milwaukee. But this conversation is about you, not me."

"Can't it be both?"

"Nope. Next time we do lunch it'll be all about me. Stop stalling and tell me about yourself. Were you born in Arkansas?"

"I was born in Missouri," I explain, "but we moved to

Arkansas before I turned two. My parents met in college and then moved to Arkansas after they graduated to be near my mom's family. My dad is from Missouri."

"Are you close to your family?"

"As close as you can be when you live hundreds of miles apart. I have a twin brother named Shannon who lives in Little Rock. My little sister is a freshman in college in Oklahoma. And my parents are still in my hometown about thirty miles outside Little Rock."

"Ooh! What's it like having a twin?"

"We're not those kinds of twins who finish each other's sentences or anything. When we were little, we were inseparable, but since we're boy-girl twins, as we got older, we drifted apart a little."

"Is he cute?"

"Who?"

"Your brother. Is he as attractive as you are?" She circles her finger in front of my face.

"Um, I don't know how to answer that question."

"Sure you do. Is Shannon handsome?"

Wendy isn't going to give up, so I admit, "I guess so."

"Do you have a picture of him?"

"I have lots of pictures of him, but not with me. I don't carry my brother's photo around in my wallet. Why do you care what he looks like?"

"You didn't mention him having a wife, so I'm trying to determine if I should add him to my list of possibilities."

I roll my eyes. I've not known anyone as boy crazy as Wendy since high school. "As I said, he lives in Little Rock. He's not a candidate for your list."

Wendy suddenly sits up straight and fluffs up her hair. "Speaking of my list," she murmurs, while smiling like the Cheshire cat.

I try not to grimace at her manic expression, and I twist in my seat to spot who she's focused on, since she didn't finish her statement.

"No," she hisses. "Don't turn around."

I swivel back toward her. "Ooookay."

She gives a little finger wave to someone beyond me, her weird smile still plastered in place. I can't resist looking again to see who could turn this normally confident woman into a mass of nerves. My gaze lands on a man being seated a few tables away. He's tall—at least six-five—with dark brown hair. His charcoal gray suit is perfectly fitted to his athletic frame. No off-the-rack business attire for this guy. I only have a profile view of his face, but I can tell he's handsome. He also looks familiar, though I can't imagine I know him since I'm new to the city.

"I told you not to turn around," Wendy says.

I face her again. "Sorry. Is it the tall guy back there?" I jerk my head in his direction.

"Yes."

"Tell me about him." I smile. "You know you're dying to."

Her face finally returns to normal, and then her expression turns dreamy. "His name is at the top of my list. He's a lawyer at the firm in the building around the corner from ours. You know: Murphy, Hamilton, and Walker?"

I shrug. "Nope. Don't know it."

"His dad is one of the partners there." She speaks to me, but she focuses on the man behind me. "He graduated from Harvard Law a couple years ago and came back to work for the family business. He's a bit grumpy, but I know there's a happy soul inside there waiting to burst out—with the help of the right woman, of course."

"And you think you're the right woman?" I take a bite of lasagna.

"Oh, I am most definitely the woman for Ash Hamilton."

My fork clatters to my plate as I choke on my pasta.

two

. . .

"Do you know the woman with the scary smile?" Jay McDavitt asks me.

"Yeah, he does," my brother Randall says, as he smirks at me across the table at Sapori D'Italia. "Wendy O'Halloran. Works at Carter-Jenkins PR. She's been in love with Ash since she first clapped eyes on him six months ago."

"She's cute," Jay says. "Or she would be if she wore a normal expression."

"Hmph," is my only reply to the latest addition to the Murphy, Hamilton, and Walker team. Jay isn't my favorite person, and for some reason, he keeps inviting Randall and me to lunch. Today my brother and I finally gave in, and I'm already regretting it.

"You're not interested in her?" Jay asks.

"Not in the least." I shake my head. "She may be cute—and smart—but she's always way too happy."

"And that's a problem?"

"Yes," I say. "Nobody should be that upbeat all the time. It's like she refuses to believe anything bad ever happens."

"Nothing wrong with that," Jay replies. "Especially in our line of work. We see the ugly side of life every day. Might be nice to go home to someone who only sees the beautiful."

"Then you date her."

"Maybe I will." He takes a sip of the drink that almost magically appeared in front of him the moment we sat down. Jay must already be a regular at Sapori. "But she has eyes only for you. Look at her."

I shake my head, as I have no intention of looking. There's no reason to give Wendy the impression I have any interest in her.

"Her friend is a stunner," my brother adds. "Take a look at *her*, at least."

"Nope."

"Why? She's—"

Randall's statement is interrupted by the clatter of a utensil against a plate followed by choking sounds. He's up and away from us in a flash. Jay and I watch my brother's quick progress to Wendy's table, where he jerks the blonde-haired woman up out of her chair, wraps his arms around her middle, and performs the Heimlich maneuver. A chunk of food launches out of her mouth and lands on the floor a good fifteen feet away. The entire restaurant applauds as the woman covers her crimson face with her hands and Randall helps her back into her seat.

"Randall Hamilton, saving the day yet again," I say when he returns to our table a minute later.

"He has a habit of rescuing ladies in distress?" Jay asks.

"Yes. He should've been a firefighter, not a lawyer."

"I rescue plenty of distressed people every day." My brother sounds defensive, as he does each time I point out he could've chosen a different profession.

"And they pay you handsomely for it," Jay replies. "Much more than if you were a fireman. You made the wise choice, my friend."

Randall doesn't reply. He and I both know he only went to law school and joined the firm because he was too chicken to defy our father, whereas I was born to bring justice and do my best to right the wrongs of the world. Not that I'm getting a chance to do so.

"What did you learn about your beautiful damsel?" Jay asks Randall. "Since her friend's heart obviously belongs to Ash, and you're attached to Colleen, maybe I should set my sights on her. She does have a great—"

"Jay," I say firmly before he can utter what I knew he was thinking—what we were all thinking.

"What? It's true."

"You don't need to say it. Have some respect."

He purses his lips but doesn't argue. Though he's a couple years older than me, I've been around the firm longer and am a partner's son. He knows better than to get on my bad side, and disrespecting women is one of the quickest ways to do that.

"As we've ascertained," my brother says, "she's gorgeous. And she has the most delectable Southern accent. Told me she's originally from Arkansas."

The mention of Arkansas unleashes a flood of memories of my childhood pen pal. I only did the pen pal thing because my fourth-grade teacher required it, but I ended up writing to Les for four years until I decided I was too old keep it up. In fact, I stopped partly because Randall made fun of me for it.

"Her name is Leslie," he continues.

I whip my head toward my brother.

He cocks his head at me. "What?"

"Nothing. Her name reminded me of someone."

"Oh yeeeah," Randall says. "Your old friend Les. He was from Arkansas, too, wasn't he? Maybe she knows him!" He chuckles. "Isn't everybody in Arkansas related to each other?"

His statement irks me, though I'm not sure why. More than a decade has passed since Les and I last wrote to each other, so I shouldn't care. But I have a rare soft spot for my old pen pal. He had a way of asking the right questions to draw things out of me, and I felt safe sharing my secrets with a virtual stranger.

Randall is mostly a great brother, but when we were younger, I could never talk about anything important—especially about girls —without him teasing me. So I told Les everything instead. It was easier writing about my feelings than talking about them anyway. But the one thing I never told him was I thought his twin sister was cute. I didn't think he'd appreciate that level of honesty.

As I eat my minestrone, I wonder where Les is now. He always said he wanted to be a journalist, and I hope he made it happen.

"Earth to Ash." Randall waves a hand in front of my face.

"Sorry." I snap out of my reverie. "What are you guys talking about?"

"The Carruthers case," Jay said. "Unless you'd rather talk about Wendy."

"Not a chance."

three

. . .

"When we leave," Wendy says, "we'll stop by their table and thank Randall one more time. And maybe I'll get to talk to Ash."

I almost choke again and take a sip of water to give myself time to come up with an acceptable response. "Let's not make a big deal out of it," I finally say, my heart racing.

"Not make a big deal out of a man saving your life? Ha!" She gives me a sly look. "What was it like having his strong arms around you? He's a handsome one, too." She frowns. "Though he has a girlfriend."

"How do you know so much about the Hamilton brothers?" I ask, avoiding her question.

"I have my ways," she says.

I raise an eyebrow at her.

"All right, fine. I made nice with Annette, the receptionist over at their office. Every few weeks, I invite her to lunch and grill her. Unfortunately, she doesn't give me much. Something tells me she goes because she wants a free meal."

"What else do you know about this Ash?"

Wendy narrows her eyes at me. "Why?"

"I'm curious." I want to learn more about the man who was once the boy I wrote countless letters to—the boy I deceived.

"Don't tell me you're interested in him, too!" she wails.

"Please don't fall for the man at the top of my list. He'll totally pick you."

"Keep your voice down," I say. "I'm not falling for anybody. I'm only asking. Plus, I haven't gotten a good look at him." Though I want to. If Ash has aged halfway as well as his brother, Wendy may indeed find herself with some competition.

No, I tell myself. *He can't find out who I am. He'll never forgive me.*

"Never mind," I say. "I don't need to know about him." And I need to stay far away from him.

Wendy pouts. "But I want to tell you about him, as long as you promise to not snatch him out from under me."

"I have no intention of doing so."

"Okay, then," she says conspiratorially, "Annette told me he hasn't had a serious girlfriend since he was in college. Not law school—college. That's at least five years ago."

I was never great at math, but I know she's wrong about the timing. Ash would've graduated the same year I did—three years ago, not five. But I can't tell her I know that.

However, she solves the conundrum for me. "He's extremely smart. Skipped a grade in high school and then finished college in three years." She sighs. "I love a brainy man." Wendy glances at her watch. "Oh! I'm about to be late for a meeting. We need to run." She flags down a waiter and asks him to bring the check as quickly as possible. "It's on me," she tells me. "After all, you nearly died."

"You don't need to pay for my meal."

"I do. If it makes you feel better, you can cover me next time."

"Deal."

When the waiter brings the check, Wendy pulls a few bills out of her wallet and sets them on the table as she stands. "Let's go. I want to stop and say hey to the Hamilton men on the way out."

"Let's not," I say, but she's already halfway to their table.

As I approach them, I keep my head down and attempt to walk on by, but Wendy grabs my wrist and tugs me beside her.

"Randall," she says, "Leslie and I wanted to thank you again for saving her life."

I avoid Ash's gaze as I focus on his brother. "Yes, thank you, Mr. Hamilton."

"Please, it's Randall. I did have my arms around you, so I think we're close enough now to use each other's first names." He grins at me. "Speaking of names, my brother here used to know someone from Arkansas named Leslie."

"Randall," Ash warns as my heart stops. His deep voice sends a shiver through me.

His brother plows ahead. "I figure everybody knows everyone else in Arkansas, so maybe you know him. Les something." His mouth twists. "What was it?" He looks at Ash, who shakes his head as I feel all the blood drain from my own.

I pull on Wendy's hand, but she stands firm.

"Bartlett?" Randall muses. "Beckham?" His forehead wrinkles and then he points a finger into the air. "Beckett! That's it. Beckett."

My body sways and I pray I'll faint so I won't know what happens next.

No such luck.

Wendy turns to me with wide eyes. "That's *your* last name."

Randall and the other man at the table both laugh.

"What are the odds?" the other man asks. "Is he your cousin or something?"

I can't look at Ash. I can't.

I have to. I need to see how he's reacting to the bombshell Wendy dropped on him. My gaze slowly moves to my old friend. His piercing blue eyes briefly shine with recognition before turning steely.

"Surprise." I give him a shaky smile, hoping against hope I'll get a grin in return.

My hope is shattered when Ash's nostrils flare, he pushes back his chair with a screech, and he stands. He shoots me one last glare and then strides swiftly across the room toward the exit.

"Ash, wait," I feebly call out.

"Hold up," Wendy says. "You two *know* each other?"

Her words snap me out of my shock, and I race after Ash without acknowledging Wendy's statement. Considering he had a head start and is about a foot taller than me, he's out the door before I'm halfway across the restaurant. I rush out onto the sidewalk, frantically looking in each direction. His height makes it easy to spot him heading toward our offices. I run after him, ignoring the pain shooting from the balls of my feet all the way up my legs from running in heels on concrete.

"Ash!" I call out much more forcefully than before. "Ash, wait!"

As he's apparently too dignified to run down the street, I catch up with him at the end of the next block as the light turns red, forcing us to stop at the corner. He spins away from me, but I skirt around him and place a hand on his arm as I suck in air. He jerks away from my touch and refuses to meet my eyes.

"Don't touch me," he says through gritted teeth. "Don't talk to me."

"Ash, I'm sorry, okay? Please let me explain."

He crosses his arms over his chest and finally meets my eyes. "You had four years to explain. Why do you think I'd want your explanation now? Why are you even here?" His eyes narrow. "How did you find me?"

"I didn't find you. I work with Wendy."

"No, you don't."

"Pretty sure I do," I retort.

"I know everybody who works at Carter-Jenkins, and you're not one of them." He sticks a finger two inches away from my face.

I move my head to the side to get away from his finger. "I started last week."

The light changes, and he shoots across the street.

I chase after him again. "Ash, let's please talk about this." I have to jog to keep up with his long stride. "Can we meet for dinner?"

He stops so abruptly I'm two steps beyond him before I can come to a halt. I turn to face him.

"No," he spits out, "we can't meet for dinner. No, we won't talk about it." He jabs a finger at me. "You deceived me. That's all

I need to know." He continues down the sidewalk, giving me a wide berth as he passes.

I want to reach out to him again, but I know that wouldn't go well.

"Please, Ash."

"No," he throws over his shoulder. "We're done."

four

. . .

I throw open the door to Murphy, Hamilton, and Walker so forcefully it ricochets off its backstop and almost smacks back into me. The receptionist lets out a screech from behind her desk.

"Sorry, Annette," I mutter as I march by.

I want to slam my office door, but I don't need anyone else wondering what I'm so worked up about. I pride myself on my ability to stay calm in any situation, and I'm currently anything but composed.

I sink into my leather desk chair and drop my head into my hands. *How? How is this real?*

The one person I've ever felt completely safe opening up to in my life is a fraud, which fills my throat with bile. Unlike my brother, I've never had many friends. In fact, I don't want many. I do want some, though, but I've always had trouble keeping them. They always complain about my pragmatic way of looking at the world. They tell me it brings them down. And in high school, college, and law school I was a year or two younger than everyone else in my class, which didn't help matters. I wasn't even of legal drinking age until after I started law school. Not that I had much interest in partying, anyway. I mostly kept to myself and focused on getting all my work done so I could graduate and get out into the working world where I could make a difference.

A knock sounds on my office door, and it opens. I know it's

my brother without looking up. Nobody else would dare to come in without me giving permission first.

Randall closes the door and drops into one of the dark blue wingback chairs in front of my mahogany desk. He props an ankle on the opposite knee, links his hands behind his head, and peruses me.

"Want to tell me what happened back there?" he asks.

"No."

"Of course you don't."

My shoulders tense. "What's that supposed to mean?"

"You never talk about anything important."

"This isn't important."

"It's not?" He puts his hands on his knees and leans toward me. "You sure?"

I sigh. "Leave me alone, Randy." The nickname slips out. He's never let anyone but me call him that, and I now only use it when I'm upset and can't stop myself.

He sits back in his chair. "Nope. Not gonna happen."

We stare at each other for a good twenty seconds before my brother says, "I'm not leaving until you tell me about it."

"About what?"

He doesn't reply.

"Fine," I say. "That woman was my pen pal."

His expression doesn't change. "I figured as much. And how do you feel about that?"

I roll my eyes. "How do you think I feel?"

"I have an idea, but I want to hear you say it."

"I'm pissed, all right?" I practically shout. "She deceived me for four years. I told …" I shake my head.

"You told her what?" he prompts when I don't finish my thought.

"I told her things I never told anyone else. Some of what I wrote I never would've said if I knew she was a girl." I briefly close my eyes. "Especially if I knew she was *that* girl."

His eyebrows raise. "What girl?"

Why did I let that slip out? No doubt my brother will keep trying to pry it out of me, so I tell him. "Les has a twin brother—

Shannon. He ... *she* sent several pictures of them throughout the years. I thought she," I wave my hand in the general direction of Carter-Jenkins PR, "was the boy and Shannon was the girl. Apparently, I had it backward, and she never told me."

"And considering she's drop-dead gorgeous, I'm guessing at fourteen she wasn't ugly. You had a crush on her, didn't you?" Randall wiggles his eyebrows at me.

"See?" I point at him. "That right there—that's why I could never tell you things. That's why I told Les ... Leslie instead."

"What couldn't you tell me about?"

I sigh. How have I gotten into this conversation? "About girls—about my feelings." I take a deep breath and force myself to look him in the eye. "You always made fun of me."

Randall's jaw drops. "Are you serious? I was joking around."

"That's not how it felt back then." I decide if I'm being open for once, I should go for broke. "Or now."

He slumps in his chair. "I'm sorry, man. Why have you never told me? I would've stopped."

I shrug. "I don't know." I'm not avoiding an answer. I truly don't know.

"So what are you going to do now?"

"Nothing."

"Nothing?"

"Nothing."

"You're going to forget this ever happened?"

"Yes." I stab the desk with my finger as I say it.

"You're not going to talk to her?"

"No."

"Did you talk to her on the way over here? Did she catch up with you after you ran out?" He moves his fingers in a running motion but then stops and cringes when he realizes he's making fun of me. "Sorry." His old habit will die hard.

I cross my arms over my chest. "I didn't run out."

"Close to it. But did you talk to her?"

"Kind of."

"What does that mean?"

I tell him about the conversation.

"And you're not going to dinner with this knockout woman? Are you dead inside?"

"I don't care what she looks like. She's a liar."

"You're a liar. You do care what she looks like."

My brother isn't wrong. Leslie is the most beautiful woman I've ever seen—she looks a little like Michelle Pfeiffer, only *better* —and I can still feel the imprint of her hand where she touched my arm, which makes the whole situation worse, if that's possible. I refuse to be attracted to the woman who betrayed me.

"You can't avoid her," Randall says. "You're over at Carter-Jenkins all the time."

I close my eyes. Doing legal work to help cover up the questionable actions of a bunch of celebrities is a far cry from my dream job, but when I joined the law firm, my dad assigned me to Carter-Jenkins PR. He told me if I could successfully handle their legal counsel for three years, he'd let me do something I thought was more worthwhile. It feels like hazing, and there are days I want to tell my father where he can stuff the public relations nonsense, but I'm determined to make it through the next year so I can do what I really want to do.

My mind wanders to wondering how Leslie ended up in PR. That wasn't her dream.

"You'll probably have to work with her," Randall says.

My eyes pop open. He's doing his best to hold back a smirk.

"Didn't think of that, did you?"

five

. . .

My office door swings open without warning.

Wendy puts her hands on her hips and glares at me. "You let me blabber on about that man like a fool, and all the while you *know* him?"

I hid in my office upon my return from the confrontation with Ash on the sidewalk, but I knew it was only a matter of time until Wendy finished her meeting and demanded an explanation.

"Can you close the door?" I ask.

She narrows her eyes for a few seconds before sticking her leg out and kicking the door shut.

"Well?" she asks, hands still on hips.

"Please sit." I motion to the deep purple upholstered chair next to my desk. "I'll tell you everything. I promise."

Wendy flounces over to the chair and plops into it. "This better be good. I thought you were my *friend*."

"I am. Please hear me out."

She hesitates but finally nods.

"It all started in fourth grade."

She sits up straight. "You've known Ash since you were ten? How? You're from Arkansas, and he's from here."

"We were pen pals."

"Ahhh. I had a pen pal named Jill from New Jersey." She cocks her head. "But she was a girl."

"I thought my pen pal was a girl."

Her forehead wrinkles. "Why would you think Ash is a girl?"

"Because Ash isn't his full name." If Wendy doesn't know his real name, he likely won't appreciate me divulging it to her, but I can't avoid it. "It's Ashley."

Her eyes open wide. "Ohhhhh. How did I not know that?"

"He thought I was a boy, I'm guessing because of my name and he would've assumed the person he was matched up with would be a boy, like I assumed they matched me up with a girl."

"But didn't you send pictures? Jill and I did."

"I sent a picture with my first letter, but it was of my whole family. I often refer to Shannon as my twin, not my brother, so it would've been easy for Ash to think Shannon was the girl in the photo and I was the boy."

She nods. "I can see how that could happen."

"We wrote back and forth for several months before he sent a family photo and I realized he was a boy. At the same time, I discovered he thought I was a boy because he asked me what it was like to have a girl for a twin. But my twin is a boy."

"So you figured it out, but you didn't tell him."

"No." I press my lips together.

"Why?"

"I was ten, and I really connected with him. I was into sports, and he was into sports. We both played tennis. We both had brothers who drove us crazy at times, and we had much younger sisters. Our birthdays are on holidays. We had a lot in common, and I enjoyed writing to him. But I had a feeling he would stop writing to me if he knew I was a girl. Or at least he wouldn't tell me anything interesting."

"You were probably right."

"Yeah, and I was wrong to do what I did."

"You were ten."

"Yes, when it started, but we were fourteen when he stopped writing back. I should've told him." I never told him because as we got older, I became infatuated with him. He was my first real crush, but I'm embarrassed to admit that to her.

Wendy scoots up to the edge of her chair. "So what did he say when you caught up to him today? You did catch up to him, right?"

I nod. "He didn't want to talk to me. He wouldn't let me explain."

"He'll come around. He's a reasonable man."

"I don't think so. He was adamant he wanted nothing to do with me. I'm going to let it go and hope I never run into him again."

"Those hopes are going to be dashed."

"It's a big city. I should be able to avoid him, even if he works around the corner."

She shakes her head. "Not possible."

"Why? Because you're going to date him?" I don't want to think about why I feel sick by that notion.

"Heck, no."

I raise an eyebrow. "But he's at the top of your list. A couple hours ago you couldn't stop talking about him."

She flicks her thumb and forefinger up and down. "Switch flipped. He's now off the list. I'll find someone else—like that guy with him and Randall at lunch. Or your twin." She points to the family photo on my desk and smirks at me. "He's more beautiful than you—and Ash. But anyway, I can't date Ash now, because the two of you are obviously destined for each other."

I laugh, because of both Wendy's final statement and her ability to shift her affections from one man to another at breakneck pace. "I don't think so. He won't talk to me."

"Think about it. You wrote letters to each other for *four years*. And now you've found each other again after all this time. It's so romantic." She puts her hands over her heart. "Imagine telling this story to your grandkids someday."

"Oh, yes, telling them about how Nana lied to Pop-Pop for four years will be a great family memory."

"You were a kid. He's a good man. He'll forgive you."

"I don't know. And no matter what you say, I'm planning to avoid him, anyway."

"You can't." Her eyes dance, which assures me I don't want to hear what she's going to say next. "He works with us."

My eyebrows shoot up. "He does what, now?"

"He's our legal counsel. The man is in our office more than his own."

I'm floored. Doing legal work for a PR firm was nowhere in Ash's grand plans for his future. Isn't his dad a partner? Surely Ash can pick his clients. Has he changed that much in the years since I've known him? And why doesn't Carter-Jenkins have in-house counsel, anyway?

"Cat got your tongue?" Wendy asks.

I shake myself and focus on my friend. "So you're saying I'm going to have to deal with him?"

"More importantly, he's going to have to deal with you."

six

· · ·

I have no idea how I'm going to deal with working with her. Well, I'm not positive I'll ever need to work with her directly, but she'll be around, being all alluring and deceptive, like a modern-day Delilah.

I've always hated that Bible story. While I'm not fond of Delilah, Samson grates on my nerves. How could such a strong man be deceived so easily? I groan when I realize I'm not much different than he was. At least I have the excuse of being a child at the time.

My phone beeps, and I press the intercom button. "What?" I bark and immediately regret my tone. "Sorry, Annette. I apologize for taking my mood out on you. What do you need?"

"I've got Wendy O'Halloran here for you."

I hold back my sigh. "What does she want?"

"Only a moment of your time," Wendy's voice chirps out of my phone speaker. "Annette told me you don't have any meetings this afternoon."

Annette will be receiving a lecture on discretion before the day is out.

"I'm coming down," Wendy informs me. "See you in five seconds!"

"Wait," I say, while knowing it's no use trying to stop her.

"Sorry, Mr. Hamilton," Annette says. "She's already …"

My office door swings open. The woman didn't see fit to knock.

"What can I do for you, Miss O'Halloran?"

"What's with the 'Miss O'Halloran'? You never call me that."

"What do you want, *Wendy?*"

"That's better." She perches on the chair across the desk from me and gives me an expectant look, as if I know exactly what she wants to hear.

"I'm going to ask you one more time," I say as respectfully as I can under the circumstances. "What do you need?"

Her expression turns earnest. "For you to give Leslie a chance."

My jaw clenches without my permission. "A chance for what?"

"To explain."

"I don't need her to explain anything to me," I lie. I desperately want to know why she pretended to be a boy, but I'm not about to ask her. I realize it makes no sense that she wants to explain it, and I want her explanation, but I'm refusing to allow her to give it to me. However, my pride and stubbornness overrule the logic.

"Oh, but you do." Wendy gives me a sunny smile.

I growl in reply, and her eyes widen, but the smile stays in place.

"This situation has nothing to do with you, Wendy."

"It has everything to do with me."

"Care to reveal how?" I link my hands together, set them on the desk in front of me, and lean toward her. I'm more than ready to refute any reason she might provide. I didn't graduate at the top of my Harvard Law class for nothing.

"I know you, Ash. You're curmudgeonly already, but if you try to avoid or ignore Leslie whenever you come over to Carter-Jenkins, you're going to kill the mood every single time. We don't need that kind of energy over there."

"Curmudgeonly?" I know I'm not the most positive person, but I'm offended by her characterization of me. And I'm a little surprised. How can she be interested in me while also thinking I'm a grouch?

"You're an adorable curmudgeon, I'll admit. But you still often remind me of a grumpy old man."

I think I'm even more offended by the "adorable" description. I shake my head to get my mind back on track.

"I know there's a heart of gold inside you, though," she says dramatically, with a hand over her heart. "You're a good man, Ash Hamilton, and that's why I know you're going to give Leslie a chance."

This woman is maddening, but how am I supposed to argue with her without looking like more of a grumpy old man? She'd make an exceptional lawyer.

I sigh and lean back in my chair. "I'm sure you have a plan for this already."

"There's a reservation for two in my name at Chez Patrice tonight at eight o'clock. Don't be late."

Wendy stands and thrusts a hand out across my desk. My own right hand automatically reaches out and grasps it before I realize by doing so, I'm agreeing to her scheme.

"Excellent," she says. "I knew I could count on you." She's out the door before I can formulate a response.

I'm stunned by how easily she roped me in. And I'm baffled by her ability to get a reservation at Chez Patrice. The latest hotspot in downtown Chicago has a three-month waitlist. I'm also surprised by Wendy's unusual demeanor. She's usually completely flustered around me, but she was in full-on confident PR maven mode just now, like she typically is around everyone else.

My mind wanders to Leslie. Though I'm still angry, I need to give her a chance to explain, especially since I can't avoid her for long. I can't imagine there's a good reason for what she did, but I won't know until I hear what she has to say. I well know you can't put together a compelling argument unless you're aware of all the facts.

I jump in my seat when my brother pops his head into my

office, also without knocking. I make a mental note to start locking the door.

"Did I see Glinda scurry out of here?"

When nobody else is around, Randall refers to Wendy as Glinda the Good Witch from *The Wizard of Oz*. Since it's an accurate moniker and not especially disrespectful—who doesn't love Glinda?—I let him get away with it.

Randall steps inside and takes the seat Wendy recently vacated. "What did she want?"

I consider what to share with him. I don't particularly want his input again, but he doesn't look like he's going anywhere. The quickest way to make him go away will be to give him what he wants.

"Apparently I'm going to dinner with Leslie tonight."

His eyebrows shoot up. "Dang, Glinda's good." A smile spreads across his face, and if I were a violent man, I'd be tempted to smack it off. "No wonder the top brass all love her over there. I'd pay good money to see her face off against you in a courtroom." He taps his finger to his lips. "You think she could pass the bar without going to law school?" He nods. "I bet she could. She's deceptively brilliant."

"You done having a conversation with yourself?"

He bobs his head from side to side a few times. "I guess. I'd ask what's got you so much grouchier than normal, but I already know."

"I'm not grouchy!" I say louder than I intended.

He chuckles. "You know what Annette calls you when you're not around?"

"I don't want to know." I'm positive my brother will tell me anyway.

"Grouchy Smurf."

I press my lips together and don't give him the satisfaction of a response, but the nickname stings. Am I really that unpleasant to be around?

"You gonna go home and change before your date?" he asks.

"It's not a date," I say through gritted teeth.

He shrugs. "Well?"

"Well, what?"

"You going to change?"

"Why would I?"

"You look better in your navy suit. It enhances those baby blues."

My jaw drops. Randall doesn't have a fashionable bone in his body.

"So says Colleen." He grins at me. "Not about you, of course. But since we have the same color eyes, I'm sure it applies to you, too. And also, you need to get over the whole boy-girl mix-up. She was a kid. I doubt she'd make the same decision now." He pushes himself out of his chair. "Enjoy your date."

I glare at him.

"Don't do anything I wouldn't do," he calls out in a sing-song voice as the door clicks shut behind him.

seven

. . .

"**Y**ou're going to dinner with me tonight," Wendy declares as she waltzes into my office without knocking.

"But I ate lunch with you." And all I want to do is go back to my studio apartment, drink a glass of wine—or three—and crawl into bed. I'm dying for a bubble bath, but as I only have a shower, that's not going to happen.

"You don't understand." She throws her arms out. "I got a reservation at *Chez Patrice.*"

My eyes widen. Wendy has talked about little else than Chez Patrice since I met her. I may be new to town, but even I know getting a reservation there is a coup. "How did you pull that off?"

She blows on her knuckles and then rubs them on her shoulder. "I'm good."

"Don't you want to take a man with you?" I hope she'll say yes. Although I'd love to try the place out, tonight isn't the best time.

"Nope. It's you and me, babe. No arguments. Wear one of your fancy dresses. People get all decked out to go there."

I only own one fancy dress, so it won't be hard to choose.

"Pick one that accentuates the twins." She points at my chest. "Those twins, not you and Sexy Shannon."

My face turns red. "Why?"

"You never know who we might see there. Your future husband might be sitting at the next table."

I roll my eyes but agree to go. "Want to share a cab?" I ask. Wendy lives near me, and Chez Patrice is at least fifteen blocks from us. It's too far to walk in heels and a nice dress, especially after dark, and I'd prefer not to take the bus, but I'm not sure I want to spring for a taxi on my own. I'm positive the meal won't be cheap.

"Can't," she says. "Sorry. I've got some errands to take care of between work and dinner. I keep a few nice outfits in my office for last-minute plans like this."

"Aunt Star, before I tell you what happened, promise you won't say you told me so," I plead into the phone when I get home from work. "And don't tell anyone else about this."

My aunt Starla is one of my favorite people, and she's the best at keeping secrets. In fact, until today, she's the only person in my life who knew Ash was a boy. Even my parents and Shannon never knew he wasn't a girl.

"Of course I won't, kiddo. You know you can trust me."

"I do."

She's never failed me yet. Aunt Star is my dad's younger sister who lives in the small town where they grew up in Missouri. When I was a kid, my siblings and I spent two weeks with my grandparents at the end of every summer, and Aunt Star was always around. She was tons of fun, and we could talk to her about anything without worrying she'd tell anyone or mock our youthful secrets and confessions.

I take a deep breath. "I ran into my old pen pal Ash at lunch. It didn't go well." I squeeze my eyes shut. "Because when we were kids, I never told him I was a girl."

She's silent for so long my heart inches up toward my throat.

"Les," she finally says, "for once in my forty years, I'm not sure what to say. But we'll get you through this, I promise. Why don't you tell me exactly what happened, and then we'll figure things out from there, okay?"

I tell her every detail.

"Please tell me what to do." I wind the phone cord around my finger as I sit cross-legged on my bed. "I want to march into his office and demand he listen to me, but I doubt that's the best idea."

"You might need to give him some time. He was blindsided by this, and in public, too. Let him have some space to process it first. Imagine how you'd feel if it were you. In fact, think about how you felt when you discovered he was a boy. What ran through your head? Do you remember?"

I remember it as clearly as if it were yesterday. "Well, I was shocked, obviously. And then I thought back through everything I'd told him, scared I'd said something I'd never say to a boy."

"Did you?"

"No."

"But did he ever write anything you think he'd never have said if he knew you were a girl—especially after you knew the truth?"

"Yes," I admit in a small voice.

As we got older, he told me many things he probably wouldn't have if he knew the truth. At first, I was too young to understand all the implications of my decision. And then when puberty hit, I felt special that a cute boy was sharing his innermost thoughts and feelings with me, though in the back of my mind I knew what I was doing was wrong. But now I realize how deeply I betrayed him.

"I'm a terrible person," I say. "How can I face him again?" I flop onto my back.

"You're not a terrible person, Les. Never think that. You're kind and smart and adventurous, not to mention almost as beautiful as your favorite aunt." She laughs at her joke. "But you did make a big mistake many years ago that needs to be made right."

One thing I appreciate about Aunt Star is she doesn't pull any punches. She tells you the truth even when you don't especially want to hear it, but she somehow manages to not make you feel awful in the process.

"What were the odds of me running into him?" I ask.

"Ridiculously low. But I don't think you running into him is a coincidence."

"What are you saying?"

"I'm not saying I think you're destined to marry him. But you were close once—maybe you can be again."

"I doubt it."

"Would you want to get to know him again?"

I sigh. "If he can forgive me. We had such a great connection all those years ago, even if it was born of deception."

"It wasn't born of deception. Your friendship started because of an honest mistake at wherever pen pal matches are made. The deception came later, at the hands of a ten-year-old. Did you ever write anything to him that wasn't true? Or did you simply lie by omission?"

"There was the big lie of omission, but I never technically lied. I sometimes worded things so he wouldn't know I'm a girl. And I disguised my handwriting so it wouldn't look girly." I cover my eyes with my free hand. "This only keeps getting worse, the longer I think about it."

"You've always been good with words," my aunt says. "Use them well when you do eventually talk to him about all this. Now, tell me all about your new job."

eight

. . .

I stick a finger between my neck and the collar of my new shirt to loosen it. I'll never tell Randall, but I went home to change into my navy suit before heading to the restaurant.

As I wait for Leslie to arrive, I look around the dimly lit room to avoid thinking about the conversation we're about to have. The clink of silverware on dishes is muted, and instrumental music plays in the background at the perfect volume. I can tell the surrounding diners are talking, but I can't hear their specific conversations. I'm not surprised people love this place.

I notice movement in my peripheral vision, and I turn my head. My gaze locks with Leslie's, and she stops. Panic flits across her features before she gives me a shaky smile and continues toward the table, trailing the hostess. Though I'm tempted to sit and stare as she approaches, I stand and pull out her chair. I catch a whiff of her floral perfume, and it's all I can do not to touch her bare shoulder as she sits. I don't know who designed the strapless purple dress that fits her like a glove, but I want to call and thank them. Then I mentally smack myself for the way my body is responding to this woman who deceived me.

"Sorry if I seem flustered," she says as she fiddles with her silverware and napkin. "I thought I was meeting Wendy." She takes a deep breath. "I'm not prepared for this."

Her anxiety oddly puts me at ease, though I also realize it

probably means I won't like what she has to say. And I'm surprised Wendy told me the truth about who I was eating dinner with, but she lied to Leslie. I'd have thought it would be the other way around, but Wendy obviously knew what she was doing, because we're both here.

"I'm not prepared either," I say, "and I knew you were coming. Leave it to Wendy to set this up." I drum my fingers on my leg. "I have no idea how she got the reservation, but she must like you a lot if she'd give up her chance to eat here so this could happen. Did you know her before you started working at Carter-Jenkins?" Why is it so easy to talk to Leslie? I shouldn't want to know anything about this woman. I also shouldn't be so turned on by her accent.

"No. But I think I'm already her new best friend." She gives me a tentative look, as if wondering whether to say what she's about to say. Then she asks, "Should I be worried about that? I like her, but I don't know her very well yet."

My chest swells at the realization she trusts my judgment and wants my opinion. "Wendy and I have a complicated friendship," I say, not wanting to mention her crush on me on the off-chance Leslie doesn't know about it. "But she's a good woman, and she's trustworthy." One corner of my mouth quirks up. "Well, if you don't count her lying to get you here."

"Her intentions were good, though."

We're silent a few moments before she laughs and points at the ceiling. "Is this a Whitney Houston song?"

I focus on the instrumental music for a moment, and the tune sounds familiar. "I can't say I'm a fan, but I'm pretty sure I've heard this tune coming out of my little sisters' rooms."

"Ah, yes, Tonya and Sonya," she says. "How old are they now?"

It's disconcerting to hear her talk about my sisters as if she knows them, but I guess in a way she does. "Tonya is about to graduate from high school, and Sonya's a junior."

"With their rhyming names, I always thought they should be twins." A look of horror crosses her face when she realizes what she said.

"They act like they are," I say in a pleasant tone, though a lump settles in my belly.

"Ash," Leslie says in a pained voice.

"Yes?" I ask, while knowing she's about to confess.

A waiter materializes at our table. "Good evening, can I get you two something to drink?"

Leslie hasn't opened the drink menu, but she immediately says, "A glass of your house red, please." Her hands are trembling, and I'm guessing she needs some liquid courage.

"Bring the whole bottle," I say. "Coke for me, thanks."

"You don't drink alcohol?" Leslie asks as the waiter walks away.

"No. I like to keep my faculties about me at all times."

One corner of her mouth quirks up. "But you want me to lose mine?"

I raise an eyebrow at her.

"If you're not going to share the bottle of wine with me," she says, "are you trying to get me drunk?"

I sit up straight and try not to feel offended. "No. I would *never* do that. It's cheaper to buy the whole bottle than two individual glasses, and most people drink more than one glass." I'm nothing if not thrifty, which is odd, considering how I was raised.

Leslie reaches a hand across the table and places it in front of me. I want to cover it with my own but thankfully catch myself before I do.

"Ash, I was joking. I don't think you'd set out to get a woman drunk. But your explanation makes sense. And you're right. I'll most definitely be drinking more than one glass." She pulls her hand back and her head tilts to the side. "Why are you being nice to me?"

"Should I not be?" I counter.

She hangs her head. "No."

She's not wrong, but I say, "Despite the way I acted this afternoon, and regardless of my Grouchy Smurf nickname," I shake my head at my surprising admission, "I try not to make a habit of being unkind to people, whether I think they deserve it or not." I wait until she looks me in the eye to add, "I'm sorry for the way I treated you."

Tears fill her big brown eyes. "You don't need to apologize. I do."

A lone tear trails down her face, and my hand twitches. I'm annoyed by my desire to reach across and brush the tear away, and I move my hand from the table to my leg to ensure I keep it to myself.

The waiter arrives with our drinks, and we're both silent as he pours wine into Leslie's glass. He waits for her to taste and approve it. As soon as he leaves, Leslie takes a gulp of wine and almost chokes on it. Her eyes water, and she dabs them with her napkin. She finally looks at me with eyes full of trepidation. She appears to be on the verge of breaking down, and I suddenly can't bear the thought.

"Listen, Leslie," I say while inwardly cursing myself, "this conversation won't be easy for either of us, and after it's over, we might not want to be in each other's presence." I can't believe I'm saying this, but I continue, "So how about we save the explanations until after we eat? Then if one of us storms out"—namely, me—"at least neither of us will leave hungry. I'd like to enjoy the meal, since Wendy went to the trouble of getting us a table here. How does that sound?"

nine

· · ·

Wendy *is* good. I don't doubt she expected Ash would do his best to make me feel comfortable, even if he's mad at me. I can't decide if his idea is wise or not, because I'm almost too nervous to eat, but he makes an excellent point. I may never get another chance to eat here, and Wendy made a huge sacrifice for us, though I still can't fathom why.

Instead of directly answering, I tease, "So … Grouchy Smurf, huh?" I hope it isn't the wrong thing to say.

It's not. Ash barks out such a loud laugh the people at the neighboring tables turn to glare. He covers his mouth, and the corners of his eyes crinkle. I giggle in response.

"Who calls you that?" I take a tiny sip of wine. I need to pace myself, if it's going to be at least an hour before my confession.

"Our receptionist."

"Annette?"

His head jerks. "How do you know her name?"

"Wendy might have mentioned it."

"Ah, yes." He rolls his eyes. "Is she one of Wendy's spies?"

"I will neither confirm nor deny your accusation."

He grins and points at me. "Which is a confirmation."

I shrug and smile. His blue eyes really pop with the navy suit he's wearing, and they linger on my mouth longer than they should. I lick my lips without intending to, and Ash's pupils dilate before his gaze skitters away from me. His physical interest surprises me, and I realize I could use it to my advantage. I immediately chastise myself for having such a thought, especially concerning Ash. A pit forms in my stomach as I consider whether I truly am a terrible person, regardless of what Aunt Star said earlier.

I clear my throat. "Speaking of Wendy, she told me you've already been practicing law for two years. But I know how old you are, so you should be graduating from law school this month. How did that happen?"

"As you know, Randall and I both went to a local Jesuit school through eighth grade, and then we attended a prep school in Connecticut for high school."

I nod. "I thought that was very fancy, you know."

He tilts his head. "Did you?"

"Oh, yes. I had to ask my dad what a prep school was. Not many of those where I come from." I shrug.

Ash chuckles. "I guess not. Anyway, after I took the entrance exams, the school told my parents I should start as a sophomore. Mom was against it, because it meant Randall and I would be in the same grade. She didn't like the idea of us competing with each other. But Dad was all for it—thought the competition would be good for us—so it happened."

"And was competition an issue?" I ask.

"No. Randall never cared much about academics, and we didn't play the same sports. I was the valedictorian, and he skated by with grades good enough to get into a decent school, but not an Ivy. Dad could've …" he trails off, and I detect a hint of a blush above his shirt collar.

"Your dad could've what?" I prompt. I want to know what he was going to say, even if he doesn't want to say it.

Ash sighs. "He could've pulled some strings and thrown enough cash around to get him in anywhere, but Randall didn't care where he went to college. For some inexplicable reason, Dad didn't force him into an Ivy. I think he knew if he did, my brother might refuse to go at all, which would kill his plan of the Hamilton boys taking over the firm someday."

"What about Murphy and Walker?" I ask. "Aren't they partners, too? Are their kids not in the business?"

"No, and neither is Walker anymore. He died last year."

"Oh, I'm sorry."

"I'm not. The man was a complete … jerk."

"You can say what you're thinking. You won't shock me."

"No, I don't curse in front of women, nor very often around men. Actually, I only do it in front of Randall, because he can somehow always bring out the worst in me."

I almost say it's the same with my brother, but I press my lips together to stop myself.

"We should probably take a look at the menus," I say. I don't want to put off the hard conversation any longer than we have to.

We spend a few minutes discussing the options, and the second we close the menus, our waiter appears.

When we've ordered, I ask, "Where did you go to college?"

"Harvard. I was only seventeen when I started, and I didn't fit in with my classmates, so I focused on my classes. As a result, I graduated in three years. And then I did law school there, too. I finished both college and law school a year before Randall did, which is weird."

I nod. I'm about to ask him how he ended up getting assigned to our PR firm when he asks where I went to college.

"Knox College in—"

"Galesburg," he finishes for me.

"You know it?" I'm a little surprised, even though the small liberal arts school is in Illinois.

"Of course. They have a great journalism department there."

"I know."

"That's what you studied?"

"I did. Does that surprise you?"

"Not in the least. It's what you wanted to do. Did you know Patrick Chamberlain at Knox?"

I almost spit out a mouthful of wine. "*You* know Patrick Chamberlain?"

He nods. "We went to church together as kids."

"Small world," I say, although maybe not as small world as

Ash careening back into my life. "I didn't know him well, but he dated a girl who lived a few doors down from me in the dorm. I wonder if they ended up getting married."

"They did a couple years ago. They've got a baby girl."

"You still keep in touch with him?"

"Not really. Our moms are friends, and I see him at church on holidays."

Our salads arrive, and we eat in companionable silence for several minutes before talking about different places we've traveled. Unsurprisingly, he's been many more places than I have.

When the waiter delivers our entrées, I'm not sure I can eat my chicken florentine. While Ash and I were chatting, I almost forgot about my upcoming explanation, but now I'm dreading it more than ever. The easy conversation proved there's still a connection between us. I don't want to lose that again, but I can't imagine I won't.

I pick at my food as Ash downs his meal in record time. We make small talk about the restaurant, the music, and the city itself, but we don't delve into more personal topics. I can tell he's trying to put me at ease, but I don't know why he's going to the trouble of doing so.

As soon as he swallows his last bite, I put my silverware down.

"I'm tired of stalling, and I can't eat any more." I push my plate away. "Are you ready?"

ten

. . .

"Not quite ready." I call for a busboy to remove our dishes and then pour Leslie another glass of wine. "Now we're ready."

She looks down at her lap. "I don't know where to start."

"Will it help if I ask questions?" Law school trained me well in that area.

She nods.

"All right." I take a deep breath and ask the question I most want—and least want—to know the answer to. "Did you know I was a boy from the beginning? Or that I thought you were a boy?"

"No," Leslie says forcefully, as she shakes her head, still looking down.

I briefly close my eyes in relief at her response. "When did you figure it out?"

She peeks up at me through her eyelashes.

I lean toward her. "You can look at me, all right? I promise I won't lash out at you again. I simply want to know the truth." Including the parts I might not like.

"Okay." She raises her head and gives her body a little shake, and I can almost see her confidence increase, which fills me with an odd sense of pride.

"I figured both out with the same letter. It was when you sent the first picture."

I nod. I can still see that family photo in my head.

"The moment I saw it I knew you were a boy. Then I read the letter."

I have no idea what I wrote in that letter, but I bet she could quote it word for word.

"At the very end," she says, "you asked if it was weird having a girl as my twin. At first the question confused me, but then I realized that like I thought I was writing to a girl, you thought you were writing to a boy. You assumed I was the boy in my family photo, which meant Shannon was the girl."

I remember asking the question, and I remember her response. "You said you didn't care if your twin was a boy or a girl—you would love them the same."

"It was the truth," she says defensively, though I hadn't used an accusatory tone.

"I know. But you didn't exactly answer the question." I cock my head. "How many times did you give me a half truth or not answer a question to keep from telling me the whole truth?"

She avoids my eyes and picks at a fingernail. "A lot. But I never did lie."

I study her face in the flickering candlelight until she meets my gaze again. "Why did you decide not to tell me you're a girl?" I thought the first question I asked was the most important one, but I've changed my mind. This one is. Her answer will determine whether we can salvage our friendship, and I realize with a jolt that I hope we can. Regardless of how this dinner came to be, I've enjoyed it. A lot.

"I was afraid you'd stop writing to me if I told you. I liked you. Our lives were so very different, but we had so much in common. I loved writing the letters, and I looked forward to getting yours and finding out more about you. I didn't want that to end."

It was the answer I was hoping for, and I pray it's the entire truth. I understand what she's saying, because it's the same way I felt about writing to Les—to her.

"When I was ten," she says, "I didn't think much about the

consequences of my actions. It seemed harmless, even though my aunt warned me not to do it."

"Aunt Star?" Leslie talked about her aunt a lot in her letters.

"Yes. She's the only person I ever told about you being a boy."

"Your parents didn't know?"

She shakes her head. "They still don't. At the time, I knew they wouldn't like the idea of me writing to a boy—and especially not as we got older. They might have been partly okay with it when I was ten, but not when I was twelve or thirteen. They would've made me stop then, but I didn't want to. You were so under-standing and," she dips her head, and a blush climbs up her neck, "you were cute. It kind of felt like I had a boyfriend, if I forgot about the fact that you didn't know I was a girl."

Her confession knocks the wind out of me.

She keeps going, "But most of all, I didn't tell them because then I'd have to tell you I was a girl, which I was sure would mean you would stop writing to me. My parents wouldn't have allowed me to not tell you the truth."

I'm relieved to hear the adults in her family weren't in on the charade. Or at least not all of them. "But your aunt thought it was fine you didn't tell me?"

"Absolutely not." She shakes her head vigorously. "The day after I got your letter, I went to Missouri for two weeks, and I showed Aunt Star your picture and the letter. She told me in no uncertain terms I needed to tell you I was a girl and also tell my parents about it. I never told her I didn't. Well, not until a few hours ago."

"And what did she say? Today, I mean."

"She told me to give you time to process everything before trying to compel you to talk to me. And I was going to give you that time, until ...," she waves her arm around to indicate our current situation.

"Right."

Her aunt gave her solid advice, but now that we're here, I'm glad Wendy forced our hands. If she hadn't, I'd still be stewing and probably despising Leslie more and more by the minute, but now I'm not. While I don't know if I would've made the same choice she did back then, I can understand why she did it.

"You didn't tell Shannon the truth?" I ask.

"No. It was weird not telling him something this big, but I knew he'd make fun of me if he knew I was writing to a boy."

I can relate to that.

She continues, "Shannon had a pen pal, too, for about four months. He hated it, so as soon as fourth grade was over and our teachers didn't require it anymore, he was done." She shakes her head. "He stopped writing to the other kid with no explanation. I was so annoyed with him."

That feels like a kick to the gut, although I'm sure she didn't mean it to be. "I'm sorry I did that to you."

"Oh!" Her hand goes to her mouth. "I wasn't trying to—"

"I know you weren't. But I'm still sorry."

She leans toward me, eyes locked on mine. "And I'm sorry. For all of it. I truly am." Her eyes fill with tears again. "Please believe me, Ash."

This time I do reach across to swipe a tear from her cheek. Her head jerks at my approach, but she doesn't pull away from my touch. My fingers tingle as I bring my hand back to my side of the table without breaking eye contact.

"I believe you. And I forgive you."

Her apology is sincere, and I'm positive she's not lying to me now. And back then, she was a kid who made a dumb decision that snowballed into something she eventually couldn't control. We've all done that in some capacity. I hope my willingness to forgive her so easily has nothing to do with how bewitching she looks in the candlelight or how her accent is more pronounced when she's emotional.

"You really forgive me?" She dabs her eyes with her napkin.

"Of course."

"Thank you," she says wholeheartedly.

"You're welcome. And thanks for telling me the truth. I know it wasn't easy."

She nods and takes a shaky breath. "Can I ask you a question now?"

"Sure."

"If I had told you about the gender mix-up when I figured it out, would you have kept writing to me?"

eleven

. . .

Now that the hard part is over, Ash visibly relaxes. He puts an elbow on the table and props his chin on his hand as his eyes roam over my face, study my mouth, and fleetingly dip lower. I force myself not to squirm under his perusal, but my skin heats up a few degrees.

"Even at ten, I had a crush on you," he says.

"What?" I squeak out and then cover my mouth, embarrassed by the high pitch of my voice.

He grins at me. "Of course, I thought you were Les's cute twin sister Shannon." He cocks his head to the side. "Though I guess all the things you told me about Shannon were about your brother —not the girl in the picture—and everything you told me about yourself was about *you*—not the boy in the picture—so maybe I had a crush on your brother."

I try to hold in my laughter, but I can't, and neither can he. We receive another round of glares from the surrounding tables, but I don't care, and he doesn't seem to either.

"To answer your question," he finally says, "I think I would've kept writing to you. But I wouldn't have told my family you were a girl. Randall would've never let me live it down. My dad never even knew I had a pen pal. Somehow, I knew he wouldn't approve of the idea of me writing to a stranger. Mom probably wouldn't have cared either way, but I wouldn't have wanted to find out."

Warmth spreads through my belly at his revelation. "You really would've still written to me?"

"While I don't know for sure, I think so. I loved writing to you, too. And to be honest, I didn't have any close friends, and it was easy to open up to you. I also enjoyed hearing about your life and your family, because they were so different from mine."

"So I kept up all the deception for nothing?" I give him a pouty look.

He chuckles. "Maybe so."

"If I'd been honest, I could've saved myself a lot of misery."

His expression turns serious. "Did it bother you that much?"

"I wouldn't really call it misery, and especially not when I was ten, but when I was older, I always had this little voice in my ear telling me what I was doing was wrong."

"Was the voice attached to a tiny woman with a white robe and halo that sat on your shoulder?"

I smile. "Yes, but she was drowned out by the tiny red man with horns and a pitchfork on my other shoulder who reminded me the truth might scare off my cute, smart, fake-boyfriend pen pal."

"That little guy can be persuasive."

"Tell me about it."

Ash considers me for a moment. "You thought I was cute? Randall always said I looked like an oversized leprechaun."

I giggle. "That's brothers for you. You looked nothing like a leprechaun. I thought you looked like Donny Osmond."

"That's funny." He struggles to keep a straight face. "So did I."

I throw my napkin at him. "You did not, Mr. Lucky Charms."

We smile at each other longer than should be comfortable, but somehow neither of us is embarrassed.

"Do you still think I look like Donny?" he finally asks.

"No." I press my lips together so I won't grin at him.

Ash's eyes widen. "No?"

"He still looks like a baby. You?" I slowly look him up and down—at least the part I can see. "All man."

His blue eyes darken a hue, and he clears his throat.

"Can I interest you in any dessert?" the waiter asks from out of nowhere.

Ash raises an eyebrow at me. "Leslie?" I consider it for a moment. I'm not ready to leave, since we're shockingly getting along so well. But I also suddenly realize I'm exhausted as well as sore from the Heimlich earlier, so I shake my head.

"We'll take the check," he tells the waiter.

Ash picks up his empty glass and holds it out toward me. "A toast, even though there's nothing left in my glass to toast with."

I pick up my wineglass and wonder what he's going to say.

"To old friends and new surprises."

"And to Wendy," I add.

"Hear, hear."

I clink my glass to his and swallow the last of my wine. He's studying me again when I set my glass down.

"What?" I say, suddenly self-conscious.

"I'm amazed we're here. Together. Friends. Ten hours ago, I thought you were a man. Nine hours ago, I wanted to wring your neck."

"You did, didn't you?" I twirl my wineglass by the stem, trying not to be disappointed by his "friends" label.

His gaze drops to my neck, and I feel it heat. "I'm glad I didn't."

My heart pounds. "Me, too."

The waiter brings the check. Ash reaches for it, but I snatch it up.

"No," he says and grabs for it. "I'm getting it."

"Nuh-uh." I hold it out of his reach. "It's my fault we're here."

"It's *Wendy's* fault we're here."

"True, but I doubt they'll take an IOU from us on her behalf."

I bring the little black folder down in front of me, flip it open, and while I'm distracted by the astronomical number flashing before my eyes, Ash plucks it out of my hand.

"I'm not letting you argue with me on this. I've got it."

Since I'm not sure how I'll cover my rent next month if I pay, I easily give in. "You don't have to, but thank you."

"It's my pleasure. If you feel the need to owe me—which you don't, by the way—you can pitch in next time."

I appreciate him allowing me to keep my pride, and then I realize the other part of what he's saying. "There's going to be a next time?"

He stills while pulling his wallet out of his back pocket and pins me with a serious look. "Only if you want there to be."

"I do." I do, I do, I do.

A smile slowly spreads across his face, and my heart skips a beat. "Excellent."

He finishes taking care of the bill, and then he stands and holds out a hand to me. I take it and sparks shoot all the way up my arm. I wobble on my feet as I stand, and he puts both hands on my waist to steady me. I gaze up into his eyes, and we stare at each other for I don't know how long until he turns me so his fingertips lightly graze the small of my back—sending goose-bumps from head to toe—and guides us to the door.

As we step out into the cool night air, his palm flattens against my lower back, and I shiver in response. Before I realize it, I'm wrapped in his suit jacket. I shiver again—this time from the sensation of his body heat warming me by proxy through the material. Suddenly, I'm glad I left my pashmina on the bus on the way here.

"How did you get here?"

"Hmm?" I look up at Ash.

"Did you walk? Drive? Take a cab?"

"Oh. I took the bus."

"The bus?" he says incredulously.

"Yeah, the stop is right down here." I walk in the direction I'm pointing, but I only make it a few steps before he wraps his hand around my arm and pulls me back.

"You are *not* taking the bus," he practically growls at me.

"No?"

"I'm taking you home."

My eyebrows shoot skyward.

"No, not like that." He holds his hands up. "We're not going to *my* home. I'm driving you to yours to make sure you get there safely. All right?"

Without waiting for me to answer, he flips open the front of the jacket I'm wearing, reaches into the inside pocket, retrieves a small card, and hands it to the man at the valet stand. A light cinnamon scent wafts up from the jacket, and I close my eyes to revel in the smell. It's somehow both comforting and stimulating.

The three minutes we wait for the car to come around are the most awkward moments of the evening so far. Neither of us seem to know what to say, so we say nothing.

I pay little attention to the four-door Volvo pulling up to the curb until Ash opens the front passenger door. My eyebrows ascend again. "This is your car?"

"What's wrong with it?" He sounds defensive.

"Nothing," I assure him. "I figured you'd drive a Porsche or BMW or something."

"I've always thought it's silly to waste money on cars."

Yet he just spent more on one meal than I paid for my first car. Then I remember this restaurant wasn't his idea.

Ash waves me forward, and I slide onto the seat. He carefully closes the door and rounds the vehicle to the driver's side. Then he puts the car in gear but doesn't take his foot off the brake.

"Where to?"

I give him my address. "Do you know where that is?"

"I know where everything is." He grins at me.

"Smartypants." I smile back.

He pulls into traffic, which is heavier than I thought it would be at ten o'clock on a Wednesday evening. As he maneuvers through the streets of downtown Chicago, I pull his jacket up higher and breathe in his scent. I watch him as he hums along to Aerosmith's "Angel" playing softly on the radio.

He glances over at me. "Are you watching me?"

"Busted."

"Stop it. You're making me nervous. I might get into a wreck."

"Really?"

"No."

I giggle. "It's truly bizarre that I'm here … with Ash Hamilton … in a Volvo … driving through Chicago. If you'd told me fifteen years ago we'd be here today, I wouldn't have believed it."

twelve

. . .

"If someone told me *yesterday* we'd be here," I say, "I wouldn't have believed it."

What a difference a day makes. What a difference a few hours make. I feel like the past ten hours have been a wild dream. But if this is a dream, I don't want to wake up. I want to keep driving around with Leslie by my side.

"Ouch!" I yelp at a sudden sting in my arm. I look over as Leslie's hand drops into her lap. My gaze moves up to her face, and she's pressing her lips together, trying not to smile.

"Did you pinch me?" I ask her with wide eyes.

"Yep. Wanted to make sure you're real."

I stop at a red light and rub my arm, but I can't blame her, since I was wondering the same thing.

"I'm real," I say, "and tomorrow I'm going to have a bruise."

"Me, too," she says, massaging her stomach.

It takes me a second to figure out what she's talking about. "Les, I'm so sorry. I should've asked if you're okay after choking at lunch."

She stares at me.

"What?"

"You called me Les. The other times you said my name tonight it was Leslie."

She's right. I've even thought of her as Leslie. I didn't do it on purpose, but maybe I didn't want to fully accept her connection to my past until now.

I can't tell if she likes that I used her nickname. "What do you want me to call you?"

"Whatever feels right."

"Okay. I don't know if I'm sure yet."

"That's fine. Can I call you Ashley?"

I whip my head toward her. She's grinning almost as goofily as Wendy did in the restaurant at lunch.

"Kidding," she says. "I have one more thing to confess, though."

My heart drops as my grip tightens on the steering wheel. I should have known there was more—that our night couldn't possibly end this well.

"I had to tell Wendy your full name."

"That's your confession?" I steal a glance at her.

She nods. "Is that okay?"

Though I'm not excited about it, it's not a huge deal. "It's fine. I don't advertise my name, but it's not difficult for people to find out. In fact, I'm shocked Wendy didn't already know. When I sign legal documents, I use my full name."

"I'm not surprised," she says. "The woman can't think straight in your presence."

I groan. "I wish she'd set her sights elsewhere. I like her, but I don't want to date her."

"She doesn't want to date you, either."

I pull over in front of a fire hydrant by Leslie's apartment building, shift into park, turn on the hazard lights, and finally turn to give her an incredulous look. "You said—and I quote—'The woman can't think straight in your presence.'"

"Let me amend my statement. That's true of the extremely recent past, but not the present."

"I sincerely doubt it. You saw her at lunch."

"I did. And then she saw a picture of my brother."

My jaw drops. "Are you kidding me? She discarded me for Shannon?"

She smirks at me. "Are you sad about that?"

"Not in the least. It's simply weird." But it explains why Wendy acted differently toward me in my office this afternoon.

"I think you should thank me."

"For what?"

"Providing her a reason to leave you alone."

Leslie leans forward and slips my jacket off her shoulders. I almost tell her to keep it, but thankfully I realize how strange that would be. Instead, I take it from her and reach back to place it on the backseat. I hope it now smells like her perfume, but I resist sniffing it. That would be even stranger. The last thing I want to do is run Leslie off. When I return my focus to her, she's watching me again.

"Thank you," she says softly.

I simply nod, because a lump is forming in my throat, which is a sensation I haven't felt in a long time. I know I should say something, but I can't, so I get out of the car and circle around to open her door. She cringes and presses a hand to her belly as she steps out.

"You're hurting." I take her other hand to guide her up onto the curb. "You should've said."

"I'll be fine." She shivers.

I don't want her to go, but I also don't want her to be cold, since she's no longer wearing my coat. She squeezes my hand, and I realize I'm staring at her bare shoulders and still holding her hand. My gaze moves to her face, but I don't let go of her. I surprise both of us when my other hand reaches up to cradle her cheek.

"Until next time?" I say as I look down into her eyes. She's not short, and she's wearing heels, but I'm still a good seven or eight inches taller than her.

"Yes," she whispers, but she doesn't move.

My focus shifts to her mouth, and I consider whether I should kiss her. I want nothing more than to discover whether she tastes as good as she smells, but I'm not sure she feels the same, and I don't want to screw this up. I swipe my thumb across her cheek, and she shivers again, reminding me she's freezing. I lower my head and press my lips to her forehead, drop my hands, and stick them in my pockets.

"You should get on inside where it's warm."

She nods, wraps her arms around herself, and steps past me. "Next time, Grouchy Smurf," she says over her shoulder as she walks away.

I smile and keep my eyes on her until she's safely inside the building, and then I stand there a little longer. I look up at the windows, wondering which one is hers.

"Hey man," a voice says. "Is that your car? You can't park there."

I turn toward a homeless man pointing a small tree branch at my car. "Yeah. Sorry. I'm leaving." I'm not sure why he cares where I'm parked, but there's no reason for me to continue standing in the cold, staring at a building.

thirteen

. . .

I step inside my apartment building and collapse into one of the two scratchy orange chairs in the dingy lobby. There's no way my legs can carry me up three flights of stairs. My forehead burns where Ash pressed his lips to it, and I place my hand where his rested on my jawline.

Why didn't he kiss me? I'm sure he wanted to. I could see it in his eyes, feel it in his gentle touch. Did he not truly forgive me? Is he punishing me by not giving me what we both so obviously want?

Maybe I wasn't obvious. Or Ash might not pick up on signals well. I know nothing about how he interacts with women. Wendy did say it's been a long time since he was in a relationship. Or perhaps he doesn't kiss on the first date. Not that our dinner was a date. And did he realize my final, "Next time, Grouchy Smurf," referred to kissing? I'm not fully sure why I used the silly nickname, because he wasn't grouchy at all tonight.

I slip my heels off and push myself out of the chair. As I pad up the stairs, I think back over the past half hour. Ash did seem to forgive me, and he flirted with me. And he *definitely* wanted to kiss me.

When I open my apartment door, a red light blinks at me from across the room. I'm too tired to call anyone back tonight, but if I don't listen to the message on my answering machine, the flashing light will keep me awake.

I toss my shoes onto the floor of my tiny closet, slip out of my dress and pantyhose—which are now ruined, thanks to a run from my shoeless trek up the stairs—and pull my Bon Jovi *Slippery When Wet* Tour T-shirt over my head. I debate whether to wash my face and brush my teeth before checking my messages, and the desire to feel clean wins out.

Finally, I hit the play button on the machine. "Leslie Beckett," Wendy's voice screeches out, "if you don't call me the second you get home tonight, you are not my friend anymore. And if you don't call by midnight, I'm calling you, even if that means I might be interrupting something … interesting." She giggles. "Because you shouldn't be doing that on the first date anyway, you naughty girl."

I flop down onto my bed. I'm too exhausted to talk to her, but I can't avoid it. There's another person I want to talk to first, though. My aunt is usually in bed before now, but she won't mind if I wake her. I dial her number, and she doesn't sound sleepy when she answers.

"Everything okay, kiddo?"

"It turns out my friend tricked me tonight. My dinner was with Ash, not her."

"Oh, wow. Did he forgive you?"

"He did."

"Was it genuine?"

"I'm ninety-nine percent certain it was."

"What about the other percent? Why aren't you completely sure?"

I feel like an idiot saying it, but I know she won't belittle me. "Because he didn't kiss me."

I imagine my aunt's eyes widening. "You wanted him to kiss you?"

"Yes. I'm positive he wanted to kiss me, too. But he didn't."

"Les, don't read anything into that. Tonight wasn't a date. Maybe he was being respectful."

"Maybe," I grumble.

"Have you been drinking?"

"I might have had a glass of wine. Possibly an entire bottle."

She sighs. "Don't get mad at me for asking this, but isn't it a little too soon after Glenn to be thinking about kissing another man?"

"I can kiss whoever I want whenever I want." I realize I sound like I'm twelve, but I'm tired and emotional and a little drunk. In all the drama of the afternoon and evening, I amazingly haven't thought about Glenn once, and I'm annoyed Aunt Star brought him up.

"True, as you're single, but it's only been a couple weeks since your boyfriend of two years broke up with you. Don't do a rebound relationship, honey. It won't be fair to the guy, and it won't be good for you. Especially don't do it to Ash, unless you want to hurt him again."

Her words are like a sword to the heart. "I don't want to hurt him."

"I didn't think you did. It's been a wild ride of a day, and you're not thinking straight. Do you feel like telling me all about tonight, or do you want to do that some other time?"

"Another time. I'm about to fall asleep."

"Okay. Talk to you again soon. Love you."

"Love you, too."

I hang up, and the last thing I want to do is to call Wendy, but I'd rather talk to her now than when she wakes me up later.

She answers on the first ring. "Leslie, is that you?"

"Yes, who else would it be at this time of night?"

She laughs. "It's not unheard of for me to get calls this late, but I was pretty sure it would be you. Tell me everything—every teeny-weeny, itty-bitty detail. Start at the very beginning. No, wait. First tell me if you kissed him."

My face burns. "No!"

"Bummer." She truly sounds disappointed. I can't believe how fast she got over Ash.

"You owe Ash big time, by the way," I say. "That restaurant was expensive!"

"Pssh. He can afford it. Ooo, but that means he paid for you! It must have gone well." If she's not wiggling her eyebrows, I'll be shocked.

"It was either pay the bill and then sell a kidney in order to keep my lights on, or let him pay. Not much of a decision there. I'm rather fond of my internal organs—and electricity."

"So it went well?"

"It did."

She's silent for all of two seconds before she says, "That's all I'm going to get? This happened because of *me*, you know."

"I know, and I'll be eternally grateful. But I can barely keep my eyes open. Can I tell you about it tomorrow?"

"I'll be waiting in your office when you get there."

fourteen

. . .

I can't sleep. I toss and turn and think about Leslie and then try to think about anything else under the sun and then think about her again.

Why didn't I kiss her? I'm not sure I've ever wanted anything more in my life than to kiss Leslie Beckett tonight, even if she pulled a big one over on me when we were kids. I shouldn't be surprised by how easily I forgave her, because I'm not one to hold a grudge, but it still blows my mind that within a handful of hours after learning the truth, I no longer care about the stupid decision she made fifteen years ago.

I consider whether I was right when I said I would've written to her if I'd known she was a girl. I think so, but I wouldn't have told her nearly as much as I did when I thought she was a boy.

I groan out loud when I recall telling her about Melissa Teague, my first in-person crush. Melissa went to my school and my church and was pretty and popular. She was my first kiss during a game of "Seven Minutes in Heaven" at Alex Conover's house in seventh grade, and the next day I heard her laughing about it after church. I'd never felt so humiliated.

There was no way I could tell Randall what happened, so I told Les. I remember his—her—response all these years later. "That girl doesn't deserve you, Ash. Ten years from now you won't remember her, but she'll read all about you in the newspaper and all the great things you're doing to help people, and she'll wish she'd never made fun of you."

Twelve years later, I haven't forgotten about Melissa, and my name hasn't been in the paper for anything related to helping people, but Les's words made me feel so much better at the time. I wonder if Leslie remembers. I bet she does. I bet she remembers everything.

I realize I'm still thinking of her as Leslie, not Les. That answers the question of which name feels right. Les was the kid I wrote to. Leslie is the woman keeping me awake.

At five a.m. I still haven't slept, and I know I'm not going to, so I shower, dress, and drive in to work. It's nice to not have to fight the morning traffic from Evanston to downtown. Of course, if I lived near the office, I wouldn't ever have to deal with traffic, but it suits me to live in my parents' pool house, even if Randall teases me about it. It saves money and I get to see my little sisters most days. I'm not into the Chicago nightlife, so the noise and bustle of downtown every night would undoubtedly bug me.

I pull into my reserved parking spot in the garage under our office tower, and for once I'm grateful to be a partner's son, since almost everyone else in the office who drives to work has to park blocks away.

Dad's car is already in his spot. I wonder if he went home last night. His office has a comfortable couch and its own full bath, so it's not unknown for him to sleep there. But my stomach clenches when I think about the few times I've caught him flirting with the new young paralegal. I tell myself there's nothing there. My parents might not be the most loving couple in the world, but I can't see him jeopardizing his carefully crafted family image by messing around on Mom.

The overnight security guard in the lobby greets me as I pass from the garage elevator to the bank of office elevators. I say hello and give him a brief nod as I press the elevator button. The door opens immediately, and I punch the button for the top floor. I sag against the wall as I ride up twenty-seven stories, which always takes longer than I think it should. At least it won't be stopping anywhere along the way at this time of day.

The elevator opens into the small, glassed-in room outside the plush lobby of Murphy, Hamilton, and Walker. I pull out my key to unlock the door, since it'll be hours before Annette arrives to buzz anyone in.

As soon as I walk past Annette's desk, I can see my office door is slightly open, and the light is on. I know I locked the door when I left yesterday, so I can't imagine why it's open now, but I'm certain my dad is in the office and the lobby door didn't appear to be tampered with, so I don't think I'm interrupting a break-in. I reach the door and nudge it enough to discover a woman's backside and legs sticking out from behind my desk.

"Hello?" I call out.

The legs disappear, and a head pops up above the desk. I stifle a laugh at the sight of the woman's wild hair and eyes.

"Mr. Hamilton, I did not hear you! I am so sorry." She scrambles to her feet.

"No, I'm the one who's sorry, Carmela," I say to my favorite custodian. "I didn't mean to startle you. Where's your cart?" It should be in the hallway, but it's not.

"One wheel is stuck, and I cannot fix it myself. So I must carry everything with me." She motions to the opposite side of my office, where a collection of cleaning supplies sits on a file cabinet next to an industrial-sized vacuum.

"Come show me," I say, heading back into the hall. "Let's see if I can fix it."

"Oh, no, Mr. Hamilton. I cannot ask you to do that. I will wait until Barney gets here at seven."

"You didn't ask. I offered. And please, call me Ash."

Her eyes widen. "It would not be proper."

She's right, and I'm irritated by that fact. If I was in charge, it would be perfectly proper, but not with Walter Hamilton at the helm. I would also allow her to speak her native Spanish in the office if she wanted to, instead of forcing her to always speak English.

"All right." I wave my arm to beckon her. "Come on, let's go fix your cart."

Carmela scampers past me and is halfway down the hall

before I can catch up to her with my long strides. I follow her around the corner and to the end of the hall to the janitor's closet. She squats down next to one of the rear wheels of the cart.

"Here, see?" She pushes the cart with her hand, and it rocks forward slightly, but the wheel doesn't rotate.

I drop to my knees beside her. "Let me see what I can do." I quickly discern that one side of the metal wheel guard is bent against the wheel. "I need some pliers," I tell Carmela. "Do you have any in here?"

"Pliers?" she echoes.

I think for a moment. *"Alicates,"* I translate. This might be one of the few times I've needed to use Spanish since college, but I'm still glad I minored in it, even though Dad threw a fit when I told him. One of these days it'll come in handy.

"Ah, yes. Here." She opens a cabinet and grabs the tool off a shelf.

As I pry the guard away from the wheel, I ask, "How's your family? Everybody okay?" I've talked to Carmela about her family a few times over the past two years. She's always eager to tell me about her husband and two young sons.

She pauses a bit too long before saying, "Everything is good. Thank you for asking."

I can tell everything is not good, so I stop working, sit back on my heels, and look up at her. Panic flashes across Carmela's face as she turns her head away from me.

"Tell me, Carmela. Tell me what's wrong."

She shakes her head. She's still facing mostly away from me, but a tear rolls down her cheek. I stand and gently turn her toward me. Then I tilt her head up until she looks me in the eye.

"Tell me. Maybe I can help."

Carmela shakes her head again. "You cannot help. I asked Mr. —" She claps a hand over her mouth.

I lightly grasp her wrist, and when she doesn't resist my touch, I pull her hand away from her mouth. "You asked Mr. ...?"

"Mr. Hamilton told me he will not help. I cannot ask again."

I'll get to which Mr. Hamilton she's talking about in a minute, but I can already guess which one. "You can't ask again because you don't want to or because you were told not to?"

She presses her lips together and shakes her head yet again, which tells me all I need to know.

I sigh. "You've been told not to ... by my father?"

She finally nods, her eyes focused straight ahead at my chest, not up at my face. I don't have the heart to make her look me in the eye again. Instead, I close the door and set up two metal folding chairs.

"Please sit and tell me everything. You can tell me in Spanish, if that helps."

fifteen

. . .

Wendy didn't lie—at least not about being in my office when I arrive. Still, I greet her with, "You lied to me!"

She grins from her seat in the purple chair. "And I will never, ever regret it!" Her feet are propped on my upturned trash can, which makes me laugh.

"Thank you," I say. "Truly."

"Would you have gone if I hadn't lied to you?"

I stop to think about it. "I don't know. Possibly not, because I wouldn't have believed he would actually show up. How did you talk him into it?"

She shrugs. "I told you I'm good. And he's a reasonable man most of the time. Now, pull up a seat," she points her toes toward my desk chair, "and tell me every juicy detail."

I don't. Well, I sit down, and I tell her some things, but not all the things. I give her the high-level details of Ash's response to my confession.

She's not satisfied with my storytelling.

"You're holding out on me, my friend. What are you not telling me?"

"That's everything."

"It's not."

"How do you know?"

"Because you're being cagey. And you smile every time you

say his name." She puts her hand over her heart, gives me the same ridiculous grin she gave Ash yesterday at lunch, and says, "Aaaaash." Then she shoots me a stern look. "Am I going to have to go pull the rest of the details out of Aaaaash?" She does the weird smile again.

"No!" I shout, before I can stop myself.

"Aha! There *is* something you're not telling me."

I don't intend to tell her everything, but I need to give her something, because I'm afraid she'll carry out her threat. "Look, there was chemistry, okay? And I'm positive it wasn't one-sided."

"I knew it!" She thrusts a finger into the air. "Within twelve months, you'll be Mrs. Aaaaashley Hamilton!"

"Keep your voice down," I hiss.

She repeats her declaration in a whisper.

"I won't."

"You will."

"I won't. My boyfriend of two years broke up with me the night before I moved here. I can't date Ash."

"Oh." She shakes her head. "No, you can't date Ash."

I decide to say what I'm thinking, since she always does. "The speed at which you change your mind boggles *my* mind."

"Hey, I'm a realist."

"You most definitely are not."

"I am. As soon as I get new information about something, I process it in seconds, and I form a new opinion based on that information."

I raise an eyebrow. "I'm not sure that's the definition of realism."

"Well, it's the definition of *something,* and I'm sticking with it. There's no use in holding onto an outdated opinion for pride's sake."

She's not wrong.

"So," she says, "how are you going to marry Ash if you can't date him?"

I sigh. "I'm not going to marry Ash." Why does that statement open a pit in my stomach?

"I bet you one hundred sixty-five thousand, three hundred

twenty-two dollars and seventeen cents your last name will one day be Hamilton."

"Since I can only dream of having that much cash, I'm not making that bet, even though you'd most likely lose."

"Then what are you going to do? You want to do the horizontal tango with the man, but you can't, and you also can't avoid him any more than you could when you thought he hated you. How's this going to work?"

I angle my head back and stare at the ceiling.

"You have to tell him," Wendy states.

My head snaps back down. "Tell him what?"

"That you can't date him—and why."

"Do I, though?"

"Are you actually considering not telling Ash Hamilton the entire, absolute, total truth about something? Really?"

I groan.

She asks, "Does he know you want to have your wicked way with him?"

"I don't want to—"

"Don't you lie to me, Leslie Beckett."

I take a deep breath and tamp down the images forming in my brain. "That doesn't mean I *would*."

"Well, why ever not? Under the right circumstances, that is."

I groan again.

"You have to tell him why you can't date him," Wendy says, "and you have to do it now."

"Now?!"

"Yep. Maybe not this very minute, but in the next day or so."

"But why?" I know I'm whining, but it's only been twelve hours since my last difficult conversation with Ash.

"Because Ash Hamilton doesn't have chemistry with just anybody. Believe me, I know. And when he sets his sights on something, you'd better watch out. He's going after it."

I'm not so sure. Ash isn't doing what he always dreamed about when it comes to his career. But Wendy probably has a point. If Ash feels all the same things I do, I need to nip any notions of dating in the bud before I get myself into a situation where I lose his newfound trust and he despises me more than he did yesterday afternoon.

When I don't respond, Wendy continues, "If he can't go after you yet, but you might want him to go after you in the future, tell him *now*."

"What do I say to him, though?"

"Everything. Tell him every single tiny little thing—all the thoughts and feelings and facts you're refusing to tell me. That's the way things have to be between you and Ash from now on, considering your past. No lies. No half-truths. No secrets. Or you'll never be anything but colleagues who avoid each other. Is that what you want?"

I shake my head.

"Then get on the phone," she points at it, "and invite him to lunch. Rip that bandage right off. No point in stalling." She grins at me. "And then call Sexy Shannon and tell him he needs to come see his twin sister."

"If you don't stop calling my brother 'Sexy Shannon' ...," I trail off.

"You'll what? I can't wait to hear the end of your threat."

How can one woman be both so endearing and maddening at the same time?

"I … I'll never tell you when he comes to visit."

"Oh, you're good."

sixteen

. . .

Three hours after returning to my office after my chat with Carmela, I'm still fuming—not at her, but at my father.

Carmela's husband Javier, who is a legitimate green card holder, went to the Dominican Republic to visit his ailing mother three months ago, and he wasn't able to get back into the US because of some mix-up with his paperwork. After exhausting all other avenues, Carmela felt like her final hope for getting justice was to ask my dad for help. Little did she know, he was the last person she should go to. I wish she had come to me instead of him when this all started.

I'm determined to get her husband back to his rightful home, but I'm going to have to do it without Dad finding out, which will be a pain. Most of the people I could go to for help would go straight to him with the news.

While I'm making a list of people who aren't loyal to my father that I can contact about Javier—which is a pitifully short list—my phone beeps. I reach over and press the intercom button. "Yes?"

"I've got a Leslie Beckett from Carter-Jenkins on line three for you," Annette says.

A nest of hornets takes up residence in my belly.

She continues, "She must be new, because I've never heard of her. She claims it's urgent, but I'm not sure I believe her. What do you want me to do?"

"You can put her through," I say as professionally as I can while feeling anything but professional.

"Hi, Ash," Leslie says when the call connects. Those two tiny words kick the hornets up a notch.

"Hey." Somehow, I can't form any other words.

"Can you meet me for lunch today?" she asks.

The hornets are now in an all-out frenzy. "Yes." I have no idea what my schedule is for lunchtime, but I'll be wherever she wants me to be.

"Does noon at Dixon's Cafe work for you?"

"Yes." Why can't I come up with more than one-syllable responses?

"Great. I'll see you then."

"Yeah. Bye." At least that was two syllables.

I hang up the phone and drop my head into my hands. I'm still in that position when my brother barges into my office.

"How'd it go last night?" He drops into the chair.

I run my fingers through my hair. "Fine." I'm surprised he didn't call it a date, but maybe he remembered not to tease me.

"When's the second date?"

There it is.

"Lunch." But I'm not sure it's a date.

His eyebrows raise. "Today?"

I nod.

Randall whistles. "Impressive."

He doesn't need to know she invited me.

"Did you kiss her?"

I glare at him instead of giving another one-word reply.

"Settle down. You never were one to kiss and tell."

Not that there was ever much to tell.

"I respect that," Randall says, to my surprise.

I lean back in my chair and fold my arms in front of my chest.

"That's all you're going to tell me?" he asks.

"Yep."

"All right then." He stands. "Great chat." He reaches across the desk, flicks my forehead, and then walks out the door, leaving it standing open.

Thirty seconds later, he's back. "Today's our lunch with Mom."

Once a month, our mother takes the two of us out to lunch. We've been doing it since Randall moved back after law school a year ago. I don't know how she'd respond to me canceling, because I've never dared to do it. Nobody cancels on Ruth Hamilton—not even her children.

My brother leans against the doorframe with his hands in his pockets. "What are you going to do?"

"I don't know."

"You know you can't cancel on Mom without a compelling reason. And you also know she'll demand to know what it is."

"I'm well aware."

"And I'm not giving her your excuse. That's all on you, buddy."

I can't tell Mom about Leslie. Not yet. "Let me see if I can change my other plans."

"A dinner date is better than lunch anyway," he says. "With lunch, there's no opportunity to do anything afterward." He leers at me.

I glare back.

"Sorry." His smile negates the apology. "I promise I'll try to stop teasing you."

"I'd appreciate it. I would also appreciate you not mentioning anything about Leslie to Mom."

"Mum's the word. Ha. *Mum.*"

I roll my eyes as he laughs at his unintended pun.

"Thanks," I say. "Unless you hear otherwise, I'm still on with Mom."

"Sounds good." He doesn't move.

"Go away."

"You don't want me to listen in on your conversation with Luscious Leslie?"

I grip the arms of my chair so I won't leap across the desk at him.

His eyes widen. "That was out of line, even for me. I shouldn't have said it. I apologize, man. Seriously."

I take in a few deep breaths through my nose before I say, "Don't you ever call her that again—not even in your head."

Randall shakes his head. "I won't. I promise." He grabs the door handle. "Why don't I give you some privacy?" The door clicks shut.

When he's gone, I release my hold on the chair and roll my neck and shoulders to release the tension in my body. Nobody can rile me up quite like my brother can. Not for the first time, I think about how our roles are reversed. Everyone in the family treats me more like the older, responsible brother and him like the younger, carefree one. Most of the time I even feel older, and not because I graduated before he did.

I reach for the phone and dial Carter-Jenkins. As I wait to be transferred to Leslie's extension, I tap my fingers on my desk. I hate that I'm already disappointing her.

"Ash?" she says. "Everything okay?"

"Yes." Except those pesky hornets are back. "I forgot I have a lunch meeting I can't cancel. I'm sorry about this, but can we do dinner instead? My treat."

"You're not treating, but yes, dinner is fine."

I suggest a restaurant far enough from her apartment that I'd need to drive her, but she counters with a place on her block. I have no good reason to insist on my choice, so we go with hers. We set a time, I tell her I'll make a reservation, and she ends the call with no small talk. I tell myself it's because she's busy and not because she doesn't want to talk to me. After all, she wouldn't have asked me to lunch if she doesn't want to be around me, right?

I pray I'm right.

seventeen

. . .

I'm both dreading and eagerly anticipating my dinner with Ash. I desperately want to see him, but I don't want to tell him we can't be together. I wish we'd been able to do lunch, which would've given us a deadline for ending the meal if it didn't go well. Plus, I wouldn't have to spend yet another afternoon agonizing over what I'm going to say and how he might respond.

I chose a restaurant on my block, knowing if it all blows up in my face, I can easily leave and walk home whenever I feel like it. If we were somewhere farther away, Ash would insist on driving me home, which would be awkward no matter how the talk goes.

Wendy enters my office, again without knocking. "You have a new client," she declares.

"Who?"

"The newest Cub. Do you know anything about baseball?"

I laugh. "I know everything about baseball." Then I pause, wondering if I should admit this, but since I know she'll find out eventually anyway, I say, "And I hate the Cubs with an unholy passion."

Her forehead wrinkles. "Seriously?"

"Yep."

"Why?"

"I'm a Cardinals fan."

"What does that have to do with anything? I'm a Brewers fan."

I take a chance based on the fact she's oblivious to one of the biggest rivalries in baseball. "Name one player on the Brewers' roster—past or present."

Wendy purses her lips while she thinks. "Mickey Mantle?"

"*Bzzzz*. You're not a Brewers fan. You're not a *baseball* fan if you don't know who Mickey Mantle played for. But that has nothing to do with this situation, anyway. If you're a Cardinals fan, it's illegal to have any positive connection with the Cubs. It's in the Missouri State Constitution."

She narrows her eyes. "I don't believe you. And you're not from Missouri."

"I was born there. It counts—kind of like how being born in the U.S. makes you a U.S. citizen."

"Well, legal or not, he's all yours."

I sigh. "What's his name?"

"Diego Sanchez."

I almost leap out of my chair. "Diego Sanchez—the best left-handed pitcher of this generation? But he plays for Houston!"

"Not anymore. He was traded overnight, and he needs a new local PR person in Chicago. He has somebody working the national and international PR stuff for him already, but he wants someone local as well. Brian was desperate to get him, but he's overloaded, as is everybody else … except you. George just made the assignment."

As much as I despise the Cubs, I can't pass up this opportunity. Not that declining is an option. I've learned that when George Carter decrees something, it's written in stone. I'm going to be stuck with Diego Sanchez whether I want to be or not. And as a baseball fan, I want to be. Shannon will totally flip when I tell him.

Then something occurs to me. "Do you know why he was traded?" I've heard no rumors about a potential trade involving Sanchez, and Houston doesn't have any other decent lefties. They're crazy to let him go, and the Cubs would have to trade at least four players to get him. I'm getting a bad feeling about this new client.

"Nope," Wendy says, "but I think you're about to find out. Go see George to get all the details." Before she heads out, she adds, "I'm here for you if you need anything. Don't be afraid to ask if you don't know what to do."

I nod. "Thanks. By the way, I'm now having dinner with Ash instead of lunch." Of course she makes me explain why and tell her where we're going.

After Wendy leaves, I head to the lobby to grab a copy of today's *Chicago Tribune*. I page through the sports section to find any evidence Diego Sanchez was about to be traded, in case I've missed something in the past few days. There's nothing.

I make my way to George's office with my stomach in knots. If I have to put a positive spin on something terrible Diego Sanchez did to get him traded to the Cubs, of all teams, I'm going to lose it.

George's secretary waves me into his office before I say a word.

"Leslie." George stands from his desk as I enter. "Have a seat." He motions toward the brown leather couch, and he sits in one of the easy chairs across from it.

As I settle onto the couch, I try not to stare at my new boss. George Carter has the bushiest eyebrows and largest ears I've ever seen.

"Are you a baseball fan?" he asks.

"I am."

"Who's your team?"

I hesitate before saying, "St. Louis."

"Ah." He raises one eyebrow, and I flinch as it wiggles. I wonder if his ears wiggle too. "Is that going to be a problem?"

"No, sir."

"Good. I normally wouldn't give a big client like this to someone new to the firm, but I know you had a little experience with some minor league baseball players in Peoria, and everybody else here is full up. Sanchez is going to need a lot of attention. Can you handle that?"

"Of course."

He stands and picks up a paper from his desk. "Here's the contact information for him and his agent."

I take the paper from him. My stomach drops when I see the

name of Sanchez's agent, Bobby Jacobs. He has a reputation for being ruthless. I'm liking this situation less and less.

"Sir?"

"Yes?" George doesn't sit back down.

"Can you tell me why Sanchez was traded?"

"I'm going to let you ask him." He checks his watch. "He's expecting a call from you in fifteen minutes."

I'm way out of my depth. My previous job was with a tiny PR firm in the small city of Peoria, after two years working for the local newspaper. Our clients were largely area politicians, a couple of B-list authors, and the rare rising star with the Peoria Chiefs, the Cubs' minor league franchise in town. Over the past week and a half, Wendy has been orienting me to this new world of PR where my clients will typically be high-profile individuals, but I'm mostly going to be flying by the seat of my pants.

One thing I have going for me in this situation is I understand baseball. It also doesn't hurt that I understand newspapers, which is key to the PR game, though the *Peoria Journal Star* is not quite on the level of the *Trib*.

I pick up the phone and dial the number for Sanchez, which has a local 312 area code. I can't imagine he's going to answer. Wouldn't he be on a plane or in an airport? And how would he already have a Chicago number?

"*Hola.* This is Diego," a male voice says.

I'm taken aback to find the man himself on the other end of the line instead of an assistant, but I quickly recover. "Hello, Mr. Sanchez? This is Leslie Beckett with Carter-Jenkins PR."

"Ah, yes, Miss Beckett. Please call me Diego."

"Okay, and you can call me Leslie."

"Will do, Leslie." He emphasizes the second syllable, and I love the sound of it. "So you are my new PR guy."

"Yes, but I'm not exactly a guy."

"Then you are my PR *dama*. Welcome to the Sanchez family, Dama Leslie."

The man is charm personified.

"Thank you," I say. "Or should I say *gracias?*"

"Sure. Speak Spanish all you want, but don't feel you have to. I'm perfectly fluent in English. I even remember to use contractions sometimes." He laughs at himself.

I'm tempted to giggle but don't want to sound unprofessional. "I know approximately five Spanish words, so I'll stick with English. Now tell me, Diego, what brings you to Chicago?"

He laughs. "You are getting right to it, eh, Dama Leslie?"

"I need to know everything, so I can ensure the people of Chicago love you."

"That's what I like to hear, Dama Leslie. Ooo, you know what? Lady Leslie sounds so much better. I'll go with the English and call you Lady Leslie. That okay with you?"

"I love it."

"Perfect. My agent says you must sign an NDA before I talk to you, but I say no. What reason would my personal PR lady have to tell anyone anything bad about me, eh?"

"You make an excellent point. You can trust me with anything you have to say." I know I'll have to sign the non-disclosure agreement later, but that's not a problem.

"Good. I left Houston because of my wife. She had an affair with one of the other players on the team, and they claim they fell in love. I refuse to work with the ...," he clears his throat, "... man anymore, so I demanded a trade."

"Wow."

"Wow is right, Lady Leslie. I wanted to banish my wife back to the Dominican Republic, but the State Department did not approve my plan." He laughs, but I can't tell if he's serious or not.

"And Houston had no problems with trading you?"

"Oh, they had problems. But I handled them." He doesn't elaborate.

"You're not going to tell me how?"

"Not unless you need to know. And I don't think you need to know yet. If you do, I will tell you."

"Okay. And you're already in Chicago?"

"Yes. They struck the deal during last night's game when the

Cubs were in Houston. I left the stadium immediately and caught the next flight here. I'm the starting pitcher tomorrow against St. Louis."

"Oh," I say before realizing it's not the best response.

"Why 'oh'?"

"No reason."

"There is a reason. Tell me. If we're going to be best buddies, you must tell me things. I need to know all about Lady Leslie. This is give and take. I tell you my secrets. You tell me yours."

Sharing my secrets with clients is not in my job description, but I decide to roll with it for now. "I'm a Cardinals fan."

"Say it's not so." He says it teasingly, so I can tell he doesn't care.

"It is *muy* so."

"Are you going to betray me to the enemy, Lady Leslie? Tell me now, so I'll know who to blame when I go down in flames."

I think I'm going to like this man. "You're safe with me, Diego."

"Yes! I knew it. You will come to tomorrow's game, and you will not cheer for your Cardinals. Can you do that?"

I decide to be honest. "I don't know."

"I am grateful for your honesty, but you will try—for me, your new best *amigo* Diego. But I won't require you to cheer for the Cubs. I don't want you to betray your own people. That is treason."

I chuckle. "I appreciate that."

"Now, I'm staying at the Drake. You know it?"

"Yes, I know it." Or at least I know of it. I've never been there.

"You will meet me here for lunch. No excuses."

Thank goodness Ash changed our plans. "I'll be there."

eighteen

. . .

"Ashley," Mom says as I lean down to kiss her cheek, "you look different. Did you get a haircut?"

Randall snorts. "He looks different because he ..." He trails off when he catches my look.

"Because he what?" Mom demands. Her gaze snaps back and forth between us as we take our seats.

I don't know if I should wait and see how my brother is going to dig himself out of this hole or if I need to use my own shovel before he buries me along with him.

He says, "This morning he learned Carter-Jenkins' newest client is one of his favorite baseball players."

I don't know how Randall already knows about Diego Sanchez. I only found out an hour ago, and I haven't had time to tell him.

Mom sniffs. "That's nice." She hates that Dad made me work with the PR firm instead of doing what I really want to do.

"What's new with you, Mom?" My brother gives me a look that tells me he's purposely taking the focus off me.

I give him a begrudging nod.

"Working on the next Junior League fundraiser, planning your sister's graduation party, and trying to convince your father he needs to get more sleep. The man thinks he's still forty."

Dad turned fifty-five last month, and Mom is right. He refuses to admit he's not as young as he once was.

"Has he been sleeping at the office a lot?" I ask, although I'm not sure I want to know the answer.

"At least once a week here lately. He's going to drive himself to an early grave. I keep telling him to hire more people."

There's no good reason for Dad to stay overnight at the office that often. I try not to think about what it might mean.

"Have either of you been to Chez Patrice yet?" Mom asks. "I made your father get us a reservation there for tomorrow night. It's all Bitsy Barlow can talk about since she and Morty went a few weeks ago. I doubt it lives up to the hype, but I want to check it out for myself."

Randall shoots me a pointed look. He's not going to give me up, but I can't lie to Mom.

"I was there last night," I tell her.

"Oh? Business dinner?"

"No." Too late I remember Leslie works for Carter-Jenkins, and Wendy set it up, so I could've said yes without it being a complete lie.

Mom gives me an expectant look.

"I was there with a friend."

"Anyone I know?"

"No." She doesn't technically know Leslie, though if I said her name, she'd undoubtedly recognize it from all the envelopes going to and from our house years ago.

Randall raises an eyebrow but keeps his mouth shut. I take a drink of the Coke Mom ordered for me and wait for her to ask who the friend was, but miraculously she doesn't.

Instead, she says, "Your father tells me a woman at Carter-Jenkins has her eye on you."

I almost spit my Coke out.

She points a finger at me and wiggles the tip. "You haven't been dating this woman and not telling me, have you?"

After a moment of panic, I realize Mom must be talking about Wendy. Leslie hasn't been around long enough, and I'm confident she would've told me if she'd met my dad. I have no idea how Dad knows about Wendy, though.

"No, I'm not dating her."

My brother smirks at me.

"I'm not sure I like the idea of you being with someone in PR anyway," Mom says. "That's always seemed like a shady type of business to me. You don't need PR if you're not doing anything wrong."

A few days ago, I might have agreed with her, but now I feel defensive. "PR isn't only about sweeping bad stuff under the rug, Mom. And some people would say law is a shady type of business."

"Don't bite the hand that feeds you, son. Or houses you. Or clothes you. Or sends you to Harvard."

"You didn't have to shell out a penny for my higher education," I retort. I feel guilty I received full-tuition academic scholarships when my family could well afford to pay and leave the scholarships for people with lesser means, but I'm not above using my own accomplishments to my advantage.

"Don't get smart with me, young man."

"I think the point he was trying to make is he's *very* smart," my brother quips.

Mom shifts her focus to him. "So are you—not that any of your teachers ever had an inkling of it. There's no question we paid for every penny of *your* education."

Randall has the grace to blush. Though I enjoy watching him squirm, I decide to help him out before Mom rakes him over any more coals.

"Are Nana and Pops able to come to Tonya's graduation?" I ask my mother.

"We don't know yet." She sighs. Her parents retired to Florida a few years back, and my grandfather had open-heart surgery a couple months ago. His recovery has been slower than any of us would like.

Mom continues, "I'm hoping Daddy will feel like it. Your sister really wants them to be there."

I want them to be there, too. I haven't seen my grandparents since Christmas. There's no good reason I haven't gone down to Florida, though. I make a mental note to visit them soon if they're unable to come to graduation.

"Do you boys remember Melissa Teague?" Mom asks us, and I nearly spit out another mouthful of Coke.

Randall gives me a shrewd look as he asks her, "Didn't she used to go to school with us?"

"Yes, and church," Mom replies. "She was in Ashley's class, if I'm not mistaken."

Her tone tells me she knows exactly how old Melissa is, and I get a sour taste in my mouth. I have a feeling I know where she's going with this.

She continues, "Melissa's mom is in Junior League with me. Anyway, she's back."

"Back from where? And why do we care?"

"You care because she's a person, Randall."

He holds a hand up. "Sorry. Didn't mean to be rude."

"Well, you were. But to answer your first, non-rude question, she went to Columbia and then stayed in New York for a few years, but she recently moved back here. She has some job in the Cubs front office. I'm sure her father pulled some strings to make that happen."

Randall says, "I'm not trying to be rude again, Mom, but I truly want to know why you're telling us about a woman we haven't seen in more than a decade."

"Because she's pretty, and she's single, and she'd make your brother a great match. I've invited her and her parents to dinner Saturday night." Mom points at me. "You will be there. If you have other plans, cancel them. And if you're secretly dating that PR woman, this serves you right for lying to me."

nineteen

. . .

Although I know I shouldn't do anything different than normal to get ready for dinner with Ash, I can't help it. Even if I can't date him, I want him to want me. Although I'm annoyed at myself for that, I justify my actions because we might be together in the future. I don't want to turn him off.

The restaurant I suggested is nice but nowhere near as formal as Chez Patrice, so I choose a black off-the-shoulder sweater and purple pencil skirt. I pull on black pantyhose and finish the look with the same purple heels I wore last night. I tease my hair a little more than usual and try not to feel bad about doing my part to deplete the ozone layer by spraying it all into place with plenty of Ultra-Hold Rave.

It's still fifteen minutes before I need to meet Ash, and it will take me all of one minute to walk to the restaurant, but I feel like the walls of my tiny apartment are closing in on me, so I grab my chain-mail pouch and head out.

"Reservation for Ash Hamilton," I say when I arrive. "I'm a few minutes early."

"Not a problem," the hostess says. "The other party is here and already seated. Follow me."

I spot Ash at a table for two in the back corner of the restaurant. His entire face lights up when he sees me, and he stands. Butterflies fill my stomach, and not only because he looks like a

GQ model in a form-fitting baby blue cashmere sweater and dark jeans. My determination wavers along with my smile. Can I really tell him we're over before we've even begun? If nothing else, it seems presumptuous.

Ever the gentleman, Ash pulls my chair out for me. As he pushes it back in, I catch his scent, which has an alarming effect on my heart rate.

"You look amazing," he murmurs in my ear. His hand brushes my bare shoulder as he returns to his side of the table, and I'm so lightheaded I'm unable to thank him or return the compliment.

How can I do this to him? To me?

Wendy's voice echoes in my head, "Rip that bandage right off. No point in stalling."

"Ash—"

"Leslie—"

We laugh, and I'm tempted to say, "Jinx," but I don't.

"Ladies first," he says with a smile.

I don't want his smile to go away. I don't want to be the reason it goes away.

"I thoroughly enjoyed last night," I say. "Well, the parts where I wasn't confessing to my childhood indiscretions, at least."

He chuckles.

I continue, "I'm so happy we reconnected and you forgave me."

"That makes me happy, too."

The look he gives me is so tender, I want to weep.

"I'm attracted to you, Ash, and not just physically—though that's very much there. You're kind, and you're easy to talk to, and you're everything I hoped you'd grow up to be."

He opens his mouth to speak, but I hold up a hand to stop him. While I want to know exactly how he feels about me, I also want to potentially spare him any embarrassment from saying something he might regret after he hears the rest of it.

I press on, "I don't think I'm wrong in saying these feelings seem to be mutual. And I wish we could act on them, but we can't right now."

His face falls briefly before he recovers and plasters on a fake smile. My heart aches from the knowledge I put it there.

I clear my throat and force myself to keep looking him in the eye. "I'm only two weeks out of a long-term relationship that ended when I moved here. I can't let you be my rebound. I won't do that to you."

Ash closes his eyes and lets out a long breath. I can feel my pulse in my ears as I watch him attempt to compose himself. If he doesn't say something soon, my eardrums might burst from the pressure.

"Man, am I ever glad I didn't kiss you last night," he says as he opens his eyes.

My eyebrows have never been so close to my hairline. "What?" I breathe out.

"I laid awake all night wishing I'd kissed you," he confesses. "But now I'm relieved I didn't." His intense gaze sends a rush of heat to my core. "Because once I do kiss you, I won't want to stop."

My body is tingling all over, and my heart can't remember how to beat properly. I want him more than I did a minute ago, if that's possible.

"Wh-why *didn't* you kiss me?" I know I shouldn't ask, but I can't help myself.

"Partly because I was afraid you didn't want me to, and partly because you shivered, and I realized you were cold."

"Are you kidding me? I shivered because I thought you were going to kiss me," I explain. "And I very much wanted you to. I was mad you didn't."

He laughs—actually laughs. "Leave it to me to misread the signals."

"So you're okay with this?" I ask.

"Okay with a gorgeous woman wanting to kiss me and date me but caring enough about me to make sure she completely gets over another man before she does so?" He nods. "Definitely."

I think I love him. And that's not the alcohol talking, because we haven't ordered drinks yet. But this is exactly why I can't date him. What if these feelings are my way of coping with Glenn dumping me? Would I feel this way about any man who showed an interest in me right now? I don't think that's the case, but I'm exceptionally grateful to Aunt Star for helping me see I might not be thinking clearly.

The last thing I want to do is to crush the heart of the man across from me, even if the wait might be agonizing—and not only emotionally. I'm sitting on my hands because I've never wanted to touch a man as much as I long to touch Ash Hamilton. His hand is lying right there on the table, and I feel like if I can't curl my own fingers around it, I'll explode.

"I thought you were going to tell me you have a boyfriend," he says, transferring my focus from his hand to his mouth, which doesn't help matters. He has a lovely mouth. "Or worse—that you don't have any feelings for me. This?" He waves his hand back and forth between me and him, and my eyes follow it like a line of ants to spilled ice cream. "This I can deal with. Am I excited we have to wait? No. But I'm more than willing to."

twenty

. . .

I think I love her. Though that may be the testosterone talking.

How Leslie and I are going to be around each other while keeping our hands—and lips—to ourselves, I don't know. But we have to hold back if we want to think straight, although not touching or kissing her is going to be a giant distraction as well. The anticipation might kill me.

The waitress finally appears and takes our order for both drinks and food, which annoys me, as it means my time with Leslie will be shorter than I hoped.

I ask, "Do you feel comfortable telling me what happened with your ex-boyfriend?" If the man broke up with her, he's an absolute idiot.

She laughs. "Compared to some of the other things I've told you over the past two days, this'll be easy."

Leslie is beautiful when she laughs. Then again, she's beautiful no matter what she's doing. There's no doubt we're going to have to limit our time together for the foreseeable future, though that's the last thing I want.

"His name is Glenn," she says. "We met my first year after college. I was a reporter for the *Peoria Journal Star,* and he worked in advertising sales. We started out as friends and eventually decided we might as well try dating. It was comfortable. Nothing earth-shattering, but we enjoyed spending time together."

She deserves earth-shattering. I want to tell her that, but it's the kind of thought I'll need to keep to myself for a while.

"I left that job after two years and took a position in PR at a small local agency," she says.

"Why did you make the switch from news reporting to PR?"

"I wish I could give you a noble reason, but it was money. I barely made enough to pay the bills, and I lived with two roommates in a run-down duplex. My financial situation wasn't going to change anytime soon in that job, so I needed something that paid better. Glenn and I had been together for a year, and I wanted to see where things might lead with him, so I didn't look into moving away at the time."

"What made you want to come to Chicago now?"

"It turned out I enjoyed PR. And you know I've always wanted to live in a big city. When I first started talking about looking for a job in Chicago, Glenn was supportive. I thought if I got a job in the city, he'd move here, too. He's in sales. He can do that anywhere. I never dreamed I'd get this job, though. One of my college professors grew up with George Carter's wife and gave me a glowing recommendation, as did my former boss at the newspaper. I'll admit, I'm not sure I'm ready for it, especially jumping right in with—" She claps her hand over her mouth.

"Diego Sanchez? I know," I say. "I'm one of the few people you can talk to about him. I spent some time on the phone with his agent today. I took the NDA over to Carter-Jenkins for you to sign this afternoon, but you weren't there."

"I was with Diego at the Drake."

"Wendy told me." And I don't like it one bit. The man has a reputation with the ladies—or at least he did before he got married a couple years ago. But since that's no longer an issue, I wonder if he'll go back to his old ways. And Leslie could be his prime target—especially if she spends much time alone with him in his hotel room. If that man even thinks about laying a hand on her ...

"I signed the NDA when I got back," she interrupts my thoughts. "There were some interesting clauses in there."

"It's not uncommon when you work with celebrities. They

often include clauses about not asking them for personal favors, tickets, autographs, and so on."

She nods.

"Back to Glenn …" I redirect the conversation.

"He was surprised I got the job, too, and he wasn't excited about it. Turns out he didn't really think I'd move away from him. He thought I'd spend some time applying and interviewing for jobs and after a few rejections I'd realize I had it pretty good in Peoria and give up on the job hunt."

Anger surges through me at the knowledge her ex didn't expect anyone to hire her. "And then when you got the job, he broke up with you?" I guessed.

"Not immediately. I think he didn't want to seem like a jealous jerk, but my last night there, he ended things." She shrugs. "Was I angry? Sure. I'm still mad at him."

She is. I can see it in her eyes, which helps me understand her reluctance to be with me.

Leslie continues, "I'll probably be upset about it for a while, which is why we need to cool things down here. But I know breaking up with Glenn is ultimately for the best. I wasn't certain we were headed toward marriage, anyway. We dated for two years and although we talked about getting engaged, we never did." She shrugs. "Maybe we both somehow knew it wasn't going to last."

I want to ask if she loves him, but I won't. I want to ask how long she thinks I'll need to wait for her, but I don't do that, either.

"One thing I know," I say, "is he's a world-class moron to not know what he had." But I'm glad he's a moron, or I wouldn't be sitting here wondering when Leslie will let me kiss her.

She blushes. "I wasn't the perfect girlfriend, by any means."

"Nobody is. But it sounds like this breakup was much more about him than about you. He didn't want to consider what you wanted or what was best for you."

She looks away from me. "Glenn's a good man. He never did anything to hurt me."

I don't like that she's defending him. "Except break up with you because he wasn't your only dream?"

Her eyes snap back to mine. "There is that. But we had two good years together." Her eyes glisten with unshed tears.

I wish I hadn't asked about Glenn, because speaking about him only reminded her of what she lost. And me talking badly about him is backfiring on me. I need to stop.

"Leslie, I'm sorry. I didn't mean to upset you." I sigh. "I don't like to see you hurting."

twenty-one

. . .

I don't deserve for Ash to be as kind to me as he is tonight. Last night I would've let him kiss me—and possibly more—which wouldn't have been fair to him at all.

Aunt Star was right. I need time to get over Glenn. For the last two weeks, I was so busy with the move and the new job it wasn't difficult to push thoughts of him and the breakup aside. But if I want to get past it and potentially start a new relationship, I can't keep ignoring what happened.

Unfortunately, I'm certain that means not seeing Ash unless we can't avoid it at work. I want him to hold and comfort me, which is the absolute worst thing we should do under the circumstances. He can't help me get over Glenn.

Our food arrives, and I don't want to discuss Glenn any longer, but I'm having trouble figuring out what to talk about. Ash senses my mood and takes control of the conversation, starting with Diego Sanchez.

I'm more excited about Diego moving to Chicago than Ash is, and he's a diehard Cubs fan. I wonder what's up with that but don't ask. I also don't tell him how at my lunch with Diego, I was pleasantly surprised that while he lightly flirted with me, he was respectful of me both as a woman and a colleague. Based on his interactions with the hotel staff, I think he would flirt with any female in his vicinity, and with his engaging personality, I doubt many women would be offended by it. However, I could see Ash not being as lenient.

When that conversation peters out, we talk about our younger sisters. Ash's face lights up when he talks about Tonya and Sonya.

"Do you see them often?" I ask.

"Almost every day." He flushes at his admission, and he focuses on his plate.

"Don't be embarrassed. I love that you enjoy spending time with your sisters. So do you go up to Evanston most days, or do they come down here?"

He meets my eyes again. "I still live up there. I took over the pool house when I moved back from law school, and I haven't left." He's trying to sound like it's no big deal he still essentially lives with his parents, but I can tell he was reluctant to admit it.

I say, "If you think I'll think less of you because of that, you're wrong. I don't know all the reasons you choose to keep living there, but unless you've changed a lot since I last knew you, I know you think things through before making decisions. I don't believe for a minute you still live there because you lack the ability or maturity to survive out in the world on your own. And considering your occupation, I'm pretty sure you don't lack the financial resources, either." I point my fork at him. "I'm happy you made the decision that's best for you, regardless of what other people might think. *That* shows maturity."

"Leslie," he says in a strained voice, "how are we going to do this? When you say things like that, I want to be with you even more. I want to spend all my time with you and find out every-thing you've done over the past twelve years and hear about all your hopes and dreams." He grits his teeth. "But we can't. I completely understand why and agree with your reasoning, but it feels impossible."

My heart goes out to him. I want to do the same, and I'm not sure how to keep from it. I don't think even talking on the phone would be a good plan. It would be too easy for the conversation to veer into intimate territory or invitations to spend time together.

Then I get an idea—maybe one of the best ideas of my life. "What if we write letters to each other?"

His eyes light up. "Like being pen pals again?"

"Yes. Only this time, there'll be no confusion about who the other person is. We're going into it eyes wide open. But we need some ground rules."

He nods, and a smile slowly spreads across his face. "I like this suggestion. What rules do you propose?"

Why do I feel like he's drawing up a contract in his mind?

"First," I say, "we take turns. No sending a letter every day. We have to wait until we get a letter and then respond to it."

"I concur," my favorite lawyer states. "And we get to ask one question in each letter."

"Only one?" I quirk an eyebrow.

"Yes," he says with mock gravity. "So you'd better make it a good one."

"And must the responding letter solely consist of the answer to that question, or are we allowed to veer off topic, counselor?"

"Each letter can contain two topics." He holds up one finger. "The answer to the question and," he adds another finger, "another topic of the writer's choice. We can also comment on what the other person said in their letter."

"Should I be writing all this down?" I tease.

Ash taps his forehead. "It's all up here. I can type it up when I get home if you can't remember it all. But of course, then I'll have to mail it to you."

I laugh.

"Any other rules?" he asks.

My smile disappears. "Yes. No mention of Glenn, how I'm doing with the breakup, or our feelings for each other." I point my finger back and forth between us. "If we need to talk about any of those things, we do it with other people."

He nods, but I wonder if he has anyone to talk to. My heart clenches at the thought he might not. I make a mental note to ask Wendy if she knows.

"Are we telling other people we're writing to each other?" he asks.

"I'll definitely tell Aunt Star, and I doubt I can keep it from Wendy. Sorry."

Ash shrugs. "I'm half convinced she works for the CIA."

"Wouldn't it be awesome if she does?" I smile at the thought.

He smiles back. "There's one kink in this plan."

I tilt my head. "What's that?"

"If you send letters to my house, my whole family will know."

I suddenly feel nauseous. "And you don't want them to know?"

"Not yet."

"You're not planning to tell them about me?" That hurts more than I want to admit.

"I will eventually," he says. "I need to find the right time to explain it all, although I'm not fully sure what to explain."

"I get it." I do, but I don't love that he's keeping me a secret from them. Then again, I don't plan to tell my family about him yet, either, except for Aunt Star. "But Randall knows, because of the ordeal at lunch yesterday."

"Yes," he admits, "which is fine. Unfortunately, Jay knows, too. You know—the other guy at lunch. He has said nothing to me about what happened, but I can't imagine he never will. If I don't mention it again, hopefully he won't, either."

"So where do I send your letters? To your office?"

"No!" He nearly shouts. "Sorry, didn't mean to be so loud. I'll get a P.O. box. How about I write the first letter, and I'll get the box set up tomorrow so it'll be ready by the time you write back?"

He really doesn't want anyone else to know about this, but I can't exactly complain. "That sounds great. So do I get to ask you a question now that you'll answer in the letter?"

"Yes. And I'll be quiet so you can think of a fantastic one."

There's a thousand things I want to know, but one question has been niggling at me since Wendy first mentioned it yesterday. "I don't need time. I already know. Why are you doing legal work for a PR firm?" I refrain from asking the second part of the question: instead of doing something to help people, like you said you wanted to do?

"I want to answer now."

"Against the rules," I say, although I want to know the answer immediately. "Also, when we see each other in person for work reasons, we can't discuss anything but work—nothing personal and nothing from the letters. All questions, answers, and comments must stay on the page."

twenty-two

. . .

"One final pen pal rule," I tell Leslie. This one is going to hurt, but it's for her own good. "Letters can be one page only. And you can't write tiny. Use your normal handwriting."

Leslie's jaw drops. "Why?"

"Because you don't need to spend all your time writing letters to me. That won't help with the Glenn situation. In fact, with that in mind, here's my final, final rule. Only one letter from each of us per week. And a final, final, final rule: you can spend no more than thirty minutes writing it. I'm trusting you to follow the honor system on that."

She pouts, and she's so adorable I almost give in, but not quite. The rules are restricting, but these letters can't be a free-for-all if I want her to have the time and space needed to truly get over Glenn.

"One page front and back?"

She looks so hopeful, I concede. "If you insist."

I laugh when she pumps a fist in the air like her team hit a home run.

Leslie pushes her empty plate aside and props her chin on her hands. "I like you a lot, Ash Hamilton."

"Hey, that's against the rules," I reply with a fake frown, though her declaration makes my heart pound.

"Only for letters." She grins. "But, as much as it pains me, it should apply at all times until further notice. I will, however, give you permission to say it back one time right now, if you so desire."

Leslie speaks with confidence, but her smile wavers when I don't reply immediately. She doesn't know I'm hesitating because I'm afraid I'll choke on the words.

I finally say, "I like you more than a lot, Leslie Beckett." I clear my throat. "The ball's in your court now. When you're ready to be more than pen pals and co-workers, I'll be waiting."

"You promise?" She shakes her head. "No, that's not fair of me. I can't ask you to make that promise."

"I promise." It's an easy one to make. There's no woman for me except the one sitting across the table.

"There's one promise I do feel comfortable asking you to make, though," she says.

"What's that?"

"That you won't try to pay the bill tonight."

Although I'd prefer to pay, I can tell by the look in her eyes that this is important to her. "I promise I won't try to pay the bill."

The waitress chooses that moment to bring the check. Leslie lets it sit on the table while looking back and forth between it and me several times. I lean back in my chair and inspect my fingernails. She laughs and then takes care of it.

When we stand, I have to stick my hands in my pockets to keep from reaching out to take her hand. Leslie stops when we step outside the restaurant door and turns to me.

"No, I'm walking you to your building," I say. "I know it's only a few doors down, but I insist."

She nods and we take off down the sidewalk.

"Thank you for being so understanding," she says. "You didn't have to be."

"No," I reply. "I didn't. But why wouldn't I, when I care about you and want you to take the time you need? I also feel I should point out that being understanding about this isn't a completely selfless move. Even if I were angry about this situation, what good would it do me to argue with you about it? Either you'd tell me to take a hike, which I don't want, or you'd give in and we'd likely crash and burn after a few weeks or months. What's in any of that for me?"

We stop and face each other outside her building's door.

"That was some honesty," she says.

"I'll always be honest with you."

She looks like she's about to cry, and I don't want our evening to end with her in tears, so I grin and say something I know I absolutely shouldn't. "Well, at least I'll be honest when it matters, which is ninety-nine-point-nine percent of the time. However, I might tell a fib to get you to a surprise party. Or I might lie and say your butt doesn't look big in that skirt."

Her eyes widen.

"Sorry." I chuckle. *That* was a lie. It looks amazing, to be completely truthful. But that's not something I should say to a pen pal, so please forget I mentioned it."

Leslie's face turns a marvelous shade of red, and she playfully swats my arm. "I don't know how to respond to that."

"Thank me and then go upstairs and call Aunt Star and tell her all about it." My arm is tingling, and not because it stings. She didn't hit me hard enough to hurt.

She bites her lip, which reminds me I don't get to kiss her goodnight. But the mannerism also reveals she wants to say something but she's not sure if she should.

"You can say it, whatever it is," I say. "Operation Pen Pal doesn't officially begin until you walk through that door." I point to the door in question.

She gives me an earnest look. "Do you have someone you can talk to about this? I don't want you to be all on your own."

I want to gather this woman into my arms and never let her go, but instead I stand two feet away from her with my hands fisted in my pockets and say, "I'll be fine."

"That's not an answer. You said you'll be honest when it matters. This matters, Ash."

I look down at the sidewalk. "I have Randall." He may tease me about the whole thing, but he'll be better than nothing.

Because she's right. I can't keep this all to myself. I'll lose my mind if I try.

"Do you trust him?"

My gaze snaps back to Leslie's. "With my life." That's no lie. He'd put his life on the line for me and I'd do the same. No question. And he'll keep anything about her between the two of us. If he could manage it at lunch with Mom, he's more than up to the task.

"Good. Promise me you'll talk to him?"

I nod. "I promise." I'm glad she made me promise, because now I won't let myself chicken out at the first hint of teasing from my brother.

"You can tell him anything I've said to you, okay? I don't mind. I won't feel like you're betraying me if you do."

"Okay. And you can tell Aunt Star as much as you want. But Wendy?" I grin. "I don't know."

"I'll be discreet." She smiles back. "I don't want my personal business to end up in a CIA dossier somewhere. Now, how long are we going to stand out here talking to each other and delaying the start of Operation Pen Pal?"

"All night?" I say hopefully. "Your shoulder could get cold, though. I might be tempted to warm it up." Her bare collarbone has been driving me to distraction all night. I'm dying to trace it with my fingertips. Oh, who am I kidding? I want to trace it with more than my fingers.

Leslie glances at her shoulder and then raises an eyebrow at me. "I'd better get inside before we say or do anything else we'll regret in the morning."

"I'm sorry," I say. "I shouldn't—"

She cuts me off. "Ash, you haven't done one thing wrong. You've been a perfect gentleman. Well, other than the butt comment, but I'll excuse that." She giggles and blushes again. "I think we've proved how much we need Operation Pen Pal."

I open the door for her, like the gentleman she believes I am, though my current thoughts are anything but polite. "I'm going to write the best letters you've ever dreamed of reading."

"I'm counting on it," she declares as she sweeps through the doorway. She unlocks the inner glass door past the mailboxes and walks away without giving me a backward glance. I know this because I watch her until she disappears into the stairwell.

twenty-three

· · ·

I can feel Ash's eyes on my backside as I stroll to the stairwell, but I force myself to keep looking straight ahead.

As soon as I enter my apartment, I kick off my shoes and flop down onto my bed. The answering machine is blinking again, but I need some time to process the evening on my own before talking to anyone about it.

I shimmy out of my skirt and hose without leaving the bed and toss them across the room. The skirt lands on top of my brief-case, reminding me of work and the fact that I'm going to a base-ball game tomorrow afternoon. I can't quite believe I'm going to get paid to watch my favorite team play—even if Diego Sanchez has forbidden me from cheering for them. I momentarily wonder what I should wear to a sporting event while on the clock, but then my thoughts turn back to Ash … and Glenn.

Like I told Ash, I haven't given myself time to mourn the loss of my relationship with Glenn. The past few weeks were so action-packed I had no mental space to think about anything but moving and my new job.

I was absolutely stunned when Glenn wasn't happy about me getting the job, and I was more astonished when he broke up with me over it. We weren't the romance of the century, but I thought we were solid. I can't believe I was so wrong about him—about us. Tears leak from my eyes and roll down into my ears. I wipe them away with my sheet and then immediately regret it when I spy the makeup I transferred onto my new peach sheets.

I heave myself off the bed and pad over to the bathroom to remove the rest of my makeup. While I wait for the warm water to arrive, I avoid looking in the mirror. I don't want to see the misery in my eyes or think about the reasons I'm sad.

Brrrrring!

I don't move.

Brrrrring!

There's no doubt the caller is Wendy, but I'm not yet ready to talk to her.

Brrrrring!

I splash water on my face.

Brrrrring!

I listen to my own voice instructing the caller to leave a message after the beep.

"Leslie Beckett," Wendy's voice blares out of the answering machine, "you'd better be home and not still with Ash. But if you're home, why aren't you answering your phone? Are you avoiding me? Call me. Byeeee!"

It occurs to me if she's only now calling, she didn't leave the earlier message. Aunt Star didn't know about tonight's dinner, so I doubt it's her, and my parents and siblings usually only call me on the weekends. I finish getting ready for bed and then hit play on the machine.

"Leslie," a low voice rumbles, "I'm sorry for everything. Please call me so we can work things out. I miss you so much, and I'll do anything to make this up to you. I love you, baby. Call me. I don't care how late it is."

I lie motionless on the bed while the machine beeps and then Wendy's message plays. My brain can't process what I heard. How does Glenn even know my phone number? I didn't know it myself until after I moved in, and I haven't talked to him since the breakup.

I roll over, pick up the phone, and punch in a familiar number.

"Hello?" a deep voice answers.

I sniffle. "Darren, is Aunt Star there?"

"Hi, Les. Yes. Let me get her." He hollers for my aunt and then says, "You okay, kiddo?"

Tears slide down my face. "No."

"Babe, you can hang up now," my aunt orders him.

"I hope you work out whatever's wrong," Darren says. "Talk to you later."

"Thank you. Bye."

The line clicks.

"He's a good man," I say to Aunt Star.

"I don't know what I did to deserve him."

"You deserve only the best," I choke out.

"So do you. What's going on?"

I tell her about Glenn's call and how I've been avoiding thinking about him until now. "What do I do about him?" I ask when I'm finished.

"What do you want to do about him? Do you want to try to work things out?"

"I don't know. I'm so confused about how I feel about any of this. If I hadn't reconnected with Ash ..." I don't know how to finish my thought.

"Okay, let's put the Ash aspect aside for a minute. If Glenn had called you two days ago, how do you think you would've responded?"

"I would've been angry, but I would've wanted to talk to him and see if we could try to patch things up. I missed him, regardless of what he said and did."

"You said 'missed' in the past tense. Do you still miss him?"

"Not as much as before Ash."

"Because now you know Glenn's not your only option?"

"That and I like Ash a lot."

"What do you like about him?"

"He's kind, and he's smart, and he's ..." I trail off when I realize I know little more about him.

"You don't know him very well, do you?"

"I guess not."

"And I wouldn't say he was kind to you on the street yesterday."

"He apologized for that."

"Anybody can apologize. Now, I'm not saying he's not a kind man. You threw him for a loop, and he probably responded as well as most people could've. But you haven't spent enough time with him to truly know what he's like. Speaking of which, have you seen or talked to him again?"

"Yes."

"You want to tell me about it?"

I describe our interactions.

"Well," she says when I've told her everything, "you may be right about him being kind. Either that or he's a great liar and really wants to get into your pants."

"Aunt Star!"

"What? He's a man, and you're ridiculously beautiful. It's not too far of a leap."

"He's not like that!"

"How do you know?"

"Because I do, okay?" If there's one thing I knew about Ash when we were kids and I'm certain is still accurate, it's that he's a conscientious man. And he doesn't play games. "And because he didn't try anything, either yesterday or today."

"All right," she concedes. "Forget I said it. Ashley Hamilton is a kind man."

"Thank you." I don't know why I'm so adamant she believes it, but I'm one hundred percent sure it's true.

"You think this pen pal thing is the best idea?" she asks.

I'm not nearly as sure about the wisdom of the plan as I was when I proposed it. "Maybe not, but we have little choice. We can't completely ignore or avoid each other because of work, and I don't want to do that. I want to get to know him again, whether we ever end up as more than friends or not. And it's already obvious we can't spend time together outside work without getting too close too fast. So writing letters seems like a good way for us to get reacquainted without muddying the waters too much while I deal with the Glenn situation." I groan. "Again, what am I going to do about Glenn?"

"I don't think you can ignore or avoid him, either. You're

going to have to talk to him, if only for your own sake. Hear him out, see how you feel, and go from there. You don't have to make an immediate decision about him. And try to keep your feelings for Ash out of it. Don't let this instant crush on him cloud your thinking."

I bristle at the "instant crush" comment, but she's not wrong.

"Will you be able to sleep tonight?" she asks.

"Probably not."

"I hope you can. Talk to Glenn soon, okay? The longer you put it off, the more you're going to worry about it."

"I know. I'll call him tomorrow night if I don't go out after work." I want to tell her about Diego Sanchez, but I'm not sure what I can say without breaking the NDA. I need to ask Wendy for details.

"All right. Let me know how it goes."

"I will. Love you."

"You, too. Night."

As soon as I hang up, I dial Wendy's number. I don't want to go over it all again, but I need to find out what I'm supposed to wear to the ballgame.

"You better be alone," Wendy says as a greeting.

"Hello to you, too."

"Yes, hi." Then she loudly says, "Hi, Ash!"

"He's not here, you dodo."

"Glad to hear it. Give me all the details."

"I'll give you some, but first, what do I wear to a Cubs game if I'm there for work?"

"You're going tomorrow?"

"Yes."

"Will you be in a box suite?"

"I don't know."

"Do you not have your ticket?"

"Diego's sending a car to pick me up at the office. He said the driver will have my ticket."

"Ooo, very fancy!"

"So what do I wear?"

"No idea. But if you tell me what happened tonight, it might come to me."

"Wendy!"

"Fine. Business casual. Wear the team colors."

That's definitely not happening. "And what are the team colors, Wendy?" I test her.

"Purple and orange. Now, tell me what happened with Ash."

I explain about Operation Pen Pal, and she thinks it's the cutest thing ever. I swear her to secrecy. Nobody else at Carter-Jenkins or Murphy, Hamilton, and Walker needs to know about this. I don't want to subject Ash to any ridicule.

"My lips are sealed."

I have my doubts, but I choose to believe her.

"Surely he'll tell Randall," she says.

"Yes. And I really hope he's helpful and doesn't mock the whole thing."

"I'll make sure he doesn't."

"Wendy—"

"Trust me. I know how to handle the Hamilton brothers."

"All right." I bite my lip. "Can I ask you something?"

"Of course."

"Is Ash a kind man? I mean, he has been kind to me, but is he kind to everyone?"

She pauses, and I can tell she's thinking. "I don't know if kind is the word I'd use, because of his general air of grumpiness, but he's fair and respectful—especially to women and people other men in his position would consider beneath them. Ash is a good man, Leslie. He has a very keen sense of right and wrong, and he always does what he believes is right—at least as much as he has control of it. The man would make a terrible trial lawyer, because if he thought—or knew—his client was guilty, he wouldn't have it in him to defend them."

Wendy couldn't have dreamed up a better answer if she'd tried, and I know she wasn't making up any of it. Everything she said lines up with what I know to be true of Ash.

She continues, "I don't know why they have him working for

us. He should be out there fighting for human rights and helping the oppressed or something."

"Couldn't he do that if he wanted to?" It's what he used to want to do. Does he not want to anymore? His first letter should shed some light on the topic.

"You haven't met Walter Hamilton yet, have you?"

"Walter … oh, his dad?"

"Indeed."

"I haven't had the pleasure."

"If you had, you'd understand. And there would be nothing pleasurable about it."

"Yikes."

"I couldn't have said it better myself. You're in for a rude awakening with the future in-laws."

twenty-four

. . .

When I leave Leslie's, my car heads toward Randall's apartment, which is only a handful of blocks from her place but in the opposite direction of home. I guess I'm going to make good on my promise and talk to him about this.

All the doormen in my brother's building know me and always wave me through whether he's home or not, but I ask tonight's guy to call up and warn Randall I'm coming. I have zero desire to walk in on him and Colleen in a compromising position.

I knock and then hear my brother faintly telling me to enter, so I fish my keys out of my pocket and let myself in. He's lounging on his black leather couch in nothing but a pair of boxers while watching SportsCenter and drinking a Budweiser. I drop onto the matching love seat.

"What's up?" He takes a swig from his bottle. I doubt it's his first of the evening. "Girl trouble? Tell your big brother all about it."

"How much have you had to drink?" I'm not going to talk to him if he's half drunk.

"This is only my second."

I raise an eyebrow at him.

"Maybe my third."

"Why do you do this?"

"Do what? Let loose? Have a little fun? You should try it sometime."

"I see no evidence of you letting loose and having fun at the moment."

"Fine." He rolls his eyes. "Colleen canceled on me tonight. Fourth time in two weeks. I don't know what's going on."

Colleen is not my favorite person. My brother deserves much better, but if I say so, he'll only defend her, which will annoy me. "Is this why you refused to promise Mom you two would go to her dinner party Saturday night?"

"Partly." He takes another swig.

"What's the other part?"

"I figured you didn't want any more of an audience to the set-up she's forcing on you."

"Oh. Thanks."

He taps his fingernail on the beer bottle. "I know what Melissa did to you back in junior high."

My back stiffens. "What are you talking about?"

"You know exactly what I'm talking about."

"How do you know about that?"

"Everybody knew, Ash. I didn't tell you I knew, because you were already so embarrassed, I didn't want to make it worse."

I did not expect that. "Really?"

"Yup. And I told Melissa you told me in confidence she was a terrible kisser, but you were too good of a person to say it to her or anyone else, so I said it for you. I'm not above taking people down a notch or two when necessary."

"You did *not* say that!"

He grins. "I did. You might need to apologize for it on your first date."

I pick one of his dirty socks up off the floor and fling it at him.

Randall swats it away. "Hey! I defended you!"

He's right, and I'm astonished by the knowledge. "That doesn't mean I'm going on a date with her."

"I bet you fifty bucks Mom will make it happen."

"Never."

"Why? Because Melissa made fun of you twelve years ago?"

"Partly." I throw his own answer back at him.

"What's the other part?" He doesn't say it mockingly.

I don't know where to begin.

"I know it's Leslie." He twirls his empty bottle around. "I'm not an idiot."

"Yeah, I know. I …"

He waits patiently while I figure out what to say, which blows my mind a little. I keep expecting him to make a snide remark, but he doesn't.

"She doesn't want to date me right now," I finally blurt out.

"I'm sorry, man." We sit in silence for a few moments. "Wait. You said, 'right now.' Does that mean she might want to in the future?"

I explain about the situation with Glenn.

"That dude sounds like a class-A jerk," he says. "She's well rid of him."

"I agree. But she needs time to deal with what happened. And I want to know she's with me because she wants to be with *me*, not because she's using me to get over him. I don't think she'd knowingly do that, but there's no way she's thinking straight after what he did."

Randall shakes his head. "That's a tough position to be in. What are you going to do? You can't avoid her."

"Promise you won't make fun of me if I tell you."

"Have I made fun of you one time since you walked in here tonight?"

"You did accuse me of not knowing how to let loose and have fun."

"That wasn't making fun. That was stating cold, hard facts. Anyway, you have to tell me now. If you don't, I'll ask you about it every five minutes for the rest of your life."

"No, you won't."

"Have you met me?"

"Yes, and that's how I know I'm going to outlive you by decades. You might ask about it every five minutes for the rest of *your* life, but not mine."

He barks out a laugh. "You're funny sometimes, you know

that? Now tell me what you're going to do before I throw this bottle at you."

"We're going to write each other letters."

His eyebrows shoot up. "You're going to be pen pals again?"

"Yep."

"I like that idea."

I stop my jaw from dropping. "You do?"

He nods. "You've always been better at writing than speaking."

"Gee, thanks."

"No, it's not a criticism. It's who you are. Most people are the opposite, but that doesn't mean it's the only way to be. You have a way of expressing yourself on paper that the rest of us can only dream of. It's a gift. I think it's why you wrote to Les for so long. You could tell him—her—things you couldn't tell any of us because you could write it down and didn't have to say it out loud."

Who is this man, and what has he done with my brother? He does sometimes get philosophical when he drinks, but I expected nothing like that to come out of his mouth. And he's right—except when it comes to Leslie. I had no problem verbalizing my thoughts and feelings to her last night and tonight.

I finally respond. "Thanks, I think. But if that's the way you feel about it, why did you make fun of me for writing to Les for so long?"

He shrugs. "Because I was a little boneheaded jackwagon. And do you think I could've realized any of that when I was fourteen?"

I'm surprised he could realize it now, which makes me the boneheaded jackwagon.

"I was also a little jealous," he admits.

I allow my jaw to drop. "You were what?"

"You heard me. I'm not saying it again. You spent more time writing those letters to Les than you spent with me. I'm your brother, for goodness' sake. *I'm* supposed to be your best friend—not some kid in Arkansas."

I don't miss his use of present tense in his statement, and my chest constricts. "But you *are* my best friend. You always have been."

He stares at me, and his Adam's apple bobs up and down a few times. I'm afraid he's going to cry. I'm not sure what I'll do if he does.

"Do you mean that?" he finally asks.

"Of course I mean it." I spread my hands wide. "Who else would be my best friend?"

"I was always worried you didn't really like me—that you only put up with me because you have to."

His words hit me like a punch to the gut. I'm hesitant to ask, but I need to know the answer. "Does that still worry you?"

He looks away from me, and I don't think he's going to respond. Then he nods.

Now I'm scared I'm going to cry. What an unexpected night this has turned out to be.

"Randy, I apologize for anything I've ever done or said to make you feel that way. I ... I don't know what else to say except I'm sorry."

He turns his head back to me and nods again. Then one corner of his mouth quirks and his eyes dance. "I bet you would know what to say if you could write it down."

Even after our conversation, I don't want to give him the satisfaction of laughing at his comment, so I press my lips together and stare at him. Before we know it, we're in an old-fashioned staring contest, both determined to not blink first and apparently not laugh first either, because his chest keeps making minor convulsions and his cheeks twitch as he valiantly tries to hold back a grin. I finally blink and let out a full belly laugh.

"I win!" he crows and then laughs so hard he falls off the couch.

twenty-five

· · ·

I get to work early so I can accomplish a few things before I need to leave for the afternoon baseball game. Thankfully Wendy isn't waiting for me when I arrive today.

When I haven't seen her by mid-morning, I get a little antsy, though. Typically, she stops by to at least say hi.

As I come up with many scenarios of why she's not here, she waltzes into my office and flings the door shut. I tilt my head and watch her flop down into the purple chair.

"You know the new guy Jay at Murphy, Hamilton, and Walker —the one at lunch with Ash and Randall?" she asks.

"Yes. What about him?"

"I don't like him."

"Why?"

"I was over there this morning—"

"Why were you over there?" I interrupt.

She flaps her hand. "I'll explain in a sec. Anyway, that *man* told me I should wear shorter skirts and tighter shirts if I ever want to get a husband instead of having to work for a living."

My eyes widen. "He did not."

"Oh, he did."

"What did you do?"

"Ash was rounding the corner as Jay said it, so he heard it, and he looked like he was going to bring the entire wrath of God down upon Jay's head. I was afraid we'd have a bloodbath on our hands, so I stepped between them. I mean, we don't need some little rodent marring Ash's beautiful face, do we?"

I shake my head. That would be a tragedy.

"So I put my fists on my hips and stood up as tall as my tiny little self could and said, 'If you ever want to get a wife who won't be plotting the divorce and making plans for the alimony payments before her daddy even walks her down the aisle, you'd better change your attitude, buddy. This is the eighties, not the fifties. Get with the program.'"

I stand and clap.

"That's exactly what Randall did," she says. "He came up behind Jay during my speech and was, frankly, in awe at my performance."

I drop back into my chair. "And what did Ash do?"

"After Jay slunk away with his little devil tail between his legs, Ash gave me a high five. Well, high for me, low for him, considering he's seven feet tall."

"Maybe not quite that tall."

"Close enough. He has to duck when he goes through a doorway, and he's more than a foot taller than me—even when I'm in heels."

"So why were you over there in the first place?"

"I went to talk to Randall about Ash."

I close my eyes and cross my fingers. "Please tell me it went well."

"Indeed, it did. I discovered Ash went directly to his brother's apartment after leaving you last night."

My eyes pop open, and I try to stop a grin from spreading across my face. "He did?" I'm relieved Ash isn't keeping everything to himself.

"Yes. And Randall promised to be gentle with him. He claimed he was last night."

I nod. "Good."

"You care about him, don't you? This isn't only raw animal magnetism? Not that there's anything wrong with that."

"It's both. Which is why it's not a good idea for us to be in the same physical space unless it's required for work."

She stands. "Speaking of work, I should get some done today. Not everyone gets to spend the afternoon eating hot dogs at the ballpark."

"Nachos and beer for me," I say. "Oh, what are the rules about drinking on the job? Do I need to stick to soda?"

"The only rule is to not get drunk and embarrass the firm. I typically limit myself to one drink, if that. I definitely don't drink alcohol if nobody else is, especially if I'm the only woman present."

"Got it." I decide I'll play it by ear.

She opens the door. "What time are you leaving?"

I look at my watch. "In about fifteen minutes. I'd better go freshen up."

"You look good," she says. "Great choice of outfit."

"You think?" I look down at my silky button-up dusky pink shirt, slim black pants, and black flats.

"Yep. Very classy."

"Thanks."

Before I know it, I'm ensconced in the backseat of a black Town Car. As we pull away, the driver says, "I need to pick up one more passenger, and we'll be on our way."

I nod at him through the rearview mirror. He turns right at the first light, drives partway down the block, and pulls over to the curb. I wonder why he's pulling over so soon. I discover why the moment the car door opens and a leg steps inside—a leg long enough to belong to only one person who works around the corner from me. The smell of cinnamon enters along with him.

"Hi," Ash says with a grin as he makes himself as comfortable as he can in the backseat of a car. Did I mention his legs are extremely long?

He clears his throat, and I realize I'm ogling him. At least I'm not licking my lips.

I glance up and raise an eyebrow at him. "Did you know about this last night?" I can't decide whether I'll be mad if he says yes.

He shakes his head. "No. Bobby called this morning and asked me to come. Wait. Let me rephrase that. He ordered me to come." Ash rolls his eyes but then his eyes dart toward the driver.

I know what he's thinking. He doesn't know if the driver works for Diego or his agent Bobby Jacobs, or if he's a random guy hired for this one ride. We need to steer clear of talking about the client and his agent while we're in the car.

"Not that I'm complaining about going to a baseball game for work," he adds.

"Right. Soooo …" I don't know what else to say. Thanks to our rules, we can only talk about work when we're in each other's presence, but we can't even do that at the moment.

"Soooo … rules." He says no more, but he doesn't need to.

I finally think of a safe topic. "Wendy told me what happened with Jay this morning."

Ash's hands ball into fists. "That guy …"

"She thought you were going to take him out. I would've paid good money to see that." I smile at him.

"Oh, yeah?" He smiles back and angles his body more toward me so our knees are touching.

We gaze at each other until I realize we're teetering on the edge of danger, and my smile fades. "Yeah." I look away from him and reluctantly shift my knee from his, though it's like trying to pry two magnets apart.

"Hey," he says softly.

I close my eyes and shake my head. "I don't know if I can do this."

"What can't you do?"

Deal with him. Deal with Glenn. Deal with any of it. I blurt out, "Glenn called me last night."

In my peripheral vision, I see him stiffen.

"Okay."

"While I was with you." I pick at invisible lint on my pants. "He left a message."

"Okay," he repeats.

"He said he's sorry and wants us to get back together."

Ash doesn't respond, and I can't make myself look at him as he breathes deeply.

"What do *you* want?" he finally asks.

I want Ash, but I also want Glenn to have not dumped me. How can I want both of those things at the same time?

I rub my temples. "Ash, I'm sorry. I shouldn't have told you that. This is why we have the rules. You can't help me deal with this."

"No, I can't." His voice is strained. I still can't look at him.

"Almost there, folks," the driver says a few silent minutes later. Then he tells us where another car will pick us up after the game.

While we're sitting at a stoplight a block away from the stadium, the driver cranes his neck so he can see us. "Excuse me for butting in, but I feel compelled to say this. I don't know why you have rules or what they are or who Glenn is or what he did, but you two?" He points back and forth between us. "There's something here. I can feel it in my bones. Don't give up on each other."

twenty-six

· · ·

The driver hands me the tickets, tells us to enjoy the game, and leaves Leslie and me standing on the sidewalk outside Wrigley Field avoiding each other's eyes. I can't move. My mind is both blank and filled with more thoughts than I can handle, all at the same time.

"I don't know where to go," Leslie says. "I've never been here before. I'm sorry I dropped that bomb on you in the car, but I need you to focus and get us inside."

And I need to get away from all these people to somewhere I can think, but that's not an option, so I give my head a quick shake and look her in the eye. "I can do that. Stay right by my side. It's easy to get separated here."

I look at the tickets and note we're in a suite. I head around the stadium toward the gate closest to where we need to be, since it's much easier to navigate outside the ballpark than inside.

"Ash, slow down. I can't keep up." I turn my head to see Leslie practically jogging to match my long strides. She's not wearing heels, but her shoes weren't exactly made for running. I slow my pace so she can catch up with me and then ensure she's right by my side until we get in line. We don't speak as we shuffle toward the turnstiles.

Once we're inside, it's difficult for us to stay together in the throng, so I finally give in and take her hand to prevent anyone from walking between us. She doesn't pull away, which I take as a good sign. I can think of almost nothing else but the fact that her hand is wrapped around my own, so it's a good thing I know this stadium like the back of that very hand.

Again we're silent as we make our way to the suite. Before we step through the door, she slips her hand out of mine, and the loss of connection is palpable. I note she also plasters on a fake smile. I don't even attempt it.

The suite is empty except for a couple of workers. Leslie heads directly to the bar and orders a beer. I rarely wish I drank alcohol, but this is one of those times. I won't do it, though, especially if Leslie is drinking. I don't know who else will be in this box with us, but it'll most likely be a bunch of men who'll drink like fish. I need to stay completely alert in case any of them try anything with her.

I grab a hot dog, add mustard and relish to it, and then take it and a Coke to a bar height table near the outside section of the suite where I can watch Leslie through the windows. She took her beer out to the private stadium seating and is standing at the railing taking it all in.

Wrigley is an amazing experience, especially for a baseball fan like her. I wish I could stand down there with my arms around her, pointing out all the little quirks of the stadium and telling her how different it'll be when the lights are installed later in the season and we can finally have night games.

If for no other reason, I can't do any of those things because we're at a work function. But I don't know if she would want me there with her or if she wishes she was sharing this with Glenn. My heart squeezes at the thought. I want her to be happy, but I don't want her to be happy with him. I know that's selfish, but I can't help it.

A man joins me at the table. "Nice view, huh?"

For a minute I think he's talking about Leslie, but then I realize he's referring to the excellent view of the field. At least I hope that's what he's talking about.

I turn to him, and he sticks a hand out. "Bobby Jacobs."

Bobby is younger than I imagined he would be. He can't be

more than thirty-five, though from his reputation and how long he's been around, I figured he was more like fifty.

"Ash Hamilton." I place my hand in his, and he squeezes it a little too hard. I force myself not to flinch. He's watching to see if I do.

"That the PR chick?" He nods toward Leslie and gives her an appreciative once over.

I pin him with a steely gaze. "That's Leslie Beckett," I say through gritted teeth, "the PR *rep.*"

"All right, man." He holds his hands up. "Message received. Hands off the PR *rep.*"

I want to growl at him, but I don't. I'm surprised he doesn't take my attitude as a challenge. Then again, maybe he does but simply doesn't want me to know it yet.

"Are you two, you know …?" He raises an eyebrow at me.

It's none of his business, but I need him—and Sanchez—to keep their distance from her, so I say, "Leslie and I have been friends since we were kids. We're close."

"Got it."

I'm not sure he does, mostly because I don't know what Leslie and I are, so how could he?

Leslie chooses that moment to turn around. When she spots Bobby, she heads up the steps and inside the suite to join us. I introduce the two of them, and Bobby is perfectly polite to her.

"Who else will be here?" she asks him after they exchange some pleasantries.

"Not too many people. Diego flew a couple cousins up from Houston. A few of my contacts here in town are coming. That's about it."

"Is Diego close to his cousins?" she asks.

"Yeah. The three of them grew up together in the Dominican. They're more like brothers than cousins. When he made it big, he moved them and their families to the US, got them set up with green cards and jobs and everything. He helps them out financially when they really need it, and he pays for flights and such when he wants them with him, but he's not letting them freeload off him, which I appreciate about him."

I appreciate it as well.

Leslie asks Bobby, "Will they move to Chicago now, you think? For that matter, will Diego move here?"

I'm surprised they didn't discuss his living arrangements yesterday at lunch. What *did* they talk about?

"Doubt it," he replies. "He doesn't like the cold. I can't see him living here in the offseason. He's planning on settling in at The Drake for now."

Loud voices speaking in Spanish reach us from the direction of the door. Diego's cousins have arrived. Bobby heads over to greet them, leaving Leslie and me alone at the table.

"He's much nicer than I thought he'd be," she murmurs to me.

"I can't decide if it's a front or not," I reply.

"Ash!"

"Surely you know his reputation."

"I also know yours, Grouchy Smurf, and it's nowhere near accurate."

I don't have time to process her statement before Bobby brings Diego's cousins over to meet us. They're not as fluent in English as Diego is, and Bobby is apparently fluent in Spanish, but since Leslie doesn't know the language, we all speak in English for her sake.

I like his cousins. They're funny and laid back and they ask Leslie and me questions like they truly want to get to know us. We chat until it's time for the national anthem, when we all head outside for the singing and then stay out there to watch Diego pitch.

Leslie sits between the cousins in the front row. They talk to her nonstop, likely telling her all about Diego. Bobby's friends have arrived and are sitting on the other side of the aisle. I'm at a loose end about where to plant myself, but Bobby motions me over with his head, and I sit with his group. I hate making small talk with people I'll probably never see again, but it's part of the job. These guys are here to watch the game, so thankfully they don't want to chat about much other than baseball.

After the third inning, I head back inside to get some more food. As I'm loading up a plate with another hot dog and some nachos, a somewhat familiar female voice says, "Ash Hamilton? Is that you?"

I spin around and chips fly off my plate. I try to catch them, but I end up dumping the entire thing on the floor.

The woman, who is none other than a grown-up Melissa Teague, claps her hand over her mouth and giggles. "Whoops! I didn't mean to startle you."

"Not your fault."

I bend down to clean up the mess, but a stadium worker is already at my side and refuses to let me help. I straighten back up, face Melissa, and force my mouth into a smile. "Melissa, it's good to see you again," I lie.

"You, too! How long has it been? Ten years?" She walks up and slips her arms around me for a hug, which is disconcerting.

"Something like that," I say with my arms awkwardly folded around her.

I try to step back, but she moves with me. I look down and notice her necklace has looped around one of my shirt buttons, and we're stuck together. After a good fifteen seconds and some laughing, we get her disentangled, and she steps away.

"I'm looking forward to dinner tomorrow night," she says as she straightens the necklace.

A strangled sound catches my ear from behind me. I turn in time to see Leslie rushing out the suite door. My heart drops. I don't know how much she saw, but I know what she heard. I briefly close my eyes and then turn back to Melissa, who wears an expectant look.

"It'll be nice to catch up with you and your parents," I say politely while hoping Leslie's okay and is heading to the restroom instead of leaving entirely. I wonder if I should go after her.

"Earth to Ash!" Melissa waves her hand in front of my face.

"Hmm?"

"You left me there for a minute." She grins at me.

"Sorry. What were you saying?"

"It's so great to be back here."

"Why *are* you here?" I ask.

Her forehead wrinkles. "What do you mean? I moved back from New York."

"No, sorry, I meant why are you here in this suite?"

"Oh!" She laughs. "I work here at the stadium in Customer Relations. I visit a few of the suites during each game to make sure everything is up to standard. I check that all is running smoothly, the guests are enjoying themselves, that sort of thing."

And she happened to walk into the one I'm in? That seems like a big coincidence, though it almost certainly is, since even I didn't know I would be in this suite until I arrived.

"Well, this customer is having a good experience so far," I say.

"Who have we here?" Bobby asks from beside me. The man is stealthy. This is the second time he snuck up on me. And the tone of his voice alerts me that Melissa is as beautiful as thirteen-year-old Ash would've imagined her to become. I hadn't noticed until now, which is odd.

I expect Melissa to introduce herself to him, but she's focused on me. Since she appears to want me to do the honors, I say, "Melissa, this is Bobby Jacobs, Diego Sanchez's agent. Bobby, this is Melissa Teague. She works here at the stadium."

"And Ash and I go *way* back," she adds with a smile.

"Oh, do you?" Bobby raises an eyebrow at me. I know he's thinking I'm a total player, but that couldn't be further from the truth.

"We went to school together a long time ago," I explain.

"Ash, we're not that old!" Melissa bats me on the arm.

I know I'm being rude, but I need to find Leslie, so I excuse myself. I step out the door, intending to head straight toward the nearest restrooms, but I stop when I realize Leslie is leaning against the wall right outside the suite's door.

twenty-seven

· · ·

I can't breathe. I don't know if it's worse that Ash already broke his promise to wait for me or that he might have been lying to me all along.

Staying at the game feels impossible, but I can't leave, because I'm here for work *and* because my purse is still in the suite. I finally manage to take a deep breath and prop myself against the wall. I need to march back in there, ignore Ash and that woman he can't keep his hands off of, drink another beer or five, and chat with Diego's cousins. But I can't make myself do it.

I'm regretting not calling Glenn back last night. The longer I put it off, the more my chest aches. I don't think I'm going to get back together with Glenn, but I won't know for sure until we talk. And I was foolish to think Ash would wait for me, especially since Glenn is back on the scene.

The suite door swings open, and I pray it's not Ash. Apparently, my prayers aren't being answered today, because there he is. I try to disappear into the wall, but it only takes him a second to spot me. I give him a quick glance before crossing my arms and staring in the opposite direction. I know I'm acting like a bratty teenager, but Ash Hamilton has some explaining to do.

He moves next to me and leans his shoulder against the wall so he's facing my side. "Leslie."

"Ashley." I shouldn't use the name he despises, but I can't help myself.

"That wasn't what it looked like in there."

"It didn't look like anything," I lie, still not looking at him. "You don't have to explain yourself to me." Although I'm dying for him to do exactly that.

"Neither of those things are true. Please be honest with me."

I can't deny him that, so I turn to face him and plant my fists on my hips. "All right, then. Are you dating that woman? Are you in a relationship and you didn't tell me, even after all that's happened the past two days?" Tears fill my eyes against my will. "Did you lie when you promised you'd wait for me?"

"No."

His simple answer deflates me a little. It also releases some of the tightness in my chest. "Care to enlighten me then?"

"Leslie, I didn't lie to you." His anguished look reveals he's speaking the truth. "The woman's name is Melissa Teague. We went to school together a long time ago. She recently moved back to town, and my mother decided I should date her. Mom invited her family over for dinner tomorrow night and sprung it on me yesterday. I couldn't say no."

I give him an incredulous look. Is he not a grown man who can make his own decisions?

"You haven't met my mother," he says in response to my unasked question.

Then something he said hits me. "Wait a minute. Melissa Teague … where have I heard that name before?"

He sighs and stuffs his hands in his pockets. "Seven Minutes in Heaven."

My hand goes to my mouth. I remember that story. "Oh, no." I want to march back into the suite and smack her.

"Oh, yes."

I tilt my head. "Then why were you all over her in there?" I narrow my eyes. "And why is she here?"

"I wasn't all over her. Her necklace got caught on my shirt when she hugged me," he explains. "And believe it or not, she works here and happened to walk into our suite."

I shouldn't like that he calls it "our suite," but I do.

Now he crosses his arms. "Why do you get to be all high and mighty anyway, after what you told me in the car? Are you the only one who gets to have second thoughts about us?"

I gasp. "I'm not having second thoughts!"

"So you're planning to tell Glenn to go fly a kite?"

My stomach churns and I look away from him as tears threaten to spill over again.

"I shouldn't have said that," he says with a light touch to my arm, which sends sparks on an erratic journey throughout my body. "I'm sorry. It's a totally different situation."

"It is," I say. "But you're right. We're not dating each other. You're free to do as you please. She's pretty, your family likes her, and what she did to you when she was twelve isn't any worse than what I did." My throat closes up and I choke out, "Why shouldn't you date her?"

"Leslie, look at me," he says softly.

I slowly turn my head toward him and look up into his eyes.

"I don't want to date her. Okay?"

I nod.

"And you have never been mean to me like she was. You got that?"

I nod again. A tear rolls down my cheek and I swipe it away. "Why are you being so nice to me?" He shouldn't be. He should forget about me and my baggage and my stupid Operation Pen Pal idea. Even if he doesn't want to date Melissa, there are plenty of other women who would be a lot less trouble for him than I am.

"I'm being nice because I care about you." His eyes tell me he wants to say so much more, but he doesn't. Those eyes briefly dip down to my lips, which tingle at the thought he might want to kiss me.

I do not deserve this man. If I care about him, too—and I do— the best thing I can do for him is to let him go. I set my jaw and say, "I've decided writing letters to each other isn't a good idea. We shouldn't have any contact except for work." I hold my breath as I wait for his response.

He studies my eyes. "Is that what you want?"

Though my head tells me to say yes, my heart won't allow it. I can't lie to him about this. "No. I want to write to you. I want us to get to know each other again. But I don't want to trap you into this …," I wave an arm around, "… whatever it is with me."

"You're not trapping me into anything. I'm choosing to see where this might go of my own free will. I know full well there are no guarantees. And I'm all in on Operation Pen Pal." His gaze never leaves mine.

I bite my lip. "You sure?"

"I told you I'll always be honest when it matters. This matters a lot." One corner of his mouth turns up. "It's too late to stop it, anyway."

My eyebrows raise when I realize what he's saying. "You already wrote and mailed your letter?"

"Maybe."

When did he have time, especially if he went to Randall's after dinner last night?

We study each other, and once again I'm certain he wants to kiss me. I'm also sure if he makes any move to do so, I'll let him, rules or no rules.

"There you are, Leslie," comes an accented voice from behind me. "We wondered what happened to you."

I tear my eyes from Ash's and smile at Diego's cousin Jorge. "Thanks for checking on me. I'm fine. We're taking care of some business out here where it's a little more private. Almost done. We'll be back in soon."

"Ah, *si*," he says. "You must come back. Diego will be mad if Lady Leslie does not watch all his pitches." He grins to let me know he's kidding and disappears back into the suite.

Ash raises an eyebrow at me. "Lady Leslie?"

"It's what Diego calls me. I'm not the PR guy, I'm the PR lady." I shrug. "I think it's cute."

The look on Ash's face tells me he thinks it's nowhere near cute, but he doesn't say so. Instead he asks, "Are we good?"

"Yes." At least as good as we can be under the circumstances. As for whether *I'm* good? That's a different situation entirely.

twenty-eight

· · ·

Diego Sanchez has no right to give Leslie a nickname—especially not a *cute* one. It's not professional. I've half a mind to tell him so if I ever meet him, but I have a feeling he would only laugh in my face.

I open the door and wave for Leslie to enter the suite ahead of me. I can't resist brushing my hand against her back as she passes. The brief touch doesn't compare to the kiss I wanted to lay on her to dispel any misgivings she might have about my intention to be with her and only her, but it'll have to do for now.

Since Melissa didn't exit while we were outside, she'll likely be waiting for my return, and I need a minute to gather my wits about me. Leslie almost gave me a heart attack when she suggested cutting off all non-work contact. I've never experienced five longer seconds than the ones when she considered whether that was what she truly wanted.

If she had said yes, I would've felt like an absolute idiot, considering I stayed up well past midnight writing my first letter and then going to the post office closest to her apartment this morning, setting up my P.O. box, and mailing the letter. There's no getting it back.

Finally, I put on my best professional smile and step inside. Melissa makes a beeline for me, loops her arm through mine, and drags me over to an empty table two down from where Bobby sits by himself nursing a beer. My eyes seek out Leslie, who has returned to her spot outside with Diego's cousins. When my gaze moves past Bobby on my way back to focus on Melissa, he gives me a look that informs me he noticed what I was doing.

Melissa says in a low voice, "Listen, Ash. Before this dinner tomorrow, we need to talk about something I did a long time ago that you may have forgotten about."

If she thinks I've forgotten what she did, why is she bringing it up?

She continues, "Do you remember playing 'Seven Minutes in Heaven' at Alex Conover's house back in junior high?"

"Vaguely," I lie.

"Well, you and I ended up in the closet together. It was my first kiss, and I was so nervous," she says, "but I didn't want anyone to know. So afterward I joked around with my friends that you didn't know what you were doing, when it was really me who was clueless.

"Then your brother told me you thought I was a terrible kisser but would never embarrass me by saying it to anyone else. I wanted to crawl into a hole, and I felt absolutely awful about what I'd done to you. So I went back and told my friends I was joking about you, but the damage was done. Word had spread like wildfire. The craziest part of it all is I actually liked you, and you'd always been so sweet to me, but I was afraid you thought I was an airhead. I should've apologized to you then, but I was too ashamed. So I'm apologizing now. I'm sorry I did that to you."

I'm astonished by her admission. "I accept your apology." I discover I truly do. "And I need to apologize on my brother's behalf. He lied to you. I never said a word to him about you. I do remember us kissing, by the way, and it wasn't bad. Neither of us knew what we were doing, but I don't think it was awful as far as first kisses go. Anyway, Randall heard what you said and was trying to defend me. I didn't know about his lie back then. When he found out I was going to see you again, he told me."

"Oh, wow." Melissa presses her hand to her chest. "I'm glad he lied, though. It taught me a great lesson about how I should treat people. I can't say I completely changed overnight, but that incident made a big impact on me. So maybe I need to thank Randall."

I chuckle. "He'd get a kick out of that."

She laughs. "I also didn't kiss anyone else for a few more years, because I was afraid they'd think I was terrible, too. Looking back, I'm thankful for that, as well. I'm sure it saved me from a lot of trouble."

I didn't kiss anyone else again until college, but she doesn't need to know that.

"I have to head out in a minute," she said, "but first I want to know what's going on with you and the blonde out there." She smirks at me.

My eyes widen. "What do you mean?"

"I'm not blind. She hightailed it out of here when she saw me hug you and mention dinner tomorrow. And then you followed her out and didn't come back for a while until you trailed back in behind her. Are the two of you dating and your mother doesn't know?"

I can't tell her everything, but since she doesn't seem upset by the idea of me potentially dating Leslie, I figure I should take her into my confidence.

"It's a complicated situation with her," I say. "I won't go into detail, but I'm not interested in dating anyone else. And no, my mother doesn't know—thus tomorrow night's dinner. I'm sorry if Mom invited you under false pretenses. I didn't know about the dinner until yesterday, but I'm guessing you've known for a while."

She nods. "We got the invitation a couple weeks ago. Well, I don't think it was an invitation so much as a joint battle plan drawn up by our mothers. Don't worry. I won't say anything to your mom about …," she points her head toward Leslie and raises her eyebrows.

"Leslie."

"About Leslie. I'm not interested in dating, at any rate. My boyfriend and I broke up before I moved back and I'm not ready to jump back into the game yet. And much like you apparently have trouble saying no to your mother, I have the same issue with mine."

I breathe a huge sigh of relief.

"You were that worried about it?" she asks.

"I'll admit I wasn't excited, but now that we both know the lay of the land, it could be fun." Oddly enough, I'm finding I like Melissa.

"Ooo, should we fake flirt with each other? Lead our mothers on?"

She gives me an evil grin, and I chuckle at her.

"Let's wait and see what feels right in the moment."

She holds out her hand. "It's a deal."

I take her hand and shake it. "Looking forward to it."

Melissa stands to leave, and I walk her to the door. When it closes behind her and I turn around, Leslie is watching me from the bar with a guarded expression. I give her a genuine smile, hoping to reassure her I'm not interested in any woman but her. Though it's best for me to stay away from her, I join her at the tiny bar.

"She apologized for what happened back in junior high," I say.

"Really?"

"Yeah. She said she actually liked me but was afraid I didn't like her back. She also claims the incident changed her for the better because she felt so bad about what she did." I shake my head. "This appears to be the week for me to receive apologies from pretty ladies for what they did to me when we were kids." I immediately realize I shouldn't have mentioned I think Melissa is pretty.

"Did you forgive her?"

"Of course I did." And I'm a little annoyed Leslie thinks I might not have.

She nods and looks down into her drink. "Of course." Then without returning her gaze to me she says, "I'd better get back to Diego's cousins." She turns and walks off.

I watch her go with a heavy heart. I'm not sure what changed from the time we came back into the suite until now, but she's pulling away from me. Instead of heading back outside myself, I join Bobby at his table.

"What did you do to make her look like her dog died?" he asks.

I shake my head. "It's complicated."

"It always is." He takes a swig of his beer.

Bobby and I talk throughout the rest of the game. The man is amazingly down to earth, especially for someone with his reputation. I'm beginning to think the reputation is the front and I'm seeing the real Bobby Jacobs.

When Leslie comes inside after the game's over, I approach her and ask, "You ready to go find the car, or do you need to stay and talk to Diego?"

She still won't look at me. "I don't need to stay. And I don't think it's a good idea for us to share a ride. Why don't you take it?"

There's no way I'm letting her make her own way home while I ride in a hired car. "No, the car is yours."

"Ash—"

"Leslie," Bobby says from beside me, "I'm sorry to steal Ash away from you, but I'm not done with this guy. We have a few more things to discuss. I'll make sure he gets back."

She nods, shakes Bobby's hand, gives me an indecipherable look, and heads out the door.

"What else do we need to discuss?" I ask Bobby. We've been talking for the past hour.

"Nothing," he says. "She was prepared to argue with you about the car, but she doesn't know me well enough to fight me over it." He glances at the door. "You'd better fix whatever's happening here, though. I need her to be in top form for Diego."

There's nothing I can do to fix it.

twenty-nine

. . .

What is wrong with me? Why did I treat Ash the way I did? Well, I know it's because I'm jealous of Melissa Teague, but that doesn't excuse my actions.

I find the car and wish I could tell the driver to take me home, but it's not five o'clock yet, and even if it were, I need to go back to the office and get some work done. Regardless of what's going on in my personal life, I have a job to do, and I want to do it right. Diego's career shouldn't suffer because I can't focus.

As the car threads its way back downtown, I stare out the window. I read every sign and look at each face in a failed attempt to not think about Ash or Glenn.

When I enter the office, Wendy is in the lobby chatting to our receptionist. She takes one look at my face and follows me down the hall. She closes my office door behind us, grasps my arm, pulls me to her, and wraps her arms around me. I squeeze her tightly.

"What happened?" she asks when I finally pull away from her and drop into my chair. She perches on my desk instead of taking her usual spot in the purple chair.

"Ash went to the game, too. We shared a car on the way there, and I let it spill that Glenn called me and wants to get back together. Then a woman Ash knows from childhood was at the game, and she's having dinner with his family tomorrow night, and they were real friendly, and I'm a mess and want to go home, but I've got so many things to do for Diego that I can't."

"Hold. The. Phone. Leslie Beckett, what's this about your ex wanting to get back together? When did this happen?"

I forgot I didn't tell her about Glenn. I was hoping I could call him, realize once and for all I never want to get back with him, and nobody but Aunt Star ever needed to know. So much for that plan.

"Wendy, please don't get mad at me for not telling you. I can't handle it."

"Okay, I won't. Tell me what's going on and we'll see if I can help."

"Nobody can help. I've gotten myself into a huge mess, and I don't need to drag anyone else into it."

"Honey, I'm your friend. This is what friends do—help each other figure out how to get out of the messes they create for themselves. Without judgment, I might add."

Tears fill my eyes. "Thank you." Then I tell her about Glenn's message and what happened with Ash at the game.

"Okay," she says when I'm finished. "First off," she holds up one finger, "you and I are going out tonight and having some fun. Second," she holds up another finger, "I don't think talking *about* Glenn is going to help. You need to talk *to* him. Do you want to call him before or after we go have some fun?"

"Before. Definitely before. I need to get it over with."

"Good." Another finger goes up. "And third, if Ash says he doesn't want to date that woman, he doesn't want to date her. Forget about her. Got it?"

I nod.

She extends one more finger. "Fourth, and most pressing, you need to get some work done. Spend ninety minutes doing whatever you need to do for Diego. Then go home, call Glenn, cry, call me so I can come over and you can tell me all about it while you get dolled up, and then we'll go out, even if it's midnight by then. I'd ask if that's okay, but I'm not taking no for an answer. That's the plan for the rest of the day ... and likely half the night."

"Okay." I'm thankful she provided a plan, because my brain is in no shape to formulate one on its own.

Wendy hops off my desk and leaves before I can change my mind.

An hour later I've made several calls and typed up a few press releases. I'm chewing the end of my pen when someone knocks on my door.

I look up and smile at the man standing in the open doorway. "Come on in."

George Carter enters my office. He leaves the door open but takes a seat—not in the purple chair.

"How's everything going with Diego Sanchez?" he asks.

"Great!" I tell him about yesterday's meeting, today's game, and what I've accomplished since I returned.

"Excellent. Normally I wouldn't give a client of this level to a new hire, but I knew you had it in you. Sure, you have more time to dedicate to Mr. Sanchez than anyone else, which is needed, but you also have something to prove, which is a good thing. It means you'll do everything you can to get him the good press he needs. But you're new in town, so if you need anything—any doors opened or access granted—let me know. I'll take care of it for you."

"Thank you, sir. I appreciate it. And I won't let you down."

He stands. "I know you won't." As he exits my office he says, "Don't work all evening. Take some time for yourself, or you won't be able to give our clients your best."

"Got it. Thanks again."

He raises a hand as he disappears.

I spend another forty-five minutes finishing up my work. Then I fax the press releases to local media outlets and head out.

As I make my way toward my apartment building from the bus stop, I don't pay any attention to my surroundings.

As I reach for the door handle of my building, a voice says, "Don't I get a kiss hello?"

I freeze with my hand two inches from the door. I slowly turn my head and lock eyes with my former boyfriend, who's leaning against the wall a few feet away. My heart races.

"Glenn, what are you doing here?"

"I had to see you, baby," he says earnestly as he pushes off the wall. "I've missed you so much. When you didn't call me back, I decided I'd drive up and see you, in case your phone wasn't working."

"You know my phone is working." I still haven't moved. "You left a message."

He steps up to me and places his hands on my hips. "What if there was a power outage and you didn't know I left the message?"

I take a step backward, out of his grasp. "You could've called again. You didn't need to drive up here."

Lines form on his forehead. "Do you not want me here?"

Why he's acting like he doesn't know the reason I wouldn't want him to be here, I don't know. It's like he's forgotten what he did—what he said.

I avoid answering his question. "I was planning to call you as soon as I got home from work."

Glenn looks at his watch. "Why are you not getting home from work until seven o'clock on a Friday night? I've been waiting here forever."

There's no way I'm telling him about Diego Sanchez. He'll try to get me to introduce him, which is not happening.

When I don't respond, he says, "Are we going to keep standing out here? Come on, baby. Let's go inside where we can talk and ... you know, see where things go." He wiggles his eyebrows.

"Things" are going nowhere in the vicinity of where he's hoping. I can't invite him into my apartment. I'm not worried he'll force himself on me, but I won't put myself into a situation where I might need to fend off his advances, either. This conversation requires a public location.

I step away from the door. "Follow me." Then I head back down the sidewalk.

"Where are you going?"

"To a diner down the street. We can talk there."

He jogs to catch up with me. "Why can't we go to your apartment? It'll be more private there."

Exactly. "I'm hungry, and there's nothing to eat at my place." That's not entirely true, but I have nothing he'd want to eat. And I'm famished since I didn't feel like eating much at the game.

Glenn follows me into the diner next to the restaurant where I met Ash last night. How was that only twenty-four hours ago?

A waitress seats us and takes our drink order. I open my mouth to ask Glenn to explain himself, but he holds up a hand to stop me.

"Before you say anything, I have something to ask you." His hand slips into his jacket pocket and pulls something out before moving it onto the table in front of me. "This isn't how I wanted to do this, but you left me no choice." In the blink of an eye, a diamond ring glitters up at me from a plush jeweler's box.

thirty

After getting back from the game, I haven't been in my office two minutes when my brother walks in and installs himself in his chair. Something seems off about him, but I'm too distracted to give it much thought.

"What are you doing tonight?" he asks.

"Going home, eating dinner, hanging out with the girls, going to bed. You?"

"Our sisters won't be home. It's Friday. They're teenagers. They'll be out. And you, my friend, are twenty-five and single. You should also be out tonight. In fact, you will be."

"I will not." I don't have the energy to have this conversation, much less go out with him and Colleen.

"You will. As my self-proclaimed best friend, you're taking me out and staying typically sober while I get sloppy drunk and almost certainly cry on your shoulder. Then you'll carry me home, tuck me into bed, leave a glass of water and some aspirin on my bedside table, and sleep on my couch because you're worried about me."

I feel my eyebrows inching farther and farther up my forehead as he outlines his plan for our evening. "Randy, what's going on?"

He slouches down in the chair. "Colleen dumped me."

"What? When?"

"Right after you left for the game. I called to confirm our plans for tonight, and she cancelled on me again. I demanded to know why, and she admitted she's seeing someone else. She'd rather be with him."

While I can't deny I'm thrilled Colleen is out of his life, my brother is obviously hurting, and I need to support him. "I'm sorry, man. You don't deserve this."

"Thanks for saying that, but you never liked her."

I sigh. "It's not so much that I didn't like her. It's that you never seemed truly happy with her." And rightly so. She mostly treated him like garbage. I never figured out why he stayed with her for so long. "You should be with someone who lights you up, not someone who brings you down. I want you to be happy."

Tears glisten in his eyes. "That's exactly what a best friend would say."

"Definitely deserving of a trophy, or at least a medal." I smile to lighten the mood. I don't need him crying in my office. There'll be plenty of time for tears later tonight when he can blame it on the alcohol.

He laughs. "Especially since you've never said anything remotely like that before in your life."

My smile fades. "I'm sorry I didn't." I've lost track of the amount of apologies I've given or received in the past three days.

"You're going to make me cry." He gives me a puppy dog face.

"No, I'm not. If you cry, it's all on Colleen."

"So are you in?"

"I'm in." I can't let him go out and get drunk on his own, although I wonder where his other friends are.

"Come straight to my place after work. Oh, wait. You can't wear a suit or shiny shoes to the places we're going."

He doesn't need to add that his clothes won't come anywhere close to fitting me. He's not a small man, but I've got three inches and two shoe sizes on him.

"I've got some jeans, a clean shirt, and loafers in the car."

"You do?"

"Yep. I like to be prepared."

"Shocking," he deadpans.

"Isn't it, though? Hold up. Where are we going that I can't wear a suit or shiny shoes?"

"That's for me to know and you to find out."

"Fine. Now get out of here. I have a few calls to make before I can head out."

"Yes, Mr. Hamilton, sir."

"Shut up and get out."

"There's the Grouchy Smurf we all know and love so well." He pushes up from the chair and heads out the door, leaving it standing open as usual.

"And close the door!" I call after him.

Shockingly, he returns, but he flips me the bird before he swings the door shut. I roll my eyes as I pick up the phone.

"Aren't you glad you're not wearing a suit?" Randall asks.

We've miraculously snagged an empty booth at the Irish pub around the corner from his apartment.

"I guess." I honestly don't care what I'm wearing, compared to anyone else. I rarely do. And I spot more than a few men—and women—in suits among the crowd at McConnell's.

"Well, I'm glad you're not."

I didn't get to Randall's until after six o'clock, and he drank a beer or two while he waited for me, so he's already on his way to inebriation.

"What are your other friends up to tonight?" I ask him.

He spins a cardboard beer coaster around in his hand and avoids my eyes. "I don't know."

"You didn't invite anyone other than your non-fun little brother?"

He tosses the coaster down. "I don't want to talk to any of them, because *she's* now with one of them."

I feel sick. "What? Colleen cheated on you with one of your friends? And now she's dating him?"

He nods. "And everyone else knew, and they didn't tell me."

I want to punch every last one of those guys. No wonder he's on a mission to get drunk. "I think you need some new friends."

Before he can respond, a waitress appears at our table. Her name tag identifies her as Tammy. She's wearing a denim miniskirt and a white button-up shirt that's missing a few buttons in a crucial area. I force my eyes up to her face as I order my usual Coke.

"No whiskey in that, hon?" she asks.

"No thanks." I give her my typical excuse. "I'm driving."

"That's handy." She licks her lips as she inspects me from head to toe. "I might need a ride home after my shift."

I try not to cringe when she captures her bottom lip between her teeth.

"You won't get anywhere with that one." My brother nods his head toward me as he fails to keep his eyes above Tammy's neck. "He only has eyes for one woman. I, on the other hand—"

I kick him under the table.

His gaze shoots to me and then finally up to Tammy's face. "I'll take a Guinness." He gives her a sultry look. "Please and thank you."

"Anything to eat?" She taps her pen on her order pad, unmoved by his attention, though he doesn't seem to notice.

"No," Randall says.

"We'll take some fries," I say. He can't keep drinking on an empty stomach. I know my brother well enough to be certain he didn't eat lunch after his call with Colleen. He doesn't eat when he's upset.

"I'm not going to eat any," he declares as the waitress walks away. He watches her instead of looking at me.

"Eyes over here, buddy," I say.

"I'm appreciating what God gave her," he protests.

"You're thinking you want to be the one to take her home, which is a terrible idea."

"Nope. Quick way to get Colleen out of my system."

"Nope. Quick way to get yourself into trouble in more ways than one."

"Why did I invite you, again?"

"You tell me, but I'm not leaving you to get drunk alone and take random women home."

"She's not random. I know her name and where she works."

"Whatever. Also, you're going to eat those fries if I have to force them down your throat."

thirty-one

. . .

"Leslie Anne Beckett, would you do me the great honor of becoming my wife?"

I'm speechless. What on God's green earth would make Glenn think I have any desire to marry him after what he did?

"Should I take your silence to mean you're so overcome with joy you can't speak?" he asks hopefully.

"No!" I push his hands and the box away. "Put that away. I don't want to marry you." I've never been more certain of anything in my life.

"But I thought you wanted to be with me. You were so upset when we broke up."

The waitress appears with our drinks. When she spies the diamond ring, her eyes widen.

"Oh! Sorry to interrupt this big moment." She glances back and forth between the two of us with a smile, clocks my not-so-happy demeanor, sets the drinks down, and scurries off.

I reach over and snap the jewelry box shut. "Why would you think I want to marry you after you broke up with me for getting a job in Chicago?"

"Baby, that's not why I broke up with you."

"That's not how I remember it," I retort.

"I broke up with you because I thought if I did, you'd stay."

The man is making zero sense. "What kind of backward logic is that?"

"I thought you would tell me you wouldn't move if it meant we could stay together. And then I thought you were being stubborn when you didn't. I figured by now you would've come to your senses."

I shake my head at the ridiculousness of what he said. "I feel like you don't know me at all. And you definitely don't love me—or respect me—if you thought it was okay to try to manipulate me like that."

"Come on, baby." He's practically whining, which he has never done before. I apparently don't know him as well as I thought I did either.

"Don't do this," he says. "I love you. You love me. We belong together. I'll even think about moving here if that's—"

"No." I stand and grab my briefcase and purse. "I do *not* love you. I do *not* want to marry you. And don't call me 'baby.' In fact, don't call me anything. Don't call me again. Don't show up here again. We're over." I fully intend to storm off, but I have one question before I do. "By the way, how did you know my phone number and address?"

"Your mom. She wants us to get back together."

I set my jaw, give him the coldest look I can muster, and march away from him. "You can pay for my drink," I toss over my shoulder.

As I make the short trek back to my apartment building, I feel like one of those cartoon animals with steam coming out of their ears.

I've barely stepped through my door when the intercom buzzes, but I ignore it, knowing it's Glenn. Instead, I head straight to the phone and dial Wendy's number.

"I need you over here now," I say when she answers. "I'm not answering any questions until you get here. Bring snacks and alcohol."

I hang up and punch in my parents' number. My mom picks up.

"Why did you give Glenn my phone number and address?" I

demand in lieu of greeting her. "You had no right to do that after what he did to me."

"Because you love him, honey. I know you can be stubborn, but I thought for sure you'd give in when you knew how serious he was about you."

"Mom, I don't care how serious he is about me." I flop down on my bed. "He has no respect for me or what I want, and he tried to manipulate me into not moving."

"But he loves you."

The intercom buzzes five times in quick succession. I glare at it.

"He does *not* love me. He loves the idea of a woman who does whatever he wants. And that's most definitely not me."

"Leslie, if you don't marry him, you might have to work forever."

I take a deep breath and remind myself my mother is of a different generation. "Mother, I like working. I love my job. And I'm not going to quit working when—or if—I get married."

"You don't mean that."

"I do."

"You spend too much time talking to Starla."

Mom and her sister-in-law have never been each other's biggest fans.

"Leave Aunt Star out of this. This has nothing to do with her. I'm not going to marry someone I don't love so I won't have to work for the next forty years. I don't want to marry Glenn—not now, not ever. If he calls you again, I want you to tell him so. Don't encourage him."

She sighs. "If that's what you think you really want, honey."

"It's not what I think I want. It's what I know I want—or what I don't want, to be more accurate. I don't want Glenn."

"Fine. Fine. I get it."

I don't think she does. But before I can state my case again, she begins telling me all about her garden, Glenn all but forgotten, which is fine by me.

"That's great," I finally squeeze into a pause after listening to her prattle on for a couple minutes. "Hey, I gotta go. Tell Dad hi."

"I will. I love you, honey. Call again soon."

"Love you, too, Mom."

My intercom buzzes as I hang up the phone. I'm afraid it's Glenn again, because I don't think Wendy could be here yet, but I cross over to the panel by the door and answer in case it's her.

"Buzz me up," my friend orders.

I hit the button to unlock the front door. Then I open the apartment door a crack so she can let herself in, and I head back over to the bed.

Less than a minute later, Wendy enters. She's wearing a skintight electric blue dress with hot pink stilettos. Her hair is teased to within an inch of its life, and there's more makeup on her face than in the Marshall Field's cosmetic department.

"Holy cow," I say. "You look bangin', but I hope you don't expect me to look like that."

She holds up a duffel bag. "Along with snacks and booze, I brought another outfit in case you weren't feeling up to clubbing tonight."

I sigh in relief. "I love you, Wendy O'Halloran."

She's strangely silent as she opens a bottle of wine and pours us each a glass. Then she hands me one, kicks off her shoes, and plops herself onto the bed next to me. "I'm guessing things didn't go so well with Glenn?"

"No. Give me snacks."

Wendy pulls a two-pack of Twinkies out of her duffel bag and tosses it at me.

"Have I told you lately that I love you?" I tear the wrapper open and hope she doesn't want me to share.

"About two minutes ago. Now tell me what happened with Glenn."

I bite off a chunk of Twinkie, moan in appreciation, and mumble around the sugary goodness, "He's here."

Her gaze darts around the apartment, as if Glenn could possibly be somewhere in the minuscule space. I don't even have a couch someone could hide behind.

I swallow. "Not *here* here. But he was waiting outside when I got home from work."

"No."

"Yes. So I took him to the diner down the street." I take another bite. "And then he proposed."

Her eyes bug out. "He what, now?"

"He asked me to marry him. Had a ring and everything."

"Okay, I need all the details. But I also need a Twinkie."

Wendy grabs the second Twinkie before I can move it out of her reach, and she shoves it in her mouth.

After I tell her what Glenn said, she says, "Well, at least now you know you don't want to get back together with him. I guess that's one good thing to come out of that total insanity."

"True. Got any other snacks in your bag?"

She pulls another package out of her duffel, and I gag. "Fig Newtons? Disgusting."

"Glad you think so," she smirks. "Now I get them all to myself."

"You're welcome to them."

Then she presents me with a large bag of Cool Ranch Doritos. I grab them and hug them to my chest. I considered writing a letter of thanks to the Frito-Lay company when they released the new flavor a couple years ago.

"Your breath will stink if you eat those," she says. "I almost didn't bring them for that very reason, but I know you love them."

"I don't care if my breath smells. I'm not planning on kissing anyone tonight." I tear open the bag and pop a chip into my mouth.

"Maybe you should."

"Nope." The next man I kiss will be Ash Hamilton. I'm sure of it now.

"All right, then I guess we don't need to go to the club."

"Your plan was to take me to a club and find me a man to kiss?"

She makes a kissing face. "Among other things. You certain you don't want that?"

"Positive." I look her dead in the eye so she'll know I'm serious.

Wendy holds her hands up in defeat. "Got it. If that's not your thing, we'll do something more low-key."

"Like what?"

"There's an Irish pub several blocks away. We can go there, drink a few beers, eat some greasy food, and then see what we feel like doing."

"You're changing your clothes, right?" I ask.

She stands and strikes a pose. "This doesn't scream 'Irish pub' to you?"

"Since I've never been to an Irish pub, I can't say for sure, but my gut is telling me no."

thirty-two

. . .

After three beers, Randall decides it's time to move on to a different bar. I try to convince him to stay. I don't see the point in traversing all over the city to get him drunk. Why does it matter where he does it?

"I need pasta," he says. "They don't have pasta here."

"They don't have pasta at any bar," I not-so-patiently explain.

"Need. Pasta. Take me somewhere with noodles and alcohol. Don't care if it's a bar."

"Fine." If he's in the mood to eat, I'll give him what he wants.

I catch Tammy's eye and motion for her to bring me the check. When she does, Randall tries to snatch it, but I don't let him.

"It's on me tonight."

"Why?"

I'm not about to tell him it's because I'm celebrating his freedom from Colleen. "Because that's what best friends do when the other person gets dumped."

"Oh. Thanks."

I pay the bill and keep my brother steady as we exit the bar. I turn him in the direction of the nearest Italian place I can think of.

"We're walking there?" he whines.

"I'm not driving three blocks. You'll be fine."

"I won't be fine. I won't be fine ever again."

I sigh. "You will."

"I won't. Who else is gonna love me, huh? Colleen was my chance!"

I stop, face my brother, put my hands on his shoulders, and make him look me in the eye. "Listen to me. She was never your chance. You deserve so much better than Colleen, you hear me? You'll find someone else. You're smart, you have a good job, you're funny, and you're nice to everyone but me."

Randall runs his fingers through his hair. "What about handsome? Am I handsome?"

I wish he was joking, but he's not. He truly wants to know.

"As much as it pains me to say it, I'm going to guess most women think you're handsome." Admittedly, he was kind of goofy looking as a kid, but he grew out of that during prep school.

"Only most?"

"Fine. Probably all women do. But, for the record, I don't. I think you're ugly as sin."

"Glad to hear it. Now take me to the pasta."

"We've talked about my love life all night," Randall says between bites of spaghetti. Thankfully the food seems to be absorbing some of the alcohol in his system. "Now it's time to talk about yours."

I groan. "Nope."

"Yep."

"There's nothing worth telling that you don't already know."

"You positive?"

I eye him warily. "Why?"

"Because you've told me almost nothing, that's why. You've eaten two dinners with Leslie. There's gotta be a heck of a lot more to tell."

"I don't know what you expect me to tell you. I'm not going to ramble on about her. If there's something specific you want to know, ask. I may or may not answer."

"Do you think she actually might want to date you someday, or was she trying to let you down easy?"

That wasn't the question I thought he would ask. "She wasn't messing with me." I have no doubt her interest is real. But I'm also not making any assumptions that anything will happen between us, especially after what she said about Glenn's call and her attitude when she left the game.

"What?" Randall says.

"What, what?"

"What's that look for?" He circles his finger in the air near my face. "You look grouchier than usual."

I smack his hand away, but I answer him. "Her ex wants to get back together."

My brother's eyes open wide. "How do you know that?"

"She was at the game today, too. We rode there together."

"And why didn't you tell me this earlier?"

"Because it's none of your business, that's why."

He slurps up some spaghetti, and sauce droplets land on his shirt. He's oblivious. "If that's true, then you shouldn't have told me. But it's not true. It *is* my business if I'm going to help you through this thing with her." He cocks his head at me. "What is going on with her, again?"

"Beats me."

"You still planning to do the pen pal thing?"

"Yes." I'm not telling him I already sent the first letter.

"But she might get back with her ex?"

"I don't know." I twirl my fork in my fettuccine. Suddenly I'm no longer hungry.

"Let me get this straight. She told you her ex wants to get back with her, but not whether she wants to get back with him."

"Correct."

"That's cold, man."

"She didn't mean to tell me anything about it."

"You gotta find out." He stabs his fork toward me.

"I can't ask her."

"Why not?"

"Because we're not supposed to talk about the ex to each other."

"That's dumb."

"It's what we agreed on."

"And she already broke that agreement."

He's right. It's not fair that she got to tell me about Glenn, but I can't find out what she wants to do about it.

"I'll ask Glinda," he says.

"You'll do what?"

"I'll ask Glinda what Leslie's doing about the ex. She'll know."

"You're not asking Wendy."

"Why?"

"We're not in junior high. And stop calling her Glinda. One of these days you're going to end up saying it to her face."

"Whatever. She won't care. It's a compliment. Speaking of junior high, are you prepared for tomorrow night?" he asks.

"About that …" I grin at him.

He sits up straight. "You told Mom you're not going?"

"I value my life. I'm going."

"Then what?"

"I saw Melissa today."

"Ash, I swear you are the most frustrating person on the planet."

I raise my eyebrows at him.

"If you were a normal person," he explains, "you would've told me about both Leslie and Melissa hours ago. But no, you gotta keep it all to yourself."

"Sorry."

"You'll get better with practice," he says, "like right now. Tell me how in the world you managed to see Melissa Teague today."

I consider how much to tell him. Does my brother really need to know all the details about Leslie's reaction to Melissa?

"You're already censoring the story in your head. Stop it. Tell me every single thing."

I decide to try telling all the details for once. If I'm lucky he won't remember half of it.

"Leslie is jealous," he announces when I finish. "No doubt about it."

"But I told her I don't want to date Melissa."

"You idiot, that was before Melissa apologized and you

decided she's an okay person and then thought it was a good idea to call her pretty in Leslie's presence. You screwed that one up big time."

I throw my head back in frustration. "I know. I realized it as soon as I said it. But I couldn't take it back."

"Her jealousy is a good sign for you, though. If she didn't have feelings for you, she wouldn't care if you might be interested in another woman."

"Maybe."

"Definitely."

It's time to change the subject. "You should come to dinner tomorrow night."

"No way."

"Come on. It'll be fun. You can help Melissa and me pull one over on our moms, which will also keep your mind off Colleen. Then you can stay the night in your old room, and we'll play tennis Sunday morning."

"You two are really going to pretend you want to date each other?"

"Probably. It'll help if you're there," I wheedle.

"All right. Count me in, and prepare to get your tail handed to you on the tennis court."

thirty-three

. . .

McConnell's Pub isn't as crowded as I'd expect for a Friday night, but what do I know about Chicago nightlife? I've only been here three weeks.

After the waitress takes our order, Wendy asks, "Did you want to button up her shirt as badly as I did? I don't need to see that."

I shrug. "Probably gets her some great tips. You gotta do what you gotta do. Plus, if we'd gone to a club, you would've seen a lot more than that."

"True. Now, are you planning to tell Ash what happened with Glenn?"

"I don't know. We're not supposed to talk to each other about him."

"But you told him about Glenn calling."

"And I shouldn't have."

"You can't leave him hanging, though. He's probably sitting at home alone crying into his beer and wondering if he's lost you to Glenn forever."

"First, he doesn't drink. I can't believe you didn't know that. Second ... do you really think so, other than the drinking part?"

She shrugs. "It's possible."

"So do I call him up and say, 'My ex proposed and I said no. Looking forward to reading your letter. Bye!'?"

"Hmm. That seems awkward. Maybe I'll tell Randall, and he can break the good news."

"You're not telling Randall."

"Why not?"

"Because we're not twelve."

"I'm telling him. Problem solved."

I sleep like the dead and wake up to a sunshiny May Saturday. There's nothing on my calendar for the day, so I decide I'll spend it exploring my new neighborhood and reading LaVyrle Spencer's latest book, *Vows*, that I picked up at Waldenbooks last weekend.

I sit straight up in bed when I remember Ash mailed his letter yesterday. I'm not sure if it'll arrive today, and I don't know what time the mail typically arrives, but I throw some clothes on and rush downstairs to the mailboxes. My hand shakes as I spin the combination lock on my box. I spot at least one envelope through the tiny window, and it takes me four tries get the combination right. By the time the box swings open, my heart is pounding. I pull out three envelopes.

The top one is from my bank. The second is from the utility company. The third has a Chicago P.O. box as a return address and is addressed in what I imagine the grown-up version of Ash's handwriting would look like.

I press the envelope to my chest and race back upstairs. I throw the other two pieces of mail on the tiny kitchen counter and carry Ash's letter over to my bed. I sit and look at it for a few seconds before carefully opening it and pulling out the folded piece of notebook paper. He has covered every square inch of both sides. I smooth out the creases and begin to read.

Dear Leslie,

I can't believe I'm writing to you again after all this time—and you're a girl. Or, to be more accurate, a woman. I want to say more, but that's against the rules, so I'll answer your question.

My dad has always known I want to practice law so I can help people. It's not about the money or prestige for me. It's about the power—the influence lawyers hold that can change people's lives. I want to use that power to make people's lives better, to bring justice for the wronged, to help powerless people fight the systems and leaders that oppress them.

When I came back after law school, I thought Dad would put me on pro bono cases or assign me to a few nonprofits we provide counsel for. But no, he had other plans for me—plans to break me and mold me into the cutthroat, high-visibility, high-earning attorney he wants me to be.

He had to know I would hate being assigned to Carter-Jenkins, and he wasn't mistaken at first. Don't get me wrong, I like the people there. George is stern and demanding but fair. Wendy understands how people tick better than anyone I've ever known. There's nobody I don't like there. But the work feels pointless in so many ways. Creating NDAs and standard PR contracts and negotiating settlements for frivolous lawsuits is not what I ever thought I'd end up doing.

However, I appreciate the unwritten philosophy behind what Carter-Jenkins does. You likely know this, but one thing George pushes on his clients is charity work. His personal motive isn't for them to get positive publicity—though they do, and that's sadly often why the clients agree to it—but because he wants people with money and influence to use those privileges to do good in the world.

Dad said I had to work with Carter-Jenkins for three years, and then he'd consider letting me do something else I'd rather do. I'm honestly not sure he will, but I'm trying to be positive. I've got a year left, and I used to think I'd simply slog through it, but lately I've been thinking I'd love to use this last year to prove my father wrong by working to make something happen that helps people in a big way. Diego Sanchez's arrival may give me that opportunity. You and I need to sit down and talk about how we might help direct him to put his vast amounts of money and influence to good use.

I've filled up all my space, and I didn't get to cover another topic, but I have enough room left to ask you a question.

Why did you choose Chicago instead of another big city?

Yours,

Ash

Yours. *Yours.*

Mine.

Is he mine?

I feel nauseous, but in a good way, if that's a thing. This letter has filled me with so many emotions, my body doesn't know what to do with them. What I do know is I want to find Ash and wrap my arms around him and do all number of other things to and with him. Which is why we have the rules.

What's interesting is I don't want to tell anyone else about Ash's letter—not Aunt Star, not Wendy, not anybody. I want to keep it all to myself, so I'll know things about grown-up Ash that nobody else knows.

I want to sit right down and write my letter back to him, but I also want to take some time to think about it before I do. While there are limits to how long the letters can be and how long we can spend writing them, there was no mention of how much time we can spend thinking about them. Not that I'd have any control over that, anyway. I have a feeling I won't have many thoughts over the coming days and weeks that aren't related to Ash Hamilton.

thirty-four

. . .

"Melissa, it's so great to see you again after all this time." I smile at her and stick my hand out. I'm tempted to put on a big show and open my arms for a hug, but since hugging isn't my thing, Mom will know something's up if I do.

Melissa places her hand in mine as she stifles a giggle. "You have certainly grown up," she says, comically craning her neck, "and up."

Mom looks back and forth between the two of us and then focuses in on our hands, which are still connected. I detect a gleam in her eye as I squeeze Melissa's hand and then slowly let go of it. I focus on the top of Melissa's head, because I'm afraid I'll laugh if I look her in the face.

"Welcome, Melissa. Come on in," my mother says, ushering her from the foyer toward the sitting room. "Your parents are already here."

I trail behind them, feeling thankful I ran into Melissa yesterday. This situation would be unbearable if I hadn't. Instead, I think I'm going to enjoy it immensely.

While Dad greets Melissa, Mom mutters to me, "Where is that brother of yours? Of course he couldn't be on time to greet our guests as they arrived."

I haven't spoken to Randall since I left his apartment this

morning. I hope he's still coming. If he doesn't show up, Mom will take it out on me, though it won't be my fault.

Mom ensures I sit next to Melissa, and we make small talk for several minutes before my brother makes an appearance. He gives me a sharp look and says hello to Melissa and her parents. Then he sidles up to me and says in a low voice, "I need to tell you something. Figure out a way to get us alone."

Why I'm in charge of figuring that out, I don't know, but I simply say to the group, "Excuse my brother and me for a minute. We'll be right back."

Mom shoots us a "you're being rude" look, but I ignore it and lead Randall out of the room and down the hall into Dad's office.

He closes the door behind us. "Real subtle there, Ash."

"You were perfectly capable of coming up with an excuse. What do you need to tell me?"

"Glinda called me."

My eyebrows shoot up. "And?"

"The ex proposed to Leslie last night."

My heart seems to have completely vanished from my body. It must have gone to the same place as my vocal cords, because they're also nowhere to be found.

"She said no," he finally adds.

I clench my jaw and close my eyes, and my vocal cords come back to life, though my heart is slow to catch up. "Why did you not lead with that part?"

"Sorry."

I open my eyes as my pulse tries to return to normal. "You just took five years off my life."

He huffs. "I said I'm sorry."

"Fine. Anything else?"

"It was a definitive no. She's done with him. Forever."

I almost collapse in relief, which is a new experience.

"Whoa, there." My brother clasps my arms. "Steady on."

"I'm fine." I shake his hands off.

He laughs. "You're not fine. You are so gone on this woman. I've never seen you like this before."

I've never felt like this before—not even close. I didn't know it was possible to feel this strongly about another person.

"Let's get back before Mom comes searching for us," I say, although I'm still a little wobbly.

Randall puts a hand on the doorknob, but instead of opening it, he says, "You undersold Melissa with the 'pretty' comment. Wow."

Now he's the one with a gleam in his eye.

"Stay away from her," I warn. "She recently got out of a relationship, and so did you."

"Look at you being all protective of your fake girlfriend."

"She's not my fake girlfriend. Don't say that again. Plus, I'm being protective of you, too."

"Not sure if I should thank you or not."

I shove his hand off the doorknob and open the door. "Let's go."

Throughout dinner, conversation flows naturally. My sisters have joined us, and they're both eyeing Melissa and me speculatively. I don't know if they're aware of Mom's plan or not, but they seem to have the same idea, because they freely tell Melissa flattering stories about me.

Mom, of course, seated me next to Melissa. I smile at her at regular intervals. A few times she places a hand on my arm as she laughs at something I say. I usually instinctively pull away from casual touches from anyone I'm not close to, but I don't have to remind myself to act as if I like her touching me. I don't feel a romantic attraction to her, but I'm comfortable with her already. I'm thinking more and more that she and I might become friends. I smile at the thought and catch Mom giving me a knowing look.

The deception is working, and I'm not fully sure how I feel about that. While this was the plan, I can't help but consider how upset I was when I discovered Leslie's deception. Am I not doing something similar—and to my mother as well as my sisters? But admitting to it now will also throw Melissa to the wolves, and I don't want to do that to her.

As we eat dessert, I wonder if Leslie got my letter today. Then I wonder how she'll answer my question. I smile again when I remember Randall's news. God bless Wendy for not being afraid to spread the word like she's at a sixth-grade slumber party.

After we're finished eating, my brother surprises me by saying, "Melissa, why don't you, me, and Ash head to his place to do some more catching up?"

I add, "And by 'my place,' he means the pool house." I let out a self-deprecating laugh.

"Yes," Mom says, "we love having Ashley so close, as do his sisters. He adores spending time with them. He's so good with children."

Randall coughs loudly and I hold back a snort. My sisters protest that they're not children, but at a sharp look from Mom, they both parrot that I'm good with kids. Melissa smiles at my mother and pokes my leg under the table.

"That's nice to hear," she says.

I detect a hint of laughter in her voice and hope Mom doesn't catch it. A quick glance at her informs me she doesn't. She's quite satisfied with herself.

"And I accept the invitation, Randall. Thank you," Melissa says.

Tonya asks, "Can we come?"

"No," our brother retorts, "children are not included in this invitation. Don't you have anything better to do on a Saturday night than hang out with a bunch of old fogies, anyway?"

The girls both grumble but confess they have other plans.

Melissa starts to stand, and I scramble to my feet to pull her chair out. My mom appears ready to burst from excitement.

Randall and I say our goodbyes to Mr. and Mrs. Teague and show Melissa out of the room. We stay silent until we exit the house, when we all howl with laughter.

"Ash, is your place presentable?" Randall asks when he catches his breath. "We can go somewhere else if not."

"It's fine." I keep the pool house in order all the time. I'm always a little afraid Mom will come in while I'm gone and judge me—and potentially later yell at me—if it's a mess.

I lead the way around the pool and into my home.

Melissa is visibly impressed. It's fairly plush as far as pool houses go, with a full kitchen and separate bedroom. It even has two bathrooms—one full bath attached to the bedroom and another locker-room style bathroom with three shower stalls that opens to the pool deck.

"This is perfect, Ash," she gushes. "If I had an option like this, I'd take it, too. I can't believe what I'm paying in rent."

"Where are you living?" I ask her as we settle onto the couch.

"I'm near Wrigley," she says. "Makes life easy because I don't have a commute, but like I said, it's not cheap."

"So how is this thing going to work with you two?" Randall points his bottle back and forth between Melissa and me. "You going to keep up this charade?" He focuses on me. "You know Mom's going to want details on how things are going."

Melissa and I look at each other.

"Same with my mom," she says. "Want to go on a fake date next week? Randall, why don't you come too? On the off chance we'd run into Leslie, we can pretend the two of us are together and Ash is playing third wheel. I don't want to make that situation any more complicated than it already is."

I don't miss the glimmer of excitement in my brother's eyes at the thought of spending an evening with Melissa, but I don't un-invite him, because I wouldn't feel right going out with only her. It's not as if I'd be cheating on Leslie, but I would no doubt feel like I was. And Randall does need some new friends. As do I, now that I think about it.

"Works for me," my brother says.

"Me, too," I say. "Where do we want to go?"

thirty-five

* * *

"How's life in Chicago?" Shannon asks. "Anything exciting happen since I helped you move in?"

"Well …" I didn't intend to tell my brother about Ash yet, but I can't lie to him anymore.

"Well, what? What happened?"

I twirl the phone cord around my finger. "Remember my pen pal when we were kids?"

"Ashley? How could I forget?"

"We reconnected."

"No way! Did you track her down through her old address?"

"No, I didn't." I unwind the cord.

"Why does your voice sound weird?" Shannon demands. "What's going on?"

"There's something I need to tell you."

"That sounds ominous."

"Ash isn't a girl."

The line is silent for a few seconds. "Did he pretend to be a girl all that time?" He's angry. Of course he doesn't think I'm the one in the wrong. And of course he'd be mad if someone did to me what I did to Ash.

"No."

He's quiet again before asking, "What are you saying, Les?"

I close my eyes. "I pretended to be a boy."

"For *four years?*"

I explain what happened.

"So let me get this straight," Shannon says. "You lied to him, *and* you lied to all of us?"

"Yes," I say in a small voice, although I never technically lied. He won't see the distinction. "I'm sorry."

"Did you not think you could trust me with the truth? Me— your twin who loves you more than anyone else in the world?"

Tears well up at the knowledge that I hurt him.

"It's not that. I thought you'd make fun of me for writing to a boy. And if Mom and Dad found out, they would've made me stop writing to him, but I didn't want to. Can you forgive me?"

"You know I will. But I'll be mad about it for a good fifteen minutes."

"I'm sorry." I swipe a few tears from my cheeks.

"What I most want to know, though, is what Ash did when he found out. And how did you run into him?"

"It's going to take a while to tell the whole story," I say. "Do you have time?"

"I always have time for you. Tell me all of it."

I make myself comfortable on my bed and tell him most of what's happened over the past few days.

When I'm finished, he says, "I'm coming up there to meet this guy. I'm not sure I believe he not only forgave you but now wants to date you."

I'm so not ready for my brother to meet Ash, but I want him to visit—for my sake and so he can meet Wendy. I don't know if I want the two of them to hit it off or not, but if I ever want Wendy to shut up about him, I need to get them in the same room.

"I'd love to see you," I say. "But Ash and I agreed not to see each other outside of work for now."

"I don't care. Your rules are not my rules. I cannot approve of what you're doing until I check Ash out for myself. If you say no, I'll come anyway. I now know where he works, and I don't need your consent."

While I want to say I'm a modern woman and don't need my

brother's approval of my potential boyfriends, I do care whether the two most important men in my life like each other.

"Fine." I sigh. "When can you come?"

"I'll start driving as soon as I get off the phone."

"Ha. Seriously, when?"

"Next weekend I have Danny's wedding, so it'll have to be the following weekend."

"Oh, yeah. Tell Danny I say congrats." Danny Taylor has been my brother's best friend since he moved to our hometown in sixth grade.

"Will do. And I'll let you know my flight information once I know it."

"Good. But I probably won't be able to meet you at the airport."

"I think I can figure out how to get to your place on my own. And I'm staying with you, so dust off the sleeping bag I stuffed into the top of your Munchkin-sized closet expressly for that purpose. Before I go, though, where are you with the Glenn thing? You still mad at him?"

I tell him about last night.

"What an idiot," he says. "Forget about him, Les. You deserve much better."

"Thanks, Shan. Love you."

"You, too. See you in a couple weeks."

On Sunday morning, I walk to a church several blocks away. I haven't been to church in too long, and when I'm sitting in the back pew singing the familiar hymns and listening to the preacher speak, I feel calmer than I have since I moved here.

The church isn't too far from the lake, so I pick up a sandwich and Coke at a deli nearby and take my lunch to the beach to eat it. I watch a family playing frisbee and daydream about doing the same with my husband and kids someday. Unsurprisingly, my future husband looks a lot like Ash.

As I sit and stare at the waves gently lapping at the shore with my chin propped on my knees, I think about what Ash said in his letter. I want him to use his power to do good in the world, too. My heart races at the thought of possibly doing that with him, starting with Diego Sanchez. I wonder what Ash is thinking on that front. From what I know about Diego, I think he might be open to using his money to help others. While I head back home, I think about all the possibilities.

When I arrive back at my apartment, I jot down my thoughts and stick the notes in my briefcase. Then I settle in to write my letter to Ash. I already know I'll be spending more than a half hour on it, but what Ash doesn't know won't hurt him.

thirty-six

I know it's pointless to stop and check my post office box Monday morning on my way to work, because there's no way I already have a response from Leslie, especially after the way we left things on Friday. Still, I'm disappointed when the box is empty.

Thankfully I have a busy morning, so I don't have much time to brood about Leslie. But when I finally have a short break at noon, I drive back to the post office because I simply can't help myself.

When I discover an envelope inside my box, I freeze. My hand shakes when I reach in and pull it out. Like the lovesick fool I am, I lift it to my nose to see if it smells like her perfume.

It does.

I stick the letter into the inside pocket of my suit coat and walk back to my car as casually as possible. When I slip into the driver's seat, I pull the envelope back out and stare at it. Then I carefully open it and slide out a light-purple sheet of lined stationery. Leslie's handwriting looks different than I remember, and I wonder if she made her writing look more masculine when we were kids.

Then I begin to read.

Dear Ash,

I'm sorry for the way I treated you when we left the game on Friday. I know we're not supposed to talk about our feelings in these letters, but I'm going to break that rule here. I'll tell you why I acted like an idiot— because I was jealous of Melissa. She got to sit by you and talk to you and laugh with you, and the two of you somehow became friends right there before my very eyes. I wanted to be the one you were doing those things with.

I close my eyes. My chest hurts. I wanted her to be the one there with me, too. And I'm not sure if I can do this thing with Melissa now. Not if it might cause undue anxiety for Leslie. I take a deep breath and keep reading.

Thanks for your honesty about your job. I'm sorry your dad did that to you, but I'm not sorry you're working with Carter–Jenkins. If you weren't, we might not have reconnected, and we wouldn't be able to work together to help Diego Sanchez spend his millions. I have some ideas about that, which you may hear about before you get this letter.

To answer your question, I moved to Chicago for several reasons. First, and most practically, it was the closest big city.

Second, I came to Chicago a few times during college on weekend trips with friends, and I adored it. I loved how it was a giant city but also still had a Midwestern feel. My family went to New York City to celebrate Shannon's and my high school graduation, and while it was exciting, it didn't quite feel like a place I could call home.

Third, I've felt a connection to this city most of my life because of you. I didn't think I'd ever run into you here, and I had no plans to look you up, for obvious reasons. But even in the days after I moved here before I ran into you, I thought about you a time or three. It felt like home because it was your home, even if I never saw you.

If someone knocked on my car window and demand I speak to them, I wouldn't be able to. Why? Because I can't breathe.

I know this is against the rules, too, but I can't help it. Shannon is coming to town the weekend after next, and he's demanding to meet you. So we need to figure out how to make that happen. Maybe we can all go out to dinner with Wendy on Saturday night. I want to make it as casual as possible.

I'm out of room, so here's my next question for you. Have you ever considered not working for your family's firm? I expect your answer to encompass all my potential follow-up questions, too. Don't give me a yes-or-no answer!

Yours,

Leslie

After reading the letter again, I carefully replace it in the envelope and put it back into my coat pocket, right over my heart. I feel like I'm living in one of the silly romance movies my sisters force me to watch with them, and I don't know how it happened. But I'm thankful it did.

While I'm driving back to the office, it hits me that Leslie told Shannon the truth about me. And it sounds like he took the news well, if he wants to meet me. Unless his plan is to kill me, though I don't know why he would, since I wasn't the one who pulled off the childhood deception of the century.

I feel giddy—giddy, as if that's a thing I've ever felt—at the thought of spending non-work-related time with Leslie again.

I'm reading Leslie's letter a fourth time when Randall invades my office soon after I return. I slide it off the desk onto my lap, but I'm not fast enough.

My brother grins at me from his chair. "I'm guessing that's not from a client?"

"It's from someone at Carter-Jenkins," I say defensively.

"Oh, they've started using purple stationery over there?"

"It's a new policy. George recently invested in a purple paper company."

"I love it when you're funny. You should try it more often."

I ignore his comment. "What do you want?"

"So about Melissa …"

He talked about her nonstop yesterday morning before, during, and after tennis. I got tired of hearing her name.

"Yes?" I refrain from rolling my eyes.

"You don't want to date her for real, right?"

"Absolutely not." I cock my head at him. "Where are you going with this?"

"What if I take her out this weekend, but we tell our parents she's with you?"

"What if you take her out, but we tell our parents she's with *you?*" That would solve my problem of not wanting to potentially hurt Leslie with this game we're playing.

Randall shakes his head. "That won't work."

"Why?"

"Because I told Mom you have a date with her."

I groan. "Why would you do that?"

"Mom asked me how everything went after we left dinner. What was I supposed to say? I thought you wanted her to think you and Melissa are dating."

I've already gotten myself in over my head on this thing and am deeply regretting it, but I guess it won't hurt to let it keep going for a few weeks while Leslie gets things figured out.

"Sorry," I say. "You're right. But I've changed my mind. You can't go out with Melissa alone."

"I don't think you get to tell me what to do."

"I do when it comes to this. It's been three days since Colleen dumped you. Don't be rebounding on Melissa. I like her, even if I'm already tired of hearing you talk about her."

"Who died and made you the dating expert? Because this can only be inherited from a stranger. You didn't earn the position from experience."

I bristle at his words, but he's not wrong. I've dated exactly one person in my twenty-five years, and the relationship only lasted a couple months.

"Sorry," my brother says. "I shouldn't have said that."

"No, you shouldn't have." I add begrudgingly, "But it's true."

"But I still get to come on the fake date?"

"Definitely." Melissa was right. If Leslie were to see us, I don't want her to get the wrong idea.

"Do I get to read the purple letter?"

"Definitely not."

thirty-seven

. . .

Lunch has come and gone before I have time to call Ash to see when we can meet to talk about Diego. While I wait to be connected to his line, I pick up the family photo on my desk. I'm glad Shannon is coming to visit, but I'm also feeling guilty about not telling my parents the truth about Ash.

"Hey," Ash says when the call connects.

How can that one syllable make my heart thump?

"Hey," I reply, smiling like a goofball.

"Are you calling about Sanchez?" he asks after a few silent seconds.

"Oh, yes." I clear my throat and sit up straight, trying to be professional, since this is a work call. "Do you have time to meet with me this afternoon about that?"

"I have nothing on my schedule after three o'clock," he says.

"You want me to come over there at three then?"

"I'll come to you. We might need to loop George in on what we're thinking."

"Sounds good. I'll see you then."

"Also ..."

"Yes?"

"I got your letter."

My eyes widen. "Already?"

"Indeed. And I'm looking forward to meeting Shannon."

My smile grows bigger. "I'm glad."

"I've blocked next Saturday evening off on my calendar."

Heat fills my chest at his proclamation. "Is it okay if I invite Wendy? I think she'll provide a good distraction in case things get tense with my brother."

"You're not afraid she'll try to jump him right there in the restaurant?" he teases.

I chuckle. "Maybe. But he can handle her. So you're fine with it?"

"Of course. And one more thing." He's silent for a moment. "Do you know Wendy called and told Randall about Glenn?"

"Yes." But I didn't know if Randall told Ash.

"I know we're not supposed to talk about him, but I wanted to let you know that I know. And I didn't think Wendy would tell my brother without your permission, but I thought you should be aware on the off chance that's not the case."

"I knew she was planning on it. I felt a little juvenile letting my friend share the news, but I didn't know how to go about telling you myself."

"Randall was prepared to ask her about it if she hadn't made the first move, so you're not the only juvenile here."

I smile. "Good to know."

Of course I can't focus for the next two hours, knowing I'm about to see Ash in person. I pull my notes out of my briefcase and add a few details, but mostly my thoughts stray to Ash. I wonder how much longer we should wait. I know with full certainty I don't want to be with Glenn anymore. But how soon is too soon?

Finally, my clock reads three o'clock, and right on cue, a knock sounds on my door. I should get up and open it, but my legs have decided to stop working.

"Come in," I say in a shaky voice.

The door opens to reveal Ash. He's wearing the navy blue suit again—or at least *a* navy blue suit. He probably has more than one. I want him to have a million.

My body is attempting to melt into my chair. I couldn't move even if the room was on fire … and it feels like it is.

"Hi. Take a seat," I say. I would motion to a chair, but I can't.

He chooses the purple chair, which surprises me, but then I realize it's much larger than the other one. I watch his every movement as he slides the chair right up to my desk, slips his suit coat off, sits, and pulls a notebook and pen out of his briefcase. The scent of cinnamon wafts my way, and my eyes drift shut.

"Ready?" he asks.

My eyes pop open. What am I supposed to be ready for?

"Leslie? You all right?"

I give myself a little shake. "Yes." No. I can't function with him sitting close enough to touch.

Can I touch him?

No.

Yes.

No.

My hand inches toward him but then stops. I stare at it and then look up at him. His expression is unreadable. My gaze focuses on his lips, which are slightly parted. I wonder how soft they are.

"Okay," Ash says as he stands. "Enough is enough."

My eyes widen as he strides to the door, and my heart leaps into my throat when he closes and locks it. Then he rounds my desk, leans down, grasps my waist, and lifts me up out of my chair. My breath grows shallow as I look up at him, and my arms raise to loop around his neck. He's so tall, my fingertips barely reach each other. His hands are still on my waist, and he pulls me flush to him. A ripple of awareness shoots down my body from chest to toe.

"Tell me right now if you don't want this, if it's too soon," he practically growls.

I'm incapable of forming words.

Ash's pupils dilate as his head descends to mine. My eyes close and my knees buckle when our lips finally meet, and his grip tightens. The kiss is tentative at first, each of us testing out the other. When one of his hands moves up and his fingers slide into my hair, cupping the back of my head, we simultaneously surrender and the kiss grows heated, feverish. Ash's other hand travels around to splay across my back, and it feels like he's branding me. Through my haze, I note that not only does he smell like cinnamon, he also tastes like it. I deepen the kiss even more. I can't get enough of him. I'll never get enough of him.

A knock sounds on the door.

We freeze.

The doorknob rattles and my heart lurches into my throat.

I whisper against Ash's mouth, "What do we do?" I'm afraid I'm about to be fired. I don't want to be fired. I can't *afford* to be fired.

He presses one more quick kiss to my lips, sets me back down into my chair, straightens my shirt, and sticks a pen in my hand. Then in a flash, he's at the door and opening it. Somehow, he's composed, while I feel like the entire universe has dropped out from under me.

"Leslie, why—" Wendy cuts off her own question when she realizes Ash is at the door instead of me.

Her gaze shoots to me, and I give her a weak smile. Her eyebrows raise, understanding fills her eyes, and a grin slowly appears on her face. "Ah, I see why. Carry on." She reaches around the door, pushes the lock button, and pulls it shut, leaving Ash and me alone again.

He leans back against the door, runs his fingers through his hair, and breathes in and out deeply through his nose. He's not nearly as unruffled as he appeared to be.

"Thank you," I eventually say, "for taking control of that situation."

"Thank goodness it was only Wendy," he says. "I'm so sorry. I shouldn't have put you in that situation." His hands curl into fists. "I would never forgive myself if you got in trouble at work because of me."

I shake my head vehemently. "No. Don't be sorry. Don't ever be sorry for what we just did." While making out in my office wasn't the smartest thing we've ever done, I don't wish we could take it back. I touch my lips, and his gaze focuses there. "We probably shouldn't do that at work again, though."

"But we will do it again?" he asks, his eyes shooting back to mine. "Because I was right. It's going to kill me if we can't."

His vulnerability is what's going to kill me. But that kiss was so explosive I know we shouldn't do it again anytime soon, even though every cell in my body is shouting at me to press my lips against his immediately.

It's too soon. I desperately don't want it to be, but it is. Although I know I don't want to be with Glenn, I'm still too irritated with him to start something serious with Ash with a clear conscience.

"I need a little more time," I say, and dismay flickers across his features before he tamps it down. "Let's give it at least until Shannon comes." He'll help me figure out the right thing to do for both me and Ash. "Between now and then, we can't be alone together, even for work stuff. We either do work by phone—with our office doors open, so we're not tempted to say anything we shouldn't—or if we need to meet in person, we bring in Wendy or Randall. Let's see if one of them can meet with us tomorrow about Sanchez."

He nods.

"And we can't talk on the phone unless it's for work. But let's not put limits on the length or timing of letters anymore." I, for one, will be able to control what I write more than what I speak. "We can write as much as we want, and we can write back as soon as we want. Does that work for you?"

He nods again. "Yes."

"One more question before you go." I can feel my face turning red for the first time since Ash walked into my office. "Why do you taste like cinnamon?"

thirty-eight

. . .

I feel like I ran the Boston Marathon … and won. I'm both exhausted and exhilarated. I'm filled with excitement at what happened, but I'm disappointed I can't do it again immediately.

Leslie thinks I taste like cinnamon. That knowledge is almost my undoing. I want to give her the opportunity to taste me again. And I want to ask why she tastes like sunshine, but I'm afraid I'll sound utterly ridiculous if I do.

Instead of doing either of those things, my response to her question is simply, "Dentyne." I keep a pack of the gum in my pocket and chew a piece before each time I know I'll see her, to ensure my breath is fresh—just in case.

"Hmm." She taps her lips with her pointer finger, which nearly makes me hurdle the desk and pull her up out of that chair again. "I used to prefer Big Red, but I've changed my mind."

I push off the door and approach her desk. Her eyes widen like they did the last time I did this, but I force myself to stop before I get to her and shove my notepad and pen back into my briefcase. She breathes heavily as she watches me, and I don't know how I'm going to leave this office without kissing her again.

After a few seconds I decide I'm not going to. I tilt her chin up with one finger, lean down, and capture her lips with mine once more. I rip myself away after much too short a time, snatch up my suit coat and briefcase, and leave without looking back.

If I look back, I'll *go* back.

Wendy is chatting with the receptionist when I pass her on my way out. She gives me a knowing look but says nothing. I'm certain she'll be in Leslie's office within seconds.

I walk back to my office in a daze. Not five minutes after I sit down at my desk, my door opens.

"Do you ever knock?" I ask my brother. "And do you ever work?"

"Why are you back?" he asks. "You said you'd be over at Carter-Jenkins for the rest of the day."

"How do you know that?" I didn't tell anyone but Annette.

"I know everything."

"I doubt it." For instance, there's no way he can know what happened with Leslie fifteen minutes ago.

"You kissed her."

My jaw drops before I can stop it.

"Ha!" He points at me. "That was a guess, but I'm right! You've got a deer-in-the-headlights look about you." He cocks his head. "Is that why you're back already? She kick you out?"

"In a manner of speaking. But she wasn't mad about it, that's for sure." She was the opposite of mad. The little sounds she made while we kissed keep replaying in my mind.

"It was too soon, wasn't it?" I barely register Randall asking.

Focus. I need to focus instead of recalling the heat of Leslie's body pressed against mine, the feel of her fingers sliding through my hair. I force out, "Says the man who wants to date someone else three days after his girlfriend broke up with him."

"So yes, then?"

I sigh. "Yes."

"She give you a timeline?"

"At least until her brother comes to visit a week from Saturday. He wants to meet me."

"The twin brother? The guy you thought was your pen pal?"

I nod.

"Good luck with that. Can I come watch?"

I snort. "Nope."

"I'm coming."

"You're not invited."

"So her brother gets to come, but I don't? I saved her life! You owe me, man. She'd be dead if it weren't for me."

My chest constricts at the thought, but I hate giving him credit for saving her. "Lots of people know the Heimlich."

"Including you, my friend. You took the same lifesaving course I did when we were teenagers. But did you save her? No. That's all on me. You're welcome."

"Fine. Thank you for saving her life."

"And I'm coming to meet the brother."

I roll my eyes. "I'll talk to her about it."

"Are you still allowed to talk to her?"

Is he taunting me? "Shut up."

"Are you, though? I seriously want to know."

"We're going to keep writing letters. But I'll ask her about you going to dinner with Shannon when I meet with her tomorrow about Diego Sanchez. By the way, you might need to come along to that meeting. Since you never seem to have anything better to do than be up in my business all the time, I'm sure that won't be a problem."

"I wouldn't miss it. After all, I haven't seen Leslie since the day I saved her life."

"You're never going to let me forget that, are you?"

"Not until the day I die. I'm thinking about saying it in my will, too, so you might get the pleasure of hearing it again after I'm dead."

"Fantastic."

After dinner, I get settled on the couch to watch TV when someone pounds on my door. It's one of my siblings, but I can't tell which one. They all knock exactly the same.

"It's open!" I holler.

The door bangs open and both girls race in. Sonya holds a Blockbuster Video tape over her head like it's a trophy. "You're watching *Dirty Dancing* with us!" They squeal as they plop down on top of my reclined body.

"Oof." I push at them. "Get off. I'm watching *MacGyver*."

"It's a rerun," Tonya says as she stands and then pulls my arm to get me to sit up. "We were nice enough to watch the season finale of your stupid show with you last week, remember? Now it's your turn to watch what we want."

"I don't want to watch a dancing movie. You can't watch it over at the house without me?"

They finally get me positioned how they want me and sit on either side of me on the couch.

"Mom hates this movie," Tonya says. "If she hears it, she'll make us turn it off."

"What makes you think I won't hate it and make you turn it off?"

Sonya shrugs. "Because you let us do anything we want."

She's not wrong. Regardless of what Mom said on Saturday, I'm terrible with kids. I've always let these two run right over me.

"How many times have you seen this movie?" I ask.

"Not enough," Tonya says.

Sonya loops her arm through mine and squeezes it. "It's soooo romantic!"

"Speaking of romantic ..." Tonya giggles.

"What's up with you and that Melissa woman?" Sonya finishes for her.

"Nothing." I press my lips together.

"Don't you dare lie to us, Ashley Theodore Hamilton." Tonya pokes my chest. "You were totally flirting with her at dinner on Saturday, and you never flirt. Plus, Mom says you're going on a date with her this weekend."

It's hard to keep a secret in this family.

"So what if I am? What's the big deal?"

"The big deal," Sonya says, "is as far as we know," she points back and forth between our sister and herself, "you haven't gone on a date since you moved back here. That's been *two years*."

"You haven't kissed anyone in at least two years," Tonya chimes in. "That's wild. I can't imagine."

I will my face not to turn red. I hope they can't hear my heart pounding as I try not to relive my kisses with Leslie in my mind for the hundredth time since this afternoon. I'm also glad they don't know it had been well over two years since I kissed anyone else.

I stick my finger in Tonya's face. "First off, you," I move my finger to Sonya, "and you aren't allowed to kiss anyone until you're at least thirty. Plus, I don't know if you realize this, but you don't have to be dating someone in order to kiss them."

"Ooooo!" Sonya puts her hands on my cheeks and turns my head to face her. "Who have you been kissing, Ashley Bashley? Did you kiss Melissa on Saturday?"

"No." At least that's not a lie.

"You're lying." She presses her fingers into my cheeks until I'm making fish lips. "I can see it in your beady little eyes."

I remove her hands from my face. "I'm not lying. And I don't have beady little eyes."

"Beady giant eyes, then."

"Whatever. What were you saying about a movie?" I'll do almost anything to put an end to this conversation.

"Yesss. I knew we'd get you!" Tonya jumps up and slides the videotape into the VCR. "Ash, go stick a bag of popcorn in the microwave. And fix us some drinks."

I roll my eyes as I stand. "Yes, ma'am."

thirty-nine

"You haven't thought about anything but that kiss since it happened, have you?" Aunt Star asks.

"No." My face burns at the admission.

"What are you going to do when you get off the phone with me?"

"Think about it some more."

She chuckles. "I appreciate the honesty, but why don't you call the new friend you keep talking about and see if she can come over or go out or something? Don't sit at home thinking about Ash."

"But I want to sit at home thinking about Ash."

"I know, but you'll probably drive yourself crazy if you do. Call your friend when you get off the phone with me. I doubt you have any food in your apartment, anyway."

She knows me well. "Fine. I'll call Wendy."

"Good. Oh, I've been meaning to tell you I'm thinking about going to a Realtor conference in Chicago in mid-June."

"How did you forget to tell me that?"

"Well, I've only been considering it for about a week, and you may have dominated the conversation the last few times we've spoken."

"Sorry."

"No need to be sorry. You've had a lot to deal with. Anyway, the conference is from Thursday morning through Friday afternoon, and then I'd stay for the weekend to spend time with the best PR rep east of the Mississippi."

"But not west?" I tease.

"That's up for debate. Also, Beckett is thinking about tagging along, if that's okay with you?"

"Yes! Please bring her. I haven't seen her in forever—not since her wedding." Beckett is my aunt Minda's daughter. It's a little confusing that my last name is her first name, but it suits her. She's six years older than me but my only girl cousin, and we've always been very fond of each other.

"I'm well aware," Aunt Star says. "If you ever ventured west of the Mississippi, maybe I'd be able to determine your spot on the nationwide list of PR reps."

"You're hilarious."

"Don't you forget it. As far as me meeting Ash while I'm there, I'd love to, but we'll see how things are going with him at the time, okay?"

"Sounds perfect. I can't wait to see you and Becks!"

Thirty minutes later, Wendy and I are both sitting cross-legged on my bed, drinking wine and eating the Chinese takeout she picked up on her way over.

"I don't know why I didn't make you come to my place," she says. "At least I have a couch. And a table."

"Hey, I have a table!" I protest.

"A table large enough for a medium-sized cat."

I want to ask how she can afford an apartment bigger than mine, but I haven't drunk enough wine or known her long enough yet to be comfortable asking such a thing.

"Now give me all the details of the kiss," she says, "since you refused to tell me at work."

"We can't talk about him at work anymore. I need to focus while I'm there and not waste time talking about boys like I'm fifteen. George isn't paying me to chat to you about my love life."

"You're not wrong," she acknowledges. "We've spent an inordinate amount of work time talking about Ash."

"I'm also not giving you details of the kiss. All I'll say is it was the most amazing kiss of my life."

"Whoa. Who'da thought Ash Hamilton had it in him?"

"You, apparently, since you had a crush on him for six months."

"Oh yeah. I forgot about that."

"Speaking of your crushes ..." I press my lips together so I won't smile.

She sits up straight. "Sexy Shannon? He's coming? To see me?"

I let my grin burst free. "Well, to see me, but I might allow you to catch a glimpse of him while he's here." I give her a stern look. "If you promise to never, ever, ever call him 'Sexy Shannon' again in my presence."

"Fine. When's he coming? When? When? When?" She's bouncing up and down on the bed. I hold on to my takeout container to keep it from spilling.

"Next weekend."

"And by 'next weekend,' do you mean the one that's coming up in four days, or the one after that?"

"The one after. Isn't that common knowledge?"

"You would think so, but it's not. I learned that lesson the hard way."

"Do I want to hear that story?"

"You do not."

I'm certain I do, but I don't push it.

"You going to tell Shannon about Ash?" she asks.

"I already did. That's why he's coming. He demanded to meet Ash."

"Ooo, I do love a man who makes demands." Her entire body shudders.

I raise my eyebrows at her.

Wendy taps her chin. "Too much information?"

"Totally ... since you're saying it in relation to my brother. Otherwise I don't care what you're into."

"Sorry. Wasn't thinking. But I *was* thinking I need to ask if Ash said anything to you about the family dinner with that Melissa woman."

I've been wondering about that, too, and I don't like the way I feel when I think about it. "No, he didn't say, and I didn't ask. I was a little preoccupied with … you know."

"Oh, I know. Your mouth was engaged in more stimulating activities. You want me to ask Randall about it?"

I ignore the mouth comment. "No, please don't ask him. Ash needed to know about Glenn, but I don't need to know about Melissa. I'd rather not know."

"All right. Back to Shannon. When do I get to see him?"

I was thinking about not mentioning dinner to her until the last second, or I'll never hear the end of it, but I'm afraid she might make other plans. Plus, she won't give me a moment's peace if I don't tell her when she can see him, so I say, "At dinner with Ash next Saturday."

She squeals. "Yes! It'll be a double date—you and Ash, and me and Shannon!"

"Not a date."

"Totally a date. Nothing will convince me otherwise." She points her chopsticks at me. "We need to go shopping. This Saturday. No excuses."

"It's still not a date, but I'm always up for shopping."

"So why was Ash in your office this afternoon? Did you have a meeting?"

"Yes, about Diego Sanchez. And we still need to meet, but that will require a chaperone, as ridiculous as that sounds for a couple of twenty-five-year-olds."

"You can't keep your hands off him, can you?"

"Kind of the other way around."

"I'm guessing it's both."

"Okay, fine. I want to touch that man at all times."

She cackles. "I love it."

"Will you help us? Do you have an hour to spare tomorrow for a meeting? You wouldn't only be our mood killer, but I'm sure you'll also have some excellent input. We're going to talk about ways we might get Diego to use his money and position to help people. I think he'll be open to it, but we need to go to him with a plan."

"Girl, that's right up my alley. I'm all in. And I resent being called a mood killer. Don't you dare call me that in front of your brother."

"There's one way you can keep me from it."

She nods gravely. "By me not calling him sssss ... you know, that word."

"Yup."

"So where do things stand with Ash now? Are you all in now that Glenn is ancient history?"

"No. Today was a ... I don't want to call it a mistake, because I'm not sorry we kissed. But it wasn't planned. We didn't talk about it ahead of time. It simply happened. But we can't do it again for a while, and I told him that."

"And he was okay with it?"

"He said he was, but I could tell he was frustrated."

"In more ways than one, I'm guessing." She wiggles her eyebrows.

I roll my eyes. "Anyway, I said we need to tamp things down at least until Shannon is here. I didn't say this to Ash, but I think my brother can help me figure out if what I'm feeling is real or a reaction to being dumped."

"I'm pretty sure it's real," she says.

"Me, too, but Shannon knows me better than anyone. He's been there since the womb."

"The twin thing."

"Yep."

"So if I marry your twin, does that mean I'm kind of marrying you, too?"

I grab my pillow and swing it at her head.

forty

At one o'clock on Tuesday afternoon I walk through Leslie's office door, my brother on my heels. Leslie sits at her desk, and Wendy has taken up residence in the purple chair.

I hate that Leslie and I have an audience for the first time we see each other after the kiss that blew my mind, but if we didn't, I'd be tempted to lock the door behind me again. I've never lacked control over my body before, but I'm struggling with it now. It's so strange that while I'm not a touchy-feely person, I want to have physical contact with Leslie every moment of the day.

The look she gives me is so full of longing I can barely breathe, but I hold myself together since both Wendy and Randall are watching me intently. Amazingly, neither of them comment on the situation. I threatened Randall to within an inch of his life to keep his mouth shut, and I'm guessing Leslie did the same with Wendy.

"We ready to do this?" I ask.

Wendy stands and claps her hands together. "Let's take this party to a conference room so we have more space to spread out. Follow me, Team Sanchez."

We let the ladies walk out first, and my brother scoots in front of me as I try to follow directly behind Leslie. He gives me a stern look and shakes his head. I'm both annoyed and thankful, because I would've touched her if he hadn't intervened.

Once we're in the conference room, Randall and Wendy word-lessly ensure we're seated so Leslie and I are neither sitting next to nor across from each other. The two of them are like a well-oiled machine. I want to scream in frustration. I'm honestly not sure why we need both of them, but neither would give in when we discovered they were both recruited to join us.

Leslie says, "Let's get started. Ash, why don't you tell us what you're thinking, and then we'll see what other ideas we have and go from there."

I pull out my notes, but I don't need them. I know exactly what I want to do. "I started thinking about this on Thursday after a conversation with a cleaner at our firm." I explain about Carmela and her husband Javier, who can't get back into the country after visiting his mother.

"The next thing I know," I say, "Diego Sanchez is coming to town, and Carter-Jenkins lands him as a client. The first thing I wanted to do was call him and ask if he can help get Javier back into the country, since they're both from the Dominican Republic, but I'm not allowed to ask Sanchez for any favors. In the mean-time, I made some calls to a few people I thought might help, but I didn't get anywhere with any of them. I'm not sure if it's because they truly can't help or because they fear Dad."

When Leslie gives me a confused look, I say, "Our father isn't a fan of immigration. Explaining we're all technically descended from immigrants does no good. He's more than happy to employ legal workers, but only if they're fluent in English."

Leslie's eyes look sad at my explanation, but she nods in understanding.

"What my brother isn't telling you," Randall says, "is Dad also pays them less than everyone else. But Ash here slips them sizable Christmas bonuses out of his own pocket."

My face turns red, and I glare at my brother while avoiding Leslie's gaze. I don't want her to think I asked Randall to brag about me for her benefit. "That's not supposed to be common knowledge," I say to him. "I'm not sure how you know about it." I've never told a soul.

He spreads his hands wide. "I told you I know everything."

One of these days I'll figure out how.

I clear my throat and continue, "So my idea is for Sanchez to set up a foundation that will help not only legal residents with their own immigration issues but also aid naturalized citizens with bringing their family members to the US legally."

"Yes!" Leslie's face and eyes are so animated my heart feels like it'll burst. "When Bobby told us about Diego helping his cousins immigrate here and get jobs and get settled into the community, I had similar thoughts. And I wonder if Jorge and Armando would be interested in being involved in the foundation as well. I bet they would." She looks at Wendy and then Randall. "We met his cousins at the game on Friday. They're great guys."

I ask, "Is anyone not in favor of taking this idea and running with it?"

"You know I'm in," Randall says. "I'd be in regardless because I love this idea, but if we're doing something that'll also stick it to Dad, I'm two hundred percent in."

"Me, too," Wendy adds. "Well, I'm not in it to stick it to your dad, but I'm all for it. I'll help in any way I can. Now, let's get into the details."

Three hours later, we have the makings of a proposal in place for Diego Sanchez and Bobby Jacobs. All four of us are amped up on adrenaline, and I feel like I could take over the world.

As we're gathering up our things, Leslie says to Randall and Wendy, "Would you two mind giving Ash and me a minute?"

Wendy raises her eyebrows at her friend. "You sure?"

My brother gives me a questioning look, and I nod at him.

"Yes," Leslie says. "You two head on out. You can leave the door open."

My heart is racing as Randall and Wendy exit the room. I wonder if they'll stop outside and eavesdrop.

Leslie sits back down in her chair and pats the seat next to hers. I round the table and sit. We swivel our chairs so we're facing each other but not quite touching knees.

"Hi," she says with a smile.

I return the expression. "Hi."

"You feeling good about this?" she asks in a low voice.

I'm not sure if she's talking about us or the proposal, so I ask, "About the foundation?"

She nods.

"I haven't felt better about many other things in my life."

"I figured as much," she says. "Same here. There's something I'd like you to think about. I don't want an answer immediately, and it's related to the question in my letter, so you can get into it when you respond if you want." She raises an eyebrow. "Unless you've already sent the next letter?"

"No." After the girls left last night, I didn't have enough mental or emotional energy to write.

"Okay, here's what I want you to think about. This isn't technically going to be up to us, but would you ever consider doing something like heading up this foundation?"

She reaches for my hand, and I allow her to take it between hers as I think about what she's asking. Though it's hard to focus with her soft, warm hands lightly stroking mine.

When I don't respond, she says, "You came alive in this meeting, Ash. You were in your element. I haven't seen you in work mode much. In fact, I've only seen you working at the game on Friday. When you were talking with Bobby, you were comfortable and confident. You knew what to say, and you got the job done. But when you were talking with Diego's cousins and asking them about their lives and their families and their dreams, and when you were leading us in here, I felt like this was the sort of thing you were born to do."

She chokes over the final words, and tears well up. I put my other hand on her knee and feel a pricking sensation behind my eyes. I'm glad she doesn't want an answer now, because I don't know what to say. I simply nod and squeeze her leg.

Leslie slips her hands away from mine and rolls her chair back. My own hands suddenly feel cold.

She stands. "Think about it, okay?"

I nod again and watch her walk away.

forty-one

. . .

Walking away from Ash after our meeting is one of the hardest things I've ever done. The feelings swirling inside me are so much stronger and deeper than anything I ever felt for Glenn. Ash Hamilton is an absolutely incredible man, and I don't come close to deserving him.

Wendy is waiting for me in my office. "You want to talk about it?"

I shake my head as I stand stock still in the middle of the room. Tears spill down my face, and Wendy rushes over to shut the door. Then she wraps her arms around me, and I sob on her shoulder as she rubs my back.

"Tell me what's wrong," she says. "Did Ash say something to upset you?"

I shake my head again. "No. He did nothing wrong. He's perfect."

Wendy gives me a squeeze, leads me to my chair, and places a box of tissues in my lap. I pull a couple out and attempt to clean myself up.

"Why are you doing this to yourself?" she asks from her perch next to me on my desk. "Why not be with him? It's obviously killing you both to not be together."

I look at my hands instead of at her. "I don't want to do the wrong thing. I don't want to hurt him."

"Leslie, I think you're hurting him more by what you're doing now than if you were to cut him out of your life, which isn't possible unless you quit this job—or get fired, which is a distinct possibility if you can't get things under control here. You can't continue on like this."

Pain sears through my chest as I focus in on the most important thing she said and ignore the rest. "I'm hurting him? How?"

"You keep letting him get close—or pulling him close—and then pushing him away. You think it's not fair to him for you to date him so soon after Glenn, but this seems less fair. Since you can't completely walk away from him, I think you need to go for it."

"But I don't deserve him. He should be with someone who's as good as he is. That's not me. Like you said, I've done nothing but hurt him from the time we were kids."

"I did *not* say that, Leslie Beckett—not even close to it. You might have done a few things to cause him some pain, but you've only done them out of a misguided attempt to potentially spare him pain down the road. You truly care for him. I can tell. You might be in love with him. This is not you reacting to Glenn. This is you discovering that a boy you cared a lot about from a distance years ago is now a man you care more about up close and personal. You didn't meet Ash Hamilton six days ago. You've known him for fifteen years. It's okay to date him, honey."

I want her to be right so badly, but I can't focus while I'm afraid someone will walk in on us. "Can you get me out of here? Get me home with nobody seeing what a mess I am? I need to be somewhere else to figure out what to do. I can't lose my job because I'm not capable of holding myself together in the office."

She slides off my desk. "You better believe I can. Fix your makeup and gather up your things, and I'll be back in less than five minutes."

While Wendy's gone, I dig my compact and eyeliner out of my purse and fix my face as best I can. She returns as I'm packing up my briefcase.

"Okay," she says, "we're going to walk out of here together. We'll talk about our plans to go shopping this weekend, your brother visiting, or whatever else we need to as we go—nothing about work, so nobody will attempt to chime in. Walk confidently, but keep your eyes on the floor to hide how red they are. If anyone stops to talk to us, I'll distract them, and you keep walking. Got it?"

I nod and take a deep breath. "Let's do it."

We make it out of Carter-Jenkins and the building unscathed. When we reach the sidewalk, I turn toward the bus stop, but Wendy skips out into the street and waves down a cab.

"You don't need to deal with the hordes on the bus," she explains as she follows me into the car.

Wendy holds my hand and is unnaturally silent as we make our way to my apartment, which I'm thankful for. I can think of nothing but how much I loved working alongside Ash while we talked and planned and attempted to make the world a better place—together.

"I want to be with him so badly," I whisper.

"Then be with him. It's okay. It really is." Wendy squeezes my hand.

The pressure in my chest eases as I consider the possibility. I haven't fully let myself think about what it might be like to be with Ash yet. Glenn was always there in the back of my mind, like a specter, taunting me—telling me I can't get over him. But I can. I have. And I've found someone so much better. In an instant, I know I can be with Ash now without reservation.

"Okay," I say. "How do I find him? Do you think he's still at work? Should I go back there? Call there when I get home? Track him down at his house? What do I do? Tell me!" I'm suddenly frantic to be in his presence—to touch him, kiss him again, tell him everything I'm feeling.

Wendy laughs. "Calm down, my friend. I've got it covered. When I left you for those five minutes, I called Randall and told him to get Ash to his place after work, because I thought this would happen. Randall only lives a few blocks from you. We'll get you all fixed up at your apartment and then I'll take you over there."

I shake my head. "I don't care what I look like. Let's go now."

"They're not there yet. I know you can't wait to see him, but another half hour won't kill you."

"Don't be so sure about that." I feel like I could spontaneously combust.

Wendy chuckles as the car comes to a halt outside my apartment building. She pays the driver and hauls me out behind her. As we pass by the mailboxes, I notice an envelope through the tiny window in my box. I know it can't be from Ash, but I have to check.

"Hold up," I say to Wendy as I spin the lock.

"Oooo," she says, "is there a letter from your pen pal in there?"

I ignore her, open the box, and pull out the envelope. My heart drops into my stomach when I see the handwriting.

"What?" Wendy asks. "You look like you've seen the ghost of your childhood nemesis."

I shove the letter at her. "It's from Glenn. I can't read it. I can't. Why does he keep messing everything up?"

Wendy takes the envelope from me and holds it gingerly between two fingers as if it's contaminated. "Want me to burn it?"

Maybe. I don't know what to do. He can't have anything to say that I want to hear, because there's nothing he could say that would change my mind. Right? I give myself a shake. Right. He doesn't hold a candle to Ash. But will I regret not reading this letter?

"You read it," I tell Wendy. "If you think I need to know what it says, then I'll read it. If not, you can burn it."

I unlock the interior door and lead the way upstairs. Wendy rips open the envelope and reads silently as we climb. I let us into my apartment, drop my briefcase and purse by the door, and throw myself onto the bed.

"What's the verdict?" I ask.

"He's a flaming idiot. You got a lighter?"

"I don't want to read it?"

"I guarantee you don't."

"Will reading it solidify my decision to date Ash?"

She cocks her head to the side. "If you need one last push over the edge into Ash's arms, this letter is definitely the ticket. But I think you should take my word for it and let me burn it and then flush the ashes down the toilet, where they belong."

forty-two

. . .

I'm not sure why my brother insisted on me coming to his place after work. He says it's because he's upset about Colleen again, but I'm not buying it. Well, he might be upset about Colleen, but that's not why I'm here. I can feel it.

In the ten minutes since we arrived at his apartment, he has talked about everything but Colleen. He keeps looking at the phone and the door and his watch.

"Randall, why am I here?"

"To help me not be sad about Colleen."

"If you're sad about Colleen, there's nothing I can do about it."

"Being here with me is enough."

I roll my eyes.

The intercom by his door buzzes, and he jumps up from the couch faster than I've seen him move since we were teenagers. "Yes?" He shouts into the speaker.

"There's a Wendy O'Halloran here for you," the doorman says.

"Send her up. Thanks, Jeff."

"No problem."

My brother slowly turns away from the intercom and avoids my gaze.

"Why is Wendy here?" I demand.

He paces by the door. "Something about work."

"Do you know how many lies you've told me in the last minute?"

"You'll get over it."

I glare at him while we wait. He yanks the door open as soon as the knock sounds. I inhale sharply when I see who's standing in the doorway, her hand still raised in a fist.

"Randall, why don't we go out for a drink?" Wendy says from somewhere behind Leslie. Her hand reaches in, grabs my brother's arm, and pulls him out into the hall. Then she nudges her friend inside and shuts the door.

I stand but don't move toward Leslie. We stare blankly at each other for several seconds, and then she launches herself across the room at me. I catch her in my arms and hold her tight.

"What's wrong?" I say into Leslie's hair. "Tell me what's wrong." If somebody hurt her, I'll kill them.

"Nothing's wrong." She shakes her head against my chest. "Not anymore."

My heart pounds in my ears. I move my hands up and tilt Leslie's head so I can look at her. "What are you saying?"

She gives me a shaky smile. "Will you be more than pen pals with me, Ashley Hamilton?"

I crush her against me again and press my lips to the top of her head. "Yes." I let out a long breath. "Yes."

Leslie clutches me as if she's afraid I'll slip away if she lets go.

"I'm here," I assure her. "I'm not going anywhere."

If someone had asked me five minutes ago what I'd do in this situation, I would've told you I'd kiss her silly. And while I still plan to do exactly that, right now I simply want to hold her in my arms.

Eventually, she loosens her grip on me and looks up into my eyes.

Then I kiss her silly.

Leslie's lips are swollen, her eye makeup is smeared, and her hair is a mess, which somehow makes her more captivating than she already was. I feel a caveman level of pride that I did that to her.

We're lying on the couch, but I'm so big I cover most of the surface area, which fortunately means Leslie is partly lying on top of me and I have to keep a tight grasp on her so she won't fall onto the floor. Her cheek rests against my shoulder, and I'm going to have makeup stains on my white button-up shirt, but I don't care.

"What made you change your mind?" are the first words I speak since I agreed to be her boyfriend at least twenty minutes ago.

Leslie lifts her head and shifts her body so she can look at me. "Wendy helped me realize I wasn't being fair to you. I kept breaking the rules and letting you get close, and then I'd retreat again. I didn't mean to hurt you by doing that."

"I know you didn't." I tuck a curl behind her ear and trail my fingers down her jawline. "You were trying to do the right thing."

"I was. But it was too hard."

Her face is only inches from mine. I want to kiss her again, but I can tell she has more to say, so I keep my mouth to myself.

"I like you too much," she says. "I want to be with you too much. You're not my rebound, Ash. This isn't my reaction to Glenn."

"I know." I smooth my hand along her hip. "You wouldn't have tried so hard to do what you thought was best for me if you didn't care about me. In theory, what you tried to do was right. But theory doesn't always translate well into reality."

She traces my lips with her fingertips. "I've never had a man talk to me about theories before. It's extremely sexy."

My lips form a smile under her touch. *"You're* extremely sexy."

And now we're kissing again.

Some time later she removes her mouth from mine and declares, "I'm parched."

"Parched?" I give her a half grin.

"Parrrrrrrched."

So am I, come to think of it. I swing my legs around and then stand, bringing her up with me in one smooth motion. Her eyes are wide when I look down into them.

"Wow," she says. "That was also extremely sexy. How are you so graceful for someone so large?"

"It's a talent."

Leslie laughs, and I decide it'll be my mission to make her laugh as much as possible from now until the end of time.

"Do you practice this particular talent often?" she teases.

"Several times a day."

She raises an eyebrow. "With who?"

"I have a life-sized doll at home." I pause. "Don't tell Randall."

She bursts into laughter and then takes my hand and leads me into the galley kitchen.

I open the fridge. "Your choices are Budweiser and … more Budweiser."

"A glass of ice water is fine," she says as she opens cabinets looking for glasses. She finds them and sets two on the counter while I pull out an ice-cube tray and crack it. She plucks a few cubes out of the tray and pops them into the glasses, and I fill them up at the sink. We do all of this with no talking or awkwardness. We're completely in sync.

We lean against the counter as we drink, watching each other the entire time. She drains her glass without stopping.

"Impressive." I tilt my glass toward her. It's still half full.

"I practice several times a day."

We grin at each other like fools. I set my glass down, pluck hers out of her hand, place it in the sink, and settle my hands at her waist. I can't believe I get to touch her now whenever I want. Well, maybe not whenever I want, but a good portion of the time.

Leslie places her hands flat on my chest and gazes up at me. "What are we going to do now?"

There are countless things I'd like to do—some of which scare the life out of me—but I lean down, kiss her forehead, and ask, "What do you want to do?"

forty-three

. . .

"We should go," I say to Ash, "so your brother can return to his own home, but we can't go to my place."

"Why not?"

My face heats. I know we need to have this conversation, because I've made the mistake of not having it soon enough in the past, but I'm not quite prepared for it.

"Do you have a secret boyfriend living there?" he asks.

I grimace. "Maybe."

"I knew it!" He gives me a mock serious look. "But the real question is: Can I beat him in a duel?"

"There's only one way to find out. Do you have a pistol, and can you meet him at dawn?"

"Any true gentleman can answer yes to those two questions."

I smile up at him. "You're too far away, Mr. Lucky Charms."

He tightens his grip on me, picks me up with zero effort, and deposits me on the kitchen counter. Then he steps between my legs and slips his arms around me.

"This better?"

I swallow. "Um, yes." I loop my arms around his neck. We're still not quite at the same height, but at least now my eyes are level with his mouth instead of the middle of his chest. I've fallen in love with his mouth, so I'm perfectly happy with my new view.

"My eyes are up higher, missy."

The lips I've been staring at are now shaped in a grin. I move my gaze up to his eyes.

He says, "Not that I mind you thinking about what you want to do to my mouth, but are you going to tell me the real reason we can't go to your place?"

"Because it's a tiny studio and my only furniture is one semi-comfortable easy chair, a miniature table with two uncomfortable wooden chairs, and my bed."

Ash nods. "And that's a problem … why?"

"We haven't even been on a real date yet. We're not going anywhere near my bed—or anyone else's bed—anytime soon. While it feels like we've known each other forever, because in a way we have, I need us to focus on getting to know each other again." I search his eyes. "Are you okay with that?"

He lifts a hand to cup my cheek. "Of course I am." He almost looks relieved, although I'm surely only imagining it. "I won't pressure you to do anything you don't feel comfortable doing. Not now, not ever."

Tears prick behind my eyelids. "How are you for real?"

"How are *you* for real?" He strokes my cheek with his thumb.

"It's crazy that a week ago, you still thought I was a boy," I say.

"It's crazy that a week ago, you weren't in my life." Now he searches my eyes. "Leslie, you need to know I haven't dated much. I've not had a ton of interest in it until you. I'm not very experienced at any of this, and I honestly don't have a clue what I'm doing." He takes a deep breath. "I don't know how to be a boyfriend."

Now I feel worse about yanking him around. I tighten my hold on his neck. "Thank you for trusting me with that. I would have no idea if you hadn't told me, because you're doing an excellent job so far." I kiss him again to show him how much I appreciate his efforts.

We jerk apart when someone pounds on the door. Ash yells out, "Come in, Randall," but he doesn't move away from me.

"How do you know it's him?" I ask.

"Jeff would've buzzed up if it was anyone else," he explains. "Plus, nobody pounds on a door quite like my siblings do."

A few seconds later, Randall and Wendy appear in the kitchen doorway. Ash turns toward them but keeps one arm around me.

"Looks like everything's going well," Wendy states unnecessarily.

"Yes," Ash says, "we're about to go on our first date."

I shift my gaze from Wendy to him. "We are?"

"We are."

I bite my lip. "Your shirt is a mess."

Randall snorts and Wendy giggles. Ash's shirt is not only wrinkled but also has various makeup stains on it. I'm not entirely certain how they all happened, considering their locations. I also wonder about the state of my face.

Ash glares at them. "I don't care about my shirt."

"If it'll make you feel better, Leslie, he can borrow one of mine," Randall says. "Although it might be a tad short."

"I have a clean one in the car," Ash states.

"Of course you do," his brother replies.

"Are you both going to keep standing there staring at us?" Ash asks the two of them.

"It's my house." Randall crosses his arms over his chest. "I can do whatever I want."

I laugh because it's such a sibling thing to say.

Ash now shoots me a glare, but his mouth twitches. "Don't encourage him. He's not funny."

I giggle. "I'm going to enjoy figuring out which of the two of you is the funniest."

"Me," Randall says. "No contest."

Wendy raises a hand. "I'm voting for Randall on this. Sorry, Ash. But we'll stop staring at you." She tugs on Randall's arm. He tries to stand his ground but soon gives in when he realizes she's not relenting.

Ash turns back to me. "You okay with going out now?"

"I'd like nothing more. I think I need to fix my makeup and hair first, though."

His hands move up to cup my cheeks. "You look perfect." I can tell by his eyes he truly believes what he's saying.

"I don't think the mirror will agree with you."

"The mirror is wrong, but I get it if you want to fix yourself up some. Do we need to stop by your place on our way to dinner?" He quickly adds, "For you to go in—not me."

My chest feels like it's going to explode at the way he's already taking care of me. "I think I can make do with what's in my purse."

He slides me off the counter. When we step into the living room, Randall and Wendy don't pretend they weren't eavesdropping. I don't care if they were.

"I'm going to use your bathroom to freshen up a bit," I say to Randall.

"Past the kitchen on the right," he says.

Wendy jumps to her feet. "I'll come help."

I grab my purse and shoes and head to the bathroom with Wendy trailing behind me. She closes the door, shuts the toilet lid, and sits while I dig my makeup out of my bag.

"Sooooo ...," she wiggles her eyebrows at me, "everything as good as you hoped it would be?"

My face heats. "Yes."

"*Everything?*"

I know what she's getting at, even if for some inexplicable reason she won't say it. "Everything we did was great. But we didn't do *everything*. First of all, we're in his brother's apartment. And secondly, we won't be doing *everything* anytime in the near future."

She needs to know where I stand on that topic almost as much as Ash does, because I don't need her comments and questions to feel like pressure either.

"Got it. I won't bring it up again."

"I don't care if you talk about it, but I need you to know that's not my focus right now. I'm afraid it would turn into the only focus, and we have a lot to learn about each other first."

forty-four

. . .

"What do you think they're talking about in there?" I ask my brother from the love seat in his living room.

"You, dingus. You really don't know much about women, do you?"

His tone isn't condescending. It's more curious, so I don't change the subject like I normally would.

"No," I admit. I gather up my shoes and slip them on instead of looking at him. "And I'm afraid I'm going to royally jack this up because of it."

"Hey," Randall says. "Look at me."

I hesitantly do.

"You might not have a lot of dating experience, but you have plenty of experience interacting with women at work and at home. You treat them with more care and respect than any man I've ever known. It's quite remarkable, if I'm honest. I don't know where you got that trait from, because it didn't come from Dad, that's for sure."

I huff out a laugh. He's not wrong there. In fact, I think my determination to treat women with fairness and respect is because our father never has. I don't want to be anything like him.

Randall continues, "Here's my dating advice for you. You love our sisters more than anyone else in the world, so when you're trying to decide what to do or say or what not to say or do with

Leslie, think about how you'd want a man to treat Tonya or Sonya. Then do that. Or don't do it, as the case may be. Got it?"

I nod.

"But don't think about the girls when you're kissing her and, you know, doing other stuff, because that would be weird and gross."

The horrified look on his face makes me laugh.

Randall's look turns pensive, and he says in a quiet voice, "Don't get mad at me for asking this, but have you ever slept with a woman?"

I drop my head into my hands. Leave it to my brother to ask me such a thing, but I don't feel like I can lie to him about it. I also realize it's something I should be able to talk about with the person I'm closest to.

"No." I'm mortified by the admission.

"Okay." There's no judgment in his tone. "Are you nervous about it?"

"A little." A lot, to be honest. "But she doesn't want to yet." I'm not fully sure what to make of that, though in a way it's a relief.

"That's good."

I finally look at him. "You think so?"

"Yep. In my experience, when you get too physical too fast, that messes with the other dynamics of a relationship. You two don't know each other all that well—at least not as adults. You need time to get reacquainted without the distraction of the physical stuff. It's hard to separate your true thoughts and feelings from your hormones if you let them run wild."

"When did you become so wise?" I ask.

"It's that extra year I have on you. Now, when you're both ready—even if that's your wedding night, which is perfectly acceptable—if you're still nervous about it, come talk to me. Okay?"

I'm blown away by how understanding he's being about this and by how much confidence his words have given me. "Okay. Thanks."

The women enter the room giggling about something. I'm

pretty sure Randall and I were talking low enough to not be overheard, so I hope I'm in the clear. At some point I need to tell Leslie what I admitted to my brother, but today is not the day, and Wendy doesn't need to be party to it.

I stand and hold my hand out to my girlfriend—*my girlfriend.*

Leslie takes it and gives me a sweet smile. "You ready?"

She's so beautiful I'm not sure I can respond, but since we have an audience, I force out, "I'm more than ready."

We say goodbye to my brother and Wendy and head out. We hold hands on the way to the elevator, and once the doors close us inside, I say nonchalantly, "I've never been kissed in an elevator."

Immediately, Leslie pushes me against the wall, goes up on her tiptoes, and pulls my head down to hers. I let her take the lead, and I'm not disappointed. She steps away breathlessly when the elevator doors open.

"You can mark that off your bucket list." She takes my hand and tows me out into the lobby. When I get my bearings about me, I guide her outside and down the street to my car. I unlock and open her door for her, and once she's safely inside I pull a clean shirt out of my duffel bag in the trunk. Then I realize I'm going to have to change my shirt either on the street or in the car three inches away from Leslie. I opt for the street.

When I slide into the driver's seat in my fresh shirt, Leslie says, "You didn't want me to see your extra belly button, did you? I know you have one hiding under that shirt."

I gape at her. "How did you know?"

"You seem like the type."

I laugh as I stick the key into the ignition. "What makes me seem like the type of person who has two belly buttons?"

"You're so big it's pretty obvious you're actually two people in one. What else do you have two of?"

"Hmm." I pretend to think for a few seconds and then start rattling off body parts. "Arms, legs, hands, feet, kidneys, lungs, eyeballs, eardrums, big toes, pinkies, armpits, nostrils—"

"Okay, funny guy."

We grin at each other for a few seconds before I ask, "Where do you want to eat?"

"I'm in the mood for Mexican," she says.

I pull the key back out. "If it's Mexican you want, we don't need to drive. The best place in this part of town is a few blocks down the street."

We get back out of the car and head down the sidewalk, Leslie tucked firmly against my side.

"Do you think Wendy is out here spying on us somewhere?" I ask.

"That's a possibility, but my money says she's still up there with Randall. Any chance something could happen between those two?"

"No," I say. "He—" I stop myself from saying he has a crush on Melissa. I don't want to potentially ruin my first date with my new girlfriend by telling her about my upcoming fake date.

"He what?" she prompts before I can think about how I'm going to deal with the Melissa situation.

"He's getting over a breakup," I say. "He recently found out his girlfriend was cheating on him with one of his friends."

Leslie's hand goes to her chest. "Oh, poor Randall. Is he okay?"

The news thoroughly dismays her, which warms my heart.

"He'll be fine."

"Not for a while, I bet. And there he was, helping you and me get together. That had to be so hard for him."

I'm a little ashamed that didn't occur to me. That makes everything he said even more meaningful. "Yeah, it might have been. But back to Wendy, I thought she was determined to date *your* brother, not mine."

"Ugh. Don't remind me. She calls him 'Sexy Shannon,' which gives me the heebie-jeebies."

I laugh. "Speaking of brothers, Randall invited himself to dinner with Shannon. He insists if your brother gets to come, so should he. Is that okay?"

"The more, the merrier. Plus, I like Randall. He seems fun."

"That's one word for him."

forty-five

. . .

At dinner we're one of those sappy couples that holds hands across the table, but I don't care what others might think of us. I'm reveling in the fact that I can now hold Ash's hand whenever I want. I think he feels the same, as the smile hasn't left his face since we sat down.

"I hate to bring this up," I say, "because we seem to have thrown all the rules out the window, but I do have one rule I'd like you to always follow."

"Anything."

"Please don't ever call me 'baby.'"

He cocks his head to the side. "I have no problem following that rule. But why do you have it?"

"Because that's what Glenn called me. I hated it then, and I hate it more now."

Ash swipes his thumb across my hand. "I promise I will never, ever call you that."

"Thank you."

He grins. "Can I call you 'petal'?"

I giggle. "Why would you call me 'petal'?"

"Because you smell like flowers."

My heart skips a beat. "That's sweet, but rule number two is you can't call me 'petal.'"

"What about 'cookie'?"

"Nope."

"Cupcake?"

I hold up four fingers. "Rule number four."

"Snookums?"

I extend my thumb. "Five!"

"Frank?"

I burst into laughter. "Yes, please call me Frank, especially when we're in public."

"Don't test me," he teases.

"I'll always respond if you call me Frank."

He pulls our hands toward him and kisses the back of mine. "Then you'll always be my Frank."

I giggle again before saying, "Now, on to more serious matters. Do you want to answer the question from my letter?"

"Are we not going to write to each other anymore?"

"Do you want to?" I do, because I want to re-read our letters someday down the road.

He squeezes my hand. "I do—with absolutely zero rules. But I'll still answer your question now."

"And my question from earlier today, too?"

"Was it today we had that meeting about Sanchez?"

"Feels like a lifetime ago, doesn't it?"

"The best lifetime." He caresses my knuckles with his thumb.

For someone who claims not to know how to be a boyfriend, Ash is knocking it out of the park.

The waitress brings some chips and salsa along with my margarita and his Coke, and we toast to ourselves.

Then Ash says, "I've often thought about leaving the firm. Dad always talks about how it's his legacy to me and Randall, but it's not a legacy I want. I don't want to be associated with a lot of the things Dad does and believes in. I want to create something better to pass on to my children—if they want it, that is. If they don't, that's fine.

"Dad doesn't understand that, either. Randall didn't have dreams of being a lawyer, but he did it because he screwed around in high school and had little choice. Dad would only pay for college if my brother promised to become a lawyer, and his grades weren't good enough for him to get any kind of academic scholarships. Plus, Randall has never been able to stand up to him about anything."

"Have you?" I ask. "Have you ever stood up to him?"

"Not at work, I'm ashamed to say. But I do when it comes to my sisters. He doesn't treat them like he does Randall and me. He doesn't expect much from them and has mentioned nothing about the firm being a legacy for them. Tonya has always dreamed of becoming a doctor, and when she told us she wanted to go to Duke and do pre-med, Dad laughed at her. He said he wasn't paying for Duke for a girl."

I'm so enraged on Tonya's behalf that I inadvertently crush a salsa-laden chip on its way to my mouth, and the remains fall onto my lap. The worst part of the situation is I have to let go of Ash's hand while I clean the mess up.

"I'm good now. Please continue." I take his hand again.

"I told Dad that Tonya was going to Duke if I had to take on an extra job to pay for it myself, and I wouldn't be afraid to tell the world I was doing so—not to make myself look good, but to make him look bad. He threatened to fire me if I did, but I knew he wouldn't go through with it. Not that I'd be upset if he did fire me. That would be much easier than me leaving of my own free will. Anyway, I didn't back down—and neither did my sister—so Dad finally said he'd pay for Duke."

"So she's going?"

"She is. It ended up she got a full academic scholarship, which stuck it to Dad in the end."

"Is everyone in your family super smart?" I ask.

He blushes and doesn't answer.

"Come on," I say. "I won't think you're bragging if you say yes."

"Then yes. Even Randall, though most people wouldn't know it. He never applied himself in school, and to be honest, he doesn't apply himself at work, either."

"So what would it take to get you to leave the firm?"

"I'd like to not quit without something else lined up. Eventually I want to start my own business or nonprofit, but for now I'd be perfectly happy doing a job I enjoy for someone else's organization."

"Like running Diego Sanchez's foundation?"

"Like running Diego Sanchez's foundation. Not that it exists yet."

"It will," I say. "I haven't spent much time with him, but I already know he's a good man, and I think Bobby Jacobs is, too. Diego will want to put his own stamp on the project, but I'm certain he'll be on board."

Ash shrugs. "That doesn't mean he would hire me."

"You hit it off with Bobby at the game, as well as Diego's cousins. I'm taking that as a good sign they'd consider you for the position."

"Maybe so. I'm also fluent in Spanish, which is helpful."

"How did you become fluent?"

"I minored in it and spent some of my college summers in Spanish-speaking countries. I hoped it would come in useful someday in my work."

"Sounds like it might." I'm in awe that he had the foresight to make that decision when he was seventeen years old.

We eat chips in silence for a minute. I love that the silence doesn't feel awkward. It's not that we can't think of anything to say. I'm processing what he told me, and he might be, too.

"How do you think your father will react to you leaving the firm?" I finally ask.

His eyes turn sad for the first time since I walked into Randall's apartment earlier. "He won't be happy, but I don't know exactly what he would do."

"Would he disown you?" I pray the answer is no, but I'm afraid it won't be.

"I don't think Mom would let him. She's the only person who has any influence over him. But he would try to make life miserable for me. He would undoubtedly kick me out of the pool house. It's about time for me to get my own place, anyway, but I'd like to stay at least until Sonya goes off to college next year. She's going to be lost when Tonya leaves for Duke in August. The two of them have always been inseparable."

I squeeze his hand. "You love your sisters a lot, don't you?"

"More than anything." He doesn't seem at all ashamed of the fact.

"I love that about you."

"I'm sure you feel the same about Shannon and Cynthia."

"I do." Though I'm not nearly as close to my little sister as Ash seems to be to his.

Our food arrives, and we finally let go of each other's hands so we can dig in.

"What would Randall do if he left the firm?" I ask.

"Probably something to do with rescuing people—firefighter, paramedic, something like that. You saw how fast he swooped in to save you from choking to death the other day."

"He'd be okay with making a lot less money?" I feel weird asking, but I don't want any topics to be off limits between us, so I might as well begin as I want to continue.

"That's the tricky part. He's not a saver like I am, and our parents didn't set us up with trust funds. Dad wants us to work for our money, which is one of the few things I appreciate about him. I've been trying to convince Randall that if he ever wants to leave law, he needs to start saving up so he can afford to do so. I haven't been successful yet."

"You sure you're not the big brother?" I ask. It rather seems like it.

"In many ways, it feels like I am. But in other ways, not as much." He doesn't elaborate on what those ways are, and it doesn't feel like something I should push him to share with me. He has been surprisingly open so far, so if there's something he's not ready to talk about, I won't force it. He'll tell me in his own time.

"It sounds to me like you're an excellent big brother to all three of your siblings." I point a tortilla chip at him. "Now, let's stop being serious and talk about silly stuff. What's your favorite ice cream flavor and why?"

forty-six

· · ·

The restaurant is only a few blocks from Leslie's apartment, so I walk her home. She stops by the outside door of the building to say goodnight, but I'm not having it.

"I'm walking you all the way to your door. You never know who might be lurking in the stairwell."

"Okay," she says, "but you're not allowed to look inside my apartment."

"That may be taking things a little too far," I say as I wait for her to unlock the lobby door. "One tiny peek can't hurt."

"No, it's not that. The place is a disaster. You don't need to witness the extent of my messiness yet."

"But now that I know about it, why does it matter?"

"It just does."

I drop the subject and follow her up the stairs, admiring the view as we go.

"Are you staring at my butt?" she asks over her shoulder.

"No," I say too quickly.

"You're a terrible liar, Ashley Hamilton."

Is it weird that I love it when she calls me Ashley?

I grin at her backside. "I'm not sure what you expect me to do. It's right in my line of vision."

We reach her floor, and I thread my fingers through hers as we head down the hall.

She squeezes my hand. "I think that might be the real reason you wanted to walk me all the way to my door."

"You'll never know." But I know both reasons are accurate.

Leslie stops at her apartment and sticks her key in the lock but doesn't turn it. Then she leans back against the door.

Her hair is windblown from our walk, and I tuck it behind her ears, letting my fingers linger on her face. "You're really not going to let me look inside?" I don't care if she does, and I'm certain she knows that, but I feel like teasing her.

She gives me a saucy smile. "Nope."

I put a finger under her chin, tilt her head up, and kiss her forehead, then each cheek, and finally her nose. Her eyes flutter closed.

"There's nothing I can do to convince you?" I ask.

"Nope."

I trail the back of my fingers down her neck, and she shudders, eyes still closed.

"Positive?"

"N-nope."

"Aha! I caught you!"

Her eyes pop open. "I mean, yes! I'm positive!" She gives me a mock glare. "Now stop messing with me and kiss me goodnight."

I take a step back, stick my hands in my pockets, and resist the urge to smile. "Are you always this demanding? If so, I might need to reconsider our arrangement, Frank."

She giggles at my use of the ridiculous nickname. "You love it, and you know it."

I do. "If you want to kiss me so badly, then kiss me."

Leslie steps into me, places a hand on my chest, and slowly slides it upward until it rests on my neck. I force myself to remain still throughout the torturous process. She swipes her thumb over my Adam's apple, and I swallow instinctively. She does it again, and a low growl escapes my throat.

"Not so fun when the shoe's on the other foot, is it?" she taunts.

Fun is definitely not the word for what I'm feeling. I press my lips together, anticipating what she might do next.

With her other hand, she encircles my wrist and tugs at my arm, and I let her pull my hand out of my pocket. She lifts it to her mouth and drops feathery kisses all over my palm before wrapping my arm around her back. Finally, she raises her hand to my shoulder. Then she cocks her head to the side, challenging me to make the next move.

When she bites her lip, my resistance crumbles. Much like she did in the elevator earlier, I press her back against the door and kiss her like I've just come home from a year in Antarctica.

Minutes later, my hands are braced on the door above her head, and we're both gasping for air.

"Go inside," I whisper and push myself off the door. I caress Leslie's cheek, press one more kiss to her forehead, and force myself to walk away from her.

Focusing on work is nearly impossible this morning. At ten o'clock my phone beeps and Annette announces I have a call from Leslie.

"Hi," my girlfriend says in a professional tone when I answer. "This is a work call."

"Got it." I can't decide if I'm thankful she set that boundary.

"I talked to Diego and said we have a proposal for him. I didn't give many details, but he seemed intrigued. He and Bobby can meet with us on the team's off day next Wednesday."

I'm surprised they have time to meet with us so soon. "Sounds great."

"Are you … no, never mind."

"What?"

"No, we need to stay professional at work."

"Okay. Want to talk about it after work? Or at lunch?" I ask hopefully.

"We have an office lunch scheduled today. But I'd love to see you after work."

"I'll swing by your office and get you a little after five. That okay with you?"

"Why don't we plan to meet in my building's lobby at 5:15?"

Does she not want anyone at Carter-Jenkins to see us together? I'm not sure how I feel about that, but I say, "I'll see you then."

I'm thinking about my teasing outside her apartment and wondering if she thought I was pressuring her when my brother saunters in—without knocking, of course. I can't believe he waited this long to talk to me.

"You're not getting anything done today, are you?" he asks.

I shake my head.

"How'd the date go?"

"Good."

"You reverting to silent Ash on me?"

It's tempting to go back to my comfort zone, but I begrudgingly admit to myself that talking to him about Leslie has been helpful. "No."

"Doesn't sound like it."

I sigh. "What do you want to know?"

"Did everybody's pants stay on?" He's not smirking at me, so I know he's serious.

My face heats. "Yes."

"Good. You cleared the first hurdle. It's the hardest one. Now you know you've got the strength to stay the course. I admire that. She'll admire it, too. You proved she can trust you."

I nod. I hadn't thought about it that way, but he's right. I still hope she didn't take the teasing the wrong way, though.

"What did you talk about?"

When I think back, I realize we mostly talked about me—and *him*—but I'm not admitting that. I make a mental note to not monopolize future conversations with Leslie, and I say, "All kinds of stuff—family, work, favorite ice cream flavors ..."

"What's her favorite?"

"Mint chocolate chip."

"Don't forget that."

"I won't." There's no chance of me forgetting anything Leslie has said to me in the past week.

"When are you going to see her again?"

"After work today."

"You're not wasting any time."

"No reason to."

He nods. "What are you going to do about Melissa?"

I sigh. "I don't know."

"You can let me go out with her alone."

"No."

"You can trust me."

"I cannot."

"Come on. You can't go on a fake date when you have a girlfriend. Melissa will understand if you cancel on her."

"I know, but I'll feel bad because of her mom. And if I cancel, what am I going to tell *our* mom?"

"That you have a girlfriend?"

"And then she'll ask why I asked Melissa out if I'm dating someone else."

"Are you scared to tell Mom about Leslie?"

"Yes. You heard what she said about not wanting me to date someone in PR. Plus, I'm not sure how understanding she'll be about what Leslie did when we were kids. I need more time to figure out how to break the news to her."

"Believe it or not, I'd already forgotten about the pen pal deception. Mom's not going to like that at all."

"Nope."

"I hate to say it, but you got yourself into this mess by pretending to be interested in Melissa. You could've told Mom the truth from the beginning."

He doesn't hate to say it. In fact, he seems to be enjoying it.

"Thanks for bringing that up. I appreciate it."

"Sorry." He's not sorry. "What if we ask Melissa to bring a friend or two along—make it a group thing?"

"That could work." I'd feel less guilty about it.

"I'll call and ask her."

"You will not. I'll call her tonight."

"You also have to tell Leslie what's going on."

"Do I?" I don't want to. I want it to all go away.

"Yes. Trust me on this."

forty-seven

. . .

Wendy is out of the office this morning, so I won't be able to talk to her until the all-office lunch. I can't believe she didn't leave a message on my machine last night to call her when I got home. Maybe she's learning some restraint.

Speaking of restraint, I'm astonished by Ash's level of it last night, and I'm grateful. I know he was only teasing when he kept asking to see the inside of my apartment, but if he had seriously asked to come in after that kiss in the hallway, I wouldn't have been able to say no.

In fact, after he disappeared into the stairwell, I slid down to the floor and sat there in a daze for at least five minutes before gathering up the strength to let myself inside. I can't let Ash walk me all the way to my door again. We're going to have to restrict our time together to only public places or group outings for the foreseeable future.

I did call Aunt Star last night, though. She didn't fully agree with my decision to date Ash, but she was supportive. She's never been one to hold a grudge against someone who doesn't take her advice.

Like I told Ash on the phone, Diego seemed intrigued by the little I told him about our proposal. Now that I know Ash would quit his job to work for the foundation, I'm more anxious about Diego's ultimate response. I want this to happen not only because it could help countless people—including Ash's friend—but also because it could alter Ash's future in a positive way.

I didn't close my office door this morning, because I need the accountability. If people can walk by and see me, I can't be sitting and staring off into space. George Carter appears in my doorway and knocks on the open door. At my smile, he enters and takes a seat. "I hear you wanted to see me."

I do, and I appreciate that he came to me instead of expecting me to go to him.

"I wanted to fill you in on where things are with Diego Sanchez."

I tell him what I've accomplished as far as normal PR work goes, and then I explain about the proposal for the foundation.

"What do you think?" I ask when I finish.

"I think it's the most comprehensive plan I've ever heard at this stage of the game, and I love it. And since Wendy and Ash were involved in the planning, I have no qualms about what you're taking to Sanchez and Jacobs. But I'm curious about why Randall Hamilton is also in on it."

I can't tell him the real reason, so I shrug and say, "Ash brought him along. I guess he was interested in the idea, and he had some excellent input. I'm not sure how involved he'll be going forward, but it was helpful to have him in the initial meeting."

George nods. "I like Randall. I haven't spent much time around him, but he's quite personable. I could see him working in PR instead of law. Not much chance of that, though, is there, with the Hamilton name above the door? His father would never allow it."

My heart sinks at his words.

He asks, "Are you settling in okay and getting to know your co-workers?"

"Yes, everyone has been great."

I wouldn't have survived either the work or the personal side of life these past few weeks without Wendy.

"Sounds like you and Wendy are spending some time together, which is good. She's the best we've ever had around here. And if she's taking time to help you, that means she thinks you have what it takes. She doesn't do that for everybody."

"That's nice to hear. Thank you, sir."

"Call me George, please." He stands. "Again, let me know if you need anything from me, but you appear to be getting along fine without me."

"I will, sir … George. Thanks again."

He nods and exits my office.

"There's something I need to tell you," Ash says.

I stare at him from across the table at a bar down the street from work, and my stomach constricts. Those words never precede anything the other person wants to hear.

"Okay," I prompt when he doesn't continue.

"Remember how Melissa and her parents came to dinner on Saturday?"

I already don't like where this conversation is headed. "Yes."

"When we were talking at the game on Friday, we decided to play a trick on our moms."

He takes a deep breath while I try to keep my stomach from rejecting the cosmopolitan I've been drinking.

Ash continues, "We pretended we were interested in each other during dinner."

My hand goes to my throat. I can't speak. Ash reaches out toward my other hand on the table, but I pull it away from him. Pain flashes through his eyes.

"Please remember I thought it would be months before I could date you. And I never intended to actually date Melissa. But after dinner—after our families thought we were into each other and we were riding on the high of our success—we were hanging out at my place with Randall. We decided to go on a fake date this Saturday, with Randall tagging along, since it's not an actual date. Melissa insisted on him coming with us, because she knew I had something going on with you. It's just the three of us having a meal together as friends. That's all."

I'm struggling to keep my tears at bay.

"Will you say something?" he asks.

I shake my head. I can't say anything without sobbing. If Ash could convince his family he was into Melissa, there's no way he didn't mean any of what he did or said to make them believe it. My heart has never ached like this—not even as a result of anything Glenn did or said over the past month.

"Please, Leslie. I'm sorry. I didn't mean for things to get out of hand like this. It was supposed to be a joke."

"It's not a joke to me," I choke out. "And you didn't cancel this so-called fake date after last night?"

He looks away from me for the first time since he began speaking. "No."

I force myself to stay in my seat instead of running out of the bar in tears. "Why?"

"Our moms already know we're going out, and if we cancel, they'll want to know why. This dinner means nothing to me, but Melissa recently moved back to town and needs some friends, and I can't let her down."

"You can't let *Melissa* down? What about me?" A few tears fall and I angrily swipe them away. "Why can't you tell your mother the truth? You're not twelve!" Then it hits me. "You don't want to tell your mom you're dating me."

He looks stricken. "Leslie—"

"You're fine with her thinking you're dating a woman who's part of your elite, rich, north-side world, but not me." I grab my purse and stand. "You're ashamed of me. Well, shame on you, Ashley Hamilton." I stab my finger at him. "Shame on you." I ignore his shell-shocked look, turn on my heel, and walk away as calmly as I can.

He's lucky I didn't throw the rest of my drink in his face.

forty-eight

. . .

"**D**on't tell him I'm coming," I order Jeff as I storm past him in Randall's lobby.

The doorman gives me a wary look. "Yes, sir."

When I reach my brother's door, I pound on it as I unlock and open it. His eyes widen when he sees the look on my face, and he holds his hands up in front of himself in self-defense.

"Whatever happened, it's not my fault!" he says.

I sigh and close my eyes. "I know," I say, even though I was fully prepared to blame him for everything. "It's all *my* fault." I drop onto the love seat. "I told you I was going to screw this up with her."

"You told her about Melissa?"

I nod. "Before I tell you what happened, do you have Wendy's phone number?"

"Yeah, why?"

"Will you call and ask her to check on Leslie?"

"Of course." He stands. "Be back in a sec."

I can hear his voice from his bedroom as he talks to Wendy, but I can't make out the words. While I wait for him, I take deep breaths to calm down.

He comes back to the couch, props his feet on the coffee table, and says, "Tell Uncle Randy everything."

I relay the conversation to him. When I finish, I say, "I can't believe she thinks I'm ashamed of her." The thought makes my chest hurt.

"Here's the thing," my brother says, "I know you're not ashamed of her, and you know you're not ashamed of her, but how is she supposed to know that? You think you know each other well because of the pen pal thing, but you really don't. She hasn't experienced you as an adult, and she has no clue what Mom's like."

I nod.

He continues, "She also doesn't understand how much you hate letting people down. Should you have called and canceled with Melissa after last night?" He shrugs. "I would've in your position, but I'm not you. Sadly, I don't care as much about letting my friends down as you do. Not that I have any friends anymore … except you."

"I get what you're saying, but how is any of that supposed to help me? I don't think telling her those things is going to do any good. Why should she believe me?"

"You've already helped yourself by having me call Wendy." He holds up one finger. "One, because Wendy knows what kind of man you are." He adds a finger. "And two, because the first thing you did after leaving the bar was to get a friend to check on her. That'll mean a lot."

"Okay. Should I call her?" I'm dying to explain, even if she doesn't want to hear what I have to say.

"Maybe later. Let her calm down first. Hopefully Wendy is helping with that. The other thing you can do to help this situation is to tell Mom about Leslie as soon as possible."

I hate how much I'm afraid of Mom's response, but I know what my brother says is true. I have to tell her, but there's one problem. "She's out of town until Saturday. I can't tell her on the phone—especially not when she's with Aunt Joan." Our aunt is scarier than Mom.

"You're right, but tell her as soon as she gets home. I don't envy you that conversation. Now, what are you going to do about Melissa?"

"I have to cancel now. Not only because of what happened

with Leslie tonight but also because I'm going to tell Mom the truth, so there's no reason to keep up the charade. Which means Melissa will also have to tell her mom the truth."

"She can tell her mom whatever she wants—whether or not it's the truth." He shakes his head. "That's not up to you."

"You think our mom won't tell her mom?"

"You're right. She'll have to confess, too."

"How did I mess this up so badly?"

"Because you're human. That's what we do."

We sit in silence for several minutes while I try not to think about how much it pains me that I hurt Leslie.

I finally say, "You didn't call Wendy 'Glinda' tonight. What's up with that?"

"Nothing," he says, perhaps too quickly.

A corner of my mouth quirks up. "How long did she stay after we left last night?"

"I don't know." He folds his arms over his chest. "A while."

I raise my eyebrows at him. "Oh, yeah?"

He narrows his eyes at me. "Leave it alone. I'm still getting over Colleen, remember?"

"The breakup didn't keep you from being interested in Melissa."

Randall sighs. "That was the rebound talking. Not that I don't like Melissa—I do, and not only because she's easy on the corneas. But I'm not ready to date again."

I look at my hands. "I think Leslie isn't truly ready, either. I'm not saying what I did was right, but if Glenn hadn't so recently screwed her over, I doubt she would've reacted so strongly to me tonight."

"You might be right. You gonna tell her that?"

I look up at him. "Should I?"

"Maybe not in those exact words, but both of you need to sit down and talk this thing out—without touching each other."

I nod. He was right about how the physical side of a relationship can get in the way.

"Ash, I'm sorry that the first time you've ever felt this way about a woman, it's been this hard. Not that relationships are always easy, but you've had a pretty rocky start here."

"It's not Leslie's fault, though."

"Actually, both of you can take some of the blame for the situation you're in, but it's mostly that Glenn guy's fault. Although if he hadn't dumped her, none of this would be an issue for you, anyway."

forty-nine

· · ·

I despise Glenn with the heat of a thousand supernovas. I thoroughly overreacted to Ash, and it's all because of what Glenn did to me.

I also hate myself for thinking I'm ready to be with Ash simply because I don't want to be with Glenn. I've proved I'm nowhere near ready, and I'm devastated I hurt Ash. The look on his face when I yelled at him is seared into my brain.

Although I would've much preferred to take a cab home, I was so angry when I left the bar I refused to justify the expense. Now, as I bump along in the bus next to an oversized man in serious need of a shower, I'm regretting my choice. But at least it's given me time to calm down and realize what a fool I am.

Somehow, I contain my tears until I enter my building. As I let myself into my apartment, my phone rings. I have no intention of picking it up, so I let the machine get it.

Soon Wendy's voice comes out of the answering machine. "Leslie, if you're there, please pick up." She pauses for a few seconds and then continues, "I know things didn't go well with Ash."

I snatch the phone up. "How do you know?" Maybe she does work for the CIA.

"He drove straight to Randall's and told him to call and ask me to check up on you. He's worried about you."

"

I yelled at the man, accused him of being ashamed of me, and made a spectacle out of both of us by storming out of the bar, yet he wants to make sure I'm okay? I fall onto my bed and let the tears flow freely.

"I messed up, Wendy." I sniffle.

"What happened?"

"What happened is I tried dating him too soon. I might be over Glenn, but I'm not over what he did to me."

"Oh, honey. Do you feel like talking about it?"

I tell her about the conversation. "I totally overreacted," I say when I finish.

"You did. But before we talk about that, let me assure you he's not ashamed of you. He's simply scared of his mother."

"Is she really that scary?"

"Yes. And he probably should've cancelled on Melissa, but that's not his style. Ash doesn't like letting people down. He sees it as a personal failure. It sounds like he was trying to do the right thing concerning both of you by not canceling on Melissa *and* telling you about it. He could've left you in the dark and you almost certainly would never have known."

I wind the phone cord around my finger. "Do you think he hates me?" I brace myself for her answer.

"Absolutely not. If he did, he wouldn't have cared about how you felt when you left the bar. He wouldn't have wanted me to check on you."

"Do you think he thinks I hate him?"

"No."

"How do you know?"

"Because he knows what you've been through with Glenn, and he's a reasonable man. And if he doesn't see sense, Randall will help him see it."

"Okay." I hope she's right.

"Now I have an apology for you."

"Why?"

"Because I practically forced you to date Ash. During our meeting yesterday I could see how good you are together and how much you both yearned to be with each other, and I allowed that to override the fact that you might not be ready yet. I'm sorry."

"It's not your fault." I shake my head even though she can't see me. "It was my decision."

"But I helped you get there. I almost literally pushed you into Ash's arms. Please let me take some of the blame."

"If you insist. And did you really use the word 'yearned'? Has anyone used that word since Victorian England?"

She giggles. "Maybe not. But I felt it suited the situation."

I'm silent for a moment. "So what do we do now?"

"I don't know. I can't tell you exactly what to do. We've experienced my terrible advice on that front. But you need to talk to him and figure out together where you go from here. Until this point, you've made most of the decisions, and Ash was forced to go along with them. It might be time to try working together to determine what's best for both of you."

"I have been ordering him around, haven't I?"

"Yes, and miraculously, he has mostly done what you demanded without argument, which is quite out of character for him. He must like you an awful lot."

I hope he still does after the way I treated him tonight.

"Why don't you give it a few hours and then call him?" she says.

"There's only one problem with your plan."

"What?"

"I don't have his number."

"How do you not have his phone number?"

I shrug. "It never came up. Do you have it?"

"No. He famously doesn't give people his home number. And it's unlisted, since he's at his parents' address. Part of me wonders if he even has a phone. Does he have *your* number?"

"No. What am I going to do?"

"I'll call Randall and give him your number. Then Ash can call you when he's ready. That is, if you're ready to talk to him. Are you?"

I blow out a long breath. "Yes."

Unsurprisingly, I'm a nervous wreck after I get off the phone with Wendy. I don't know how long it might be before Ash calls me. I also don't know for sure where he is or if Randall can track him down to give him my number.

I'm starving and, as usual, have nothing to eat, but I'm not leaving if Ash might call. So I call Domino's and order a pizza for delivery, feeling guilty for ordering from the chain when there are so many local pizza places around, but I'm desperate and it's cheap and easy.

While I wait for both the pizza and the call, I turn on the TV to distract me. I flip to NBC in time to watch the winning *Wheel of Fortune* contestant shop for her prizes at the end. I always hope someone will choose the ceramic Dalmatian, but I've yet to see it happen.

When the game show ends, a rerun of *Highway to Heaven* comes on. I watch mindlessly, mostly thinking about how it's difficult to imagine Michael Landon as anyone other than Pa Ingalls. But then again, for the first few years of *Little House on the Prairie*, I couldn't think of him as anyone other than Little Joe Cartwright from *Bonanza*.

My intercom buzzes, jerking me out of my reverie. I buzz the pizza guy up and dig through my purse for cash. We make the transaction, and I carry the pizza box over to my bed. No eating at the table for me tonight. I'm all about comfort, even if my sheets end up greasy.

I'm inhaling my fourth piece of pepperoni with mushroom when the phone rings.

fifty

. . .

The second Randall relayed Leslie's phone number to me, I rushed home so I could call her in privacy. Now, as I wait for her to pick up, my heart races. My entire body is tense as I sit on the edge of my couch with the phone to my ear. I have no idea how this conversation is going to go, but I'm relieved she wants to talk to me.

"Hello?" Her voice is full of uncertainty, which pierces my heart with a thousand tiny needles.

"Hi." I close my eyes. "Leslie—"

"I'm sorry," she blurts out. "I was out of line, and I'm so sorry I hurt you. I never want to hurt you, Ash."

My heart is leaping around like a frog on steroids. "I'm sorry, too. I should've canceled with Melissa. To be honest, I should never have started that ridiculous farce with her."

"No, you don't have to apologize," she says vehemently. "You did nothing wrong. In fact, you were trying to do the right thing by telling me, and I blew it all out of proportion."

"I did at least three things wrong. I didn't tell you about Melissa, I deceived my mom, and I didn't tell her about you. I'm going to talk to Mom about all of it on Saturday as soon as she gets back from her trip to see my aunt. I promise."

One thing I realized on my drive home was if Mom can forgive me for deceiving her, she'll have a hard time justifying not forgiving Leslie for deceiving me when we were kids. And if she doesn't forgive one or the other of us, well then ...

"You don't have to tell her if you're not ready." Leslie is breathing heavily, like she's trying not to cry. "And I don't know what you should tell her about me, anyway."

My heart stops, even though I'm sure she's about to say what I was going to suggest. I say it so she doesn't have to. "Because we can't date yet."

"No, we can't." She sounds sad but resolute. "I'm so sorry, Ash. I jumped the gun, and I ruined everything."

"Hey," I say gently, wishing I could comfort her with my touch instead of only my words. "This isn't your fault. I wanted it as much as you did. I could've said no—that we needed to wait longer—but I didn't. And you didn't ruin anything. We're still good. We simply need more time. Right?" I hope I'm not off about this.

"Right."

Most of the tension leaves my body with that one little word.

"I hate what Glenn did to you," I say. "And I want to help you get past it, but I don't know that I can. So I think we need to really limit our contact."

"I agree. Should we go back to our original plan?"

I grit my teeth. I don't want to say this, but I have to. "No. We shouldn't have any contact outside of work—not even letters."

Spending all our time wondering when the other person will write, analyzing what they wrote, thinking about what we'll write back, and writing the letters won't be helpful to our cause. I realize I'm making assumptions on her part, but based on her reaction to me tonight, she needs this break as much as I do.

Her voice catches when she says, "Okay."

"*Is* it okay?"

"Not really, but it's what we need. For how long?"

"As long as it takes." I pray it won't take very long, but I'm willing to wait forever if I need to.

"What about Shannon?" she asks. "He's coming to town specifically so he can meet you. He already bought his plane tickets."

"I thought about that. I think he should meet me, but you shouldn't be there—or Wendy, obviously."

"She'll be devastated."

Leslie huffs out a laugh and my body relaxes fully at the sound. I finally lean back against the couch and make myself comfortable.

"Oh, but she still needs to meet him. What if they're soulmates?" I tease.

"Yeah, right."

"Well, she loves you already, so why wouldn't the same happen with her and your twin?"

"I hate to admit that makes sense."

"Before Shannon meets me, feel free to tell him all of it—even about Melissa. I don't want you to think you need to hide anything from him for my sake." I pause, hoping I'm not about to cross a line. "But maybe don't tell him about what we did in your office ... or on the couch ... or in the elevator ... or in your hallway."

She giggles, and my heart soars. "Definitely not. Speaking of which, I don't know what you were smoking when you said you're not experienced and don't know how to be a boyfriend. With the exception of the Melissa thing, it's like you know what I want—what I need—without me having to say a word."

She's not wrong about that last part. I may not have dated or even kissed many women, but somehow my mind and body know what to do when I'm with her. I can also effortlessly flirt with her, which is new.

"You make me feel ...," I search for the right word, "... safe. I feel comfortable with you emotionally and physically in a way I never have before. These past few days, I felt like no matter what I did, even if it wasn't quite right, you wouldn't reject me. You might not like something I did, but you would still like *me*. But I also was afraid you wouldn't tell me if I did something you didn't like. In the future when something I do isn't right, or when something could be *more* right, I want you to tell me, like you did today." I pause. "Well, maybe not exactly the way you did today, but you know what I mean."

"Okay," she says softly. "The same goes for you. I want you to always feel comfortable telling me what you need. And please don't stop admitting when you've messed up—or confronting me when I've messed up. I promise I'll do my best to not react the way I did tonight."

"And I promise I won't hide things again like I did about Melissa. I want you to feel safe with me, too. I'm sorry I didn't make you feel that way today."

"But you did, Ash."

Did I only imagine that scene in the bar? "I beg to differ."

"Granted, I didn't feel great when you told me about Melissa, but my reaction was more about me than you. The thing that made me know without a doubt that my heart is safe in your hands is when my phone was ringing as I walked through my door after leaving you. I said some harsh things that hurt you, and the first thing you did was make sure I was okay." She sniffles. "That meant more than anything."

"I'm still sorry I didn't handle the Melissa situation better."

"I know you are, but you're fixing it, and that's what matters most."

My arms ache to hold her. "Remind me why I decided we shouldn't have any non-work contact?" That may have been my dumbest idea ever.

Leslie chuckles. "Because you're a much better man than Glenn could ever dream of being."

"Oh, yes. That's right. But not so much better that I'm not going to keep you on this call as long as I possibly can."

"You wouldn't have to try very hard to keep us on the line all night long. But we really shouldn't do that."

"If you insist," I say. "But before we hang up, tell me something funny that happened to you this week. I want us to end this call on a happy note."

"Oh, that's easy. I have the perfect story."

I smile and kick my feet up onto my coffee table. "Let me hear it then, Frank."

She chuckles. "We're back to Frank now, are we?"

"If that's okay with you?"

"Always. So when I left for work this morning, I met my neighbor—the one directly across the hall. She opened her door as I was locking mine. I think she'd been listening for me. Anyway, we exchanged basic info: names, occupations, why I moved here, and so on. Her name is Maud. She's a librarian and has lived in the building for decades, and she's sixty, maybe?" Leslie giggles.

"Why is it funny that she's sixty?"

"That's not what's funny. As I was telling her I needed to leave for work, she said, 'You and that young man of yours sure put on a show last night in the hallway.'"

"Oh, nooo." Heat creeps up my neck.

"Oh, yesss. She was watching us through the peephole!" Leslie lets out a full belly laugh. "She claimed she didn't watch the whole thing, but she heard us talking and couldn't resist taking a peek. I think we made her week. And I guess now we know to keep quiet in the hallway. I can't wait to meet the other neighbors." She giggles again.

I groan. "I don't think I ever want to meet any of them."

"Come on, it's funny!"

"If you say so."

"All right then, Grouchy Smurf, you tell me a funny story."

"Nothing funny ever happens to me."

"Well, does anything funny happen *around* you?"

"Hmmm." I wrack my brain because I can't let her down. "Oh! I've got it."

"Good. What?"

"You know Jay?"

"From your work? Unfortunately."

"Then you're going to love this." I grin. "He was rude to Annette this morning, which honestly isn't any different from most mornings. After lunch, she somehow attached a length of toilet paper to the back of his suit jacket without him knowing. He walked around the office all afternoon with toilet paper streaming out behind him."

Leslie laughs. "I wish I'd seen that. How long did it take him to figure it out?"

"He's not the most popular person in the office, so nobody

told him about it until Dad saw him late this afternoon. He was hopping mad. He said, and I quote, 'This is a place of serious business, not a carnival!'" I snort. "As if people walk around with toilet paper hanging off them at carnivals."

"You know, I'm not looking forward to meeting your dad someday, but I think I'll find him fascinating."

"Morbidly fascinating, maybe."

"I'm going to have fun messing with him."

I smile. "I hope you do." We could keep talking all night, but we shouldn't, so I say, "Okay, I'd better go."

"Wait a minute," she says.

"Yes?"

"You said Melissa recently moved back to town and needs some friends, right?"

"Yes. Why?"

"Because I recently moved to town and need more friends than Wendy. Do you think Melissa and I would get along?"

My jaw drops. "Are you serious? You want to be friends with Melissa?"

"Maybe. Do you think that's weird?"

"A little, if I'm honest. But I do think you might get along. You have several things in common." They both love baseball, they seem to have a similar sense of humor, and they're both coming out of long-term relationships.

"So can I have her number? I think her Saturday evening is about to open up."

fifty-one

· · ·

I feel energized after my call with Ash instead of devastated. It's not that I'm excited we put the brakes on our relationship yet again, but for the past month all I've thought about is the drama with the men in my life—first Glenn, and now Ash. And it's not that I won't still think about Ash, but since I now have no good reason to think about when he might call or write, or what I'll say to him in my next letter or when I see him, I feel an odd sense of freedom.

I surprised myself almost as much as Ash when I suggested I might become friends with Melissa. I can't hold a grudge against her for what she did to Ash when they were kids, considering what I did to him. And she shouldn't lose out on potential friend-ships because of my stupidity. Thanks to me, a friendship with Ash—and possibly Randall, too—is off the table for her unless I befriend her. The least I can do is meet her and see if we click.

Ash asked me to wait a half hour to call Melissa so he'd have time to contact her first and cancel their plans. In the meantime, I call Wendy to give her the update on my talk with Ash, and then I dial Aunt Star's number.

"You were right," I say when she answers. "It was too soon." I cry for the first time since I got off the phone with Ash.

"Oh, Les. What happened?"

I tell her all the details of the encounter at the bar and my phone conversation with Ash.

"Maybe it's good you tried it," she says. "Now you know without a doubt that waiting is the best thing to do. You won't wonder if you made the wrong decision."

She makes an excellent point. "Yeah, I think you're right. I don't feel nearly as stressed about it now as I did before."

"But you still want to date him down the road?"

"Definitely. Now, what do you think about me trying to be friends with Melissa?"

"I don't think there's any harm in it. Who knows? You might end up being best friends."

"Wouldn't it be funny if we did?"

"For sure. By the way, I got signed up for the Realtor conference, and Beckett is on board to come with me. I made us reservations at the Drake Hotel."

"Wow! That's fancy." And expensive. "Can I stay with you?"

"That's the plan."

"Excellent."

"It's good to hear you sound content. Our last few phone calls worried me a bit. I almost decided to drive up to see you this weekend. I still can, if you want me to."

Tears fill my eyes, but for once they're happy tears. "No, I'll be fine. But I love you for wanting to come take care of me."

"Promise you'll go out and do something fun this weekend."

"I will. Wendy and I are going shopping on Saturday, and I'm hoping Melissa can join us for dinner."

"Good deal. Okay, kiddo, I gotta run, but I'll talk to you again soon. Thanks for keeping me updated."

"Bye. Love you."

"You, too."

I don't know why I'm nervous about calling Melissa, but I am. When she doesn't pick up by the third ring, I think she won't answer, but then she does.

"Hi, Melissa?" I reply to her greeting.

"Yes. Who's this?"

I take a deep breath. "My name is Leslie Beckett. I'm—"

"Ash's Leslie."

I feel a prick in my chest. "I guess so. Yes. Did he tell you I might call?"

"No, but I did talk to him twenty minutes ago." She sounds courteous but guarded. I figure I should get to the point.

"Okay. I know he canceled on you for Saturday—because of me—and I want to make it up to you. He told me you recently moved back home to Chicago, and I'm new to the city, so I thought we should get to know each other. Would you like to go to dinner with me and a friend on Saturday?"

She's silent for a few seconds and then lets out a soft laugh. "I guess I can't bow out by saying I already have plans, can I?"

My heart sinks. "No, but I understand if you don't want to go. This is a totally oddball thing for me to do."

"I think it's kind of sweet. I can see why Ash likes you so much. I'd love to go to dinner with you and your friend. Thank you for asking me."

"Really?"

"Really. Now, where should I meet you and when?"

I sleep soundly for the first night in ages and wake up ready to face the day and whatever it might bring, though I hope it's uneventful for a change.

When I leave my apartment, I call out on a whim, "Good morning, Maud," and pause for a moment.

"Morning, Leslie," her muffled voice calls back from behind her door. "Have a good day."

"You, too."

It's a gorgeous sunny day, and the wind brings a welcome warmth with it instead of the chill of the past few weeks. This is one of those days when I wish I lived close enough to work to walk there, but since that's out of my budget, I convince myself the bus isn't too bad. At least I don't have to change buses anywhere and the ride only takes about fifteen minutes.

True to form, Wendy appears in my office soon after I arrive.

I cock an eyebrow at her. "I have a question for you."

"What?" She plops down in the purple chair.

"Do you work for the CIA?"

She stares at me and then lets out a burst of laughter. "What would you do if I said yes?"

"Not believe you."

"What if I said no?"

I tap my lips with my pointer finger. "Not believe you."

She grins. "Then I guess you'll have to wonder. What's on your agenda for today?"

"Tons of calls to get Diego some interviews and speaking engagements. We want to start pushing the narrative about him wanting to give back to this city that has welcomed him with open arms. And you and I need to meet in the next day or two to nail down our presentation for next Wednesday."

"Hmm." She twists her mouth. "Diego is going to be single soon, right?"

I roll my eyes. "Wendy, you will not be dating Diego Sanchez."

"Hey! I resent that!"

"First off, you signed an NDA before we looped you in on the foundation stuff. You can't ask him for favors."

"Um, excuse me? I don't have to ask anyone for favors … if you know what I mean." She actually winks at me. "Men come to me."

"Whatever. Secondly," I say with mock irritation, "are you throwing my brother out with yesterday's garbage, like you did to Ash?"

"I didn't throw Ash out." She flicks her hand. "I tossed him to you."

I raise an eyebrow at her again.

"Okay, fine," she says. "He never wanted me, anyway."

I study her for a minute.

"What?" she asks. "Why are you staring at me like that? It's creeping me out."

"If you knew he didn't want to date you, why did you keep him at the top of your list? Why did you act like a lovesick teenager in his presence? I saw how you acted that day at lunch."

"What would you say if I told you it's because I knew he didn't want to date me?"

My mouth falls open. "Wendy O'Halloran!"

She shrugs.

"Explain yourself," I demand.

"Two things," she says. "First, he presented a challenge. It's like neither my brain nor my body would accept that he didn't want me. The more he brushed me off and tried to avoid me, the more I wanted him. It was weird."

"I don't think that's weird. It's fairly normal."

"Hmm. I'll take your word for it. Then second, I knew my obvious crush on Ash kept a few guys here and at the law firm off my back. Since I wasn't interested in anyone else that was available, I figured why not keep it up?"

I lean forward. "Which guys are you talking about?"

"That's not important."

I narrow my eyes at her. "You said you weren't interested in anyone else that was available. What does that mean? Was there someone else who *wasn't* available?"

She reaches down and rubs the toe of her shoe like she's wiping off a scuff, but the cherry red patent leather is flawless. A slow smile spreads across my face when I get what she's not saying, though I don't understand why she's not saying it, considering how open she usually is about her feelings.

"Randall."

Her cheeks turn pink. "No."

I thrust a finger toward her. "Yes!"

"Fine. Yes." Her face is now the color of her shoes. "But he was dating Colleen."

"Not anymore." I consider her for a moment. "Why are you being so secretive and embarrassed by this? You were more than willing to let everyone know about your interest in Ash, and you've not been subtle about my brother, either. What gives?"

She sighs. "It's because everybody knows I had a thing for Ash. What if people think I have some weird brother kink?"

I laugh so hard I double over. "Wendy, it's not like you want to be with both of them at the same time." My laughter dies. "Do you?"

"No! The very second I knew about you and Ash and your pen pal past, my body and brain knew he was meant for you, and they stopped wanting him. Truly, Leslie. I no longer have anything but friendly feelings for Ash."

"I believe you. But since when do you care what people think about who you have feelings for?"

"I knew people made fun of my crush on Ash, and I didn't care." Her voice softens. "But this is different. I don't want my feelings for Randall to make him the butt of anyone's jokes. I don't want anyone to tease him about me."

I tilt my head. "You really care for him, don't you? It's not just a crush."

"It's not."

fifty-two

· · ·

On Friday morning, I arrive at work before six o'clock so I can talk to Carmela. I find her vacuuming in Randall's office. Since she can't hear my voice over the noise, I'm certain I'll scare her again, and I do. When she spots me, her hand raises to her heart. Then she shuts off the machine.

"Mr. Hamilton, I did not see you there."

"I'm sorry I scared you. I wanted to tell you I haven't forgotten about you and Javier. I've made some calls, and I'll be talking to a few more people soon about your situation. I'm very hopeful we'll be able to help you, but it might not happen immediately."

I hope I can get Diego's help. Even though we're not supposed to ask him for favors, I'd like to tell Carmela and Javier's story as part of our presentation to him next week, and my gut tells me he'll offer to do something about it.

She nods. "I understand. I am thankful for any help you can give us."

"Do you know others who have had problems like this? Issues with travel and immigration, whether the people are here legally or not?"

She hesitates before nodding. "Yes, many people. I know some who are scared to leave the country and go see their families because they are afraid what happened to Javier will happen to them."

"Okay. Thank you for telling me that. I hope we'll be able to help more people than Javier."

Carmela's hand goes to her heart again, but not because she's frightened. "That would be wonderful, Mr. Hamilton. But I feel that is asking too much."

"Again, you didn't ask. I'm offering." Even if Diego decides not to move forward with the foundation, I've learned enough about immigration issues over the past week that I know I have to do something about it—with or without him.

I'm about to ask if I can share her story with Diego when an idea comes to me so quickly, I can almost see the imaginary light-bulb over my head. "Carmela, are you free next Wednesday morning at ten o'clock?"

Her brow furrows. "I am usually sleeping then, but if you need something, I will be happy to help."

"Well, you'll be helping me, but you may also be helping your-self. Would you be willing to share your story about Javier with a few of my friends at a meeting on Wednesday?"

She thinks for several seconds and then nods. "Yes. If you trust these people, then I trust them. I will tell my story."

The rest of the day passes uneventfully, and before I know it, Saturday is almost here—or "doomsday," as Randall has been referring to it. He can't stop reminding me about my talk with Mom tomorrow.

He's at my place after work on Friday, which hasn't happened since he first moved back a year ago. A month after he came back, he met Colleen, and after that I saw little of him outside of work.

The Cubs are out of town, which means they're playing a night game, so we've tuned into WGN. We're watching the game while reminiscing about junior high and what happened to all our former friends, few of whom we still keep in touch with. Most of them left the area for prep school or college and haven't returned.

"What about those two girls Melissa was always with?" Randall asks from the couch. "What were their names?"

"Crystal and Shelley."

"Ah, yes. Crystal was the blonde."

"Yep."

He takes a swig of his beer and says nonchalantly, "I had a thing for her."

"Please tell me you're joking."

"What?" he asks defensively. "She was cute."

"And dumber than a bag of sticks."

"Like I cared when I was thirteen."

"Do you care now?"

"I do. I kinda even want a woman who's smarter than me … although she'd be a rare find." He chuckles at himself.

"I know a woman who is most definitely smarter than you. Goes by the name of—"

"Ashley." His tone is full of warning.

I don't heed it. "Nope, her name is not Ashley."

He grabs a coaster from the coffee table and flings it at me. I snag it with one hand and flip it back onto the table without a word.

"So Leslie and Melissa are going to dinner." I note he doesn't also mention Wendy's name, although he knows she's tagging along, too. "How do you feel about that?"

I sigh. "I'm okay with it, because even though Melissa completely understood why I had to cancel on her, I still felt bad. So if she and Leslie get along and become friends, hopefully that'll make this whole mess worthwhile. But, at the same time, …"

"They'll spend a good chunk of their time together talking about you," my brother finishes for me.

"Yeah." I don't love the idea of the two of them comparing notes on me.

"Get used to it. That's what women do. They talk about us, and there's nothing we can do about it."

His declaration makes me a little uneasy—not only the women-talking-about-us part, but also the stereotypical attitude he has about it.

"If I recall correctly, you and I have spent a good chunk of the past couple weeks talking about women."

"Touché."

Pounding sounds on my door.

"Speaking of women," Randall says.

"It's open," I holler.

Our sisters rush in, again holding a movie case. Sonya plops down next to me on the love seat and loops her arm through mine. Tonya sits on Randall's feet on the couch. He yanks them out from under her and sits up.

"What cringeworthy movie have you picked out to torture your brothers with, girls?" he asks.

"*Some Kind of Wonderful,*" Tonya replies.

Randall gags. "We're not watching that."

"Maybe you're not," Tonya pokes him in the chest, "but we are." She circles her finger around to encompass the rest of us.

"Nope," I say. "Not me, either."

Both girls gape at me and Randall laughs. "You can't wear him down tonight, ladies. It's two against two, and we're bigger and stronger."

He grabs the video from where Sonya set it on the coffee table and shoves it underneath him. I wince on his behalf. The situation can't be comfortable. Those cases have sharp edges.

Tonya reaches toward him, but Randall sticks his finger in her face. "If you touch my butt, I'm telling Mom."

How he thinks that conversation would go any worse for Tonya than for him, I don't know.

"Ew, gross," Tonya says with a shiver. "Like I have any intention of touching your butt."

A smug smile spreads across my brother's face as he links his fingers behind his head. "Now, let's all settle in and watch the Cubbies."

I can see what's coming next from a mile away, but I say absolutely nothing. Tonya's hand shoots out and tickles Randall's exposed armpit. When he jumps, her other hand snatches the video out from under him.

Randall curses, and Tonya points at him. "Ha! I'm definitely telling Mom about that." Our mother has zero tolerance for cursing, especially in the girls' presence.

"Ton-Ton," he uses the name Sonya called her when they were toddlers, "you wouldn't dare."

"I would … unless you watch this with us." She wiggles the video in the air far enough away that he can't grab it again.

He lets out a long-suffering sigh and then looks at me. "You're not going to help me out here?"

I shrug. "You're the one who got us into this mess with your potty mouth. Figure it out." Plus, I've found myself halfway enjoying the girls' movies lately, but I'm not about to admit that to any of them.

"Fine," he says, "but it better be a daaaaa…ng amazing kind of wonderful."

"Hold up," Sonya says. "There's one more thing you have to do to keep us from telling Mom about that word you said."

Randall closes his eyes and in a defeated tone, asks, "What?"

"Tell us who Ash has been kissing."

Sonya stretches up to peck my cheek, Tonya giggles, and Randall's eyes pop open. His gaze snaps to mine and I shoot eye daggers at him. He'd better have my back on this, even if I just failed to have his.

"Can't do it," he says to our sisters. "Brother code and all that."

"Fine," Tonya taunts. "I'm telling Mom."

"Fine," Randall mimics. "We're not watching your movie."

"Here's what's going to happen." I point at Tonya and then Sonya. "You two are not telling Mom anything." I point to Randall. "You are watching the movie." I ignore his groan, even though he did save me. "But every thirty minutes, we pause the movie and check on the Cubs game. If it's the ninth inning and a close game, we'll finish watching it before going back to the movie."

The girls stare at me.

"What?" I look back and forth between them.

Tonya says, "You never tell us what to do."

"He tells me what to do all the time," Randall protests. "He tells *everybody* what to do."

"Not us," our sisters say in unison.

"There's a first time for everything." I pat Sonya's leg. "Now go get me a drink."

fifty-three

. . .

"I have one rule for today," Wendy says when she arrives at my apartment Saturday morning. "We're not talking about the Hamilton boys or your brother. We are modern women, which means we should be able to spend a day together without talking about men."

"That works for me." It'll be a nice change. Wendy and I have spent a lot of time together in the past few weeks, but I know very little about her other than which men she's interested in. And she could say the same regarding me. "I'm a little ashamed of how much my love life has dominated our conversations."

"I have a feeling we'll be talking about Ash at dinner, though."

"Yeah, we probably can't avoid that, but I hope we can get to know Melissa, too."

"All right, the not talking about men starts … now." She plops down on my bed. "Why aren't you ready?"

"I've never done a shopping day in the city," I explain. "I don't know what to wear. Do I look casual or classy? Should I wear cute or comfortable shoes? And what about dinner? Are we coming home to change before we go?"

Wendy points at the bag she dropped on the floor inside my door. "We'll come back here. I brought my dinner clothes with me. That's when we're going to look classy. For now, look cute and for sure do comfy shoes. In fact, if you don't have any shoes that are both cute and comfy, that'll be the first thing on our list."

In the end, she chooses my outfit, and we head out to conquer the shops of Chicago. Our first stop is Filene's Basement, where we comb through the shoe department. I find some purple Keds on clearance that I think fit the bill, but Wendy disagrees.

"They're cute for a thirteen-year-old, not a twenty-five-year-old," she declares. "You need sexy cute."

"Sexy cute? I don't think that's a thing."

"It's a thing. It's something guys find sexy and girls consider cute."

"Sexy *and* cute *and* comfortable? Not gonna happen. We're more likely to see a unicorn galloping down Michigan Avenue."

Within minutes she finds me a pair of genuine leather kitten-heel wedges with a peep toe that are almost as comfortable as the Keds.

"What did I tell you?" she says as I model them in front of the mirror. "The heel gives you a little lift in the booty, which you honestly don't need, but it doesn't hurt. The peep toe is sexy, I think they're cute, and you claim they're comfy. Plus, they're on sale. What's not to love?"

"You think I can wear these the rest of the day?"

"No. You need to break them in before wearing them on an all-day shopping expedition. You know what else they'll be great for?" She doesn't wait for me to guess. "Baseball games when you're there for work."

She's not wrong. Melissa wore something similar at the game last week.

We spend the rest of the morning in the women's clothing department and then head to a little bistro for lunch. I would've missed the place entirely, as the nondescript entrance is right next to Bennigan's, which is overflowing with tourists.

As we sip our Clearly Canadians and wait for our soup and sandwiches, I ask Wendy about her family.

"As you know, I have two much-younger brothers. They're still teenagers."

I wonder exactly how old Wendy is. She hasn't said, but I'm guessing she's one or two years older than me.

"I know you're wondering how old I am, so I'm going to tell you, but you will not tell anyone else. Got it?"

"Got it."

"I'm thirty."

I try to keep my eyes from widening, but I'm unsuccessful.

"I'm going to take that look as a compliment," she says. "And yes, I realize I'm several years older than ... those people we're not talking about today, but I'm hoping that won't matter."

I don't know Randall that well, but I don't think the age difference would bother him. And I know for sure my brother wouldn't care.

"Anyway, my mom got pregnant in high school, they had a shotgun wedding, and then my father left when I was two. I don't remember him being in my life at all, although I've seen him on a few rare occasions throughout the years. Then Mom met my step-dad—who I call 'Dad,' because that's what he's always been to me—when I was six. It took him a couple years to convince her he wanted to marry a woman with a child. Actually, I helped convince her, because I was dying for him to be my dad. Then a few years later my brothers came along."

"Did you go to college in Wisconsin?"

"I came here. I went to Northwestern."

Again, my eyes widen.

"What?" she teases. "Don't think I'm good enough for Northwestern?"

"No, I ..." I actually don't know what I thought other than I was stereotyping her.

"Don't worry about it. My dad's a lawyer, and I was valedictorian. Put those two together, and it's a ticket for a good school."

I nod. "So did you stay in the Chicago area after graduating?"

"Keep your eyeballs in your sockets for this. I went to the University of Chicago and got my MBA."

"Wow." I'm seriously impressed.

"I worked part-time for a PR firm during grad school, and I

loved it. They hired me after graduation, and I was there full-time for more than five years."

Wendy's education and years of experience all help explain how she can afford a nicer apartment than I can. My salary is much better than it was in Peoria, but the cost of living is astronomically higher here.

The waitress brings our soup, and we spend a few minutes eating and talking about the restaurant.

Then I ask, "So how did you end up at Carter-Jenkins?"

"My old job was fine, but I didn't like some of the internal politics going on at the firm. I knew George's reputation and his desire to get his clients to do good things in the world, so I called him one day about seven months ago and told him why he should hire me. He did."

I laugh, because that doesn't surprise me at all. "You were your own PR rep."

"Indeed, I was. Oh! I completely forgot to tell you. Ash called me yesterday."

"We're not supposed to—"

She flaps a hand at me. "I know, but this is about work, so it's fine. You know the woman who cleans their office that got him started on this whole Diego Sanchez foundation thing? He asked her to come talk to Diego with us, and she said yes!"

"That was an excellent idea. Diego's going to have a hard time saying no with her there."

"My thoughts exactly. But that's not the main reason Ash asked her. He's hoping when Diego hears her story, he'll immediately help her husband."

My heart swells when I realize how Ash worked this out. "Since he's not allowed to ask Diego for favors, Ash thought he'd put the situation in front of him and let it be Diego's idea to help."

"He's a brilliant man."

"And a ridiculously kind one."

fifty-four

. . .

"Mom, can I talk to you for a minute?" I'm standing in her bedroom doorway as she unpacks her suitcase. Her flight arrived several hours late, and my nerves are almost shot.

"Of course. Come sit." She pats the bed next to her.

I feel like a little boy coming to confess to mommy when I sink down onto her flowered bedspread, but I'm not suggesting an alternative.

"You have your date with Melissa tonight, right?" She gives me a knowing look. "What time are you picking her up?"

"About that …"

She stops in the middle of pulling a shirt out of her suitcase. "Ashley Theodore Hamilton, what have you done?"

I stop myself from groaning. "I … when you told me about the dinner with the Teagues, I wasn't lying when I said I wasn't dating anyone."

Mom crosses her arms, the shirt still dangling from one of her hands. "I sense a 'but' coming."

"But there's someone I *want* to date, and it's not Melissa."

"Then who is it?" she demands.

"I'll get to that in a minute. Last Friday I was at the Cubs game, and I ran into Melissa. We talked about the dinner and discovered neither of us wanted to be set up. She recently broke up with a long-term boyfriend and isn't ready to date again, and

I'm interested in someone else. But we knew you and her mom wanted us to hit it off, so we pretended we did."

"Ashley—"

I hold a hand up to stop her, shocking myself as much as her. "Let me finish, please. We did hit it off—as friends. Afterward we decided it wouldn't hurt to go on a fake date so we could tell you we did and then maybe you'd ease up on us."

She narrows her eyes. "So why did you decide to come clean?"

"Partly because I felt bad for deceiving you, but mostly because of the other woman."

To my surprise, Mom gives a sharp nod of approval. "And who is she?"

"She works at Carter-Jenkins—"

"I knew it!" Mom jabs her finger at me. "You lied to me."

"I didn't. It's not Wendy—the woman Dad would've known about." I take a deep breath. "Do you remember my pen pal from when I was a kid?"

"Les? Yes. What does he have to do with this?"

I close my eyes for a moment. "Because it turns out Les isn't a boy." I flinch when Mom's hand goes to her stomach. "Leslie Beckett is a girl. Well, obviously, now she's a woman, and we're … well, it's complicated."

Mom puts her hands on the edge of the suitcase and grips it tightly while squeezing her eyes shut.

"You … I … Ashley, you have left me speechless for the first time in your life."

Then she straightens, crooks her finger at me, and heads toward the door. "Come with me. You're going to tell me this whole story, but I'm going to need a stiff drink."

I trail her downstairs and into the sitting room.

She prepares herself a gin and tonic at the wet bar and then takes a seat in one of the two chairs by the fireplace. "Sit."

I obey.

Mom tips her head. "Well?"

"When Leslie and I first started writing to each other, she thought I was a girl, and I thought she was a boy. We both assumed we got matched up with someone who was the same gender."

"That makes sense," Mom says, "considering your names can go either way. But from the way you said that, you figured it out at some point."

"I didn't, but she did."

Mom's eyebrows raise. "I see."

"About six months after we started writing, I finally sent her a photo. It was a family photo."

"I remember it."

I nod. "And then she knew. The girls were way too young to have been me."

"But how did you not know from her pictures?"

"She has a twin brother, Shannon. Both of them were in every picture she sent. I thought the boy was Les and the girl was Shannon."

"Why did she decide to not tell you the truth?"

"She was afraid I'd stop writing to her if I knew she was a girl, and by then we were growing attached to each other."

Mom gives me a probing look and I try not to squirm under her gaze. "Do you think you would've kept writing?" Her calm voice and demeanor are unsettling. I expected her to be livid by now.

"Maybe, but I can't say for sure."

"Believe it or not, I'm glad she didn't tell you the truth. I'm certain ten-year-old Ashley wouldn't have continued writing to a girl, at least not for long. You wouldn't have been able to keep it from Randall, and he would've teased you mercilessly. But you needed that pen pal." She reaches over and puts her hand on top of mine, which startles me.

"You're not like your siblings, Ashley. You don't wear your heart on your sleeve, yet you feel things more deeply than any of them. They're impulsive, but you think everything through from every angle before you act. You needed someone to talk to that understood you. I was surprised you wrote to Les for as long as you did, but I wasn't about to stop you, because I could see how much it meant to you."

Tears prick my eyes. "You're not mad at her?"

"Mad about something a ten-year-old did fifteen years ago that probably did you more good than harm? No." She finally removes her hand, sits back in her chair, and takes a sip of her drink. "Tell me how you met up with her again."

I describe our chance meeting at Sapori D'Italia but stop before telling her how I responded to discovering my pen pal was not a boy.

"You were angry, weren't you?"

I look at the fireplace instead of at her. "I might have stormed out of the restaurant."

"I see why you'd be upset with her," Mom says, "but you're obviously not anymore. How did that happen?"

"Her friend tricked us into meeting each other for dinner that night. Leslie explained the situation, I forgave her, and we started catching up on the past fifteen years of our lives. Things kind of went from there. We've had dinner a couple more times, and we're partnered on a work project." She doesn't need to know all the highs and lows of the last ten days.

"You said earlier that it's complicated. Is that because you work together?"

"Not really. It's because her boyfriend of several years broke up with her a few weeks ago when she moved here. She needs to get over that before we can date. But I don't want to date anyone else—not even fake date them."

"I wish you had told me this last week."

"I only ran into her the day before our lunch. I wouldn't have known what to tell you." Not that I would've told her. Who could've predicted she'd respond this way?

"So you really like her?"

I can't stop the smile—nor the blush—from spreading across my face. "I do."

Mom beams at me. "She makes you happy?"

"More than I've ever been."

My mother, whom I've seen cry exactly once in my lifetime, wipes a tear from her cheek. Then she puts her hand on mine again. "I'm glad you've found someone, Ashley. I can tell from the look on your face that you truly care for this woman."

I nod. If I say anything, I'm afraid *I'll* start crying, which will make this situation more surreal than it already is.

"On to more practical matters," she says. "There's no way to keep the pen pal thing from your father. He'll find out eventually, and he doesn't need to hear it secondhand. I'll tell him."

"He's not going to like it."

"I don't care if he likes it or not. He's going to accept it."

"If you say so." I have my doubts, though.

"Now, I need you to promise me one thing—no, two things."

"What?"

"One, that you do your best to make sure Leslie meets me before she meets your father or he finds out about her. We can't let him scare her off. And this meeting should probably be soon, considering she could run into him at the office. Can you make that happen?"

Since Leslie and I aren't supposed to spend any time together, that could be a problem. Even after the way Mom is responding now, I'm not sure I want to send Leslie to her alone. But maybe she doesn't need to be alone.

"What are your plans next Saturday night?" I ask her.

"Your father will be out of town, so I was planning to enjoy the peace and quiet."

I choke back a laugh.

"Go ahead and laugh," she says.

I do and then ask, "How about you meet Leslie and Randall for dinner?"

"Why would Randall be there instead of you?"

"Because Leslie and I have decided not to spend time together for a while."

"And you don't want to subject her to me all on her own?" she teases.

"Honestly, no."

Mom chuckles. "I understand. And where will you be during this dinner? Eavesdropping from the next table, wearing a ridiculous disguise?"

"No, I'll be at dinner with her brother."

Her eyebrows raise. "The twin?"

"Yes."

"She wants to make sure he approves of you?"

"More that he wants to make sure. She's not one to need anyone's approval."

"Aha. I think I like her already. Next Saturday it is. I'll talk to your brother to work out the details."

"What's the second thing?" I ask.

"What?" Her forehead wrinkles. "Oh, the other promise you need to make is that you won't tell anyone about this conversation—at least not how understanding I was. I have a reputation to uphold, you know." She winks at me.

I give her a solemn look. "I promise to not tell anyone other than Leslie."

"That's what I was hoping you would say."

fifty-five

· · ·

"Melissa," I stand and put my hand out to shake hers when she arrives at our table, "it's so nice to meet you. I apologize for not introducing myself to you last week at the game."

She grips my hand firmly but not painfully. "I could easily have introduced myself. But it's great to meet you now."

I introduce her to Wendy, and we take our seats.

"Soooo," she says, "I won't pretend this isn't awkward, but I'm glad we're doing this."

"Yeah? Same here."

"I'm here for the show," Wendy quips. "Ignore me. I'll be drinking my wine and taking notes for the Hamilton boys."

I elbow her. "You will not say one word about what happens tonight to either of them."

"You know Ash and Randall, too?" Melissa asks Wendy.

"Yes. Leslie and I both work for Carter-Jenkins PR. Ash acts as legal counsel for us, and I'm in their offices a lot, so I know Randall too."

Melissa turns her attention to me. "Are you and Ash officially dating?"

"No. My boyfriend of two years broke up with me when I moved here a few weeks ago, and I'm not ready to be in a serious relationship yet. I don't want casual with Ash, so we're waiting."

"I get that," she says. "My boyfriend of three years cheated on me a few months back, which instigated my move back here. I'm over him, but I'm not over what he did to me. The woman was in our friend group, though the two of us weren't close. And the rest of our friends picked the two of them over me. I'm still quite bitter about the whole situation."

"Dang," Wendy says. "That's rough. But good for you for taking control of your life and starting fresh. I admire that."

"Really? I often feel like people think I ran home to Mommy with my tail between my legs," Melissa admits.

"Do you have a good job?" Wendy asks, although she knows the answer.

"Yes, I work in the Cubs front office."

"Do you enjoy it?"

"I adore it."

"Do your parents subsidize your lifestyle?"

I don't know why I'm amazed by Wendy's brazenness.

"No. I'm determined to make it solely on my own."

My gaze is ping-ponging between the two of them. So much for Wendy being an observer.

"Then you did not run home to Mommy, and your tail is waving enthusiastically. You made a wise decision to move where you're close to people who love you but where you can also be independent and work in a job you love. If anybody has a problem with that, they're simply jealous."

Melissa has tears in her eyes by the time Wendy finishes. "Thank you for saying that."

I point my thumb at Wendy but look at Melissa. "PR master right there, my new friend. Wendy cares about people—not only about making them feel good or look good to outsiders. She reveals the true positive aspects of a situation, and if there's a negative side, she helps the person deal with it privately. She doesn't sweep it under the rug and hope for the best. That's why they pay her the big bucks."

Melissa nods. "You must be doing okay, too, if they gave you Diego Sanchez as a client."

"That was mostly luck. I've only been here a few weeks and had little on my plate, and I had some experience doing PR for a couple of Peoria Chiefs players at my old job." Since Melissa works for the Cubs, I know I don't need to explain to her who the Chiefs are.

"You were in Peoria before this?" she asks.

"Yes, and Galesburg before that, but I'm from Arkansas. Thus the accent."

"Galesburg? You went to Knox? Do you know Patrick Chamberlain?"

I laugh. "That's the first thing Ash asked me, too. We weren't friends, but he dated a girl on my hall. Ash told me they're married now."

"I met her and their baby at church on Easter," Melissa says. "So if you've only been here a few weeks, how did things happen so fast with you and Ash?"

"We were pen pals when we were kids."

"Oh yeah," she says, "our fourth-grade teacher set us up with pen pals. Mine's name was Karen. We wrote back and forth for a year or so." She pauses. "Wait a minute. You were pen pals with a *boy?*"

Wendy and I look at each other and laugh.

"What?" Melissa asks. "Tell me why that's funny."

I explain the misunderstanding and my resulting deception.

"Wow. So he wrote to you until he was fourteen, never knowing you were a girl?"

"Yep."

Her face goes slack, and she sets her wineglass down. "Did he tell you personal stuff?"

I know where she's going with this, and I decide it's best to come clean. "Like about 'Seven Minutes in Heaven'?"

Melissa buries her face in her hands. "Oh, noooooo."

"For the record, he's an amazing kisser." A shiver involuntarily runs through me at the memory of his kisses.

She peeks through her fingers at me. "I can't believe you want to be my friend, knowing I did that to him."

"Is it any worse than what I did to him?"

"I'd say yes," Melissa says. "You didn't humiliate him in front of the whole school."

"Ash explained what you told him at the game. If he can forgive you, so can I. You were a kid."

"Okay," Wendy cuts in, "I've been sitting here patiently and quietly while you've talked in broad strokes about what appears to be an absolutely fascinating story, but I can no longer sit in silence. I need all the details *now*."

"I'm going to let you tell it," I tell Melissa.

"Well, Wendy," she says, "to put it bluntly, I was the mean girl in junior high. I've repented of my ways and hopefully nobody sees me like that anymore, but I was a little twit as a young teen." She then tells us the entire story, sharing details Ash didn't tell me, including the part Randall played, which endears him to me even more.

Wendy is both riveted and incensed. "You made fun of the most respectful man I've ever known because you were embarrassed and thought *he* was going to be mean to *you*? I'm not sure I can be your friend now." She shakes her head. "I don't care what Ash and Leslie have decided about it."

"Hear me out," Melissa pleads. "I was so ashamed, especially because I liked Ash. But I was an idiot. Instead of apologizing to Ash like I should have, I avoided him for the rest of junior high, and then he left town for prep school, and until last week, I didn't see him again except from a distance at church on holidays. But in the end, I'm glad Randall lied, because it helped me become a better person. I decided I needed to be more like Ash and treat people with kindness. It took me a while to completely change my ways, but I like to think I have." She gives Wendy an imploring look. "Can you forgive me? Please?"

Wendy purses her lips for a moment. "I do, since you apologized to him and claim to have changed for the better. And yes, we can be friends."

From what I've learned about Wendy over the past few weeks, I'm not surprised she forgives as easily as she changes her mind on other matters.

"Thank you." Melissa takes a sip of wine and says, "Now tell me about Randall. He's not dating anyone, right?"

It's surprising the topic didn't come up last Saturday, but

maybe he was still dating Colleen at the time. Though if he was, wouldn't she have been at the dinner, too?

Wendy kicks me under the table, and I try but fail not to flinch.

"What?" Melissa looks back and forth between the two of us.

I can't tell her the real reason we're being weird, but I can give her something. "He and his girlfriend recently broke up." I decide not to explain why, even though it's eerily similar to her own situation.

"Oh." She doesn't hide her interest. "Like how recently?"

"Within the last week or so."

"Hmmm." She sounds intrigued. "Not that I'm ready to date again anyway, but it's nice to dream, you know?"

I avoid looking in Wendy's direction. This could get very awkward if both of my friends have a thing for my future boyfriend's brother.

"Yeah," I say. "I think he's taking a break from dating for a while, too." I don't know that for certain, but it's an educated guess. It's time to change the topic from the Hamilton men, so I say, "Tell us about yourself, Melissa."

fifty-six

. . .

"**A**re we ready?" I ask my brother, Wendy, Carmela, and Leslie on Wednesday morning. We're in the conference room at Carter-Jenkins, waiting for Diego Sanchez and Bobby Jacobs.

"I am," Wendy says. "I don't know how he can turn this down, unless he's completely heartless."

Leslie puts a hand on Carmela's shoulder. "Are you feeling okay about everything?"

Carmela sucks in a shaky breath but nods.

"Are you sure?" I ask her. "Because you don't have to do this."

"I am positive, Mr. Hamilton. I need to do this not only for my Javier but also for all the others who need help."

After Carmela agreed to speak to Diego, I got permission from Bobby Jacobs to have her sign an NDA so I could tell her what she needed to know to get her up to speed on our proposal. Not only did she agree to talk to Diego, but she also provided excellent input on the needs and some potential solutions.

At precisely ten o'clock, George Carter ushers Diego and Bobby into the room. George plans to stay for the presentation, which should help sell it to the two men.

Leslie makes the introductions, I offer the men a drink, and we're ready to begin.

"Gentlemen," Leslie says, "we asked you here today because we believe Mr. Sanchez—"

"Diego," the man himself inserts. "Call me Diego—all of you. Please."

We all nod.

Leslie continues, "We believe Diego is a man of both integrity and generosity. Diego," she focuses on him, "we know you love the people of your home country, and after meeting your cousins at the game, we discovered how you helped them immigrate to and settle in your adopted country. Because of your connections and financial resources, you could aid them in a way most people couldn't. Our proposal is that you create a foundation in your name to help other immigrants in ways they can't help themselves. And we have one of those people here with us."

Everyone is silent for a moment.

"Ash?" Leslie prompts.

I'm so distracted by Leslie's confidence and mere presence that I missed my cue to pick up where she left off. I jerk to attention. "Yes. I first had the idea for this foundation a few weeks ago when I was talking with Carmela," I motion toward her, "one of the cleaners at our firm. She told me about a situation that left her and her family feeling hopeless and helpless, and she'd like to share her story with you."

All eyes shift to Carmela.

She sits up straight and looks Diego in the eye. "Thank you for meeting with us, Mr. Sanchez."

"Like I said, call me Diego. And you may speak to me in Spanish if that is helpful."

Carmela glances at me and I nod in agreement, but she says, "Thank you, Mr. … Diego, but I would like to speak in English so everyone here can understand what I am saying."

Diego nods his approval.

"My name is Carmela Reyes, and I am an American citizen. My parents legally immigrated here to Chicago from the Dominican Republic when I was a child. We have all become naturalized citizens. On a trip back to our homeland when I was sixteen, I met my husband Javier. Three years later, we married, and he moved here legally as my spouse. He has not yet applied to become a U.S. citizen because he says he needs more time to make sure he wants to denounce his Dominican citizenship. We have always carefully filled out the paperwork for his green card and sent it in on time, and he should be in good standing with the U.S. government." She takes a deep breath. "Several months ago his mother got very sick. He went back to see her, and God saw to it she recovered from her illness." She makes the sign of the cross.

Carmela continues, "But when Javier tried to return home, he could not do so. They say there is some mix-up with the paperwork, but there should not be, and nobody can tell me what to do to fix it. Our two young sons are distraught and afraid their papa can never come home again. Mr. Hamilton noticed my distress one morning and asked me to tell him what is wrong. He promised to help me, and I believed him. He is a man with much money and power, and he is a *good* man. I know he will help me. But what about all the other people who do not have a Mr. Hamilton? What happens to them? Mr. Diego, I ask you to please consider the plan these kind people have put together that will help people like me."

Diego stretches a hand across the table to her, and she reaches her own toward him. He clasps it between both of his and says in Spanish, "Carmela, I will do everything in my power to get Javier home to you and your sons. And I'm excited to hear about this plan. Did you help create it?"

She nods, eyes wide.

"Good. Then I know it will be excellent." He lets go of her hand, sits back, focuses on Leslie, and says in English, "Hit me with it, Lady Leslie."

When Diego and Bobby leave the room several hours later, tears are glistening in all three women's eyes, and I feel a pricking behind my own. Diego has agreed to it—all of it—and has more ideas than we proposed.

George says, "I've never seen the likes of what just happened in this room. Well done, all of you. Countless lives will be changed because of what you're creating here." Then he shakes all our hands and leaves us in our shell-shocked states.

I decide in that moment I want to be like George. I want to create and leave a legacy like what he's doing here at Carter-Jenkins, not to mention what Diego is doing. Not once during the entire meeting did Diego or anyone else refer to how this foundation could affect his standing in the world—for better *or* for worse. It'll bring some very positive press, but not all of it will be. Some people won't like what he's going to do. However, the man doesn't seem to care about any of that.

Carmela worked overnight and then came straight here afterward, so I know she likely hasn't slept in more than twenty-four hours. She must be exhausted, but she was full of energy throughout the meeting. She filled in gaps, added her thoughts and opinions, and dared to challenge Diego on a few issues.

When our eyes meet, tears stream down her face. "He is going to help us," she says. "He really is."

Leslie moves to Carmela and wraps an arm around her. "Yes, and it's in no small part because of you."

Wendy takes a turn hugging Carmela, and Leslie mouths to me while pointing to Carmela, "He's going to hire her." Then she points at me and smiles, kicking my heart into overdrive. "And you."

fifty-seven

. . .

I want to throw my arms around Ash so badly I physically ache. To distract myself, I offer to walk Carmela out.

"We have a car coming for her," Ash says. "Let me call and tell them she's ready."

He makes the call from the phone in the corner of the room, and I can't keep my eyes off him.

Carmela whispers in my ear. "You love each other, don't you?"

My head snaps around to face her. "Wh-what?"

"I can tell," she says.

I close my eyes, internally groaning at how obvious we must have been, though we avoided looking each other in the eyes as much as possible.

"Do not be ashamed." She places her hand on my arm, and I open my eyes and turn to fully face her.

She says, "I do not think the men could tell. But I saw the way you looked at each other when you thought nobody else was looking. The pride on your faces—it made my heart smile. Mr. Hamilton deserves a good, smart woman like you."

My face heats, and I look at the floor. "I care for him very much. We … it's complicated." And I'm not sure I'm ready yet to admit to myself that I love him.

"Can you make it not complicated?"

"We're working on it."

Carmela can't be more than a few years older than me, but she seems much older and wiser … and stronger. Not being able to spend time with Ash this past week has been brutal, but I'm sure it's nothing compared to what she's feeling.

"I can't imagine how hard it is for you to be apart from your husband." I hug her again. "I admire your strength."

"Me, strong?" She laughs. "No. I cry every day. Many women are much stronger."

"You cry because you miss your husband and maybe because you feel powerless," I say, "not because you're weak. I saw today how strong you truly are. You asked a very rich and powerful man for what you need and what many in your community need. That's not for the weak of heart."

"It's not," Ash says from my side. "You were impressive, Carmela." He smiles at her and then turns his gaze on me. "As were you, Leslie."

Heat rushes up my neck again, and Carmela giggles. Ash looks back and forth between the two of us, no doubt wondering what's going on, but we don't enlighten him.

"You ready to go home?" he asks Carmela. "The car will be here in a few minutes. I'll walk you downstairs."

Carmela says her goodbyes to the rest of us and the two of them leave the room.

"Shall we take a short break until Ash gets back and then debrief?" I ask Wendy and Randall.

"Think you can handle it without me?" Randall asks. "I need to get back before Dad realizes I've been gone more than half the day. I'm not sure how I'll account for these non-billable hours."

Wendy's eyebrows raise. "Your dad doesn't know you're here?"

He shakes his head. "And he doesn't know the real reason Ash is here, either. He's going to lose it when he finds out what we've set in motion. I fear for Ash's job, honestly, and his home."

"I'm sure it'll all be okay," I say. How can his dad be that upset with what we're helping Diego do, even if he doesn't fully agree with it?

"I'm sure it won't, and Ash wouldn't disagree. He told you

Dad's not a fan of immigration, but that's a gross understatement. He hates immigration with a rabid passion unless he can somehow exploit it. Exactly what Dad will do when word gets out about this, I don't know, but it won't be good. Ash is going to keep my involvement quiet, but even if Dad finds out, I don't regret being part of this, and I never will."

I collapse into a chair. "Why didn't Ash tell me this?"

"Probably because he doesn't care what Dad will do. He wants this to happen more than anyone."

My stomach clenches. I need to talk to Diego about potentially hiring Ash, and soon. I no longer care about the no-asking-for-favors clause, and I don't think Diego will either.

"Sorry to leave you ladies on such a down note," Randall says, "but I gotta go. Thanks for letting me be part of this." He stands, pats my shoulder, squeezes Wendy's, and heads out.

"Leslie, these men …" Wendy is rarely at a loss for words, but she is now.

"They're pretty amazing, aren't they?" I'm so proud of Ash for standing up for what he knows is good and right, even though it may cost him his job.

We both sit quietly as we process everything that happened today until Ash appears in the doorway. His eyes lock on me, move over to Wendy, and then back to me.

"What's going on?"

"Come in and shut the door," I say.

He does, and then he sits across from me. "What's with the change in mood?"

"Discovering you might lose your job and home over this," I explain, my eyes full of tears.

Ash pounds his fist on the table. "Dang it, Randall."

"Don't get mad at him," Wendy says. "He loves you, Ash, and he knows we care about you, too. We needed to know, although I doubt there's anything we can do about it."

Ash shakes his head. "No, there's not. I don't intend on telling Dad about this, but it won't be a secret forever. He's going to find out eventually, and then I'll have to pay the price, whatever it is.

Regardless of what kind of creative punishment he decides to mete out, I'll never wish I wasn't a part of this."

I suddenly realize Ash and Randall aren't the only ones who might be punished for this project. "What about Carmela?" I ask, a knot forming in my stomach all over again. "What if your dad finds out she was involved?"

"It doesn't matter if he does. I talked to George about the situation yesterday. He's hiring her. She gave me her resignation letter this morning. I'll make sure HR gets it by the end of the day. She starts here on Monday, at double what Dad was paying her."

Carmela is right. I love this man. He's kind and thoughtful and smart and may well have sacrificed his career and home for something he believes in. My heart races and my lungs don't know what to do in response to this revelation.

Wendy, oblivious to the emotions swirling inside me, says, "I bet Diego will hire her out from under George. He was extremely impressed by her."

"So was I," Ash replies. "She was meant to do more than clean offices. She should be running one. After seeing her in action, I bet George will figure out a different position for her than cleaning."

It's my turn to say something about Carmela, but my lungs still won't function properly. Ash and Wendy are both giving me concerned looks, so I cough and squeak out, "I think I need some water."

Ash strides over to the food and drink table set up on the side of the room and pours me a glass of water. He places it in my hand and then lightly brushes his fingertips across my shoulder before circling the table to his chair again. I close my eyes and revel in the brief contact. When I glance at Wendy, her eyes narrow at me. I look away from her.

"We ready to go over next steps?" Ash picks up his pen.

I nod firmly and set my glass on the table. "Let's do it."

fifty-eight

. . .

"I might not have the power to get my wife sent out of the country," Diego Sanchez says over the phone, "but Javier Reyes will be back home where he belongs by Monday."

My mouth drops open and it's a few seconds before I can reply, "Diego, that's …"

"The most amazing thing you will hear today? Yes, it is, Ash Hamilton."

"How did you get that done so quickly?" It's eight o'clock on Thursday morning. The man didn't know Javier existed twenty-four hours ago.

"I have some friends in the State Department." I can hear the smile in his voice.

"Apparently."

"Now that I've taken care of that, I need you to do two things for me."

"Anything." I lean back in my chair, no idea what he's going to ask, but trusting he won't ask me to do anything I won't want to do.

"First, come up with a list of people who could run this foundation of mine. I'm asking Leslie to do the same, and Bobby and I are making our own lists. Send it to me by Monday."

"I can do that." I wonder if it's ethical to put my name on the list, particularly because I'll almost certainly be without a job soon.

"Second, and more importantly, tell Leslie Beckett you love her, do whatever you need to do to make sure she knows you mean it, and put the poor woman out of her misery."

My heart stops. "What?"

"You heard me. I saw the way she longed to touch you and how you undressed her with your eyes every chance you got. The sexual tension in that conference room was ..." He makes an explosion sound. "Do something about it, man. Put us *all* out of our misery. Nobody needs to experience that again."

"Diego, I apologize if I wasn't professional in that meeting."

"Oh, you were professional. Too professional. Stop it. Take that woman to dinner, take her to bed, fly her to Paris for the weekend, whatever. I don't care. Do something other than look at her like she's the most precious thing you have ever seen."

I sigh and decide honesty is the best policy here. Diego's not going to let this go. "I want to, but it's—"

"Complicated. I know. Bobby told me. Under duress, you understand. He is usually a vault, but I have my ways. I am ordering you, as your new friend and co-conspirator in the Diego Sanchez Foundation, to uncomplicate it. I will check back in a week to make sure you have accomplished this mission. If you haven't, I will talk to the lady myself. Got it?"

If the man is going to be this pushy, maybe I don't want to work for him. "Diego ..."

"Okay, fine. I'm meddling. It's your life. Do what you want. I will not force you to do anything. But think about what I said, yes?"

"Yes."

"I like Leslie. I like you. You are both good people and extremely smart. This foundation the two of you dreamed up is going to make many, many people happy. Now go make yourselves happy. You want to be happy, Ash Hamilton?"

"I do."

"You will be happiest when you make her happy. This I have

learned … though you might not know it from the state of my marriage. But I am right. Believe me."

"I do." There's nothing I want more than to make Leslie Beckett happy.

"My prediction is I will hear you say those two little words in front of a preacher within the year. I would bet my new foundation on it. And if I'm not invited to hear you say those words to your Lady Leslie, I will never forgive you."

"What are you going to do if Dad fires you?" my brother asks from across the table at McConnell's Pub after work. He's on his second beer, and I'm on my second order of fish and chips.

"Somebody will hire me." I'm not worried about it.

"Somebody that's not afraid of repercussions from Dad? Good luck with that. You might need to move to Des Moines."

"I don't want to work for anyone who's scared of hiring me because of Dad."

"You make a good point, but that still doesn't conjure up the existence of someone who's not terrified of our father."

I know at least one man who would have no fear of Dad. And I'm counting on Leslie to put my name on the list she sends to him by Monday.

My brother studies me. "You want Diego to hire you, don't you?"

I drum my fingers on the table. "I've thought about it."

"Then tell him."

"I can't."

"Why? Because of that stupid NDA clause? Whatever. He won't care. Tell the man you want to run his foundation. He would appoint you in a heartbeat."

I shake my head. "I can't do it. I can't ask him to do that."

"Ashley, you need to ask for what you want in this situation, like you do in most other areas of your life. Diego Sanchez is the kind of man who responds to straightforwardness. In fact, part of me thinks if he wants to hire you, but you don't put your name at the top of the list you're making for him, he *won't* hire you simply because you didn't go for it. He wants somebody who goes after what they want. He knows you'll jump through hoops to help other people get what they want or need—that's what this foundation is all about. But I think he also wants someone who's not afraid to stick up for themselves."

"You really think I should do it?"

"Yes. And what do you have to lose? He won't punish you for asking for what you want. If he doesn't want to hire you, he won't. But he won't hold it against you."

My brother is right. There's no reason I shouldn't ask Diego for the job.

I call Diego at the Drake first thing Friday morning, hoping he hasn't left for the ballpark yet.

"Ash Hamilton, are you calling to tell me you completed your Lady Leslie mission?"

"Not yet." I've decided to wait until after our respective dinners tomorrow night to talk to her. I feel like those conversations will help us figure out how to best move forward together. "I'm calling about the other thing you asked me to do."

"You have a list for me? You can fax it over here to the hotel."

"No need. There's only one name on it," I say with as much confidence as I can muster.

"Oh, yes? And whose name would that be?" His tone reveals he already knows.

"Mine."

"Ah, and why should I hire you?"

I knew he would ask that, and I'm prepared. "Because I was put on this earth to do work like this. I've always wanted to use my power and position to help people, and this is the perfect opportunity. I have the skills, education, and drive it'll take to not only set up this foundation but also to run it. In addition, I'm fluent in Spanish."

"Will you stay with me forever?"

"I'm not going to ask you to marry me, if that's where you're going with that," I joke. "And I don't intend to stay with the foundation forever. But I'll stay long enough to ensure it's running smoothly and effectively, and I plan to train up someone to take my place whenever I feel it's the right time to leave. And I believe that person should be from the immigrant community, as should most of the other employees." I doubt it's lost on him that I'm speaking as if the job is already mine. Something tells me he'll appreciate that.

"I can guarantee I won't be able to pay you as much as your father does."

"I don't care."

"All right, Ash Hamilton. I'll think about what you said and get back to you soon."

fifty-nine

. . .

On Friday afternoon, I know I need to finish my list for Diego, but there's only one name on it. Even though Ash is the only person I want to recommend for the position, I don't know anyone else I think would be a good fit—especially not anyone in the area. Diego wants the foundation to be headquartered in Chicago, and I don't know many people here yet.

Finally, I decide to make Ash the only person on my list, and I also write a letter explaining why I think he's the man for the job. When I leave work, I walk the few blocks to the Drake and drop it off at the front desk to be delivered to Diego's suite.

Then I catch the bus home, hoping I'll arrive before my brother does.

I don't. He's standing outside the door with his backpack when I approach the building from the bus stop. The second I spot him, he looks up, and I run to him. He spreads his arms wide, and I drop my briefcase and hurl myself into them. He squeezes me tight and then cups my shoulders and sets me far enough away that he can look me in the eye.

"Why are you crying?" He brushes a tear from my cheek.

"I'm so happy to see you." I swipe more tears away. "I love you so much." I hug him again.

"Love you, too. Now can we go inside? This wind is brutal."

"Wait until tomorrow," I say as I lead him inside. "A cold front's moving in."

Shannon takes my briefcase from me and carries it upstairs. "What are we doing tonight?"

"Going to dinner with my friend Wendy. Then we'll see what else we feel like doing. Maybe go dancing, or if we don't feel like it, we might go back to her place to watch a movie. She has a couch."

"Oooh, fancy."

I shoot him a grin as I unlock my door. "I know. We'll get to experience how the other half lives."

"This isn't a set-up with me and your friend, is it?" He sets his backpack and my briefcase on the floor and then dives onto my bed.

"You have a problem with that?"

"Not if she's gorgeous." He smirks at me.

"She's a redhead." I head to my closet to pick out something to wear for dinner.

He sighs dramatically. "It'll be instant love then."

I laugh. "She's great, and I honestly don't know if it's a set-up or not. I know you'll like her, but she has a thing for Ash's brother."

He holds up his fists. "Could I beat him in a fight?"

"Nope. He has several inches and a good thirty pounds on your puny little butt."

"Hey, I have an excellent butt, thank you very much."

"Ugh. Stop. I don't want to think about your butt." I pull a shirt and pair of jeans out of the closet.

"You brought it up."

I head into the bathroom to change but leave the door cracked so we can still hear each other. "What do you want to do tomorrow?"

"Is it too late to get Cubs tickets?" he says. "Or we could try to buy some off the street."

"We won't have time to go to the game, get back here, change clothes, and get to dinner on time."

Ash is planning to meet Shannon at a restaurant near enough

to the apartment that he can walk there, while Randall will pick me up and drive me to Evanston to meet his mom.

I haven't yet told my brother about Diego Sanchez, and I'm about to when he says, "I still think it's weird that I'm going to dinner with Ash while you go to dinner with his brother and mom. Why are we doing this again?"

I stick my head out the crack in the door. "You're the one who demanded to meet Ash. You don't get to complain about the situation." I disappear back into the bathroom.

"Still. It's weird."

I finish changing and then make myself as comfortable as I can in the easy chair, since my brother is sprawled across my bed.

"Yes, it's weird. But it's what we need to do for now, okay? This whole thing has been a little strange, but we're muddling through as best we can. Go with it, please."

"All right. I'll be fine. What time are we meeting your friend?"

"We don't need to leave for a half hour or so."

He nods. "Anything exciting happening at work?"

"As a matter of fact, yes."

"Oh, yeah?"

"I have a famous client. I had to sign an NDA, so I can't give you details, but I can tell you who it is."

"So it's somebody I've heard of?"

"It's Diego Sanchez."

He sits up. "Excuse me, what? How am I only now hearing of this? And why can't he get us tickets to the game tomorrow?"

"Like I said, I can't talk about it, and I can't ask him for tickets. It's in the contract."

"Let me get this straight. You work with Diego Sanchez. You've met one of my all-time baseball favorites. You failed to tell me this while you claim to love me 'so much.' We shared a womb, and you betray me like this?"

"I'm sorry, Shan. I should've told you. I meant to, but with all this stuff with Ash, it's taken a back burner in my mind."

"Aw, Les, I'm sorry. You've been through a lot. But can you tell me what Sanchez is like? Is he a jerk? Does he have a gigantic ego?"

"I can honestly say he's a good man. Yes, he has an ego, but what famous athlete doesn't? He's friendly, and he's an extremely generous person."

"Then he should be fine giving us tickets to tomorrow's game."

"Shan—"

"I know. I'm sorry. I'll leave it alone." He flops back down onto the bed. "Diego Sanchez. Wow."

We've been with Wendy for fifteen minutes, and my brother is one hundred percent smitten. The two of them are getting on like long-lost best friends. I don't think I've said more than ten words since I introduced them, and they haven't noticed.

Wendy giggles at something Shannon says, and my attention goes to her face. She's looking at him with more than casual interest, so she must not be as attached to Randall as I thought. But who knows with her? I hope she doesn't end up breaking my brother's heart.

"Have you met Diego Sanchez?" Shannon asks Wendy and then points his thumb at me. "This one didn't tell me about him until today. Can you believe that?"

"Shush," I say. "Keep your voice down."

"Yes, I've met him," Wendy says. "We had a big meeting with him on Wednesday."

"Wendy," I warn. She's already halfway through her second glass of wine, and her tongue is loosening.

"Whoops. Sorry. Not supposed to talk about it."

"Talk about what? What was this big meeting about?" Shannon asks her, purposely avoiding my stare.

Wendy zips her lips. "Can't tell you." Her gaze shifts to me. "Did you tell him to hire Ash?"

My brother turns wide eyes to me. "Hire Ash to do what?"

I jab my finger at her. "Wendy O'Halloran, stop talking about Diego Sanchez this second." I turn my focus to my brother. "Shannon Beckett, forget you heard any of that."

He raises an eyebrow at me and then pours more wine into Wendy's glass. "Drink up, Wendy. And then tell your new best friend Shannon everything."

I pinch his leg under the table, but he doesn't react.

Wendy smiles seductively at him and says, "Wanna know another secret? I call you 'Sexy Shannon,' and it drives your sister absolutely bonkers."

Shannon bursts into laughter as I drop my head into my hands and groan.

sixty

· · ·

Shannon isn't the male version of Leslie, but there are some similarities. His hair is dark, while hers is blonde, but their eyes are the same shade of brown. Their mouths are carbon copies. And they're both easy for me to talk to. I intended to be honest with Shannon about everything, even if he asked me highly personal questions, but I thought I'd have to force myself to open up to him, like I have to do with almost everyone. I was wrong.

He asked how I felt when I found out the truth about Leslie, and I told him how my feelings changed throughout that day. He wanted to know if I've had second thoughts about dating her with all we've been through in the past couple of weeks. I said I haven't and never will.

I'm not surprised by anything Shannon says until he asks, "Why might Diego Sanchez want to hire you, and why would my sister want him to? I thought you worked for your family law firm."

My eyebrows raise. "Leslie told you about the Sanchez thing?" I know they're close, but I'm shocked she would break the NDA.

"No, she refused to. Wendy let it slip that Leslie was going to tell him to hire you, but she didn't say for what. Are you not going to tell me, either?" He pops a fry into his mouth, appearing indifferent to my response, but his piercing look informs me he's anything but.

I shake my head. "No." I give no excuses, because he should understand why.

He nods and swallows the fry. "Good. That's what I was hoping you would say, even though I'm dying to know."

I chuckle. "So I passed the integrity test?"

"That one, at least." He smiles back, and seeing Leslie's smile on his face disorients me for a moment.

"But," I finally say, "I'll tell you I don't intend to stay at the family firm much longer. Leslie knows this. My father is *not* a man of integrity, and I've lost the desire to be associated with the things he and his firm stand for—or against. Not that it ever truly was a desire of mine. And yes, there's the possibility of working for Sanchez, but even if that doesn't pan out, I plan to leave as soon as I can find another job, or sooner if necessary."

"You would quit your job without having another lined up?"

I know what he's getting at. "Yes. Some things are more important than making money. But I have savings, and I'm not lazy. I'll find another job. And to put your mind at ease, I have no intention of mooching off your sister—ever." I point my fork at him.

"Glad to hear it."

"Anything else you want to know about me?"

"I can guess you don't especially get along with your dad, which might not be a bad thing. What about your mom and siblings? Do you get along with them?"

"I do. People have been known to call my mom scary. She's one of those people who expects you to do what she says, when she says it, and how she says it. That can make for some tense moments, and I'll be the first to admit I often do what she wants even if I don't want to, simply because it's easier than fighting her. But mostly our relationship is peaceful, and she always has my back when I need her to."

"She doesn't sound much different from most moms I know."

I nod. "My two sisters are in high school, and they're typical teen girls. I spend a lot of time with them, and I'd even call them friends now, which is weird. They're not little kids anymore."

"I feel the same about Cynthia," Shannon says. "It really is strange. What about your brother—Randall, right?"

"Yes. He's a year older than me. We were close as kids and then drifted apart a bit as teenagers and even more when we went off to different colleges and law schools. But since he's been back in town the past year, we've spent a lot of time together, and he's my closest friend. I'd do anything for him, and he'd say the same. He loves Leslie, too."

The moment the words leave my mouth I realize what I said, and while my heart races, I keep my face passive, hoping Shannon didn't notice.

He did. "You love her?"

I do. "I didn't mean to say that."

"But you meant it?"

My pulse pounds in my temples. "She should be the first person to hear it, not you. No offense."

"None taken. I get it. But you don't think it's too soon?"

"Can you put a timeline on falling in love? And can you control it?" I sure can't—not with Leslie. I love her with all my being, and I can't imagine there will ever be a time when I won't.

"No. And no," Shannon admits.

"I understand you don't want your sister to get her heart broken again. And I never want to hurt her, though I can't promise I never will. But Leslie is a wise and strong woman. She'll make the decision she feels is best for her, whether that means loving me back or walking away from me. She gets to decide who she gives her heart to. I can't make that choice for her, and neither can you."

We hold each other's gaze for several seconds until he nods. "I can't argue with that."

"What was Glenn like?" I hope knowing a little about him might help with understanding what Leslie is dealing with.

Shannon takes a long drink of his beer before replying. "I didn't love the guy, but I also didn't hate him. He didn't have much of a personality. I always felt like theirs was more a relationship of convenience than anything. When she talked about him, it was like she was talking about a good friend, not someone she was dying to spend the rest of her life with."

I wonder how she talks about me.

"In fact," he continues, "she rarely had extreme emotions about him. Even when he dumped her, while she was angry about his reasons why, she wasn't devastated. She was more upset with herself for not seeing the signs sooner."

"You never questioned her about her feelings for him? Or him about his feelings for her?"

He smirks. "Like I'm doing with you now?"

I laugh. "Exactly."

"No."

"Why?"

"Like you and your brother, since we didn't go to the same college, we slowly stopped being a daily part of each other's lives. And I've been so busy with work the last few years I didn't pay as much attention to Leslie's life as I should have. I feel partly to blame for the Glenn fiasco, because maybe if I'd talked to her about him, she could've avoided all that mess."

While I'd love to blame him, too, I know I can't. "It wasn't your fault."

"Maybe not, but I still wish I'd been there for her more than I was."

sixty-one

. . .

"Y ou ready to face the lioness in her den?" Randall asks me on the drive north to Evanston in his silver Porsche 944. Ash wasn't kidding about his brother's spending habits, though I can't complain about the ride itself.

"Is your mom really that bad?" I don't believe she is, or Ash wouldn't have been okay with me meeting his mother without him.

He pauses before saying, "She's a good old gal most of the time, but she does like to get her own way."

"Don't we all?"

"Good point, but Mom is more demanding than most people."

I squeeze his arm. "Thanks for going with me. It'll help to have someone on my side."

"Ash seems to think Mom will be on your side, too."

"I hope so."

I stare out the window for the last few minutes of the ride.

A valet takes the car at the entrance to what Randall informed me is his mother's favorite restaurant, and he escorts me inside. A young man takes our coats, and the hostess leads us through the dining room to the table without either of us saying a word. The employees obviously know the entire Hamilton family. We're halfway across the room when Randall's steps falter and he curses under his breath.

"What's wrong?" I murmur.

"Dad's here."

My heart stops. "What? Why?"

He halts and turns to look me in the eye. "I don't know, but I have your back. I promise you that." Then he holds his elbow out and I loop my arm back through his and squeeze tightly.

"Thank you."

He leads us forward and I spot the couple at the table in the corner. Although they look older than in the pictures Ash sent me, I would recognize them anywhere. Ash's mom is smiling at me, and his dad looks like he's about to murder someone. She stands as we approach, but he doesn't.

Randall says, "Mom, Dad, this is Leslie Beckett. Leslie, this is my mom, Ruth, and my dad, Walter."

"Nice to meet you, Mr. and Mrs. Hamilton," I say with a confidence I don't feel.

His dad gives me the once over and doesn't even offer a brief nod. But his mom surprises me by rounding the table and giving me a hug.

She whispers in my ear, "I'm sorry about this, dear. He wasn't supposed to know."

I'm not sure what Mr. Hamilton wasn't supposed to know—that I exist, that I'll soon be dating his son, that this dinner was happening, or all the above.

We take our seats, and Ash's dad says, "So, Leslie, why do you think I should let you date my son after the way you deceived him as a child?"

Randall reaches for my hand under the table, and I grip his fingers. "I apologized to Ash for what I did when I was ten years old, and I feel terrible about it." My eyes narrow at him and I decide to throw caution to the wind and stand up for myself and for Ash. I refuse to let this man run all over me. "But to be honest, I don't think you get to have any say in who your son dates. He definitely doesn't need your permission—nor do I."

Out of the corner of my eye, I watch Mrs. Hamilton barely suppress a smile, while Randall squeezes my hand.

"You're the feisty one, aren't you?"

"Walter," his wife warns, "let's be civil and get to know Ashley's young lady. That's why we're here."

He downs the amber liquid in his lowball glass in one gulp, sets it down, and says, "I'm always civil. And that's not why I'm here. I am here because all of you," he circles his finger around to include the rest of us, "and my other son seem to be deceiving me. Speaking of Ash, where the devil is he?"

"Why do you think we've deceived you?" Randall asks his father.

Mr. Hamilton turns his steely gaze on his son. "For starters, I discovered you and your brother have been wasting my firm's time and money by thinking you can help a bunch of godforsaken immigrants who have no right to be in this country."

Mrs. Hamilton's eyebrows shoot up, and she only halfway attempts to suppress her latest smile. My heart warms to her, as I take her reaction to mean she'll be in full support of the foundation.

"Who told you about that?" Randall demands.

"Does it matter?" his father retorts. "You will cease this activity immediately. And this duplicitous woman," he jabs his finger at me, "will apologize for dragging you into it."

"She will not," Mrs. Hamilton replies before I can. "Walter Hamilton, you are acting like a boor. Stop it this instant."

He presses his lips together and glares at her. It boggles my mind that this man raised Ash and Randall. They did warn me, but I didn't fully believe it until I experienced him for myself. Tears fill my eyes at the thought that the man I love grew up with this man as his father, yet somehow Ash turned into the most amazing man I've ever known.

I don't want Mr. Hamilton to misinterpret my tears, so I stand and grab my purse. "I need to use the ladies' room." Then I walk away from the table with my head held high.

I reach the restroom, dab my eyes, reapply my eyeliner, and take more than a few deep breaths. Another woman enters, and I give her a fake smile through the mirror. The bathroom is fancy enough to have cushioned chairs, so I sit for a minute to compose myself. I don't want to return to that table, but I can't let Ash down. If he can deal with his father, so can I.

When I push through the door, I run smack into Mr. Hamilton. His hand closes around my upper arm, and he drags me down the hallway.

I wrest myself from his grasp. "What do you think you're doing?"

"What do *you* think *you're* doing? You're going to ruin my son's life. Ash is destined for great things, and I will not let him be influenced by a woman like you."

The man only met me a few minutes ago. How does he know anything about what I'm like?

He continues. "You will apologize to both of my sons, and you'll ensure they have nothing to do with this Diego Sanchez publicity stunt. You dragged them into it, and you will get them out of it. And then you'll never speak to either of them ever again. Do you hear me?"

I snort. "I hear you, but I have no intention of obeying you."

"You will obey me," he says with a snarl, "or else."

What is his deal? "Or else what?"

"Or else I fire them, disinherit them, and kick Ashley out of my home. That's what."

All the oxygen exits my lungs, leaving me with little ability to respond with a weak, "You can't do that."

"I can and I will. I will not allow some little strumpet from Arkansas, of all places, to ruin my family legacy."

I want to tell him Ash doesn't want his legacy, but it's not my place to do so.

"I will also ensure you never work in this city again."

Does he have the ability to make that happen?

He crosses his arms in front of his chest. "Do you agree to what I said?"

My mind is swirling so much I'm uncertain what he wants me to agree to, but whatever it is, I guarantee I do not agree, so I say nothing.

"I'll take your silence as a yes. And you will not say a word to anyone about this conversation." He turns on his heel and strides away.

Once he's out of my sight, I lean against the wall and gasp for breath. I can't return to the table, but I also can't let Randall wonder what happened to me. Thankfully, the bathrooms are near the entrance to the restaurant, so they won't see me leave. I ask the hostess to relay a message to Randall that I'm not feeling well and am leaving. Then I rush outside. I shiver in the cold night air, but I can't chance going back in for my coat.

Now I need to figure out how to get home on my own. I don't know the bus routes up here, so that's not an option. Not that I'm in the mood for the bus, but I'm not sure I have enough money for a cab. At that moment, a taxi pulls up and lets a young couple out at the door, and I slip into the backseat before I can talk myself out of it. I give the driver my address, hoping there's enough cash in my wallet to cover the fare. As we drive away, I turn and look back at the front of the restaurant in time to see Randall run out. I duck my head so he won't see me. I'm in no state to talk to him if he tries to wave us down.

Then I let the tears flow freely. I don't know what I'm going to do. Although I already know Ash can deal with being fired, disinherited, and kicked out of his home, I don't know if the same is true for Randall. I don't want to be the catalyst for any of those things happening to Ash, either.

My thoughts run in circles all the way home.

It turns out I have exactly enough money to pay the driver, and I drag myself upstairs to my apartment. When I open the door, Shannon is sitting in the easy chair, cocooned in the sleeping bag.

"What's going on?" we ask at the same time.

He attempts to stand up, but he gets tangled in the sleeping bag and slides to the floor.

I rush over to help him. "Why's it so cold in here?"

"I heard some people in the hall saying the boiler's not working right, but they think it should be fixed by morning," he says as he slithers out of the bag. "I've made us a reservation at a hotel a few blocks away. Pack up your stuff, and let's get out of here. Then I want to know why you're so upset and are already home. Something tells me we're going to need time and warmth for that conversation."

I quickly change my clothes and throw my toiletries and pajamas into a duffel bag. Then my brother puts my heavy coat on me, takes me by the hand, and walks me to the hotel.

sixty-two

. . .

I'm lying on Randall's couch watching TV when he rushes through the door. I've never seen him look so frantic, and I sit up in alarm.

"What happened?" I demand. He shouldn't be home yet.

"She's gone." His chest heaves as he gulps in air.

My heart moves into my throat, and I leap to my feet. "What do you mean she's gone?"

He tries to sit, but I grab the front of his shirt and haul him back up to face me.

"Where is Leslie?" I grit out.

"I don't know. Dad was there, and he was awful, and then she went to the bathroom, and then he said he was going outside to get some air, and then we got a message from the hostess that Leslie was sick and she left."

"You didn't go after her?" I shake him a bit.

"I did. Ash, please let me go." Randall wraps his hands around my wrists, and I loosen my grip on his shirt.

"I'm sorry." My legs are no longer capable of holding me up, and I fall back onto the couch. "So you went after her?"

"Yes, I ran straight out when we got the message, and there was a taxi pulling away, and I think she was in it. It took the valet forever to get my car, and then I raced down here to her apartment building, but I didn't know which apartment was hers, so I didn't know who to buzz or where to go if someone would let me inside."

I leap up, finding new strength. "I'm heading over there."

"I'm going with you."

The two of us run down the stairs instead of waiting for the elevator. Jeff stands when we dash by and calls out, "Can I help you gentlemen with anything?"

We ignore him.

I sprint the five blocks to Leslie's building, not stopping for red lights. I fling the outside door of the building open and repeatedly press the buzzer for her apartment. Nobody answers. I close my eyes and try to remember the number of the apartment across the hall from Leslie's. I think I get it and jab the buzzer.

After several interminable seconds, a woman's voice says, "Hello?"

"Hi, is this Maud?"

"Yes, who is this?"

Randall finally catches up with me and collapses against the wall.

"This is Leslie Beckett's ... boyfriend. You know, Leslie across the hall from you?"

"Oh, yes. I remember you." There's a smile in her voice. "Do you need me to buzz you up?"

"Yes, please. Leslie's not answering."

The door buzzes and clicks, and we rush through. When we exit the stairwell on Leslie's floor, an older woman stands in the doorway across from Leslie's door. She's wrapped in a thick robe and is inexplicably wearing gloves.

"I tried knocking, but nobody answered," she explains.

"Leslie!" I call out as I pound on her door. "If you're in there, please let me in."

Nothing but silence comes from her apartment.

I turn to Maud. "Have you heard her tonight?"

"The door opened and closed a few times in the past hour." She glances away from me briefly and continues, "I also heard a man's voice, and it wasn't yours."

Anger surges through me as I consider the possibility my dad followed her here, but then it hits me. "Shannon. It was probably her twin brother Shannon."

"Ah, he had a Southern accent, like hers," Maud replies. She cocks her head at me. "Is something wrong? Is Leslie okay?"

"Yes, something's wrong, and I don't know if she's okay," I explain. I pray she's with Shannon and is somewhere safe. "I really need to find her."

"All right," she says. "If I see her, I'll tell her you came by to check on her."

"Thanks. I appreciate that."

I walk dejectedly down the stairs, Randall on my heels. When we head outside, I realize I didn't wear a coat, and the night has turned frigid, but I decide I deserve the punishment. I should never have let Leslie meet my family without me.

I turn to my brother. "How did Dad end up there?"

He holds his hands palm up. "You tell me. But somehow he knew about the pen pal thing *and* about Diego Sanchez. Regarding Diego, he told me, and I quote, 'You will cease this activity immediately.'" He snorts. "I'm not ceasing anything. I don't care what he does to me."

My jaw tightens. "What did he say to Leslie?"

Randall relays the entire conversation. By the time he finishes, I'm primed to maim my father.

"You're not going home tonight," my brother says. "You're staying with me, where you're not close enough to Dad to kill him. Because if you do that, I won't be able to resist helping you, and I won't do well in prison."

"I have to go home. What if Leslie tries to call me?"

"Does she have your number?"

"Yes, why wouldn't …" I trail off, remembering Wendy had to call Randall to give me Leslie's number, and I never gave her mine in return. "No, she doesn't. But we can leave a message on her answering machine, and we can also call Wendy and give my number to her, in case Leslie checks in. In fact, we need to call Wendy to see if she knows where Leslie is."

"We'll call Wendy to see what she knows, but we'll tell her to have Leslie call my place if she hears from her. You're not going home, and you will not argue with me about that."

"Fine." I'm not in the mood to argue with him, anyway.

We enter the lobby of Randall's building, and I stop in my tracks. Randall turns back to me with a quizzical look.

"Mom, what are you doing here?" I didn't realize I'm angry with her, too, until I laid eyes on her.

She stands from her seat on the lobby couch. "I came to see if you found Leslie."

"Why would you care?"

My brother whirls on me. "Ash—"

"Randall," Mom cuts in, "it's fine. He has a right to be upset with me. Let's go upstairs and talk."

We're all silent on the elevator ride. When we reach the apartment, I say to my brother, "Call Wendy and see if she's heard from Leslie, while Mom explains how she let this happen."

Mom takes a seat at the dining table as I pace along the other side.

She twirls her necklace around and says, "I was getting ready to leave the house for dinner when your father arrived home."

"I thought he was out of town," I say.

"I thought so, too. He asked where I was going, and I told him I was headed out to dinner—though not who with—and he insisted on accompanying me. The man wouldn't take no for an answer. You know how he can be."

I nod.

"Please sit down, Ashley. You're making me even more jittery than I already am."

I don't want to sit, but I do as she says. My mother is never jittery.

She continues, "It was too late to call and warn Randall, but I was hoping for the best, because I didn't think there was any way your dad could know anything about Leslie. I was wrong, and I still don't know how he knew any of it. He didn't hear it from me."

Randall takes the seat next to Mom. "I think I know."

"What did Wendy say?" I ask, without acknowledging his statement.

"She hasn't heard a word from Leslie tonight, but she'll let us know if she does. She said to tell you not to worry. Shannon will take good care of her, wherever they are. There's no way they're not together."

Wendy is right. Shannon would've arrived home before Leslie did. But that doesn't help much when all I want to do is see Leslie, hold her, and tell her I love her and want to be with her until the end of time, no matter what my father might say or do.

"So how do you think Dad knew about Leslie and the Sanchez thing?" I ask Randall.

"Jay."

I close my eyes.

"Who's Jay?" Mom asks.

"He's a new lawyer on the team. He's a pretentious, backstabbing, misogynistic, jack…," my brother's mouth snaps shut when he remembers who he's speaking to, "…hole who wants nothing more than to be like Dad. Actually, he's already like Dad. I bet Dad had him spy on us. Jay knew about the pen pal thing because he was there at lunch when we first saw Leslie. And I've caught him lurking outside my office and Ash's several times, but I didn't think much of it at the time. He must have overheard us talking about Sanchez and tonight's dinner plans."

Mom says, "That makes sense. I also know without a doubt when your father left to 'get some air,' he cornered Leslie, even though he denied it. So I took the car, left him there, and came down here to check on Leslie and you boys." She focuses on me. "I like her a lot, Ashley. She stood up to your father, which most people won't dare to do. And she responded to his insults with grace. I heartily approve."

I slump down in my chair. "If she'll still have me after this— whatever *this* is."

sixty-three

. . .

I'm lying on my side on the hotel bed, wrapped in the sheets and bedspread, looking at my brother, who is sitting cross-legged on the other bed with his elbows propped on his knees.

"You ready to tell me what happened?" Shannon asks.

I tell him about Ash's dad and what he said. Then I say, "How could he do that to me? How could he make me responsible for two men's livelihoods and standing in their family? H-he's an evil man."

My brother gets up, throws my covers off, and pulls me into his arms. I let him hold me as I cry.

"Les," he says, "I love you, and I know this hurts, but you're not responsible for what that man does. He's only trying to make you believe you are. That's what men like him do."

I sniffle. In theory, he's right. But in actuality, I do hold the power to stop Walter Hamilton from carrying out his threats.

"Ash told me he's planning to leave the firm anyway," Shannon says, "whether he has another job lined up or not."

I turn my head so I can look him in the eye. "He told you that?"

"Yes. And he told me a lot more. I like Ash. He seems like a very good man. Maybe even good enough to deserve you. And he won't be upset at all if he gets fired. In fact, after what happened tonight, I'd guess he'll quit before his dad has time to fire him."

"But what about Randall? He doesn't deserve any of this. I don't know how he'll survive without an income or his family."

"Again, that's not your responsibility. Randall is a grown man. If he can't take care of himself, that's not your problem. Plus, something tells me he knew what he was getting into with this Diego Sanchez thing, anyway."

"He's not like Ash," I say. "He's impulsive, and he's not good with money."

"That's his problem, not yours. Now, you haven't mentioned how you feel about this man threatening to ruin your own career."

"I don't care about that."

"No?"

"No. All I want is to be with Ash and for him to be happy. I don't care what my job is or where it is, as long as I'm with him."

"You mean that?"

"I do."

"You love him?"

"I do—more than anyone." I poke his chest. "Even you."

"I think I can deal with that." He kisses the top of my head, slides off the bed, and covers me up again. "Now go to sleep. There's nothing we can do about any of this until morning."

I want to call Ash, but I don't know his number, and I don't currently have the strength to tell him what his father said to me anyway, so I let myself drift off to sleep.

"Les, it's time to get up," my brother says as he shakes my shoulder. "We need to check out soon."

I groan and roll over onto my back. "What time is it?" I mumble.

"Nine-thirty. Check out time is ten."

How did I sleep so long?

"Do you have somewhere you can stay tonight if the heat still isn't working in your apartment?" he asks. "Can you stay with Wendy?"

I stretch and rub my eyes. "Yeah, she has a couch."

He grins. "I know. I spent a few hours sitting on it the other night. Now come on. Let's get out of here so you can go find your man and tell him you love him."

My face heats. "Can I say it so soon?"

"Yes."

"What if he doesn't say it back?" My chest clenches at the thought.

"He will. Trust me."

I narrow my eyes at him but don't ask why he's so certain. "But me talking to him will mean his dad will carry out his threat."

"Ash won't care. And how will his dad know you've talked to him?"

He makes two good points.

"I need to talk to Randall first," I say. "I can't let these terrible things happen to him with no warning."

"All right. We'll call him first thing when we get back to your apartment." He grabs my hand and pulls. "Now get up."

I take a quick shower, since I don't want to take one at home if it's still frigid there. Then I throw my few belongings into my bag, and we head out.

When we arrive back home, it's blessedly warm again. I sort through the pile of notes on my table and find Randall's phone number. My hand shakes as I dial it. Shannon sits next to me on the bed and puts his arm around me.

It rings four times, and the answering machine kicks on. After the beep, I say, "Randall, this is Leslie. I need to talk to you. Will you please call me back as soon as you can? Also, I'm sorry I ran out on you last night. Okay, bye."

"Do you want to call Ash, even though you haven't talked to Randall?" my brother asks.

"I don't have his number."

"How do you not have his number?"

"I haven't needed it."

"Would Wendy have it?"

"She didn't last week, but maybe somehow she does now. I'll call her and see. Not that I'm going to call him yet, though."

Wendy answers on the first ring. "Leslie, is that you?"

"Y-yes. How did you know?"

"I've been worried sick about you, as have Ash and Randall. In fact, I think Ash might commit justifiable homicide if he doesn't track you down soon and find out what his dad said to you. The man is distraught. Where have you been?"

Tears fill my eyes. I love Ash so much. And I love Wendy and Randall for caring about me, too. "When I got home last night, the heat wasn't working, so we went to a hotel. We just got back. I tried calling Randall but didn't get an answer, and I was calling you to see if you have Ash's number."

"I do. Randall gave it to me last night in case you called." She rattles off the number and I write it down. "Call him. Now."

I hang up the phone and it immediately rings again. I snatch up the receiver. "Hello?"

"Leslie, are you okay?" Randall asks breathlessly.

"Yes, are *you* okay?"

"Yeah, I was getting out of the shower when … that doesn't matter. Are you sure you're fine? Where've you been?"

"I'm fine." Relatively speaking. "The heat was out in my apartment when I got home last night, so Shannon and I went to a hotel."

I finally notice the light blinking on the answering machine. There's no doubt who the message is from.

"I'll give you Ash's number, but it won't do you any good for a while. He left here a few minutes ago to go confront Dad and try to force him to tell him what he said to you."

Nausea settles in my belly. "Ohhh, that's not good."

"What's not good?" Shannon whispers in my ear.

I shake my head at him.

"I tried to stop him," Randall said, "because I'm afraid of what he might do, but, well, he's bigger than me. And he's so worked up about not being able to find you. When I realized he wasn't going to listen to me, I said I'd go with him to confront Dad, but he made me stay here in case you called. We've been so worried."

"I know. I'm sorry."

"I want to hear what happened, if you're willing to tell me before telling my brother. But first I need to call Mom and see if she can head Ash off at the pass."

"Okay, call her and then call me back." I hang up.

I tell Shannon what Randall said and then chew my fingernails while my brother rubs circles on my back as we wait.

When Randall calls, I tell him everything his dad said to me in the hallway. Then I say, "I don't want to throw you under the bus, but if I do, I can't see Ash again. It's an impossible situation."

"It's not impossible. I don't care what Dad does to me. I'm tired of him controlling my life. To tell you the truth, while I'm enraged he did that to you, this isn't a bad thing for me. I'm not sure I would've ever had the courage to leave the firm otherwise."

"But your family ..." He shouldn't lose them over this.

"My family, other than Dad, will stick by me."

"Even your mom?"

"Especially Mom. As soon as she figured out what happened last night, she rushed down here a few minutes behind me to find you. She stayed until after midnight, hoping you'd call."

Dread fills me. "And then she had to go home to your dad."

"Don't worry about my mom," he says. "She can take care of herself. She has decades of experience, though for the life of me I can't understand why she puts up with him."

sixty-four

· · ·

I screech into the circle drive in front of my parents' sprawling home and storm up the steps. The door opens before I can pound on it, and my mother slips out onto the porch.

"Leslie's fine. Randall talked to her."

I sway on my feet and Mom reaches out to steady me. Then she wraps her arms around me and holds me tight.

"He's not here, anyway," she says. "He left for the club ten minutes ago."

I'm not surprised that the morning after my father blows my world apart, he goes about his Sunday as usual on the golf course. I let go of Mom and say, "Then why did you come out here to stop me?"

"Your sisters don't need to know about this. You can come in, but if you see them, don't say a word to them about what happened."

"No, I'm not coming in. I'm going to her."

"Call and see if she's home first. For all you know, she's on her way here to you, or she's at your brother's place."

We go inside and I close myself in Mom's office to make the call. I memorized Leslie's number the day Wendy gave it to me. My heart races as the phone rings.

"Hello?"

The sound of her voice leaves my lungs unable to function.

"Hello? Ash? Is that you?"

"Yes," I breathe. "It's me. Can I come to you?"

"Yes, please." I can hear the tears in her voice. "I need you."

I hang up the phone and sob for the first time in my life.

On my way to Leslie's, I want to drive twice the speed limit, but I realize having an accident or getting stopped by the police will hinder my rush. Randall didn't tell Mom what Dad said to Leslie —if he even knew—so my stomach is still in knots as I wonder what horrors Dad might have inflicted upon her.

Miraculously, I find a parking spot on Leslie's street. I race to the building and through the outside door. Shannon stands on the other side of the interior door, a backpack slung over his shoulder. He opens it for me, orders, "Take good care of her," and then exits the building when I rush past him.

I stop outside Leslie's door and take a deep breath. Then I knock softly. The door swings open immediately, revealing the most beautiful woman in the world, even with her messy hair and bloodshot, tear-filled eyes. I kick the door closed behind me and engulf her in my arms. We rock back and forth in silence, my lips resting on top of her head, her cheek nestled against my heart.

When her erratic breathing evens out, I ask, "Can that chair hold up under the both of us?" There's no way I trust myself to go to her bed, but I'm not letting go of her.

She nods against me, and then I scoop her up into my arms, stride over to the chair, and settle down into it with her sitting sideways on my lap. The chair creaks, but it doesn't give way.

Leslie puts a hand on my cheek and looks into my eyes. "I love you."

"I wanted to say it first," I protest, but then I cover her hand with my own and add, "I love you more. Leslie, I never knew I could love anyone like this. In a few short weeks, you've become the most essential part of my world, even during the times we couldn't be together." I move her hand from my cheek to my mouth and kiss her palm. "I think about you every second of every day, and I never want to stop."

I shift her hand to press against my chest, slide my other hand behind her neck, and remove all distance between our lips. Unlike our previous kisses, this one is slow and gentle, though no less passionate. I can feel Leslie's love for me in the way her mouth and tongue move against mine.

An indeterminate amount of time later, I get her settled back into a comfortable position on my lap with my arms encircling her. "You want to tell me what my father said to you last night?"

"I don't want to tell you, because it's awful, but I will."

My hold tightens around her. It'll be a miracle if I don't end up in jail because of what I'm considering doing to my dad.

"He told me if I didn't kick you and Randall off the Diego Sanchez project and promise to never speak to you again, he would fire you both, disinherit you, and boot you out of your home."

I don't trust myself to speak for several seconds. When I finally do, it's a curse.

"Ash," Leslie chastises me, "don't let him change who you are."

I shake my head. "I've never been angrier in my life."

She places her hand over my racing heart. "I understand. But you're going to need to let it go."

"I'm not sure I can."

It's one thing for him to make those threats against me. It's quite another for him to make them to the woman I love. I take deep breaths in a futile attempt to dispel the rage unfurling inside me.

"I'm asking you to try—for me," she says with a soft kiss to my lips. "For *us*. I'm not asking you to forgive him right now, but please don't let your anger over what he did overshadow what's happening between you and me. We deserve more than that. We *need* more than that, especially after these past few weeks."

She's right. "I promise I'll do my best to let it go, but I need you to tell me everything so I'll know exactly what we're dealing with. Is that all he said to you?"

Leslie turns her head away, which gives me her answer.

"What else did he say?" I ask in as steady a tone as I can muster while turning her face back toward mine.

"He said if I don't do what he says, he'll end my career in Chicago."

I growl in response. Her fingers flex against my chest and I cover her hand with mine again. She flips her hand over and laces our fingers together.

"I don't care about that," she says, "but does he really have that much power?"

I shake my head. "No. He wields a lot of influence in the city, but there are people who won't give in to him. And I can guarantee George Carter is one of them. I've never understood why George ever agreed to work with us."

She cocks her head and studies me. "When did that begin?"

"I was the first person from our firm to work with them."

"Hmm." She looks thoughtful.

"Hmm, what?"

"Did you know George before that?"

I nod. "His family are members of my parents' club. He would always talk to me when I was a kid and when I was home in the summers after I moved away for school."

"What did you talk about?"

I finally get where she's going with this line of questioning. "Mostly what I wanted to do with my life."

"I think he saw something in you, even then. And when your dad went to him to put his scheme into place to try to break you, George saw an opportunity."

My mouth slowly forms a smile. "Maybe so."

"Carter-Jenkins is going to need new legal counsel," she muses.

My smile grows bigger. "Maybe George will hire Randall to be your in-house counsel. I've often wondered why he didn't have in-house counsel anyway. It has to be cheaper than hiring our firm."

Leslie sits up straight. "George already told me he'd like to hire Randall but didn't think he'd ever leave the family business." She pushes off me. "Let's call him now."

I chuckle and tug her back toward me. "That can wait a few minutes. Speaking of jobs, I called Diego on Friday and told him he should hire me."

She straddles my lap and wraps a hand around the nape of my neck, sending tingles down my spine and to places they don't currently need to go.

"I'm proud of you for doing that," she says.

My chest swells.

She adds, "And you were the only person on the list I gave him."

I rest my hands on her hips. "I was?"

"Of course." She kisses the tip of my nose. "You're the only man for the job."

"I love you, Leslie Beckett." Who would've thought saying those five words could fill me with such joy?

"And I adore you, Ashley Hamilton."

She presses kisses all over my face and whispers in my ear, "You trying to grow a beard?"

"I had more important things to worry about this morning than shaving."

"Mmm. I like it."

She moves her mouth below my ear and I tilt my head to give her better access. When her tongue flicks my skin, I stifle a moan.

"Go on. Let it out." Her lips tickle my neck as she speaks, and I shiver. "I want to learn all your sounds."

Her mouth trails to the other side of my neck and my fingers dig into her hips when her body slides all the way forward.

"Leslie, you need to stop," I grit out between clenched teeth.

"I don't want to wait anymore—not for anything," she says against my skin as her fingers toy with the top button of my shirt. "I'm ready for all of it."

The button pops loose and I freeze. She senses it, because she leans back.

"Ash?" Her eyes search mine. "Are you not ready for all of it?"

Am I? My hormones are screaming yes, but my head is telling a different story.

Leslie smooths a hand down the side of my face, stopping at my jaw. "It's okay if you're not."

I didn't think I could love her more, but I was wrong.

"Talk to me," she says softly as her thumb strokes my cheek. "What's going on inside this head of yours?"

"I … I wasn't expecting this today."

"If you don't want to …" She pulls her hand back and suddenly looks unsure of herself, and I hate that she might think I don't want her in every way.

"It's not that I don't want you—want this," I assure her as I take her hands in my own. "I do." I suck in a steadying breath. "But it's been less than two weeks since you said we weren't going to jump into bed anytime soon. I don't want you to make this decision in the heat of the moment and regret it later." My face burns. "Also, I don't have any protection, because I didn't think it would happen so quickly."

The heat in my face intensifies when I add, "And I'm a little nervous. I should have told you this before, but I've never …" I close my eyes, hoping she doesn't think I'm less of a man because of what I'm telling her. "I've never …" I can't make myself say it.

My heart stops when her hands pull out of my grasp, but then they cradle my face, and her mouth is on mine. "You beautiful, wonderful man," she murmurs against me.

"What are you saying?" I breathe into her.

She leans back enough to look me in the eye. "That you're strong and thoughtful and amazing and I don't deserve you."

My chest tightens. "You deserve everything."

"Maybe so, but so do you. You deserve infinitely more than being unsure about this. It wasn't fair of me to think mine was the only opinion that mattered here. And you're right, this isn't the time for me to make this decision, either. I want both of us to be one hundred percent ready in every way, no matter how far in the future that might be."

I nod because it's impossible to speak around the lump in my throat.

"We'll talk about this again when I'm not sitting on top of you." Her mouth quirks into a grin. "But for now, can we make out in the chair?"

I clear my throat. "Under two conditions."

"Anything."

"First, tell me where Shannon is."

"He went to Randall's. We already said goodbye, and your brother is taking him to the airport."

"Good. And second, you've got to stop straddling me. You're killing me here."

sixty-five

. . .

"Lady Leslie, what happened to Ash Hamilton?" Diego demands at two minutes after eight on Monday morning. "I tried to call him at work at the crack of eight o'clock, but they informed me he does not work there anymore. They said the same about Randall. I demand to know why my ace team is falling apart!"

I switch my phone to the other ear. "Calm down, my friend. They're not leaving you, but they have left the firm."

"The *family* firm! What are you not telling me?"

"Their father was very much not on board with them working on this project with you," I say diplomatically, "so they quit."

"They quit." His voice is devoid of all emotion.

"They did. They believe in what we're doing with your foundation."

"But ..."

I haven't yet experienced a speechless Diego Sanchez. I rather like it. "Randall is now in-house counsel for Carter-Jenkins," I inform him.

When we all met with George last night, he didn't care one whit that he'll have to deal with the fallout of breaking his contract with the law firm.

"And Ash is hoping something else will come along for him very soon," I say meaningfully.

"And is Ash still hoping for *another* something—or someone—else to come along soon, or has that happened since last week?" Diego asks with a grin in his voice.

Ash told me what Diego said to him about me. "It happened." I can't stop the grin from taking over my own face.

"Yes! I knew it! I will be his best man."

I chuckle. "We're not planning a wedding yet," though I won't be surprised if we are soon, "but I'm guessing when the time comes, he'll ask his brother to fill that role."

"Fine, but he'd better ask his new employer to be his second-best man."

Now I'm speechless.

"You heard me, Lady Leslie. I am hiring your Ash. You know what tipped it over the edge?"

"My letter?" My chest fills with warmth at the thought.

"Nope." After a beat, he laughs. "Although that was an excellent touch."

"Then what did it?"

"When he told me he wants to get the foundation running and then train up someone from the immigrant community to take over. He understands my people don't need a bunch of white Americans coming in to save us. Yes, we might use the assistance of a few specific white people to get things going, but I want this foundation to be built around people who have the drive to help because they have been there themselves."

Tears filled my eyes as he started speaking, and now they're spilling down my cheeks and onto my silk blouse, but I don't care.

"Your Ash will do great things, Lady Leslie, both for the Diego Sanchez Foundation and whatever he does next. You mark my words."

I don't need to mark them. I know what he says is true.

A knock sounds on my door, and before I can respond, Ash's voice says, "It's me."

"Come in," I call out.

"Is that him?" Diego asks. "Is he there? Let me talk to him. Don't you dare tell him before I do!"

Ash enters, and when he sees the state I'm in, his eyes fill with alarm. He pushes the door shut and rushes toward me, and I hold out the phone to him. "I'm fine. It's for you."

His gaze turns questioning, and he swipes the tears off my cheeks with one hand while taking the phone in the other. Then he gives me a lingering kiss before sitting on my desk so he's facing me.

"Hello?" he finally says into the phone.

"Ash Hamilton, I hear you are in need of employment." Diego's voice is loud, but I can barely hear him from my chair, so I stand between Ash's legs, drape my arms around his neck, and move my ear near the phone. A thrill goes through me that I can be this close to him now.

"Did a little birdie tell you that?" Ash smiles at me and strokes my cheek with the back of his fingers.

"If by 'a little birdie,' you mean a woman named Annette, then yes." Diego huffs. "You Americans and your ridiculous idioms."

Ash chuckles. "Did you call to complain about Americans and harass me about my lack of employment?"

"Ash Hamilton, I like this non-professional side of you. And I like that you have made Lady Leslie *your* Lady Leslie."

"I like that, too." He wraps his free arm around me and pulls me tightly against him.

"So do I," I say into the mouthpiece. "Very much."

"Lady Leslie, stop listening in to private conversations," Diego orders.

"Hey, you're the one who called me," I reply.

Ash kisses me quickly while my mouth is in the vicinity of his.

"All right, Ash Hamilton and Lady Leslie Soon-to-Be-Hamilton, I'm here to humbly ask Ash to lead my foundation."

I press my hand against Ash's chest. His heart is racing, and he's looking at me like he wants nothing more than to devour me.

"This seems to be the day for people to be speechless," Diego says. "Say yes."

"Yes," Ash replies. "Yes, I will lead your foundation." He can't keep his eyes off me. "Can I call you back later to discuss the details?"

"Call me after today's game. You have my number. Now hang

up the phone and kiss your lady the way you've been dying to ever since you walked into that office."

Ash's mouth is on me before he gets the phone back on the hook. I help guide it into place, as I have no desire for Diego to hear us. I briefly wonder if Ash locked the door.

"I love you, Lady Leslie Soon-to-Be-Hamilton," Ash murmurs against my lips.

"And I love you, my much-more-than-pen pal."

epilogue

. . .

Punta Cana, Dominican Republic, January 1989

"Good morning, Lady Leslie Finally-Hamilton." I smile at my wife as she stretches herself awake beside me. "Or should I call you Frank?"

She gives me a lazy smile in return before scooting over in the king-sized bed and kissing me. "You can call me whatever you want for the rest of our lives."

Then she snuggles up against me and lays her head on my shoulder. "How did I end up so far away from you in the night?"

Although she was barely a foot away—and only because I didn't want to wake her by pulling her close—I know what she means.

"I have no earthly idea, but you weren't that far away from me *all* night." I twirl a finger into one of her curls.

She cranes her neck to look up at me with pink cheeks and twinkling eyes. "No, I definitely wasn't." She lays her head back down and traces circles on my chest with her fingertip. "What are we going to do today?" Her hand drifts lower.

"If you keep doing *that*, we'll never leave the room."

I feel her smile against my skin.

"You have a problem with what I'm doing?"

"Not at all. But Diego signed us up for every single activity the resort offers, so we should probably do at least a few of them. You know he's going to check in to see how many we did and will tease us endlessly if we stay in the room every day and do nothing else."

Soon after starting work for Diego, I learned he owned a resort near his hometown, and he's a hands-on owner. He ensures his workers are treated and paid well and there's no corruption at any level of the organization. He also gave Leslie and me a week in a luxury suite as a wedding gift.

"I don't care if Diego teases us," she says. "What does he think people do on their honeymoon?"

"Apparently deep-sea fishing, SCUBA diving, snorkeling, surfing—"

"Yeah, yeah. I get it. Which are we doing today?"

"I've always wanted to try surfing."

She looks up at me again and her hand stills. "Really?"

I nod.

"Surfing it is," she says. "But can we do another activity first?"

The corners of my mouth turn up. "What did you have in mind, my lady?"

She shows me instead of telling me.

Later, when we're getting dressed for the day, Leslie pulls an envelope out of her handbag. "I forgot Diego gave me this for us to read when we got here. He said it's for both of us, but mostly for you."

I take the envelope from her, pull her with me to the couch, and then haul her onto my lap. I open the flap and slide two papers out. I read the top one out loud first.

DEAR ASH AND LADY LESLIE HAMILTON,

CONGRATULATIONS, AND WELCOME TO MY RESORT. I HOPE YOU ENJOY THE ACTIVITIES, BUT I WILL UNDERSTAND IF YOU CHOOSE TO NEVER LEAVE YOUR SUITE.

Leslie giggles. "What did I tell you?"

"You were right, as always."
I press a quick kiss to her lips before I continue reading.

> WHEN I LEARNED ABOUT HOW YOU TWO WROTE LETTERS TO EACH OTHER AS CHILDREN, I KNEW I NEEDED TO GIVE YOU THE LETTER LESLIE WROTE TO ME WHEN SHE ORDERED ME TO HIRE ASH.

I turn Leslie's face to mine. "You wrote him a letter?"
She nods.
"Why did you never tell me?"
She shrugs. "I guess I never thought to." She gives me a peck on the cheek. "Keep reading."

> LADY LESLIE'S LETTER IS A PERFECT WEDDING GIFT— MAYBE EVEN BETTER THAN A WEEK AT MY AMAZING RESORT.
>
> ASH, I TOLD LESLIE I HIRED YOU BECAUSE OF WHAT YOU SAID TO ME, BUT IT WAS ALSO PARTLY BECAUSE OF WHAT SHE SAID ABOUT YOU. EVEN THOUGH I ALREADY KNEW SHE LOVED YOU, I ALSO KNEW SHE WAS PROFES-SIONAL ENOUGH TO ONLY TELL ME THE TRUTH.
>
> YOU ARE TWO OF THE BEST PEOPLE I KNOW. I AM SO PROUD OF BOTH OF YOU AND THE WORK YOU HAVE DONE FOR ME AND THE PEOPLE WE HELP AT THE FOUNDATION.
>
> CONGRATULATIONS AGAIN. I WISH YOU ALL THE HAPPINESS IN THE WORLD.
>
> YOUR SECOND-BEST MAN,
>
> DIEGO

I set that page aside and begin reading the second letter, which is handwritten on Carter-Jenkins letterhead.

Dear Diego,

You asked me to give you a list of people who could run your foundation. I don't have a list. I have only one name: Ash Hamilton.

This foundation is his brainchild, and he took great risk in planning and presenting it to you. I can't give you all the details, but he put his job on the line for this. That's how much he believes in it.

I've known Ash since we were ten years old, and even as a young teenager he dreamed of one day changing the world and making it a better place for all people. That's still how he wants to use the talents, education, and experiences he's been given.

Ash is the smartest, kindest, most respectful man I know, ...

I choke up, so Leslie picks up reading where I left off.

... and he treats everyone equally: men and women, rich and poor, no matter their race or color. It's rather astonishing, especially considering his upbringing. He also has a clear sense of what's right and fair, and without fail he stands up for what he believes is right.

Those qualities make him the best person to launch and run the Diego Sanchez Foundation. Ash will work harder than anyone to make it a success, and he'll make you proud. I'm certain of it.

Sincerely,

Lady Leslie

"Leslie, I …" I don't have the words to finish my sentence.

My wife sets the letter down and takes my face in her hands. "I love you so much, Ashley Hamilton, and you've made me so proud with everything you've done with this foundation, despite the obstacles and all you lost because of it. You are the strongest, most caring, *best* man I've ever known. I'm so glad you're mine."

IF YOU ENJOYED THIS BOOK, JOIN AUTHOR DANA WILKERSON'S ROMANCE MAILING LIST!

When you join the list, you receive writing updates, sneak peeks of upcoming books, the potential of joining an upcoming launch team, book recommendations, and much more. Come join the fun!

To join, go to danawilkerson.com and click "Sign Up."

Get ready for
Wendy's story in

Throwback RomComs Book 2

Coming
Summer
2023

About the Author

Dana Wilkerson is the author of the Throwback RomComs series. She has been a professional writer and editor for almost two decades and was the collaborative writer of two non-fiction *New York Times* best sellers: *The Vow: The True Events That Inspired the Movie* (Kim and Krickitt Carpenter) and *Balancing It All* (Candace Cameron Bure).

She is also the author of the Totally 80s Mysteries cozy mystery series as D.A. Wilkerson.

Dana lives in Oklahoma and enjoys traveling, reading, being an aunt, binge-watching crime shows, and attending Oklahoma City Thunder basketball games.

Find Dana Online

Facebook, Instagram, and TikTok: @danawilkersonbooks

Website: danawilkerson.com

Totally 80s Mysteries

Available on Amazon